Principal
And The
TEACHERS

TO: KEMP

Blessings; enjoy life daily.

Jewel E Dearman

Also by Jewel E. Dearman

UNYIELDING BRONZE

Jewel E. Dearman

Principal And The TEACHERS

Jewel E. Dearman

DARKLOVE PUBLISHING
Dallas, Texas

3

Principal and the TEACHERS

This is a work of fiction.

Library of Congress Cataloging-in-Publication Data

Dearman, Jewel E.
Principal and the TEACHERS / Jewel E. Dearman
P.   cm.
ISBN 0-9661361-1-X

Printed in the United States of America

Jewel E. Dearman

DEDICATION

To my lovely wife Gerri of eighteen wonderful years.

Principal and the TEACHERS

Jewel E. Dearman

PREFACE

Eroticism is in all of our lives, whether fantasy or reality, and Principal and the TEACHERS slowly evolved as an entry of this erotic literature. Read no further if you are intimidated by the art of making love or sexual gratification. The novel is in good taste with excellent characters and a fine story between its pages. I pride myself in the ability to diversify and almost apologetically state: This novel had to be written, for erotica is a healthy and pleasant stimulant; it is not however something that should be exploited, but read and enjoyed within the confines of one's privacy. Afterall, erotica etchings, engravings, drawings and paintings, can easily be traced to the first century BC; and in addition to that, erotic literature, especially poetry, dates to early biblical times. A good example of this appears in Song of Songs. There will be those who discuss the morality and religious aspect of erotica, but we must let them talk; afterall, obscenity, etc. is the first thing that enters their mind. They too, probably never think of the virgin they had and never married or the orgasm they never received during an intercourse. "Each one should judge his own conduct. If it is good, then he can be proud of what he himself has done, without having to compare it with what someone else has done." Galatians 6:4.

7

Erotic literature has its finer appreciation; certainly during time lapses when an opposite sex is not responsive or available and self-pleasuring becomes a realistic gratification tool, heightened of course by leisurely reading literature as Principal and the TEACHERS. Eroticism itself rejuvenates instant sexual explosions and that loss of adventure from the status quo or from years gone by; perhaps preventing frustrations, headaches, and sleepless nights from lack of a good sound screwing or a sensational cunnilingus performance from your mate. There is no denying that feminine and masculine sexually does exist and sexual pleasure hereto covers the earth in abundance. This is not to say that I advise sex outside of marriage. There is nothing disgraceful about the art of making love; for instance, a scene reads: When Rory Davanpourt and Clara A. Feldon returned home and cleared the bathroom, rinsing the Metfield filth from their bodies, the bed awaited. They slid upon its sheets and their exuberance came forth. Clara could faintly be heard saying, eat slow and deliberate, Rory...eat slow and deliberate. Clara's body gave Rory's nostrils an appetizing fragrance, a sensual scent and extremely mouthwatering which lubricated all that it touched. Her neck, breast and stomach were still moist as she slowly guided his head pass her gorgeous spiral-dimpled navel toward the tasty angle of her thighs where their moistures would meet. Her throbbing tingling nerve endings sensed another one of their astonishing love making sessions.

Clara could feel his warm wide palms around her smooth irresistible bare brown behind. Rory's firm manipulative fingers were caressingly massaging each glossy round cheek. She could also feel a warm broad fleshy object slivering slowly and thoroughly about; truly the beginning of an ultimate oral massage; and he was on the way to graciously eating her delicious zabaglione. Rory had the perfect expansive mouth and broad lips to cover a large area with his tongue as he ate. Most, of the time now, Clara had numerous instantaneous orgasms which, gradually progressed to a stormy screaming passionate frantic sensation, but today she had instructed Rory to eat slow and deliberate. For some reason she wanted to nurture and savor this one; obviously a woman's choice. Rory loved nothing better as did Clara for kisses to be planted upon her vulva. Seductive, lip and tongue kisses which gave quivering pleasure, touching her luscious outer and inner labia, prowling inside her delicious vaginal opening, and ultimately pursuing her clitoris at her request, but with an aggressive enthusiasm that always quelled his appetite. Early on, Clara massaged her breast when Rory ate her zabaglione, but later directed her palms against his cheeks to make sure both got their fill of her powerful orgasmic delicacy.

Clara's tender sweet folds were swelling and opening generously to meet the challenge of Rory's long skillfully roving, teasing, devouring tongue; a juiciness penetrated his taste buds, bringing greedy eating habits to her genital area. Alternate thrilling wet kisses between each swishing titillating wandering movement brought her now gyrating energized body to a new arousal point. She loved his gentle aggressiveness upon her, as was evident by her constant sighs and moans; his head was weaving, slow but to perfection, enjoying her soft marvelous appetizing delicacy, she thought, the last time she opened her eyes. The unhurried vigorous intensity of Rory's exquisite performance had her naked arms and fine bowlegs moving wildly. In this pleasurable excitement, Clara's lovely thighs flew attractively apart; his saliva drooling mouth lowered to a new depth of carnal enjoyment. Her colorful pink puffy rounded sensitive lips now surrounded his thick lips, and her sensation heightened; her flexible palms, those passionate embraces, gripped his non-resistant head, pulling him in further within her sumptuous fleshiness. She could feel his magnificent tongue flicking, wonderful spots, leading her to breathless ecstasy; his powerful attached mouth quivering like she'd never felt; his astounding nose caressing her ravishing red clit...numerous clitoral kisses...and then it was over.

One only needs to be reminded that this is a work of fiction and no attempt should be made to imitate such fictional characters; this novel is written solely for one's reading pleasure. It is imperative though, that we as human beings enjoy the beauty of nudity and sex, erotic or exotic, as it was spiritually intended. "A man does well not to marry. But because there is so much immorality, every man should have his own wife, and every woman should have her own husband. Now, to the unmarried and to the widows I say that it would be better for you to continue to live alone as I do. But if you cannot restrain your desires, go ahead and marry—it is better to marry than to burn with passion." 1 Corinthians 7:1,2,8,9.

Jewel E. Dearman

PART ONE

Principal and the TEACHERS

1

"Rory, we are counting on you to get the job done!"

Those were the last words spoken to Rory G. Davanpourt at the breakup of a Top School Official Administrative meeting. Moments earlier, within the birch paneled commodious board-room, ten well-seasoned gentlemen had come together for an important construction meeting, involving the new junior high school. Presiding was Dr. Sauninger T. Metfield. Overlooking them all was Ordon T. Metfield; who like his grandson, Sauninger, wore small round gold-rimmed spectacles, coupled with a distinguishing part, down the center of his head. Dr. Sauninger T. Metfield was proud of the man who had raised him, and on every available opportunity duplicated grandfather's ways and actions. It appeared, at times he was actually insecure in being himself. Even that same monomania expression could be seen in their hardened beady black eyes. The late Ordon T.

13

Metfield's large oval shaped photograph hung on the wall, out of respect for his achievements to education in the Washington, D.C. community. Dr. Sauninger or Metfield as he preferred, (the latter naturally blended in with his proud heritage) sat there waving his hand conductorialy to the pitch of his voice; puffing a large cigar that carried smoke upward, across the face of his dear old grandfather, Ordon T. Metfield, who seemed to be inhaling and blowing the pungent fumes onward into the ceiling fan. Katherine, the boardroom maid prepared a fresh pot of coffee and left the room.

Metfield, sporting a charcoal suit (vested as most of the others) was still gloating over the unbuilt school's new name: Ordon T. Metfield Junior High School. All of the gentlemen present, however, had some significance to the prior educational generation; as they were the new-breed on the board. New in the sense that they were next and were still in control of things; but currently, all of them were at least sixty-two. Metfield, himself was seventy-four. The guys were a close knit group and a sort of informal bunch of men who made decisions by majority voice vote or simply as suggestion. When Paul O. Wilhelm suggested: "I think the new school's name should be Ordon T. Metfield Junior High!" That was how certain things got done and so it was.

None of the ten men were relatives, that is, by blood, however, Charles S. Fernfort and Alvin P. Gilder had married the famous Charwood sisters; Margaret and Delores, respectively. They were the first two sisters in the community to graduate from Fisk School in Nashville, Tennessee (now Fisk University). Rory G. Davanpourt and Willie B. Deinham had also married the wealthy William sisters; Charllotte, now deceased and Maybelle, respectively. Alfred K. Stuckworth and Albert K. Structworth did have the same uncle, but this was understood to be some sort of filial breeding mistake; and as a result they did not claim the other as blood kin. However, their daughters; LaQueeta Stuckworth and Janetqua Structworth, both thirty-four, had a curiosity and were pursuing the mystery up the family tree. The last two; Edward C. Scott and Linnie D. Scott of the same, namesake also argued that their family trees had no interwoven links. Edward C. swore he was from the excellent stock of Scotts, from Philadelphia, while Linnie D. contended to be of the fine Scott family in Baltimore. The group though, functioned extremely well as Edward C. Scott speaks:

"Metfield, we need to get some well qualified young man to be principal of our new school."

"Yes Edward, I was just thinking of that; someone of the new order from the ranks of the old order, was my precise thoughts."

"That should be no problem," states Charles S. Fernfort; "we all have college trained progenies who would adequately warrant and eagerly take such a fine position."

"So true!" chimes in from Albert K. Structworth.

It was apparent this position was to be from the inside; and before voices became silent, practically everyone in the room had made some sound; looking of course, to have a favor thrown in their direction.

"Well, boys, just simmer down;" as Metfield let go of a huge illimitable smoke cloud "Rory has not said anything, and I suggest that he take care of this task for us."

"Well ... I don't know about that!" states Rory.

"Yeah, Rory," states Alvin P. Gildor.

All the others roared in with an overwhelming approval. Each man liked and respected Rory G. Davanpourt and each hoped, he would select someone they dearly knew. Rory's beloved Charllotte had departed, leaving him childless.

The meeting adjourned and the words; "Rory, we are counting on you to get the job done," was the last thing said. It was not clear as to who spoke them, but the short and simple sentence was truly echoed by each one of them. Wide smiles were upon Rory, as they departed.

Rory left the meeting to visit his mother, as he did after every important meeting. The elderly Mrs. Rachel Meadlarkin Davanpourt was interested in their doings at those board meetings, and always had some strong relevant, if not terse input. After all, she had rose to the rank of sub-principal (more of a token thing from longevity) during her tenure in the school district.

As Rory drove, he thought to himself; at times even talked to himself concerning his new assignment. There was no urgency; the school was at least eighteen months until completion. As long as he acted within the next six months, the staffing of Ordon T. Metfield Junior High's pedagogues and leader was sure to be filled rather easily. The evasive undertoningly instructions from Sauninger T. Metfield and the group dictated little choice as to the prospective candidates. The message had come through loud and clear to Rory; it was to be a son from their elitist group. Of the twenty-seven offspring in question; and Rory did not know exactly how many, without a serious assisted head count, but he knew there were only six boys.

Two of the young men, Ordon T. Metfield II, thirty five and Sauninger T. Metfield, Jr., thirty three, however, belonged to none other than Sauninger T. Metfield and his lovely wife Charmayne Strutley Metfield. Of course, Metfield had already seen to them having lofty administrative positions. They personally now, only had to look out for their wonderful freckle-faced daughter, Johnnie-come-lately, Renatra Metfield, who was soon to graduate from some prestigious girl's college in the south. Renatra, a pretty young thing that possessed the same shapely body of her mother, Charmayne, and sure one day to have as equal an appeal at luring the opposite sex into her soft tan tender flesh. Paul O. Wilhelm had a son, but there were some strong rumors as to his rectitude; running afoul with the law, writing a few – five more digit zero's on his checks, than the – two digit zero bank account could handle. Real bad checks. If not for the fine reputation of Paul O. Wilhelm and his wife Brenda Dueverette Wilhelm from the outstanding Dueverette family; along with their two beautiful daughters, Analicia and Felecia, who themselves were lawyers; Paul O. Wilhelm's status with the guys would itself have been doomed. There was little talk of his son; only chatter that evolved his beautiful intelligent lawyers. Naturally, Rory did not expect to hear from Paul O. Wilhelm.

The list was growing narrower but the choosing was getting even tougher; real tough now that Rory had time to focus on who remained. Not the sons, mind you, but the Charwood sisters; Margaret Charwood Fernfort, wife of Charles S. Fernfort and Delores Charwood Gildor, wife of Alvin P. Gildor spoke extremely high of their only son, Ilique K. Fernfort and Dulique C. Gildor, respectively. The Charwood spirit usually found its way into the administrative meetings through the weaker husbands. Just this morning, Charles S. Fernfort mentioned his wife thought the new school should have a free lunch program as well as a free bag-meal to take home in the evening. Margaret Fernfort felt it was entirely impossible to study on an empty stomach, when they arrived at home and there were no parents around to at least fix a snack. Alvin P. Gildor also spoke up for his sister-in-law, Margaret Fernfort; because if his wife Delores found out later, he did not support her sister's project, there would be a long night before retirement. (That project by the way was tabled until the next meeting.) Those Charwood sisters stuck together, and its weight forced a carryover into their husband's behavioral pattern.

The last young man in question was the son of Albert K. Structworth and his wife Trudie Lovett Structworth; a strong willed woman, from the more than hear-say, strong willed Lovett family. Young Clifford A. Structworth was also strong willed, after his mother, no doubt, and usually objected to her viewpoint generally selecting the opposite. Rory knew Mrs. Structworth and would call directly to inform her of the new position. If he figured right, this would leave the job, ultimately to be fought for between the sisters; the Charwood sisters.

Rory smiled as he pulled into mother Davanpourt's driveway. She was an early riser, and it was apparent at eleven a.m., this sunny April day, mother Davanpourt was up and stirring. The walkway had water splashes, made when the hose crossed over to spray the flowerbeds. Tiny balls of water still stood on the

17

yellow and purple pansies. The tall orange blossoms were in evidence also of a recent watering because their peduncle leaned only a few inches from the ground. And the red roses climbing on the white picket contraption in front of each corner porch post, had freshly fallen petals, lying gaily upon the gray wooden porch and around its trunk below. Rory enjoyed the sweet fragrance of the roses as he climbed the thick-oak sturdy two steps. Rory lightly rang the doorbell; no more using his key after nearly scaring mother Davanpourt to death about ten years ago. Stephen H. Davanpourt, his father had, for twenty years, left the earthly chores to his wife. So Rory did what any sensible only child would do; look in on his elderly mother every chance he got. This was the only option since she refused to move in with him.

"Hello son!" as they embrace for mutual kisses. "you have been to another of those old board meetings, haven't you ...I can smell that stinking cigar of Metfield's. Sit down, let me hear all about it."

The ninety-three year old tall slender, Rachel Meadlarkin Davanpourt had all alert faculties, moving hurriedly to the blue and white linen-laced kitchen table. Rory always made and poured the tea for them, so he prepares the blue kettle on the stove, first thing. Generally, there were teacakes inside the tall blue vase, but this morning, they had to settle for some of mother Davanpourt's lemon flavored cookies. Certainly, a surprise for Rory, and one of his favorite sweets. Mother Davanpourt, loved seeing her son smile; they were all, each other had. She counted her blessings daily – one by one; and one of those ones included her handsome Rory.

"Okay son, let's hear it!" Rory sat down near her, around the table's corner.

"Well mother, I was given the task of finding the principal for the new junior high school. It is a rather simple task though; I narrowed it down to the Charwood sister's sons."

"You mean Margaret Charwood Fernfort and Delores Charwood Gildor's, Ilique and Dulique? Good heavens son; why

18

those girls will not speak to each other for a year, if one of them gets it. Rory, you cannot do that; you would tear the family apart. Those Charwood girls support each other a hundred percent, except when it comes to the other's son getting the upper hand. Son, you are too young to remember (Rory was only sixty six, and really, probably too young.); the year, I don't recall myself, but they actually had physical blows when one of those boys was chosen over the other for the leading role in an elementary school Christmas play. Our Stephen had to tear them apart. And it was all due to the stupidest thing you ever heard of – a play. Delores Charwood thought her son Dulique should have gotten the part because he was older by two months. It caused so much of a stir that the director of the play asked Margaret Charwood if it was okay to switch to her nephew. And of course Margaret Charwood said – "no way." Well, as it turned out, Ilique kept the part, but as a small kid will do – forgot everything. I mean this kid went totally blank every time it was his turn. The director read the lines each time while poor Ilique just stood there, looking out into the audience, at .his mother. Margaret Charwood then blamed her sister for his silence, because of the prior confusion; which obviously, in her opinion, was Delores Charwood's fault. And as the argument escalated they started landing blows on each other."

"Now son, I am telling you, up front; be careful when it comes to these Charwood sisters. Maybe, they have learned some sense by now, but I don't think so! Of course, the Charwood girls were much younger then, but there is no way you should chance it. You know yourself, son; sometimes a family is all the other has, left in life."

"Well mother, what do you think I should do; there were only six boys to began with."

"Who were the others, son?"

"There was Metfield's two, who already have good paying positions."

"Yes son, Metfield takes care of his own real well; his grandfather Ordon T. Metfield, who raised him was the same

19

way. I always did admire that in him; that young Charmayne Structley was real fortunate to get a man like that Sauninger." Her voice trailing off.

"Then mother, there was Paul O. Wilhelm and Brenda Dueverette Wilhelm's son."

"Oh, my Lord, that Robert Wilhelm; that boy was always into something; talking about a bad apple. I felt so sorry for the Wilhelm's until their beautiful daughters came along; Analicia and Felecia. I have never been able to tell them apart, but they are darling things. They hugged me in church last Sunday and I truly claim them as my grand kids. And on top of being beautiful, they really made something of themselves. Because of those girls, the Wilhelm's can walk proud and hold their heads up again."

"The last one mother is Albert K. Structworth and Trudie Lovett Structworth's son."

"I don't know much of him son, but his mother has been known to be a pretty obnoxious woman. If it was not for Albert K. Structworth's personality, nobody would ever speak to that heifer."

Rory poured them some more tea. Mother Davanpourt waited patiently to sling another question or remark if necessary. She sipped the new hot tea; all the time, never taking her small charming eyes off her son. She no longer ate any of the cookies; several laid beside her cup untouched. Rory had brought her great news in the morning and she was busy eating that; so to speak. She was also thinking of something and Rory knew it. Rory had been raised to respect a person's thoughts. His dad, Stephen, always use to say, "you must respect the inner person … give a man time to get himself together; and then he'll come out." That is how Stephen H. Davavpourt explained it; so Rory remembered, and waited patiently for mother Davanpourt to split her lips. He could see it coming.

"Son, I don't like to cause trouble, but why don't you name a woman to that post. I know your old fraternity might not like it, but believe me, it's overdue. Sometimes, I think those old men are too senile to do any real modern thinking. I was close, to being principal, years ago myself; hear me now; so that should tell you it's time for a change. Look at the Wilhelm girls; into law and all. Doesn't that tell you, we can and will do any job a man can do."

Now it was Rory's turn to pause. He rubbed his hands together as if he was getting cold. He knew there was a lot of merit in what had just been spoken. There was no tea in his cup as he turned it to his parched lips; so he staggered toward the kettle. Still standing, Rory slowly poured himself a cup, without offering mother Davanpourt a refill; but never taking his newly bright eyes off her. Rory's first mind was to tell her, "Oh no, that will never work," but he calmly said:

"Mother, do you mean, select one of the fellow's daughters? I really do not know if any of them are qualified!"

"Well, son, you told me your task was to find a principal!"

Mother Davanpourt had put something on her son's mind, that even he felt absurd; but admitting as much, took even more courage. Rory was like all other male chauvinist; qualifications and other excuses, when it came to breaking the norm, especially if it meant putting a woman over something important. Mother Davanpourt had put her cup on the table and was now giving Rory her serious – believe me – look; hands crisscrossed against her bosom, and eyes focused in a stare.

"Son, I can see you are agonizing over that one; what else happened at the meeting today?"

"Oh, I almost forgot; the new school's name will be Ordon T. Metfield Junior High."

"That is so nice son; Ordon would be so proud if he was with us today. That man was deserving of everything he got, posthumous or whatever. Ordon was the first principal of the old colored high school. He worked so hard and caught hell from so many people; most of them were his own. I don't know son, why we have to cause our own people so much trouble. Ordon blazed a trail that will be forever cleared. I hope your old fraternity put a plaque inside the school telling who he was and what he was about. Otherwise, the young people will not know his accomplishments. Ordon T. Metfield and others like him will never get into no history books son; so it is up to people like you, to see they get their justice."

Mother Davanpourt was wound up, and had long since forgotten about her tea and lemon cookies. The blue tablecloth was ruffled about, mostly in front of mother Davanpourt, where she had pushed the long side back onto the table. The opposite end of the table showed not only the white lace, but a portion of the oak wooden table; nonetheless a relic itself. Mother Davanpourt still had the table to herself as Rory never did sat down again, after the discussion of the female principal.

"Mother, I must be going, I just remembered, my attache case was left in that boardroom; I will call you later this evening."

Believe it or not, Rory was really telling the truth; although it was getting plenty warm in mother Davanpourt's kitchen. After considerable thought though, Rory now was going to do a check on all the daughters of their group; "just for the hell of it," he told himself. What started out to be a simple task was now becoming a real chore. Rory's thoughts were heavily on his lips as he backed his car out to leave the administration building; "I really don't care what the fellows think, fair is fair, the women have an ..." Then there was a crash; Rory had backed into another car, also backing out. Pieces of something could be heard hitting the concrete.

Rory immediately pulls his car forward a foot or so and hops out. In two of his large steps, he is crossing the rear of his auto; heading for the driver's side of the other auto.

"Hello ma'am, are you hurt?"

"I do not think so; we did not hit each other that hard. The jolt did frighten me though. There must be some damage to the cars; I heard the sound of something falling."

"Are you sure, you are okay ma'am; I want to be sure before you get out."

"I am sure, and quit calling me ma'am; I am not an old lady."

"I did not mean anything ma'am ... I mean -"

"Oh, my name is Clara A. Feldon. Could you move to one side sir, so I can get out."

"Yes, but only if you call me Rory! My name is Rory Davanpourt; here, take one of my cards."

"Okay Rory, could you move so I can see what damage I have caused you."

Rory opens Clara's door and stand behind it as she turns her gorgeous brown bowlegs and shoeless feet outward. Still sitting, Clara reaches in the passenger seat pulling forth a pair of green two-inch pumps. Clara put one on, then the other; crossing, her pretty hairy curvy legs each time to do so. Rory tries not to notice the bottom of her smooth thighs; well, at least he tries not to make it so obvious, he is looking.

"Isn't that against the law to drive with no shoes on Clara?"

"It might be, are you the law?"

Clara is smiling as she cast her friendly light brown eyes upward toward Rory.

"Oh no, I am just an old school administrator."

Clara finally gets both feet on the ground and walks toward the rear of her auto. The mid-thigh green skirt is really showcasing Clara's bowlegs.

"Oh my God, my whole taillight is gone!"

"It is only your lens cover, Clara; I will buy one and install it myself."

"That is not necessary Rory, it was just as much my fault as yours."

"No – no – I insist, I will get the cover today and replace it later on; if I find out how to reach you."

"This is my address; I should be home by six this evening, but you really do not have to do this."

"I will see you around that time Clara."

Rory headed for the auto shop. His mind went back to the daughters of their group. Of course, he knew getting a woman for the principal was going to be a tough sell. The guys or us

23

fellows, he thought, is not in the habit of putting our women at the head of anything of this magnitude.

"Sir, I called around for this lens cover; no one has it, but that is no problem, I can have it the next working day. Can we order it?"

"I suppose so, if there is no other choice. Today is **Friday** – what is – I mean is Saturday a working day?"

"Oh, no sir, you will have it on Monday!"

Rory did not mean to compound his problems. He promised Clara her lens cover by this evening and now we are talking an entire weekend. His new thoughtful intentions were to call Clara and tell her what the situation was, but when he looks at the slip of paper Clara had given him, there was no number, only an address. Rory finished ordering the cover, promising himself to call the operator for Clara's number later. Rory's thoughts; then went back to his mother's idea of a woman for the job. "This is going to be a real shocker for the fellows," Rory smiled to himself, "but they will get over it. Yes, mother is right; that is a great idea; this is going to be fun; oh, the fellows will just love me ... now I must find the right daughter."

It had finally sank in on Rory that a woman should be seriously considered for the principal's position. Once he got a complete list of the daughters, there should be no problem. Rory smiled again to himself, uttering out loud, "yes sirree – guys should listen to their mothers more often – they have great ideas." A fruitful day, thought Rory, a fruitful day; then he remembered that he must call on Clara around six. But first the number, as soon as he arrived home.

"There is a number sir for Clara A. Feldon, but it is unlisted!"

"Is there anyway I can get it operator?

"No sir, I am sorry!"

Well, it looks as if Rory's fruitful day just turned into a squashed tomato. The look upon his face was disappointing to say the least. He poured himself a cold pepsi to clear his head; a little fizz always helps out. A conclusion, of course, was simultaneous; he had promised Clara he would come over and replace the lens cover; and that is what he must do. Come Over, now, being the sincere committal. Rory waited until six and headed that way.

"Good evening Rory, the car is down the street a ways; come on in." Clara lived in some apartments in Southeast; not very far from the large Frederick Douglass mansion. Street parking is not always great; especially when one can never seem to find a spot directly in front of their building.

"There is something I have to tell you Clara; the lens cover will not be in until Monday."

"No problem Rory, I can still drive; but isn't that against the law to drive with no lens cover?"

"Probably, and I might be the law!" Rory and Clara could not help but laugh together.

"Okay Rory, what do you suggest ... that I drive anyway. This is going to be a long weekend for me without my car ... I must have my car."

"Oh, no problem – I will rent you a car!"

"I could never accept that Rory – please excuse me, have a seat – unless I share the cost. You must pardon my manners – can I get you something to drank – I mean a soft drank; you can tell I am not use to entertaining."

"I will take some water Clara, on the rocks, of course. Sharing was not what I had in mind – I will pay for the rental."

"Then there is no way, I can accept a rental car! I cannot have you going out on the limb for me, when it was partially my fault. There is just no way I will allow you to do that!"

"I understand what you are saying Clara – women today and independence and all that."

"It has nothing to do with independence and women; if I was a guy my thinking would be the same Rory. We are talking about doing right. I don't know where you men get off, labeling women, always giving us labels."

It appears that Rory had touched a mean nerve in Clara. He was ready to go now. If there had been any way he could have eased out of there, he would have. Now, his squashed tomato had turned into a fiery feminine expounder. A quick calming solution would have to be presented, thought Rory.

"Okay, Clara, what do you have to do this weekend – I mean, where do you have to go?"

"Excuse me!" Clara's hands were locked onto her shapely hips and her head was cocked to the extreme right when it finally finished moving. She looked if though she was ready to be shot out of a cannon.

"I mean – Clara, my auto will be available for your use."

"I am sorry Rory, I cannot take your auto and leave you stranded."

"Okay, then let me chauffeur you around for the weekend. I will even take you to work on Monday. And for a head start, how about dinner this evening, Clara?"

"Rory, you are so nice, but I will pay for dinner, okay!" Rory did not know quite what to say, so he merely smiled.

So it was; Clara paid for dinner. Rory even ate the grilled chicken breast dish she suggested as being healthier. Rory found Clara much more amiable when not threatened. And somewhere during the course of the meal, Rory's thoughts began to focus on Clara A. Feldon as his woman principal. Her qualifications were in order, excellent as a matter of fact, when it came to education. There were even hours toward a doctorate; which she intended on having within the near future. Currently, Clara was a teacher at Dunbar High. The drawback in all of this, Rory noted, was Clara had no experience in Administration. Other negatives also found their way to Rory's mind: Clara now lived in Washington, D.C., but was not from the family of the fellows; and did not know anyone that knew someone. *Important.* That was going to make it extremely difficult for Clara, he thought, to pass the simplest of test among his peers. Now if she were one of his kin, it would not be a total Herculean task. First, there would have to be a softening period among the fellows, before one could even think about trying to convince the other rather illustrious members – a young female was right for the principal's position

26

at Ordon T. Metfield Junior High. An outside female had virtually no chance, whatsoever, he thought.

Yet, the more Rory listened to Clara A. Feldon and saw the seriousness of her attitude, the more she stood out as being the lady or person for the job. To be sure; before the weekend was over, he would take Clara by his mother's to see what she thought. After all, it was mother Davanpourt's idea. Rory promised not to breathe a word of his thoughts to Clara before mother Davanpourt's wisdom. Rory was now anxious to leave Clara for the evening and call his mother to set up a visit.

"Rory, would you care to come in for a while?"

"No Clara, I really must be going, but the chauffeur will see you tomorrow at ..."

"At nine in the morning Rory; I should know what I want to do by then."

The to do list had been explained to Rory as whether to keep a beauty shop appointment; a trip to the mall; visitation of a girlfriend; bookstore browsing; or a casual and relaxing day at home. Clara explained Saturday as a day of feeling free, to Rory.

The evening had been wonderful for Clara and now sitting in the car, waiting on its abrupt ending seemed a shame; it had been far too short. Clara was unusually talkative, especially after being apologetic for being so brusque earlier. "The adolescent of the night," thought Clara, "with such a mature man is considerate of an extension." Finishing one topic, quickly moving on to another before a lull transpired, gave Clara the satisfactory prolongation she yearned for. Time well spent.

"Rory, you will have to pardon me for talking so much of myself tonight."

"Think nothing of it Clara!"

Without Clara's immediate comprehension, Rory had inquired of her short transference life. Clara's father had been killed in Vietnam; the father she never knew; only photographs remained behind to keep her memory unlocked. She spoke often of her uncle Henri who lived in the city and of which she truly adored. He was important. Clara's family had come to the city

27

from Fayetteville, North Carolina; like so many other North Carolinians, seeking and finding a much better way of life in the Nations Capital.

What about you Rory?"

"There is not much to tell Clara. I suppose I am a country boy like most of my colleagues; born in one place and raised in another. In my case, that happens to be Charlottesville, Virginia; the life of which is in my blood somewhat, because of the summers there with my grandparents. So I am very cognizant of where we have come from as a people."

The night and conversation had worn on into the early morning. Rory was aware of the time as he unpretentiously observed the green florescent-lit clock within his dash. Rory's intention of discontinuing the evening was spoiled by Clara's enjoyment of his company. Calling mother Davanpourt tonight had long ago diminished to an early Saturday morning chore. After all she was an early riser. Rory was enjoying Clara's company, equally so; except his mind was totally consumed in getting the principal's position filled. Clara on the other hand had found a warm and caring seasoned man to just sit and listen. To Clara, Rory was so big and strong, yet so gentle; she slumped and relaxed in his car seat, feeling downright protected upon a shadowy street, she had long become fearful of traveling alone. "His long muscular arms stretched over the steering wheel," thought Clara, "should be squeezing the tenderness of my breast." Crazier thoughts zigzagged through her abdomen as she watched the open-mouthed, distinguished gray haired Rory yawn. Rory was a full gray-bearded-half bald distinguished looking man of sixty-six. A rather, tall gentleman, who carried the weight or importance of his position in an authoritarian manner. One could tell at one glance, Rory G. Davanpourt was in charge of something. Better characterized as one who had the power to do things and he strutted, his power with an air about himself. Obviously, some of this power must be rubbing off on his charming guest. Clara's skirt slid well beyond her

28

pulchritudinous thighs as one of her brown bowlegs moved back and forth. Rory never noticed.

Clara A. Feldon wondered as she sat there, not wanting to control her thigh movement, if Rory had any inclination what her feelings might be at this moment. Her actions were purely reactionary, to the beautiful relaxing dinner and evening, Rory had shown her. He had been so attentive, listening and responding with mature verbal reasoning. Clara A. Feldon crossed and braced her legs at the ankles as her sexual arousal became greater and her thigh movement intensified. She thought, "I want Rory to feel what I am feeling; I want him to know I want him." Underneath her skirt and in the midst of the heat and lubrication, Clara A. Feldon felt her magnificent lips of pleasure puffing up and pushing against her panties, and likewise her thigh movement was entertaining the tip of her clitoris, which had started peeping from its hidden cellar. This excitable rosebud slowly eased forward for great expectations. Clara A. Feldon's eyes focused on Rory was as sensual as one could expect at a time like this, but Rory in the dimly lit setting never noticed. Her thigh movement continued and Clara A. Feldon visualized Rory being there at their junction; saying to herself, "his hands, his fingers, his penis, his head, his lips, his tongue, should be down there swirling. Why is this my first time with him."

"Excuse me," Rory stated as he threw his hand over his mouth, yawning. "Clara, I must see you in, it is Saturday already."

"Sure Rory, I guess we lost track of time."

2

Rory walked Clara A. Feldon to her door, saying goodnight; still not noticing any sensual signs, but that did not make them go away. Clara's labia minora and labia majora (her magnificent lips), not to mention her crimson clit, was now fiercely pressing against her tight silk panties; justifiably to the point of self-pleasuring them if no male opportunist appeared. No sooner than Clara A. Feldon closed the door, her hands commence to firmly press her blouse and bra against her breast in removing them; doing likewise, pressing her skirt and panties against her already saturated vagina. She did not know what to expect from Rory along these lines as she crawled, clothes free, into her bed, cupping and tenderly massaging each breast, rolling soft fingers over her incredible vibrant nipples, before resting one over her watering throbbing vagina. Fondling, pinching, and caressing her erect nipples, going from one to the other, while affectionately rubbing her vaginal lips brought delightful

30

stimulating results. She wanted to, but refused to imagine what Rory would do at this point, saying to herself, "I cannot wait until our first lovemaking session." Clara A. Feldon was romantically pampering her smooth shaven folds of damp flesh, performing a teasing intimate provocative fingertip caressing, as she lay spreaded-wide upon her king-sized bed. She then said in a sensual whisper, "If Rory was here now, without a doubt, his pointed-tip broad tongue would be somewhere upon my naked body.

Rory managed to get to bed by four in the morning, after sorting through some of the other female children of his group. He wanted to make sure Clara A. Feldon stood out or least was equally to the task. And sadly enough, to his surprise, there were two with impressive credentials: Janetqua Structworth and LaQueeta Stuckworth; and due to being almost ten years older, also had some valuable experience. No doubt, that is why his answering machine had messages to call them, from Albert K. Structworth and Alfred K. Stuckworth. The Scotts had also called; that would be Linnie D. Scott and Edward C. Scott; though Rory could not imagine why. Their girls, Helene and Bretanya, respectively was barely out of college.

At seven, the sound of the alarm; Rory stumbled to his feet. This **Saturday** had not started out as Clara had interpreted, "a day of feeling free." First, there was the call to his mother, and the calls on the machine; and the commitment to Clara.

"Hello mother, I need a favor; your opinion on a young lady for the principal's position. I want to bring her by this weekend; what would be a good time?"

"Oh son, I am so proud of you for taking my advice. This is wonderful; when can I meet her?"

"Mother, that is what I just asked; it is up to you, either today or tomorrow."

"Oh Rory, I am so excited; I have to get ready for new company – not today – not today! How about tomorrow, after church. That is it son, I will prepare dinner for the two of you.

31

The church bus generally has me back home by two o'clock. Son, I cannot wait."

"Another thing mother, I have not told the young lady the real purpose of her visit; if you know what I mean."

"Oh son, that is not good; secrets are not good. I will do this, only if you promise to let me acknowledge my approval in her presence."

"Okay mother, it's a deal; we will see you tomorrow."

There were no answer on the other calls, except to his good divorced friend, Linnie D. Scott from Baltimore.

"Rory, I am so glad you called; what are you doing today? I have four tickets to the Oriole's game tonight, and I promised my daughter, Helene, the entire day over there. She has never spent much time in my birthplace, basically due to my broken promises. We are not going to leave until around ten this morning; how about it?"

"Man, you caught me at a bad time; especially for the day. There might be someway I can maneuver into tonight Linnie, but I will have to call you back around nine-thirty."

"Hey Rory, that will work; look to hear from you then."

Rory finished up his toiletries, as it was approaching nine; and headed for Clara's place. It seemed like only a few minutes ago, he thought, they had been together. Everyone obviously was sleeping in, as he drove into the next block, for a parking space. This was a shade or two different from Prince Georges County where Rory lived. It was, however, a nice morning for a stroll. The city's pigeons, along with other winged inhabitants were competing peacefully for their morning's breakfast upon and near the sidewalk. The bird's familiarity with people only allowed one or half a step before jumping quickly, a foot or so, out of your path.

"Well, good morning, Miss Clara A. Feldon; your limousine is here for you!"

"Good morning Rory, come on in; you are not being funny, are you?"

"Feel good Clara; just having a little fun!"

"In that case you can sat down!" And the biggest smile Rory had seen lately danced across her face.

"Rory, as you can tell, by my attire, I am not quite ready. The morning seems to have gotten here so quickly.

And Clara was off to the bedroom. Clara's bright multi-colored peignoir bore no outline of the beautiful brown bareness hidden underneath.

"Keep talking Rory, I can hear you real good from in here! Did you have any trouble parking?"

"Oh, no Clara!"

"I will be ready in a few minutes; the make-up slowed me down; I do not normally wear that much on Saturday."

"Why are you putting it on today, Clara?" Laughing out loud.

"You are being funny today, Rory; will I have to put up with this all day?"

"Only if you ride in the rear seat!"

It was early, but the two of them were in real good moods.

"I am curious Clara; what is the A for?"

"It stands for Arletra."

"Why don't you use it instead of Clara; that is a very pretty name."

"I did at one time Rory, but people seem to have problems with it; calling me everything under the sun. And not only that, my name was being spelled every way but the correct way. So finally I gave up or gave in; whichever is appropriate."

"Do you always give up so easily, Clara?"

"There. I am ready, how do I look?" Doing a three hundred sixty-degree spin.

"The make-up looks great," Said with a wide smile. "And you look fantastic, Arletra – did I get it right?"

"Thanks for the compliment, Rory; both or rather all three of them."

Clara had on slacks – white ones, which magnified the shapely curvaceous body underneath, but practically hid the well-proportioned bowlegs. Also out of sight under the buttoned up bright purple blouse was her eye-filling breast and necklace.

33

Today felt, special, thought Clara, so she had slipped on her lucky cross-necklace. The miniature gold cross, embedded with emeralds and rubies (At least twenty of the tiny gems, each, surfaced the front.) adorned her neck; hanging just beneath her pronounced, but hidden cleavage. She did look nice.

"Okay Clara, where is the chauffeur headed?"

"I figured Rory, to let you take me to breakfast, and we can decide from there."

"My, my, that is a big turn around!"

"Well Rory, I thought about last night as I lay awake. It disturbed me a little that you were not allowed your manhood expression. So today, I am going to be real ladylike. And after breakfast, the shots are all yours."

"Are you serious? That is perfect; can I use your phone, Clara?"

"Sure Rory, what is it?"

"How would you like to spend the entire day in Baltimore? This friend of mine has invited me, and a guest to spend today there with, he and his daughter. I told him no, for today, but left tonight open – he has tickets to the Oriole's baseball game. Anyway I promised to call him back by nine-thirty."

"Sure Rory, that would be an adventure for me. Do you know, I have only been there one time and have never been to a baseball game."

Rory made the call. Linnie and his daughter, Helene picked them up; and they all had breakfast before heading to Baltimore. There was a wide grin across Linnie's face when he saw Rory with this young beauty queen.

The introduction struck a chord with Clara.

"Linnie, this is a good friend of mine, Clara A. Feldon!"

"Wrecked cars yesterday; wrecked Linnie today," thought Clara, as his demeanor fluctuated from the unbelief to the unconvinced. Linnie quickly inquired of her education, to get to the main question – the year of graduation, to ascertain age. Rory pressed Clara's hand to the seat, noting to Linnie that she had gotten out a couple of years early. Linnie's mouth stood open and his ears stood out; and thanks for his baldhead or his hair would have stood up. His mind was having trouble conceiving the fact; Rory G. Davanpourt was dating a beautiful young lady, a few years older than his daughter, Helene. It seems if Rory still felt good; and was now having more fun. He asked Clara rather loud; "what time did you finally get to sleep?" Again pressing her hand to the seat and smiling.

"Thanks to you Rory, it was almost three o'clock this morning." As she leans over and smack Rory on his cheek.

This surprised Rory, but he was having too much fun observing Linnie's expressions, to even hint, he and Clara did not sleep together last night. Clara was enjoying herself as she locked her arms around Rory's, squeezing her fingers between Rory's firm grip. The softness of Clara's hands, for the first time, caused a swelling in Rory's body. The breakfast was packed with stares and smiles from one to the other. *Unbelievable and intrigue*. After breakfast, when Rory excused himself to the men's room, Linnie hastily followed. First opportunity alone.

"Rory, you old rascal you. You have been holding out on us; Clara is a beautiful young lady."

"Thank you Linnie."

"Plus, she seems so intelligent; how long have you known her?"

"Believe me Linnie, not long enough!"

"Man – O' – man – O' – man, you are even stepping livelier this morning."

"Well, you know what they say Linnie; those young women add a little pep to your step." They both laugh.

"Man, you are full of surprises; I would never have guessed you for a young looker like that. Does she have a sister?"

"I am sorry Linnie, she is an only child."

"I cannot get over you, holding out on us. If I had not extended you this invitation, you would still be holding out on me. When are you going to bring her around for the fellows to meet her?"

"Real soon, no doubt!"

"I am not going to mention this, because I want to sit back and watch, their eyes go silly-Willie. She is right for you too Rory; the happy look on her face says she is in your corner."

"Really?"

"You bet Rory; and speaking of being happy, I have not seen you this cheerful since before your Charllotte passed on. She brings you joy and I'm happy for you; that is what life is all about."

"I feel pretty good, Linnie; we had better get back, the girls are probably wondering about us."

Clara and Helene were busy laughing and talking when the fellows returned. Rory noticed the happy look on Clara's face; it even showed in her eyes when she asked.

"Are you guys ready to head to Baltimore?" Their eyes met.

Baltimore – five miles – the highway marker read as their automobile sailed by. Clara and Helene were leaning over the seat toward each other, still full of mid-day chatter as it neared twelve o'clock.

"Linnie, what does the agenda look like?"

"Well Rory, I wanted to go by my boyhood home...."

"You mean it is still standing! What is it propped up with?" Everyone laughs. "Go on Linnie; sorry for the interruption."

"No problem; you know, they built things to last in those days Rory. The girls ... or young ladies might want to do some shopping before we camp in the Harbor area; then the aquarium; and the time to play ball should be real close" There was a chorus of cheers for the shopping from Clara and Helene. Helene politely stated:

"Dad promised to buy me any outfit I wanted." She was talking to Clara, but bobbing her head toward her father.

"And I will honey, just don't you worry."

Clara looked at Rory, with a downward tilted head, and eyes purposefully larger. Rory, obviously still in a good mood, intentionally heightened a smile, giving Clara a fluttering blinking of his eyes. They both laughed. Linnie was now doing all the talking as they neared his old neighborhood.

"The neighborhood is still pretty much the same; a transformation has taken place only in the sense that some younger people have moved in...huh, there appear to be a few more vacant lots than four years ago," Suddenly dropping his head. "Helene, that is the old homestead, honey." Linnie spoke these last words lowly and regrettably.

The house Linnie was born in, to his surprise, had a "For Sale" sign in the weedy yard. Plastered against the boarded up windows and doors were old faded posters of would be politicians. The pillared porch's top sagged from that broken down column. He nevertheless had expected more. Linnie had initially spoken as if Helene had never seen the place before; she had, but not looking like a deserted homeless house. So, what was to start his high-flying tour had somehow been removed from the parade of homes to the list of dilapidated ruins.

"How could this happen?" Linnie's trembling lips transmitted sottovoce mumbles.

No one knew what to say as Linnie slowly drove away.

The shopping mall was a welcomed sight, for no other reason, the silence broke. Helene, a pretty young lady, with black curls hanging over her forehead, just above the left eye; held her father's hand as the two couples browsed the mall. Linnie was smiling again as he teased Helene about passing up all the cheap stores. Linnie D. Scott earnestly loved his only child and the feeling was mutual. The two of them strolled along, hand in hand, carrying on like lovers, instead of father and daughter. They had not seen each other much since the divorce over six years ago. There was some catch-up time here; and if she had asked, Linnie would have found a way to buy the entire mall for her.

Clara and Rory also held each other's hand. Rory thought nothing of the seriousness of this perambulatory journey, other than whether he should respond as he felt; that being to buy Clara an impressive gift. He had not felt this good in a long –

long time. Clara A. Feldon on the other hand was thinking the least of a present, though she, like any woman in a mall coveted a shopping bag attached to her fingers. No. Clara actually felt Rory's firm grip and visualized no end to his grasping or fondling, to stretch the imagination into her bedroom; a flashback to the early morning hours when Rory appeared, focusing his eyes on she in her robe, dashing to the bedroom. Clara thought, what would have happened if she had disrobed, displaying her nude body upon Rory's entrance. Clara could not help but pierce her nails into Rory's hand and wedge her hips against his leg. Rory, lastly, felt the nudge and sensation, placing a kiss upon Clara's cheek.

To Helene, the shopping trip was a success; Linnie dangled two expensive lady's garments upon his back. They were both extremely happy; now almost skipping along. And for Clara and Rory, nothing was bought, but they found a plenty while shopping – each other. Rory had offered to get her whatever she wanted, but she happily refused, leaning more into him each time. Linnie kept yelling at the "lovebirds" to keep up as they headed to the car for the Harbor place.

Sitting atop the Harbor place's patio food section, to catch their breath, Rory and Linnie would engage in a conversation while the ladies rambled through the vendor booths below and nearby. No one was hungry after, their late sumptuous breakfast. This however did not curb the fellow's beer thirstiness. Rory leaned against the tubular chrome rail from his seat, while Linnie, sitting opposite, placed both elbows on the circular table, extending them upward to his cheeks; where his head rested. Linnie's comfortable position only allowed him to remove one arm as he downed the cold beverage. Even as he talked he preferred to support his gray mustached-mouth in this manner. A bright illumination came through the irenic blue sky above. There was no hint of rain as the scattered hovering white clouds seemed to be guarding and admiring the harbor's ever changing calm sparkling bluish sapphire-emerald waters.

"Linnie, that is a fine looking daughter you have; where is she working these days?"

"Rory, you must be a mind reader, her employment is what's on my other agenda for today."

"Not a mind reader Linnie; I just figured with a lovely lady like that, you did not need me to help keep you company in Baltimore. I understand ... so, what's up with her employment?"

"Well Rory, she complains all the time ... well, a time or two anyway, about the assignment she was given at her school. She is an English teacher and has gotten stuck teaching Speech. Helene is coping, but I know she is unhappy, after spending all that education on English. Rory, you do not have a daughter, but a father just hates to see his little girl in less than a happy mood."

Through all the squeezing of his hand by Clara A. Feldon, Rory was still trying to figure out how he was going to convince the fellows to hire her as Ordon T. Metfield Junior High School's principal. This was a perfect opportunity to add an ally in his corner.

"Oh, no problem Linnie; though I am primarily to be concentrating on the principal's position. But, I see no reason why your girl Helene, should not be one of the new school's English teachers. As a matter of fact, tell her not to worry about getting the job."

"Do not mention this to her Rory; Helene knows nothing of what I am doing. This is just another way of her old man, seeing a need and trying to help out. But I did want you to take a first hand look at her."

"Speaking of help Linnie; I believe I am going to need a little help from you."

"Oh yeah!"

"Uh, huh; I do not have a daughter as you just mentioned, but I do have a girl I want to help, in Clara. You see, she has the credentials to be the principal."

"A lady principal, Rory! Are you joking?"

"No, I am not! When it first came up, I was pretty much like you. Unbelievable. Now that it has has time to sink in, I feel it is a wonderful idea and certainly due."

"Well, when you think about it Rory, women are doing everything these days; there's even some women principal's somewhere, I suppose. Whatever I have to do to help you, just let me know. Why Clara could be the principal of my girl, Helene; they seem to have hit it off real good too."

"Oh Linnie, please do not ask Clara anything about this, because, she does not know anything about it."

"Rory, you mean she does not know!"

"That is correct Linnie; just trying to help a girl in need."

"Rory, you are something else." And they both laugh. "The first thing that must be done is to try and convince Brother Sauninger T. Metfield, this is a good idea. And the next thing, without a doubt, is for the fellows to know she is extremely close to you. Establishing those close family ties among us, you know, is also very important. Her name alone suggest that she could fit in as an insider, but the fact of selecting a woman; there is bound to be some hem and hawing, among the fellows. To be truthful Rory, there will be major opposition to a woman as principal."

"Who do you think Linnie, will have the greatest objection?"

"All initially, until they get over the shock of a woman; and the talk, even before you were selected to do the honors, had one of the Charwood sister's boys, Ilique or Dulique, getting the nod. Now Rory, since you have opened up a can of worms with female leadership, there will be others such as Albert K. Structworth and Alfred K. Stuckworth daughters."

"Those two did call me Linnie, but I have yet to get in contact with them."

"They would be two strong individuals in your corner Rory, so you had better contact them to see what they want. You and I both know, deep down within, it is not going to be a numbers game, or majority vote that win. It's going to boil down to the ones making the most noise in Sauninger T. Metfield's ear.

40

Clara sounds remarkably intelligent, so let her talk before the fellows; that, along with her beauty could give her the necessary edge."

While Rory G. Davanpourt and Linnie D. Scott were upstairs mapping strategy for Clara A. Feldon's new journey; the women were below, looking at souvenirs, engaged in a conversation about Rory.

"Girl, you look so happy; how did you meet a man like Rory?"

"Oh ... Helene, we sort of just bumped into each other, one day!"

"I am looking for me a man like that; one that will bury his head and slide his tongue deep into my darkhollow. I saw you pressing yours against his legs; you look if though your man is doing great things for you. Am I right girl?"

"Rory is okay, Helene."

"Don't be so modest girl; I bet you cannot wait to get back home tonight for Rory to give your darkhollow a good tongue swishing. You do make him do that, don't you girl?"

"Sometimes ... uh ... do not be so nosey ... that is personal Helene! Darkhollow; is that what you call that thing between your thighs?"

"It sure is girl, my vagina is special and darkhollow fits my deep dark groove; I suppose you got something better!"

"Well, for me Helene, I have a delicious hot zabaglione awaiting the arrival of my man's tongue."

"A delicious hot what ...that sounds like sensuous disease to me girl."

"It's that, only in the sense Helene that it could be contagious to my man's appetite."

"I was kidding Clara, it really sounds sexy; so what's the story?"

"It's a dessert that I fell in love with while an exchange student in Italy; in short, a delicious hot chocolate pudding. Once I tasted the delicious hot zabaglione Helene, I told myself, that was me and what I wanted my man to be sliding his tongue through. Talking about smooth and creamy; I have never ever had anything in my mouth that taste so good, and that is exactly how I want my man to feel when he is eating and licking on me."

"Sounds good girl, but darkhollow works for me."

"Anyway Helene, enough of that, I do not want to spend my day talking -."

"Don't get uptight girl; I am merely inquiring from a curious perspective. I have heard that seasoned gentlemen can really keep our slits nice and lubricated with their tongues. Is that true girl?"

"You might say that Helene!"

"Well come on girl, tell me about it; is that licking any good or what?"

"Sure, Helene it is good! But it is more than just licking; you never give up do you!"

"Well girl, is it better than the traditional? I mean, do you enjoy his mouth and lips more?"

"I enjoy them both Helene, but it's much more than all that."

"Yeah, but what I mean; which did you have the most climax? I hear it is normal to get as many as three orgasms, everytime if our darkhollow's lips are caressed properly. Is that normal girl?"

"I suppose so Helene."

"You don't have to tell me girl, how many, your zabag ... produce, but do you get multiple orgasms?"

"Sure Helene, but my toleration, is getting a little thin!"

"Okay girl, one last question, and please elaborate honey! Since you have had both Clara; which do you really prefer?"

"I prefer the eating of my delicious zabaglione Helene, because I not only control the number of orgasms I get, but I control the size of them and when I want it. That is basically done through good communication. For instance, his warm wet tongue goes where I want it to go. If I love the spot, and is ready, I let it stay there; otherwise I move his powerful tantalizing-tongue to another part of my tasty zabaglione, that is less sensitive and not as far along. By doing this, you can determine whether to have multiple orgasms or one great big one. Me personally, I like to mix them up. There is just nothing better than variety; plus your man enjoys it more, when he knows you are enjoying it more. It really seems so much more appetizing, you know, for him when he has a mouth full of your delicious creamy luscious juices. One thing you must remember Helene is to never turn your man a loose from eating your darkhollow immediately after the big climax. Most men think it is over when you stop screaming and hollering; most of us even think it is over. I find the best part is having small tremors, as I lay there completely exhausted; with him eating everything my delicious hot zabaglione has produced. Once, he is taught right, he graciously goes on enjoying himself for hours; even with you immobilized and in fantasyland. It does take us a while to drain, you know; so there is an ample supply of good juices for his enjoyment. I can even take and enjoy the traditional at this point if he wants that too, but that is solely for his additional pleasure. Generally, he goes in a quick minute anyway. Anytime, your man is full of your sweet delicacy, he is not capable of anything else for long; of course, neither are you. My man's tongue flicking upon and in my deep wet hole is both exhilarating and intoxicating, leaving me completely drained and immobile every time girl. And you are right Helene, I cannot wait to get back home, so I can get Rory to wrap that long tongue of his around my clit; believe me when I tell you, it will be like giving it up to him for the first time. I am talking about making the greatest of my fantasies disappear. Now, did I elaborate enough."

"Girl you make me horny just talking about having your bag eaten."

"Now girl, that is your problem; you asked for it Helene! And the word is zabaglione." Both Clara and Helene are laughing out loud.

"Whatever Clara, I cannot wait for my seasoned gentleman to come along. I am a fast learner, and based on half of what you told me, the next guy is going to have to come with lip-smacking my style or move on. Seasoned huh!"

"Helene, I hope you interpret, seasoned, as experience, because I am sure there are a few young brothers who are adequate."

"Yeah … sure, Clara! I would probably need two of them at the same time. Girl, I was just pulling your leg; I have trained a few guys to my way of doing things. We are talking purely amateurs though. You are so right on that communication, and it works well for me, orgasm after orgasm, when my man listens. And for our conversation, I have had a good one or two."

"I knew that; let's go see about the guys Helene." They laugh some more.

"Hi Helene, hello honey; Linnie and I were wondering out loud, whether you two were hungry or not. This beer has stirred up an appetite in us. We thought of having a snack and heading for the aquarium. Looks if though you two did some more shopping; what is in the bags?"

"Oh, just a few souvenirs, honey."

Helene and Clara had the works; glasses, mugs, plates, shells; all either saying Harbor place – Baltimore, MD or both.

"I am hungry daddy; how about some of those crab legs?"

"It is fine with me; how about it Rory?"

"Sure thing; honey what do you think?"

"I am with the crowd Rory!"

Rory never noticed as he tackled the crab legs, but he had a scrutinizing audience in Helene and Clara. Instead of using the forceps provided for manipulating and extracting the meat from the crab legs, Rory, used his fingers and mouth exclusively. His skillfulness in doing so intrigued the ladies. Rory's strong fingers forced a gap in the crab legs and gently sucked the meat out. His long tongue appears to have wrapped around the meat as it was sucked upon those thick lips of his. Clara and Helene continued to be intrigued as Rory seemed to have forgotten about the napkins; opting to licking a double set of fingers, carefully gliding his pointed fleshy tongue through each and

44

every crack and crevice. All of Rory's sucking, licking, and eating were gentle and smooth; deliberate yet decisively. Clara and Helene were amazed to see, mouth, lips and tongue work so cohesively with an outside object, as Rory did with the crab legs and his fingers. They smiled at each other; Helene smiling enviously, now knew what Clara was getting and for the first time really understood why she was so happy. Clara, smiling assuredly, now knew what was available and could see Rory's long tongue inside of her delicious hot zabaglione searching for wonderful new flavors, and those big lips completely covering her zabaglione's furrows. "That man," she thought, "has a tongue and a half; I got to have that, and soon."

Clara then looked at Helene, smiling moreso, saying to herself; "If Helene only knew." Rory had started all of this by introducing her as his good friend. She thought; "And I am definitely going to end it by making Rory thrust that thinking cap of his between my very moist thighs."

"Linnie, this is good stuff!"

"Yes it is Rory; give Helene the credit, she picked it."

"Thanks Helene, you made a very good selection."

"I could tell you liked it Rory."

Clara smiled, but said nothing. She would save her remarks for later.

As they boarded the ferry to the aquarium, sitting in the harbor, Rory pointed out a yacht to Clara with the name, Clara, on its side.

"Now why can't we ride that honey?"

"That is a good omen Rory; make a mental note of it; you will get your chance to ride me specifically."

Clara smiled and winked at Rory who only smiled in return. From this point on, Clara promised, Rory would know exactly what was on her mind. He would know what she wanted and what he had to do, promising herself, it would not be long in coming, possibly tonight. Clara found it hard to believe sensuous feelings occurring in her so soon; it was only yesterday that she and Rory had met.

Rory held Clara's hand as they ferried across the tranquil waters lying still from a soothing fishy breeze. Now this is how Clara envisioned her Saturday's, "a day of feeling free." The low hanging puffy white clouds seems to be within Clara's grasp as her gleefully filled eyes stared into them. Neither of them spoke, preferring to enjoy the peaceful atmosphere of the moment. There were no distractions. Rory's mind sailed back into a cruise, he and his beloved Charllotte had enjoyed together. Moisture glistened in his eyes, thinking how happy they had been. Turning his head upward, Rory stared; it was toward the heavenly blue skies, where he knew his Charllotte was watching; Rory could feel her presence. Their forty years of loving inseparable living brought a joyful expression upon his face. A ray of light fell upon Clara's cross from inside her unbuttoned blouse as he lowered his head. The red and green gems radiated a benevolent look to Rory's already blithesome façade. Unknowingly, Rory squeezed Clara A. Feldon's hand. The strong and gentle grip sent a tingling through Clara's arm. She looked into Rory's blessed face and smiled, knowing and feeling stronger than ever, this was her present and future. Rory's gray, well-groomed, beard turned silver under the bright glaring day, reflecting an even more illumination upon Clara's countenance. It was too early – much too early – perhaps; for either of them to express what was surely at the bottom of their hearts. Love. After all Rory had a position to fill and Clara; well, she had a moist delicious hot zabaglione to be filled.

3

Once inside the aquarium, Rory and Linnie again paired off, giving Clara and Helene an opportunity to chat or better put; more time for Helene to be intrusive. Clara found Helene to be an open-minded innocent person with a funny disposition; good sense of humor. And after the initial irritability of inquisitiveness; found Helene to be quite amusing. The difference obviously contrasted with Clara's serious mind – tolerable moodiness – which, Helene thought adorable. These two had hit it off real good after only a short time together; of course, with Helene doing all the interviewing and questioning. Clara even began to entertain herself on what next provocative question would come from Helene's pretty wide-lipped mouth; apparently stretched from talking all the time or laughing a lot; here to be – one and the same – openness.

"That cross ... around your neck ... it looks expensive; where did you get it girl?"

"My Uncle Henri gave it to me; he brought it from Africa, Helene."

"Is he wealthy or have a lots of money or something like that girl?"

"Something like that Helene!"

"I would love meeting a man like that; here lately I have had the worse luck." Without spilling her embarrassing secret to Clara, of her last close man, a rare momentary tightening of her jaws took place. She thought of his bills on her VISA card: A set of tires and four suits, totaling more than three thousand dollars. Reggie "the slickter" in Helene's opinion had lit out after she seriously pressed for some rent money during the ninth month of a year's lease. So what; if he took her to work and picked her up every day, it was her car. And the Exxon card in Reggie's pocket did have her name on it. Thoughts of Reggie's other side, however, caused a broad smile to her pretty face and a quick palm swiping across the front of her blouse, over the sensitive breast underneath. Reggie was gone, but Helene felt his slick movements upon her.

Helene had fallen into that category with so many of her sisters: Believing the "male shortage" and virtually allowing absolutely the worse thing to happen or be inflicted on her by a male; that thing becoming horrendous, only when she gets fed up with it and give the good-sucking leech the proper alternative. The clincher though is being able to smile about it today, because it was partly, her own fault.

"I bet he is one of those older men or seasoned gentlemen, isn't he girl!"

"No Helene, he is not that old; only forty-four."

"Well now girl, that is old for me; I am only twenty two. But to be honest, I am looking for someone a little more seasoned; sort of like what you have in Rory. Girl, he is one handsome man."

"Thank you Helene; I appreciate your compliment in my selection."

"Yeah, you sure can pick'em girl! That uncle of yours, is he married?"

"No Helene; never been married. Why do you ask?"

"Well, I thought you might be able to hook us up girl!"

"And get in my family; I don't think so! Anyway, I thought he was not seasoned enough for you!" Clara laughs.

"Who knows girl, I might be able to teach him a thing or two, to make up the difference; so when do I meet him?"

"Let me think about it for awhile Helene."

"Hold it, let me back up for a minute girl; is this uncle of yours good looking and fine as Rory?"

"Well, he is not as large as Rory, but then, not many people are; however, Henri and my mother look alike and she, in my opinion, is simply beautiful."

"Are you saving this fine man for somebody else girl?"

"No Helene, I told you to let me think on it! I will let you know today; I promise."

With Helene chattering about men, there was no way for Clara A. Feldon to forget about Rory's long thick tongue and his large wide hands. She pictured those powerful gentle hands holding her derriere, and Rory making a declivitous onslaught upon her delicious zabaglione as was done with the crab legs. Certainly, she thought, "an easier slit to manipulate amid her curvaceous bowlegs and no doubt delicious by decuple." Clara was sure of the digestibility of her sweet zabaglione; it was however, the precise conveyance to Rory that the edible softness would be devoured, which presented the question. Presently, Clara thought, she and these fish had something in common. Both were very wet and entrapped.

"Helene, what do you think of these poor imprisoned fish?"

"What do you mean Clara?"

"Look at them Helene; what do you really see?"

"I see beautiful fish, every color imaginable, swimming around in a body of water Clara."

"Exactly Helene; a controlled body of water, of which they cannot possibly get out."

"You make it sound so devastating Clara!"

"It is; how would you like to be caged, against your will, Helene?"

"There is a difference between me and some dumb old fish swimming around in a tank; anyway, they look perfectly happy to me Clara."

"That is the erroneous perception, I am sure, most of you sightseers get. Those fish would be much happier and much more productive in their natural habitat Helene."

"I understand what you are saying Clara; and what do you suggest?"

"They obviously should be free and not confined. Free, to be with whomever, and to do what they are capable of doing in their natural lifetime Helene."

"You sound like some kind of preservationist Clara. Maybe, you should join one of those societies that share your views. It seems to me, you are comparing these "poor fish" with human beings; with yourself for instance."

"The correlation is similar, don't you think so Helene?"

"Well – yes and no Clara. The yes being: Look at it as the caretaker being your husband; Rory for an example, allowing you to stay at home everyday while he provided for the two of you -."

"That in my opinion is definitely a loss of my freedom and I could never allow such to happen Helene."

"Okay Clara, look at this angle. What if there was something you could not do for yourself or was physically incapable of doing a particular function. And look at it like this Clara, these fish don't have to worry about being eaten by another specie."

"I suppose you are right Helene!"

Clara's mind was jolted back to reality and to her appetence which when satisfied would eliminate her wet and entrapped body. On the other hand, her intended victim, Rory's esusient appetite had applied to the crab legs, his beloved Charllotte, or the new principal for Ordon T. Metfield Junior High.

"Linnie, do you really think presenting Clara to the fellows in person is a good idea ... I mean prior to them knowing I had considered a woman."

"It might be the only way Rory. The initial impact will be startling, but will wear off fairly quickly, if Clara A. feldon is present."

"Man, I hope you are right!"

"I know I am right Rory, because that is the effect it had on me. If Clara had not been here for me to talk to, one on one, I would still be saying you're crazy. The impact of a woman was great, but Clara A. Feldon's intellect and seriousness soothed my wound."

"Speaking of soothing Linnie, maybe we should spike the coffee; at least a double dose of caffeine. Or better still, how about soaking the donuts with rum." Both laugh.

"Oh Rory, I don't think we will have to resort to anything like that; but seriously, make sure Sauninger T. Metfield has his old stogie lit. I would hate to have him fumbling for a match when he hears the word; Woman. Though it would be fun to see!"

"Yeah Linnie, about as much fun as when sister Delores Charwood came to a meeting and spoke up for her absentee husband, Alvin P. Gildor. Man, I thought Metfield was going to have a stress attack; wanting to know how she got there, and at whose invitation."

"That was funny Rory, seeing Metfield squirm in his seat; especially when sister Charwood held her ground insisting; a rightful proxy in her husband's incapacitated unavailability."

"Yeah, that was funny. Sauninger T. Metfield is probably still trying to figure that one out. His intelligence or lack thereof, would not allow him to ask sister Charwood for a repeat. To be honest Linnie, I am not so sure I understood. And more than likely would have done the same; just let her speak her peace and leave."

"Metfield was cool, but was he ever hot. He could not comprehend sister Charwood's gobbledegook, but found himself being challenged. And Rory, I have discovered one thing about Sauninger T, Metfield, he hates to be challenged; especially if it is as powerful as sister Charwood."

"She was powerful Linnie! Those words came out with such force; it appeared as if her whole rotund body was being thrown at him. Metfield really had no sensible choice, other than to inflate that large stomach of his and take it."

Delores Charwood Gildor was as silver-tongued as they get when it came to expressing herself. Rory was correct, Sauninger T. Metfield had, "no other sensible choice." Margaret Charwood Fernfort in contrast, was identical except, she had to be provoked to be as aggressive as Delores. The Charwood sisters had plenty of fire; two virago individuals who could easily make one sit up and take notice.

"Whoa ... it is humid in here!"

Rory and Linnie had reached an area of the aquarium, (and immediately joined by Clara and Helene) which included some tropical plants, and upon close inspection, a few small colorful birds hopping among the branches, happily chirping their apparent favorite lullaby. This was especially noticeable to Clara; the captive creatures and the freedom and all, but she did not dare mention anything. The fear of another justification lecture from Helene simply was not worth it. Plus, Clara A. Feldon had a policy of trying not to fall into a predictable pattern; though that was not always possible. And too, the diaphoretic conditions did nothing to lessen her already moist area. Tiny balls of perspiration quickly formed on Clara's forehead, nose, and top lip. It would be moments, she thought, before the little makeup she had on, was a thing of the past. Even Helene's pretty face had begun to glisten from the humidity. Her neck was not as fortunate; water was actually being wiped away with a tissue in her dainty hands. Looking at each other simultaneously, one of them spoke:

"Fellows, we are going to have to find the lady's room!"

The lady's room was a welcomed refuge, even giving them an opportunity to get some other important toiletries out of the way. Who is to say who needed the room the most, because a need is a need. And while this break would in no way prevent Clara's moisture, it would definitely give her the chance to at least prepare for the rest of the day. It was, afterall still pretty early; only two-forty seven in the evening as Clara glanced at her watch. Then there was the baseball game, which was next on their agenda.

"Clara, before I forget; I have really enjoyed being in your company today. It is hardly ever that I meet a person, to feel so close, so quickly. You are warm in your sort of serious way and I would love having you for my sister, if I had one."

Clara, discontinued putting on lipstick; for she had felt the identical sincere warm-heartedness, but did not know how to express herself to another woman. The two women spontaneously embraced each other tightly, patting the other on the back as tears welled in their eyes, streamed down their cheeks and fell to the spotless blue tile below. Tears of joy in finding a female friend other than moms to really be comfortable talking to; to open one's heart in confidence. Women have a way of being sentimental and some, like the talkative Helene, have no problem verbalizing their compassion. Continuing their tender-heartedness, helping the other with the colors on their lips, cheeks, and eyes, brought smiles to their brown, red, black, and blue decorative faces. The two emerged from the lady's room as two caring friends, holding hands; faces intricately made over, and grinning a lot. It was obvious, more than mascara secrets had been exchanged. Even Rory and Linnie noticed a difference, glancing at each other, not mumbling a word as their pride got in the way.

"What do you say, we move on back to dry dock, people!"

Linnie sensed the aquarium no longer held the group's interest and opted to speak accordingly. Then too, today's agenda was his. Not to be out done by his original community tour, which self-destructed, Linnie was determined to show his guest some high points of his Baltimore community.

4

"We have several hours before the game folks; so I am going to show you people something to take back home with you."

Everyone looked at one another before Helene spoke up:

"What is that Dad?"

"Just hold your horses honey; get in the car my good people. Although we need more time, my skeleton tour should be enough to make you hungry for the appreciation of my old hometown."

Linnie was just a singing to himself as he drove; before shortly reaching a building where the sign read "The Great Blacks In Wax Museum." Once inside everyone understood what Linnie had meant about "hungry for the appreciation ...." That appreciation, shining in everyone's eyes as they went through the museum; it went much-much further than the "old hometown" though. The horrors of the Middle Passage was by far the most touching; but the wax look-a-likes of bygones such

54

as Billie Holiday, Sojourner Truth, Zora Neale Hurston, and others were truly breathtakingly impressive. Linnie rushed everyone through as they tried to stop and read.

"Time is short folks, we have places to go." The next site was a slow drive by Coppin State College.

"Rory, this is where I graduated, and where you and I will have to return for a visit of Cab Calloway Jazz Institute. Clara and Helene are a bit young for this super star of our times." Clara and Helene only laugh.

"Dad, how about where mom graduated; let us go by there!"

Though, Morgan State University was not on Linnie's agenda, there was time, and there was a request from the dearest one to his heart.

"Clara, you have to see this huge statue of Frederick Douglass on campus. Mom has this picture holding me as a baby there. You and I must take a picture there. Dad, is your camera still in the trunk?" Helene had this magical glow about her now.

"Sure, but more than likely honey, there is no film in it."

Helene gave her father an ungraceful look because she knew he was never without his camera or film. He always told her "a camera without film is not a camera." Linnie promptly recognized his daughter's changed expression.

"Oh, I am just kidding honey, the camera is loaded and ready."

Helene had her father take several photographs of she and her new friend, Clara. Clara even got Rory to pose with her; planting a kiss on his cheek, the instant one of the photographs were taken. Rory again responded graciously, folding those strong arms around Clara's waist; demonstrating the moment's happiness. There had been happier times for Rory, but it had been by his admission, "a long time ago." Temporarily, the principal's position had faded to the edge of his mental faculty. Having a good time echoed all, of their demeanor as the twelve-foot statue imposed its Brobdingnagian figure upon them. Lost in the cheerfulness was the game, until Linnie spoke out.

55

"Folks, we must be going, there is just enough time to reach the ballpark for the start of the game."

Clara and Helene had never been to a baseball game and swiftly got caught up in exuberance for something totally new; they agreed that a snack or whatever was offered baseball fans was to be their first order. And it was no secret, Linnie and Rory had their sights on some nice cold beer. Rory, however, had some nachos with his beverage. Seated, between the ladies; Clara and Helene again saw a magnificent display of his long-thick tongue. He held the container outward from his chin appearing to, anteater, the cheese drenched tortilla before his hands touched it; forming a "V" at the tongue's tip, pulling the food forward. The cracking and smacking sound was only out done by the cheese ring around Rory's wide-broad lips, which he simultaneously disposed of with one or two swipes of his organ of taste. Such awesome display was indeed excitable to the ladies.

Helene again showed her covetousness by smiling at Clara; thinking to herself, exactly what would happen to her deep darkhollow when she met Henri. She presently had no inamorato, so a stimulating imagination did not have far to travel. Clara on the other hand was thinking of later tonight; the quelling of her rivulet, which had began to flow again. Rory would have to do something, she thought, to wipe out the moisture; having no one else to do the honors, Rory was the only likely candidate. Clara envisioned the nacho annihilation tool approaching her mons pubis and slowly slipping downward. This, Clara thought, was the perfect manner to end a long carefree day. It seemed to Clara, she had known Rory much-much longer than the two days. Her left hand rubbing his knee as Rory explained the game, was an indication of both; familiarity and acknowledgment. She even felt comfortable stroking the inside of Rory's upper thigh over the large spongy-throbbing elevation; but stopped and held on after four or five times, in respect to Helene's voracious stare. Clara was indeed enjoying this new game of balls and bat, expressing as much to Rory.

"I love this game Rory, despite the fact of it being long and hard. Of course that might be the best part, because it gives one, time to grasp."

"You seem to have a good handle on it Clara!"

Rory, now held the program over Clara's hand as she commence to manipulate her fingers; afterall, it was her turn to bat; and according to Rory's smile, his instructions were paying off. Rory was embarrassed, but felt too good not to allow Clara to continue. Clara knew this was her moment to get her point across and she capitalized on it. Those amorous-eyes of Clara A. Feldon's were focused upon the face of Rory.

"I love the way you eat nachos Rory."

"Oh, really!"

"I also love the way you eat crab legs!"

"Oh really; is that so!"

"Uh, huh Rory, I believe I just love the way you eat!"

"Is there something special about the way I eat Clara?"

"It sure is Rory; I love the way you slide that long-thick tongue of yours around the food. That says a lot about you."

"And what is that Clara?"

"For one, you do it skillfully, with so much care; and next, you never seem to lose any of what you are eating, which tells me that you love to eat."

"That depends Clara"

"On what Rory!"

"It depends on, if what I am eating is good."

"Oh, I see; is there any way I would know before time Rory."

Rory looks at Clara and smile, saying, "Maybe you can provide me with a sample."

"The sooner the better, I take it, huh?"

"Oh no Clara, I am not in a hurry; I have the stamina and fortitude to wait."

"We'll see Rory."

"It is purely a mind thing, you know Clara."

"Like I said Rory, we'll see!"

Clara was again moving her legs inward and outward; much the same as last night, but this time Rory took notice. Clara's two-inch inflamed thumb-size clit pressed firmly against her tightly fitted nylon panties; more would have to be done to subdue this prized swollen energized serving of flesh. At this time her vagina was wetter than the fish in the aquarium. Clara thought, "If there was some way I could slide my fingers through that delicious lubrication without Helene noticing, I would have Rory tasting how good it is at this moment." And abruptly after a second thought she said, "I must" ...sliding her hand casually inside her pants as if straightening her blouse ...over her clit, beyond ... thoroughly, saturating, two fingers near her thumb ... resurfacing the glistening two prongs across Rory's nostrils onto his lips into his mouth. Rory calmly placed his hand over hers, partially covering his face. Then an amazing artistic display of mouth-tongue masterly occurred. He sucked her fingers, vigorously rolling his tongue from the outer-inner rounded edges through a crevice ... eating the way she expected her delicious zabaglione to be eaten. Within seconds, Clara slid her left hand inside her panties again, purposely to massage her pulsating clit. Rory could feel her tender hand movements against his as he held the program to block Helene's view. Hmmmm ... a ball ... a swing ... a hit through an infield gap ... screams ... Clara was really into this game. Clara A. Feldon had seen what she wanted and had communicated what she desired to Rory. She believed he more than understood. Now it was only a matter of time before Rory's long-thick organ of taste made its way into her delicious zabaglione. "If I play it right," she thought, "he will eat tonight; I must keep the pressure on." Doing just that from the sixth inning until they reached home was a challenge Clara A. Feldon welcomed. After all, she had broken the ice with Rory and understood his comment "purely a mind thing," which obviously was her conquering answer.

58

Rory's mind. And by the way, the Washington Senators won the game five to four.

On their way home from Baltimore, it was extremely quiet; lateness of the hour, a long day, and tiredness being the major contributors. Helene lay asleep; head and shoulders making a bed inside the corner of the front seat and door. Clara had stretched across the rear seat resting her head in Rory's lap. She could feel his strong arms lying powerless across her waist; noticing too, his eyes were closed. She could also feel his large penis pressing lovingly against her cheek. The day had been wonderful as was evidenced by such relaxation. Linnie cleared his throat, it appeared, at regular intervals, assuring his passengers they were in good hands.

Upon reaching Clara's apartment, Clara vaguely heard Helene say, "I will call you early next week girl." Rory had to practically carry her each step of the way, before vivacity rebounded into her slumbering body. Courtesy, however, prevailed at the door, when she asked Rory to come in. Though tired, Clara thought how nice it would be if someone could tuck her in; probably reading that bedtime story, her father never got a chance to read. Rory was now her chosen candidate; he was so strong and gentle, plus Clara A. Feldon felt secure with Rory around and very comfortable in his presence.

"Help me undress Rory."

Rory, unhesitatingly unbuttoned her blouse and pants, removing each garment. Then he politely carried the black bra and bikini panty clad beauty to the bed.

"Help me with my bra Rory."

Rory did likewise, accidently touching Clara's bare breast in doing so. Looking at Clara's beautiful brown exposed body caused excitement to reverberate inside his mouth. The narrow strapped panty was the next and last item to come off; Rory let them be. Clara lay sprawled on the blue spread bed, naked to the waist; with a body beckoning for attention and to Rory's surprise, a sleeping beauty; Clara had quickly dozed off. It was difficult to determine what was shining most; the lucky charm necklace with its precious gems, or Clara's sumptuous body with all its dazzling charms. It had been a long while since Rory had seen anything so magnificent; her perfect arched-eyebrows, upon her innocent soft brown radiant face; her remarkable ripen velvety delicate breast; her flawless navel spot; her shapely hips, trailing into gorgeous thighs and graceful bowlegs which lay stretched wide. Rory was right, it was a mind thing; and for the moment his mind was imagining things; like the beauty underneath Clara A. Feldon's black panties. Rory imagined Clara's love nest, open and spacious as the gap dividing her curvaceous bowlegs. Then he imagined his tongue occupying the spaciousness of Clara's vagina, swishing, nibbling, devouring, and caressing gently and lovingly to Clara's pleasure and delight. *An intimate dinner.* Clara's lucky necklace seemed to be having a profound consumptive effect, and obviously what she desires. At Rory's age, one would think some type of aphrodisiac was going to be necessary for arousal, but the sight of Clara's beautiful body appears to be sufficient. Clara would be pleased to know her lucky necklace had really worked. Rory's lips had swollen, his tongue had elongated and expanded, and his mouth had filled with saliva; each equal to the task of dining on Clara's sweet delicacy immediately. Rory bending over Clara with an imagination going wild, kissed her on the cheek; covered her beautiful body, and whispered her a low melodious-goodnight. Clara had again missed getting tucked in; through no fault of her new aficionado though.

Rory set Clara's clock for eight in the morning and quietly left for home. En route, Rory's body felt enriched, rejuvenated, and powerfully energized. He had made a promise to Clara, which he longed to keep as soon as possible; it appears his stamina and fortitude was wearing thin. His beloved Charllotte no longer occupied the greater portion of his brain, Rory had been content, but mother Davanpourt had been prayerful, someone would enter into her son's life.

Rory called Clara soon after eight; a wonderful **Sunday**.

"Hi Rory; thanks for setting the alarm; was it for any particular reason on your part?"

"Yes, your chauffeur is again at your service. Are you going to church today ... or better still; how about attending church with me. Afterward, my mother has invited us to dinner."

"Rory, that is so nice, but not today!"

"Why not?" Dejectedly expressed.

"Don't sound so dispirited, Rory; I did not mean it like you took it. I mean; the dinner sounds fine, but I sang in the choir and have a lead for today; so I must attend my own church. Why don't you just join me and maybe next time, we can attend yours. The dinner would be wonderful afterward Rory."

"That is great; Clara, you are wonderful and so speedy in working things out; reaching a very good conclusion. That is the mark of a good leader; making quick, timely, sound decisions when they have to." There was excitement in Rory's voice.

"Thanks for the compliment Rory. You can pick me up at ten this morning. I want you to know, I am excited too and very-very happy."

In fact, excitement was the order of the day. Clara A. Feldon, and Rory G. Davanpourt glances one to the other in the car. They held hands the entire eight church miles. Even in the large African Methodist Church, excitement was pure explosive rapture.

"Here Rory, let me pin this visitor ribbon to your lapel! Good morning Mrs. Taylor; Mrs. Johnson; Mrs. Williams."

The red and white ribbon was enough to hold Rory hostage during the fiery spiritual manifestation; blending as the marquetry-crosses into the furniture; yet standing out in spite of such. And the three widows, all well over seventy, who spoke to Clara in the foyer made him all the more visible. Their conversation took precedent to the Reverend's sermon of, "The wounds shall be healed."

"Mattie (Taylor), look at that, Ms. Feldon is looking at him from the choir stand."

"I see it Bobbie (Williams); isn't that awful!"

"What did you say; who did you see girls." Exclaimed Mrs. Pasty Johnson who could neither see nor hear too good, without informing others nearby. Rory was seated diagonally left on the next bench, easily within good ear distance.

"We will tell you later Patsy!"

"Undoubtedly, Bobbie, there is something going on between them!"

"What did you say; what did you say Mattie?"

"Hush; hush patsy, people can hear you!"

"Yes; that young thing ought to be ashamed of herself Mattie."

"What was that Bobbie?"

"Ain't that the truth Bobbie; that old buzzard is old enough to be my husband."

"What was that Mattie?"

"Look at her, just look at her Mattie, grinning like a Cheshire cat!"

"Where is the cat Bobbie?"

"Yeah, those young girls have all the luck Mattie."

"And listen to her sing, "How Great Thou Art," looking right at him Bobbie."

"Yeah, and from the way she smiling; I would say he is the one she thinks is so great, Mattie."

"That is so awful Bobbie and a shame before God for me to witness such a thing; she will surely rot in hell for such carrying on."

Rory, too heard the melodious soprano's soothing words to this relaxing song, "And hear the brook and feel the gentle breeze." Words, which sent him back to his beloved Charllotte, drawing a solemn smile across his face. He recollected when he had been active in the church; deacon, Sunday school, usher board, choir, bible class, prayer service. And in passing, Charllotte had taken all those things away from him. Never understanding or coming to grips why God had taken away the one he loved so dearly, so early; only fifty-seven. It seemed like yesterday, that they laughed and made eyes at each other, in a sanctuary, much like this one. Now, listening and looking into the eyes of Clara brought a newness of life and religious reverence into his heart. Oh, he had been back to church, off and on during those lonely nine odd years; but the holiness and active participation was no longer there. There was not even a sign or feeling of guilt in his absence. But today, this moment, he felt something; that pious sincerity. And that was certainly more than Mattie, Patsy, and Bobbie, felt. Their piosities were locked into Clara A. Feldon's business. Good gossip and being first class hypocrites.

Rory sat there real benevolent like, meditating from down deep within. No oral testimonial virtues would come forth today, but prayers were emanating from Rory's heart this very moment. A prayer for his aging mother; a prayer for Clara A. Feldon to be accepted by the fellows. A prayer for the sick and shut-in, and the bereaved family requested by the minister; a prayer for the church; a prayer for the less fortunate; and lastly, a prayer for his own soul and well being. Afterward, Rory began to feel real good; his body felt lighter, floating like. He could hear himself repeatedly saying "Amen and Praise the Lord," as the services proceeded. Unaware of anyone around him, talking unfavorably, Rory even clapped his hands and laughed, seemingly for no reason at all.

Rory continued to listen as the preacher's message echoed against the walls and pierced his ears: The faithless and non-believers will not enter the Kingdom of God. You must believe … you must believe … in our Lord and Savior Jesus Christ. Those words bounced around inside Rory's head until he thought; what an excuse, what an excuse, I have been using; hiding behind Charllotte's departure for no longer being active; for no longer believing. Today forward would be different, he continued to think, saying Amen … Amen … Amen, aloud; patting his feet, to an inner rhythm of his soul. Rory never heard Bobbie:

"Look at him Mattie; pretending to be Holy!"

63

"Yeah, robbing the cradle Bobbie; his conscious is beating him to pieces!"

"Peace ... there is peace in here Bobbie," Quotes Patsy, who still was not hearing her friends conversation too good, but was correct in her assessment of the surroundings; especially Rory's, whose countenance bore it out.

"Look at Clara, Bobbie; she is even caught up in his devilment, moving that head of hers from side to side."

"Yeah, that poor innocent child!"

"What child are you talking about Mattie?" Rather loudly.

"Sch ... schh ... he will hear you; we will tell you later Patsy."

What would Bobbie Williams and Mattie Taylor, tell Patsy Johnson. That Rory's heart had been rekindled; that the spirit had swooned into his body; that he had surely heard the word of the Lord; or that he was a no good so and so.

It would not have mattered to Rory; even if he had heard the sisters; for he was totally consumed with a good righteous feeling. A white handkerchief, rubbed the sweat from his brow as the sanctuary appeared to warm up. His large strong hands held the white cloth firmly, waving it as if to say, "I surrender ... I surrender ... Rory's world was revolving around an axis of its own. The Reverend's fire and brimstone message was having its effect. He had entered the church with a tottering belief and undoubtedly leaving with a renewed dependence upon the known Higher Power and his God. He felt good all right; his mental state was conscientious of the inspirational uplifting. Oh, this feeling was going way back, way back to an almost old-fashioned spiritual kindling; a rejuvenation which caused Rory to think about getting active again. Suddenly, he was beginning to miss the old days; that was when, by his admission, the Lord was truly present. And today, this moment, Rory again, by his admission, realized the "Footsteps" belonged to his one and only merciful, loving God. Rory's thoughts settled onto his own mother and father's God-fearing upbringing and his beloved

Charllotte's spiritually. He knew at this instant, he had to get back; get back active.

Rory looked at Clara A. Feldon and returned her smile. Clara, he thought, looked real good, in the gold and black choir robe; maybe a compliment to this effect would be a responsible remark later. Goodness came all over Rory at this moment and complimentary thoughts occupied his mind; Clara's beautiful brown face; her shiny black hair, her sweet-sounding voice; her adorable charming disposition. Somehow, Clara A. Feldon stood out radiantly at a distance, as Rory's keen-eyes zeroed in on her.

The close of service brought the minister to Rory's side as they both held one of Clara's hands.

"Mr. Davanpourt, we welcome you back to our congregation any time; Clara, here, is one of our favorites. Without her, most of our services would be without the necessary fire and spirit."

"Thank you Reverend Smith; your message was very inspirational and rewarding. I can assure you, my return is ineluctable."

Three other wellwishers also stood nearby; looking directly into Rory's mouth as he spoke. Their barrage sent the Reverend on to others leaving the church.

"Hello Clara, you sang so beautiful today; you always uplift my weekly burdens. Is your handsome guest a relative?"

"Oh, hello Mrs. Taylor; Rory, these are three of our staunchest members, Mrs. Mattie Taylor, Mrs. Bobbie Williams, and Mrs. Patsy Johnson."

Rory politely bows to each of them saying, "how do you do; it is so good to meet you."

"Clara, did I hear, he is a cousin of yours?"

"No, Mrs. Johnson, he is definitely not a cousin in the real sense; maybe a kissing cousin."

Clara laughs and pull Rory away from her known nosey church members; leaving, of course a lively discussion.

"Oh, that is so disgusting Bobbie for her to admit in church what they are doing."

"It sure is Mattie, and she thought it was so funny. I fail to see the humor in it myself."

"What is the rumor about Bobbie?"

"I said humor Patsy, HUMOR; oh – we will tell you later!"

"Come on ladies, let us go get something to eat before the evening services."

5

Eating was exactly what was on Rory's mind; some of mother Davanpourt's fine home cooking. And did she ever have a feast; there was food, everywhere, lined on the stove and on the dining room table, covered under a bright white tablecloth. Prior to entering the house Clara had noticed the red climbing roses; along with the colorful pansies and other multi-colored flowers both in the flowerbeds and pots upon the porch. The entire atmosphere, she thought, reminded her of the old home place, back in North Carolina. When her mother moved to D.C., she had given up the country space for a row house and hardly any room for blooms and greenery. It is so sad, she thought, how so called progress seemed to be so retrogressive.

"Mother, this is Clara A. Feldon."

"Clara; meet, mother Rachel Meadlarkin Davanpourt!"

"Son, don't be so formal; you can call me mother Davanpourt; that is what most of my friends call me."

"And Mother Davanpourt, you can call me Clara."

They casually shook hands and held them for minutes, just admiring the beauty in each other; mother Davanpourt had her wavy silver strands pulled tightly into a stately chignon.

"Is there, anything I can help you with mother Davanpourt?"

"No – no Clara – you just wash up and have a seat at the dinning room table; son, show our guest where the bath room is."

The black and white marble tiled bathroom was very spacious, with what looked to be eighteenth century fixtures in brass and black; highlighted of course, with a white tub standing on brass legs, of all things. This room was magnificent, thought Clara, noticing the pale blue and black dirty-clothes hamper, upon which one could sit. Hanging in the center of the window, falling near the tub's top was a bushy green and white leafed Ivy plant. It looked as full and hearty as the dining room table. Four sets of towels; dark blue, pale blue, black, and white, hung over a four feet brass towel rack, standing freely, between the front of the tub and the ancient white wash basin, displaying two antique faucets. Clara gazed into the oval ornamental mirror; slowly washing her hands. This process, through no fault of her own, other than admiration, if you will; took more than ten minutes. When she did emerge, mother Davanpourt was sitting at the covered dining room table.

"Sorry it took me so long mother Davanpourt, but I was captured by your elegant bathroom; it is simply magnificent." Clara simultaneously raises her left hand, showing three straight fingers, allowing the thumb to form a circle with her small finger. Quoting the words magnificent twice more while shaking the hand sign.

"Thank you Clara; please have a seat, anywhere." Mother Davanpourt was seated on the far side of the table, striking her usual comfortable pose, with her arms folded securely across her bosom.

"Where is Rory? As she takes a seat across the table from mother Davanpourt. "I am sorry for the delay."

"He went to the store for me; to get me some sweet Garrett. I told him he could do it after dinner, but he insisted on doing it right now. He knows how particular I am about that old bad habit, after I eat. Yesterday, I was so concerned about not forgetting anything for dinner today, that I completely forgot to get me some. That tells you right there that I could really do without it."

Clara is laughing.

"Excuse me mother Davanpourt, but that brings back pleasant memories of my grandmother. I use to find pretty colorful buttons and put them in her snuff can and jar. You know, sort of like getting those prizes in the cereals. She always found it amusing, never telling me not to do it. My mother thought it was mischievous, but grandma, told her, "It was all right.""

"My – my that was cute of you and very loving on your grandmother's part; sounds like, she is an extraordinary woman. I have often wondered what it would have been like to have a few grandbabies to spoil."

"Oh, I was not spoiled mother Davanpourt; it really taught me to have love and respect for my fellowman."

"That is what I meant Clara. Anyone in their right mind knows grandmothers only bring out the very best that young ones have to offer." They both laugh.

"Speaking of the best mother Davanpourt, I have something for you."

Clara dashed to the living room where her shoulder bag is on the sofa; returning with a neatly gift-wrapped package.

"Mother Davanpourt, this is for you."

"Oh my, the wrapping is so pretty; I never ask what is in a present Clara, but may I open it after we eat. I just love pleasant surprises after a blessed meal. Your grandmother is blessed to have a person like you in her life, and I know she adores every moment of your good-heartedness. Tell me, where does she live and what is the wonderful lady's name."

"Mrs. Clarissa Herndon; she still lives in Fayetteville, North Carolina. I understand I was born in that same house and named for her. Of course, my parents did not give me the full name, because mom said it was a bit old timey."

"Yes – yes, I have seen a lot of that; trying to get away from the old and go with what we think is the new. And I suppose there is nothing wrong with it, as long as we don't let our moral values suffer. Herndon – Herndon – Herndon, it seems to me I know some Herndons from North Carolina; was your mother's family very large Clara?"

"Not really, mother Davanpourt; there were only two; Henrietta, my mother and her twin brother Henri. Uncle Henri does live in the city, but my mother lives in Correa, Maine."

"No – no, I am talking about some older heads; Rory may be able to help me with those first names … my – my;" Looking at the large round clock ticking on the wall. "Rory sure is taking an awfully long time Clara."

Clara notices her arm for the first time, only to find her loose fitting band has dumped the watch to the bottom of her wrist. Nonchalantly, she turns the watch forward, forgetting to check the time; partially due to more questions from mother Davanpourt:

"Clara; Rory told me you are a teacher now, but what are your future plans?"

"I do not want you to get me wrong mother Davanpourt; I love children and I love teaching, but my goal is to move onto the administrative side of things. Of course, even with my educational credentials that is going to take some time; especially with no experience in this male-oriented society of ours. I am prepared to keep plugging away though."

Mother Davanpourt had heard all she wanted to hear from what she thought; this lovely young lady. She had been prepared to coax Clara A. Feldon into reaching for higher heights, but found that to be unnecessary. It seems, she thought, women were

70

waking up to the challenges before them and seeking to compete in all facets of the workplace. Clara's words "to keep plugging away" was a familiar ring; for mother Davanpourt had used those same words, while seeking and eventually getting to be vice-principal, in her day. Sort of, you know.

"Clara, you can achieve anything you set your sights on. The idea is to stay focused – never lose that drive; and like you, yourself said, keep plugging away."

"My main concern mother Davanpourt is education; the best education for our children."

"I understand Clara ... well son, it is about time you made it back; what did you do, make a jar of that stuff yourself."

All three laugh as Rory taps Clara on the back; putting the small sack on the buffet near the china cabinet, filled with china and crystal from a different era. Mother Davanpourt uncovered the food while Rory washed up and rejoined the two at the table, sitting at the head; where mother Davanpourt had made him sat, since Stephen H. Davanpourt had sought refuge in the Higher Kingdom.

"I am ready at last folks; Clara – could you lead us in a word of prayer?"

"Son, that is so impolite to ask your guest to do your job."

"Forgive me Clara; consider my actions a mere faux pas for the moment."

"Oh, I do not mind mother Davanpourt; could we please bow our heads."

"Our Most Gracious Father in Heaven, we come on this great day to first say, Thank You, for having kept us safe during the night, watching and protecting us in Your most compassionate way."

"We also come to say, Thank You, for allowing us to wake up clothed in our right minds, and enabling us to have the full usage of our limbs. We were able to see a beautiful day today that You had already prepared for us; we are ever grateful that when we arose this day, our minds were focused on You and Your forever goodness to us. With You on our minds Lord, we were able to make it to our places of worship just one more time to say, Thank You."

"Lord, we Thank You, for Mother Davanpourt, and we Thank You, for Rory. We ask that You would continue to bless and keep each of them in Your care. We Thank You for this lovely dinner that has been so elegantly prepared by Mother Davanpourt. We ask that it will nourish our bodies, but most of all, help us to know and understand that the real Chef is found in You Lord, who daily continues to supply us with the necessities of life."

"We ask that as we each travel down the road of life that You would continue to guide and lead us in the direction that leads to Your will for each of us. We all seem to be in some path that yearns for the growth and development of our children and their future; only asking that You would allow us to be used as instruments and beacons of light in a sometimes dark world. Lord, we Thank You for this opportunity to be together, and Your richest blessings will always be appreciated. We ask all these things in Your name Jesus Christ our Lord and Savior. Amen."

After hearing such long and wonderful prayer, mother Davanpourt had no sooner said Amen, than uttering the next sentence:

"Son; Clara is, without question, the person for your position; what she lacks in experience is offset with a willingness and capability to learn. Plus you can coach her if she has any problems; I will expect nothing less of you son."

Clara, meanwhile, was just sitting there, looking one to the other, not understanding much of the conversation until Rory's statement:

"Clara, what mother is talking about as we enjoy this delicious food that you so graciously blessed, is a principal's position for the new junior high school. I asked mother to sort of check you out in my planned absence. Little did I know she had an errand for me anyway; sorry I circled a few extra blocks prior to returning. My stomach has been growling for the past half hour, but I wanted to give mother enough time to size you up, so to speak."

"Clara, you will find that my son's choice of words are not always the best; sizing you up, or any young lady is not what I would want or expect of him or any of his fellow board members, you'll surely meet. I believe he meant, getting to know you properly."

"Oh, I am not offended now, mother Davanpourt; we have already had a discussion on Rory's use of the king's language."

"Excuse me ladies; old habits are sometimes hard to break. Well Clara, would you be interested in being the school's principal?"

"Of course, she is interested son; I just told you she was the person for the job."

"Sure Rory, I am interested; when will the school open?"

"It opens in about eighteen months or after the next school year. But first, there are a few things that must be cleared up; such as, the hiring; or the approval of hiring a female. There might need to be some convincing among the fellows of this being an appropriate and positive direction to pursue for a new school. There will be some opposition, I am sure; especially from Sauninger T. Metfield. The new school is named for his grandfather, Ordon T. Metfield."

Mother Davanpourt looked at Rory saying:

"Don't worry about Metfield, son; he owes me one."

They had heard her, saying Metfield "owes me one," but it seems as if they did not hear her. Rory knew from her expression, she wanted her space. Clara just poised herself after Rory's silent, "its okay."

Mother Davanpourt's arms were again, tightly across her bosom, and she stared seemingly, through the window on the far side of the room. She never saw the bluebird perched on the sill lubricating its feathers. Her thoughts began to flow: It seems as if it was a long time ago, she thought; and it was. Over seventy years to be exact. But in this moment of reminiscing, it seemed like yesterday to mother Davanpourt; then Rachel Meadlarkin:

"Rafeal, I think, they done found out; here comes old man Thomas V. Brontlier in the wagon with yo Leslie Mae."

74

"And she promised not to tell; quick Rachel, get in the bed and under the cover; let's pretend we sleep."

Little did Rafeal Meadlarkin; Rachel's twenty-two year old brother, know, the days for pretending and secrets were over. Rafeal had made his twenty year old sister, Rachel, cross her heart and hope to die: To never tell their secret; he had gotten Leslie Mae Brontlier pregnant.

Rachel hovered over Rafeal as they both sneaked a continuous peek behind the daisy-patterned flour-sack curtained drawn window. A day of dread loomed for Rafeal. Even the mule pulling the wagon seemingly, dreaded this day, trudging along grudgingly in the shivering cold weather. Smoke was steaming from the mule's nostrils, as it was from old man Brontlier's. Poor Leslie Mae looked to be frozen, or scared, or both. Frozen-scared stiff. She had on her old hooded checkered-green, blue, and red coat; covered further with a dirty white blanket – cream – tan – well – soiled white.

Old man Brontlier jumped off the wagon, tying the reins to the hitching post, landing his field-weathered boots up the three steps, and onto the porch in the same motion. One could see, he was in a hurry. This is when Rafeal and Rachel quietly scurried to bed, pulling the cover over their heads. Leslie Mae remained hunkered down; looking pass the mule's hindquarters and swishing tail; nervously to the ground.

"Maybe, she is scared," thought Rafeal, "but I ain't scared of nobody; not even old man Brontlier." As he lay still, solidly underneath two hand-made quilts, topped with a blanket. A thunderous knock on the door and a loud boisterous yell, did have its effect though:

"Willie Meadlarkin, we need to talk; this is Thomas Brontlier, we need to talk; open up!"

Rafeal could feel Rachel shaking as he lay next to her.

"What are you scared of Rachel? I ain't scared of nobody!"

"I am scared for you Rafeal, you don't have to be."

Papa Meadlarkin had opened the door. The next words heard were:

"Leslie Mae – git down and git in here!"

A few seconds and tiny feet later, the door shut.

"What can I do for you Thomas? Is everything all right?"

"Yo boy done got my girl pregnant!"

"What? Rafeal, git in here!"

"Rafeal, I think papa wants you."

"Yeah, I heard." Rather squashily.

"And remember, I didn't know nothing Rafeal!"

"Rafeal, you heard me – git in here!"

Rafeal's bony legs and feet hit the floor. He was wiping his freckled-face and half-shut eyes; yawning as he entered the room.

"What is this I hear about you getting Mr. Brontlier's girl pregnant. Is that true?"

"I … think so papa, we … hadn't got round … to telling you and mama just yet." His head and eyes were sort of hanging low to the floor.

Mama Thelma Meadlarkin hugged Rafeal, as she always did, when his behind was subject to be heated up, to no avail. What was done was done in this case. Rafeal breathed a sigh of relief and looked at Leslie Mae. You could tell they were in love as their eyes glittered into each other's. Leslie Mae, however, still kept her arms, hanging long, and crossed in the front of the old checkered coat. It was as if she thought someone was going to steal it or ask her to open it up.

"Well there, now Thomas, the boy admits it; we are prepared to do by you and the Mrs., what is right. We can have them two married in a week or so."

"Well, Willie, that is not quite, why I'm here; me and the Mrs. sort of figured on sumptin else. You see, we promised Leslie Mae to Mr. and Mrs. Ordon T. Metfield and their son, Benjamin R. Metfield. He has already asked for her."

"You mean that damn old educated fool and his wife, Thomas."

"Yes Willie, I am talking about Professor Ordon T. Metfield."

76

"So you think yo girl is too good fuh my boy, Thomas!"

"Nah, that's not it Willie; its that we had already planned the wedding and everybody has agreed to it."

Of course, nobody had asked Leslie Mae; and of course, she was only sixteen and still in school. Both she and Rafeal were in the eighth grade. At least that was the last grade Rafeal attended before dropping out for the last cotton crop. Rachel though younger had managed to make it to the twelfth.

"You see Willie, that boy, Benjamin Metfield is about to graduate from Hampton Institute; and what me and the Mrs. see, is a way out for Leslie Mae. She don't understand now, but later on, she will thank us for what we trying to do."

"I am still listening Thomas!"

"Me and the Mrs. figured you and the Mrs. ... and we can't afford it, but that you would take five hundred dollars to sort of forget this ever happened. I hate this happened Willie, but you and me is farmers, and there is just not much for our kids, unless they get some outside help. I can give you two hundred fifty right now, and get you the balance as the crops pay off. I am asking you Meadlarkins as our friends, to help us; that boy and the Metfield's don't know our Leslie Mae is carrying yo boy, Rafeal's baby."

One could tell Leslie Mae's grief was beyond tears as Willie Meadlarkin holds his hand out for the cash.

Rachel had heard the whole thing and could not help but shed a silent tear. She had no idea that unions were suppose to happen in such a cruel manner; whats love got to do with it, huh. The door to the three-room shack closed and Rafeal returned to the bedroom. Rachel noticed him as he looked Mr. Thomas Brontlier and Leslie Mae away. Leslie Mae looked back as long as the wagon traveled the long sparsely grass path to the main road and then, for as long as the tin-roof shack was in her view. The wagon wheels grooved the brown-graveled, red-dirt road, which had as many ruts as was formed on Leslie Mae's forehead. Her perplexed frown accented the hopelessness and helplessness within her life. It was hard to tell if she was crying, but it was not hard at all, to tell that she was grieving. Rafeal crawled into bed and said nothing, but Rachel could feel his hurt. He was taught that men were not suppose to cry and she whispered to him – I have and will always cry for you Rafeal. Rafeal drew closer to his caring sister and hugged her tightly as she cried the both of them to sleep.

That was the last time Leslie Mae Brontlier and Rafeal Meadlarkin saw each other. Shortly after the wedding, both Benjamin Metfield and Rafeal was called into the first big war. And as fate cries, Rafeal was killed; but died a hero for some feat "above and beyond the call of duty;" yes, he received a medal of honor. Leslie Mae read of the Medal of Honor ceremony, but could only be there with her lonely heart. Benjamin Metfield returned from the war to a healthy bouncy baby boy, Sauninger T. Metfield, who now stayed with the Ordon T. Metfield's, who simply did not have the courage to write him of his wife, Leslie Mae's death.

Leslie Mae never smiled again after the sale. She loved and wanted Rafeal so bad. Her daddy's words on the way home that evening was, "Girl, you better not breathe a word of this to nobody." When she failed to respond, he said, "Do you hear me girl." Leslie Mae only nodded. "And you will stay married to him as long as I am around ... do I make myself clear!" Again, Leslie Mae nodded.

Thomas Brontlier and his wife knew Leslie Mae was grieving, but figured she would come around after the baby was born. No one considered her feelings for love and the word of Rafeal's death only agonized the grieving process, more so. Leslie lived only long enough to see the crying baby boy leave her tired and grief-stricken body. Leslie Mae shook her head without murmuring a word, and simply passed away – a fixed smile camped upon her lonely face.

Leslie Mae could not bear to mail the following letter, composed to Benjamin Metfield, and had given the original and copy to Rachel Meadlarkin for "proper disposition:"

Dear Benjamin

I cannot live with a lie in my heart - the baby to be born is not yours. It belong to my first love, Rafeal Meadlarkin; a proud farmer, who incidentally was killed in the war, the other day. My heart and soul is burdened with sadness. Please forgive me for betraying you. Also, forgive my parents for making me do such a terrible thing; they simply wanted me to have a better life than that of a farmer's wife. I wanted to tell them a many times, the mistake in not believing a young girl's heart.

Your parents don't even know and I could never tell them, because they seem to be so happy with the anticipated arrival of their first grandchild. And though I grieve, I will have this baby for their sake. When you return, promise me, you will do what is right – though by law – it is your child.

I am giving a copy of this letter to Rachel Meadlarkin, who knows of this tragedy and who shares my misery. She has been asked not to be the first to divulge this tormenting secret; and only to verify the fact when called upon. She can do it because, Rachel is a strong daughter of a farmer, whom I love and respect.

Again, Benjamin, please forgive me; I truly wish for your sake, life could have been different. Goodbye and may God bless you.

Sincerely

Leslie Mae Brontlier

Rachel had her instructions and after the war, reluctantly delivered the letter to Benjamin Metfield.

"Mother, are you all right?" As he noticed, she had began to cry."

"Oh, I am sorry son, and please forgive me Clara. I was thinking of something that happened a long time ago. It is nothing that concern you two directly."

Mother Davanpourt cleared her throat, wiped her teary eyes, regained her composure; hugging and kissing Clara, who had been holding her hands during the consolable period. Only bits of food had been eaten by anyone.

"Rory, you leave that Sauninger T. Metfield to me."

Mother Davanpourt wanted to tell her son about the entire tragedy, but had promised Leslie Mae, not to divulge it first. Somehow, she thought, Sauninger T. Metfield was going to have to come forward with the truth. He was not a Metfield, but her nephew – a Meadlarkin. The tears shed today had been for him and his cowardice. The tears were for his two boys, Ordon T. Metfield II and Sauninger T. Metfield, Jr. and his lovely daughter, Renatra, who were all living a lie. Unbeknownst. The tears were for all the times, she wanted to visit and love her brothers's family. Mother Davanpourt was right; Sauninger T. Metfield owed her one.

The good Lord had blessed Rachel Meadlarkin Davanpourt with long life because she had a story to tell; she had a wrong to right; she had to live to see the record set straight.

"Thanks mother, we will let you know how all future meetings with the fellows turn out."

"I am really sorry for this outburst Clara; and sorry I spoiled everyone's appetite. There is absolutely too much food for me to consume, so you and Rory will have to take most of it with you."

Mother Davanpourt not only had pot roast with all the vegetable trimmings inside, but she had Rory's Sunday special – fried chicken; two of them.

"Mother, do you have any of those little green onions to go with these collard greens? And Clara, be sure to pack enough cornbread! Mother, which dessert do you want to keep?"

"Son, you and Clara split the pecan and potato pies the way you want; also take the lemon pound cake. Clara you better watch this man or he will eat all that sweet stuff."

Clara's mind sort of dipped to the side of the road, saying to herself, "I certainly hope so; seems like my mother's saying will definitely be applicable with Rory. Cook those good meals for your man ... tell him how you expect to be loved ... sit back and enjoy yourself while he eats." Then Clara was reminded of their togetherness later on, where she planned on serving her own assortment of "sweet stuff." She thought lovingly, also of mother Davanpourt, the entire time they were packing; putting the food away, and cleaning the kitchen and dining room. Rory started washing the dishes and Clara pitched in later to finish the task.

"My – my, you two make a lovely couple!"

Rory and Clara looked at each other and smiled. Finally Rory managed a sarcastic remark:

"Clara A. Feldon, I am surprised you know how to manually clean dishes."

Clara looked over her shoulders to see how far away mother Davanpourt stood before whispering the following words into his ear:

"There is a lot of manually things you will be surprised at before the evening is over, Mr. Rory G. Davanpourt." Laughing and throwing soapy-suds in his direction.

Mother Davanpourt was correct; they make a lovely couple because today, they are a happy couple. Rory had been on a spiritual high earlier and now he was on a natural high, just watching the pleasure-giving bowlegged beauty move about. Mother Davanpourt smiles as she speaks to Clara:

"Clara, I know I will see you again; put your mind and heart into that position, because it rightfully belong to you. Rory knows you can do the job and will convince the other old timers to search their hearts for the right individual. Here is my number; call and let me know how things are going. I want you to know I have a personal stake in this assignment for us and womanhood."

The two women left each other embracing, kissing, again holding the other's hands in deep admiration. To mother Davanpourt, she felt a daughter in Clara. Rory and Clara laughed all the way home about first one thing and then the other. A bunch of petty-pretty nothings. Even finding a parking space in front of Clara's apartment.

Her thighs ... his tongue

Her thighs hid a sumptuous treasure
A vulva – so beautiful – so sweet
His tongue sought its sensuous pleasure
... to caress ... to love ... to eat

And though neither Rory nor Clara knew it at the time they left mother Davanpourt's or even at this time, but their next few days would find them making love in a most spirited and sensuous fashion; erotomania. It too seems fitting to warn the weak-hearted not to read further, for such eroticism could lead one to their lover's bedroom, etc. on an irregular basis.

"Have a seat Rory, if you will, while I freshen up."

The shower could be heard to be running from the bath in Clara's bedroom. Rory liked the idea of being acquainted with a woman conscientious of a scrubbed anatomy. Before a complete article was read in the current Ebony magazine; Clara reentered the living room, motioning to Rory, saying casually:

"It is your turn now; the towels are laying at the foot of the bed." The two straps on the front of Clara's sheer blue negligee was being fumbled about with her long thin fingers, until one strap freed itself, allowing the garment to stand open; revealing two beautiful brown medium-size breast. Looking disinterested and unimpassioned; Clara stepped to one side as Rory leaned to kiss her cheek. A swing mood had rapidly occurred which showed her deemphasizing the current affair. "If you need anything Rory; perhaps another towel, let me know, I will wait for you in the bed." There was now no zip or enthusiasm in Clara's voice.

Clara's unloving expression deepened when a daguerreotype of a man, dressed in a military uniform, on the nearby dresser came into view. She could not help but think of the one thing deserting her most in his absence; Clara A. Feldon would have given anything to have sat on her father's lap.

Clara's eye-filling breast, though, still stood at attention. Rory noticed the adornment of two lovely nipples in his passing; thinking how, one should feel good about herself with such smooth sightly assets. It was obvious to Rory; Clara's mind had lost its original focus. His experience, however, had taught him to concentrate attentively on a woman's primary climatic goals, or two, problems accumulated prior to a rendezvous in the bedroom, if they insisted. Rory knew a later discussion would be better after needed tension was relieved, and hoped Clara would allow him to proceed. He felt, making love first was more of the correct therapy. Rory's key was to wear down Clara's irritability with silence and action. If she said nothing, then he would say nothing. Then it boiled down to re-stimulating Clara, gently; touching her warmly and lightly.

Toweling off as he set foot back into the bedroom, Rory found Clara lying on her back, eyes closed, with the negligee open; framing her shapely nude body. The white walled room was well lit. And in addition to the evening sun against the closed venetian blinds, both table lamps and ceiling light had been turned on. There would be no shadows to conceal Clara's lovely glistening vulva or Rory's large-thick tongue. Whatever it was that bothered Clara, thought Rory, she now has enough light to frighten it away, or the least, to meet it face to face. He had never been accustomed to this much brightness, but was fearful of mentioning his old ways to her at such an enraptured time.

What a beautiful sight, thought Rory, as Clara A. Feldon lay sprawled on the bed with her gorgeous thighs and impressive bowlegs gapped open; vertically angled, fully extended. *Beau ideal.* Clara's invitation was also fully extended, with one hand inside her thigh and the other atop her firm breast; a definite signal on what must be done. Rory remembered Clara's words on yesterday, "I love the way you eat." His lips and jaws quivered all the way to his temple; saliva streamed into his mouth, preparing, his tongue and lips for a sumptuous meal. Rory would make Clara A. Feldon happy again, eliminating her gloominess with each stroke of his tongue. So Rory greedily, occupied the angled space, head first, facing the corner within an inch; looking forward and directly into Clara's delicious moist folds. Rory had prepared himself to waddle through a beautiful thick-wiry meadow, but Clara A. Feldon's luscious vulva was shaven clean. "Was this the new generations approach," Rory thought, "if so they are missing part of the fun of it all. There is nothing like trampling through a coarse black patch of curly-locks." Rory smiled as he admired the beauty before him. *Truly a chef-d'oeuvre.*

Clara A. Feldon said nothing, but she could feel Rory's presence. The warmth from Rory's moustache-lips found its way into the corner of her smooth delightful thighs, generating sultry steam. Clara lay motionless with thoughts paining her of paternal loneliness. As the steam got warmer and warmer, Clara sallied downward gently touching Rory's large broad lips. The silence was broken as their lips gave rise to a smacking sound. Clara A. Feldon's glabrous sumptuous vulva had lips comparable to the magnificent wide lips of Rory; and now they were pressed tightly against the other. *Vis-à-vis; mere teasing and luxurious foreplay.* No other sounds were heard. No other voluntary movements were necessary as Clara felt her breast rising and her nipples hardening, underneath her hands, which had grasped them; she suddenly wanted them sucked, pulling

Rory's mouth onto her swollen nipples. Rory, enjoying the sweet aroma and slight moist surface of Clara's puffy-round folds, moved reluctantly, but knew the breast trip was a mere brief stop over. Two of his senses had already dictated where quality time would be spent this evening. Clara held one breast, then the other, directing Rory's time of possession before alternating. Rory was aware of what to do as his mouth encircled the upper crust of Clara's breast to include the nipple; simultaneously, gently passing his tongue about. Clara lost grip of her breast as sensation after sensation gyrated through her body. She could feel warm liquid stirring on her inner vaginal lips.

Rory massaged and caressed each soft tissue individually, collectively, and synchronously. His large palms cupped them within; his strong fingers gently squeezed inward and outward in a rotation motion, as if playing a musical instrument allowing Rory's elegant tongue to manipulate the sound – the stimulus – the effect. Sweet music – sweet juices flowed from the tip – the nipple; and Rory consumed it all, catching most on the sides and underneath; moving swiftly, gently and steadily – one to the other. Rory's tender loving tongue rolled with the sound – the music – the juices; sucking – licking – entertaining Clara A. Feldon's vibes:

"Rory ... Rory ... Rory ... Oh Rory -"

To Rory, the sounds were beautiful; the music was enchanting, and the vibes – well – they were oh – so sweet. Rory even thought this journey nutritious; lots of juices continuously flowed from the nipples. Rory imagined what it would be like below; his massive tongue stiffened, growing another inch or two; forming an enormous structure. He was ready to move on. Clara felt Rory's imposing tongue, seemingly wrap around her breast at the same time. Clara A. Feldon also felt the juices streaming through her breast as Rory still gently sucked each of them. Rory's swift tongue, oscillating titillatingly on and around the tip of Clara's soft tissues caused a swelling of her entire lovely breast, creating ecstasy within her extremely moist twitching vagina. Clara opened her eyes to watch Rory play her instruments. Upon seeing Rory's long-thick tongue again, but twice the size, she immediately envisioned it splashing inside her vaginal lips, the same as when eating the nachos. Clara even saw the same creamy cheese on his thick lips.

Clara's sight of Rory's tremendous tongue brought excitement to her body like, never before. This was by far, she thought, the largest piece of flesh, she had ever seen coming out of anyone's mouth; larger and longer than any penis encountered. Clara A. Feldon realized there was much more to Rory than expected. Unreal. Heat burst into Clara's dazzling vulva; its walls initiated a gripping motion, and fluid oozed out of its pulsating opening.

"What a man ... what a man." She blurted out these words extremely excitingly loud.

Rory suddenly, knew Clara was having a good time as she tightened those strong bowlegs around his body and screamed:

"Ooooh, this is so good!"

Then those sprightful bowlegs fell apart; her hands pushed Rory's head away, downward away until it rested far below her navel. Clara A. Feldon lay all worked-up, upon the king-sized bed.

"Rory, I did not know my breast was so sensitive. You are wonderful! That was great! Could we rest for a minute or two before we go on? The next episode will last longer, but your taste buds will enjoy every moment." Clara gives out a big smile.

Rory looked upward and smiled in agreement. The minute, however, was over when Rory raised up and saw Clara's potent vaginal opening, enshrined between two powerful brown thighs, completely saturated with sweet juices. They both knew the other was steaming, but Clara A. Feldon had promised herself, she would let Rory know what she was all about, expressing her maturity at the same time, if possible. Then she gently moved aside, pushing Rory on his back and spreading his legs apart as she crawled between them, sitting facing him, gapping and laying each of her legs over his. Rory's eyes stared into her hairless swollen-lipped delicacy, causing more throbbing in his, seemingly ten inch plus penis, which now rested between Clara A. Feldon's palms. With a firm grip and an irresistible urge, she leaned forward, placing her tongue's tip on the gorgeous shiny pulsating knob. Curving it over each precious ridge, to groans and sighs from Rory, as his eyes began rolling around all funny like; and he felt the fiery sensitivity within his scrotum sac. Clara could feel his body tense up when she slowly moved her hand up and down Rory's large shaft, still ravishing her tongue over his pretty red knob. More groans, sighs, and now moans surfaced from Rory's mouth, which stood open in a circular form, as if he was prepared to suck her fingers like at the ball park. His eyes were now closed.

Clara A. Feldon was in no hurry as she slowly massaged Rory's brick-hard plallus with her soft warm hands. Her lips latched loosely onto his smooth knob while her jaws bulged to sounds of a swishing tongue inside, lavishing stimulating sensual pleasurable strokes. Rory had now began to mix screams and hisses with, the constant loud groans, moans, and sighs. This excited Clara more, making loving him that much more enjoyable; she still concentrated her kissing, licking, and sucking action upon his precious knob where tasteful pre-juices already provided an additional incentive. Clara A. Feldon had now stopped her hand massaging, preferring to explore a bit, touchingly teasing his lovely balls, sending Rory further into hysterics. Most of the fluid, which enabled Clara to glide over his delightful knob was provided by her own saliva glands; responding favorably to his flavor and his jubilant scintilating sounds. She was really off into it now, working her mouth and tongue on his luscious knob like it was her favorite lollipop. Licking, kissing, smacking; going round and round, up and down, in and out, circling and swirling, rapidly bringing them both to their peak; so much so that Clara A. Feldon had placed her other hand inside her juicy vagina and was vigorously rubbing her clit. Rubbing, licking, rubbing, kissing, rubbing, sucking; his screams were louder and more excitable. Rory made phantasmagorical noises as if in real pain, but Clara knew this was joyful gratification. Clara A. Feldon also knew it would not be long, as she caressed his lubricant knob, sliding her teasing tongue over it, feeling his throbs and sensing his end, as she commenced her terminal suction sucking. More screams, loud breathing, more sucking, and now it was time; she removed her mouth, grasping his stiff rigid long shaft in her hand with smooth rapid upward and downward strokes until creamy semen came forth, covering her hand, while she simultaneously, rubbed herself toward sexual pleasure.

Suddenly Clara A. Feldon noticed his parched mouth and long dry tongue hanging out, begging for moisture; her moisture, so she politely rose and lowered her saturated zabaglione into his mouth where his tongue eased forward for some vaginal massaging. And in seconds there was enough lubrication and sweet juices for the both of them. His appetite soared instantly to an all time high as he prepared himself to lovingly eat Clara A. Feldon's juicy zabaglione thoroughly. The sweet aroma again filled his nostrils and Rory's long-thick tongue moved her large luscious lips to and fro. Clara flinched and said:

"I am ready Rory! Rory, I am ready! Its yours ... eat what you want ... eat what you want ... I'm yours ..." Spoke Clara impetuously.

Rory heard Clara A. Feldon's invitation, easing her over onto her back, spreading her marvelous bowlegs; and again he was burying his mouth upon her lustful swollen crimson lips, gliding his tongue over her tender folds of delicious juicy laden flesh. To capture her magnificent beauty once more, Rory raise up to view Clara's beautiful brown body sprawled on the bed with her gorgeous thighs gapped open. Warm juices flowing from the internal heat sparkled in Rory's eyes. As the moisture glisten, Rory cannot help but slide his tongue across his lips, in anticipation of again sliding it into the long slit before him. Clara had again closed her eyes; and like a magnet Rory was drawn downward to the finest set of lips he had ever seen, and while only a foot away, he paused to again admire this delicious eatable wonder. His mouth profusely began to water as Clara's clitoris had already started to peep through. Knowing this was going to be good, Rory savor the whole thing by moving even closer, close enough to smell her sweet scent. So close in fact, his nose touched Clara's quivering hot vagina and more juices flow. Clara A. Feldon's fragrance teased Rory's taste buds and now he wants to eat everything in sight. Through restraint however, he took several deep breaths, drawing the flavorous aroma through his nostrils. Unfortunately or fortunately, depending upon one's point of view, some of the candied juices are sucked in and end up on the palate of Rory's tongue. Clara is being patient, but is only a second from pulling his whole mouth inside of her steamy vaginal opening.

Whatever was bothering Clara, had apparently been moved to a back burner; oddly enough, Rory thought of it, saying to himself, "Maybe it was mother and her crying or the thought of getting offered a principal's position. Whatever it was, I'm not worrying about it at a time like this. Clara has just given me one of the greatest sexual encounters of my lifetime, and if nothing more, I am going to reciprocate."

Clara A. Feldon smells so good, and Rory continue to sniff and draw in gulps of watered down air. Of course, by now, Rory's nose has entered the succulent delicious opening, simply because Clara has sucked him in with one of her rhythmic moves. She now wants action and not teasing, and Rory is more than willing to accommodate her; pulling away just enough to get his breath and to take another visual assessment of what beauty is before him. And as he figured the juices are still there, only more so. The pinkness of Clara's lovely vulva's inner lips and the liquid is now blending to stir up a strong appetite. Clara knows her zabaglione is adorned well; well enough for Rory to want to eat. And from every indicator, Rory will eat and eat a lot, but for now there is too much precious juice flowing. *A natural hors d'oeuvre.* Something must be done about first things first. Rory look closely at the oozing cream; his tongue extends long and he began to lap inward, much like he was on the creamy nacho cheese. The juices are very good to Rory; and what more, Clara is beginning to enjoy this affair, because she is making those sensuous cooing noises. Clara opens her eyes to see Rory's huge tongue in action. She promises to watch as much of Rory's onslaught as she possibly can. The juices are so good to Rory that he cannot seem to get enough; so he ease his long-thick tongue between the drenched groove until their lips touch. Clara is ecstatic, but continue to watch Rory do well.

Rory lick the last of the sweet creamy juices and commence to eat – gently at first – then vigorously as Clara pulls his head in tight. Rory is having trouble breathing as Clara's zabaglione is wide open and has consumed his sinciput. Clara is frantic, but still pretty cool, because she knows there is more to come. He don't care about no breathing as he continue to eat inside Clara's juicy slit; saying to himself, "this is real good eating." Something tells him to tell Clara; tell her man, the little voices say. And he does; raising his head to see Clara massaging both her breast, looking straight into his creamy vagina covered mouth, with hers standing wide open. "This is real good eating honey ... this is real good eating..."

"Thank you Rory ... thank you ... it gets better as you get deeper ... keep doing what you're doing ... just go as far as you can go ..."

Clara and Rory are both enjoying themselves. Rory again attack Clara's luscious insides; following her instructions, slowly inching deeper and deeper. Clara was now getting deliriously vocal.

"You are in virgin territory honey ... take your time ...I can feel you baby ... stay on course sugar ... deeper ... deeper ... hold it ... hold it ... work that spot some more ... this is good Rory ... this is good ... are you loving it honey ... talk to me Rory ...are you loving it."

Of course, Rory, was loving it; that is precisely why he failed to surface with an answer. He loves her talking to him though. Clara could feel his warm firm tongue probing inside of her; moving slowly as if trying to create some familiarity, swirling around the soft spongy sensitive walls, gliding through the sweet wetness, wiggling and searching to her delightful moans. Enjoyable sighs and squirming circular behind movements which, seem to be in agreement with such pleasurable tongue circumambulating. Both, her body and mind appeared to be floating higher and higher as his long slippery tongue explored every inch of her delicious tasteful juicy delicacy. Clara could also feel herself about to explode. So Clara nudge Rory's cheeks with her thighs, shouting, "its time Rory ... its time ..." Rory looks in her direction and Clara gives him a wink and a sigh as her thumb size clitoris is now in full view. They have communicated perfectly, as they both know, it is time, to remove his long tongue buried deep inside of her generous delicacy and head outward.

Clara is ready and Rory knows the transition must be good; so he pulls his long-thick tongue to the surface and give Clara's red and pink lips a whopping sucking kiss, to help send her on a joyful trip. Rory then stroke near Clara A. Feldon's clitoris with his tongue, letting it slide loosely within his lips; where he holds it, licking it with his tongue, sucking it with his lips, simultaneously caressing it with the tip of his tongue. Clara A. Feldon's delicious zabaglione, commence to flood Rory's mouth with hot sweet juices. Non stop. He loves it; he eats it. Rory is eating again ... eating ... eating... as he has never eaten before and as Clara A. Feldon has never been eaten before. Clara feels her heart pumping extremely hard as Rory's tongue and mouth is crawling all over her tender swollen folds; she feels a tremendous climax coming as Rory is viciously eating. Clara cries to herself, "what loving this man is putting on me." She is now having orgasm after orgasm and she still wants more. Rory's long-thick tongue is now alternating between Clara's overpowering vaginal opening, where she pulls Rory in deep, and between her supersensitive clit. Clara is steadily producing tons of warm, real warm juices for Rory's digestion. Her hands are clasped around Rory's head as he continues to alternate; murmuring something about real good eating. His mouth is forced wide open as Clara's tasty zabaglione flood even more. Clara A. Feldon knew Rory was having a good time because he had told her; "he loved eating what he enjoyed."

Clara felt drained, but she would not turn Rory's head loose; so he had to keep on eating until he was released; and there was plenty to eat. She was not holding out for a bigger orgasm, but the way Rory was eating, it seems if one was always there. Rory could again feel her body tense up; he could again feel another one coming; she even told him it was coming and to keep on alternating. Silent breathing slowly turned into harsh growling breaths. Hot air gasped between her widely parted lips with each smooth tongue stroke upon and through her other widely parted lips; soft slushing-mushy strokes which made splashing – squashy sounds to her ears. Sensitive sounds which sent more juices gushing into Rory's mouth, making the watchful Clara A. Feldon envious of his swiftly roving tongue slashing upon and through her sweet stuff. Even her mouth watered to watch such appetizing action, as Rory appeared to be enjoying it so much. Clara strained to hold back another ultimate release which, had been rapidly building and again was now about to explode. With each stroke she slid deeper and deeper into another mesmerizing, frenzied, sensational feeling; her behind twisted and turned, meeting Rory's tongue which was constantly curving onto her tender spots, dipping it inside and outside upon her clit with each revolution. She has yet to figure out what his mouth and lips were doing; it seems if Rory was playing her swollen vaginal lips like a harmonica. Maybe that is why she kept getting orgasms and looking for bigger ones. Rory's head kept turning to the side and each time this dynamic mouth and lip act slid from one end of Clara's vaginal lips to the other. Side to side with his tongue doing all sorts of wonderful things within her very wet slit. She kept wanting more and more; this harmonica thing was driving her into nymphomania and she still craved for more. Finally she said:

"I feel the last of it Rory … please let me guide you or I'll never let you stop eating."

Clara stopped his mouth and tongue onto her clit for the finale. Rory gently manipulated the engorged object real slow and easy with his tongue. Rory could not believe the stamina Clara A. Feldon had as her body got even, more tense. Her hands had fallen off his head, but she continued to watch Rory; to instruct Rory.

"Go slower Rory ... it won't be long."

Clara had not had loving like this for awhile – like never – and she wanted it to last forever – this evening. Even the experienced Rory had never been seized like this before and now he wanted it to last. So he slowed his tongue to a crawl; moving it every now and then. Somehow, it seemed if Clara's flavorful vagina tasted better – certainly sweeter – like nectar, he thought. Rory was, loving, this new sweetness, this new sugary flavored goodness. There was no need to hurry. Apparently that was Clara's motto – go slow – get more. And it was truly working – well – until Rory's body overheated. There was no holding back for Rory as he placed his strong gentle hands around Clara's behind; holding her to his face like the nacho dish. Clara A. Feldon's fiery-colored round swollen folds, gapped wider as Rory's entire long-thick tongue forged a new trail; piercing more untapped spots. An unusual warm slithering could be felt within. Clara's vermiculating body proceeding seemed to bring new excitement to Rory's tongue. Clara looked up to see her derriere dangling in the air; swinging in Rory's hands, and his long-thick tongue moving furiously out and in, within her appetizing zabaglione. Then Rory placed this large thick object over her delicious delicacy, licking its entire surface to include her clit. The excitement found its way into Clara and she screamed; again flooding the warmest of her sweet juices in Rory's mouth. Incessant flooding. Afterward, Clara admitted to Rory that his action was so draining, she would only need it once a month. Of course, Rory wanted it more often, and asked that she leave the subject open.

"Clara, there is something you remind me of; looking into her swollen vaginal lips."

"And what is that Rory?"

"A flower – a cherry blossom – those now in bloom."

Clara, secretly however, had a more sensual exotic name, "her delicious hot zabaglione," her creamy Italian chocolate pudding. "What the heck," she says to herself, "if Rory wants a cherry blossom and continues to ravish his long fat tongue upon, about, and through my petals, I will pleasingly give him all the nectar his mouth can hold.

"A cherry blossom – and how is that Rory; I compare it with a delicious hot zabaglione."

The taste for one thing – sweet as nectar; and the gorgeous look – with that large red clit ... I love that substantial clit."

"Thanks Rory! A flower huh ... does that mean you are going to be my honey bee." Smiling.

"I don't see why not; I feel like buzzing in it again right now. But I like your description so much better; its far better than mine and so much more digestible, for sure."

And Rory commence to licking the surface of Clara's sweet wet delicious hot zabaglione again. Clara lay still, not knowing what to expect. Rory's long large thick tongue was swishing all over Clara; even inside her thighs and onto and inside the crevice of her beautiful brown buttocks. Before long, Clara A. Feldon's clit had reappeared glowing as red as ever, begging for Rory to massage and manipulate it again. Clara felt good and warm and after only a few swishing of Rory's tongue deep into her delicious hot pudding and a few kisses around her clit; it was over as soon as it began. Clara locked her bowlegs around Rory's head, not letting him move an inch. His tongue was stranded deep inside Clara's delicious hot zabaglione touching her tender crimson walls. Rory digested the remaining juices, and they both momentarily fell sound asleep. *Bravo for the encore.*

It had been a while since either of them had been with another, let alone, sleep with another, so all during the night, their itchy hands wandered across to the other's side, affectionately feeling, caressing, and seductively touching delicate fleshy body parts. Rory was still fascinated by the bareness of, Clara A. Feldon's delicious dining area. She was far different from his Charllotte. Lying here, just thinking about the beauty of Clara's smooth colorful vaginal folds was having an arousal affect upon Rory. "Clara's large oval shaped love nest with its full-rounded lips and large opening which grasped, held, and massaged my tongue," he whispered to himself, "has really brought my bod back to life." He admitted to himself; before Clara put loving her this way – soaking his tongue inside her vagina – it had somewhat entered his mind. And after one look at her magnificent hairless wonder gapped wide open with its added invitational juices glistening, he had to send his tongue licking and his mouth eating, what definitely appeared to be wholesome food.

Now Rory is glad he did eat Clara A. Feldon's delicious hot chocolate pudding, as he lay here still savoring her sweetness upon his tongue. One of his hands has found its way upon her soft breast, with its still erect nipple, while the other hand is gradually probing up Clara A. Feldon's inner thighs, meticulously caressing her outer and inner vaginal lips instinctively with his scanning fingers. The smoothness under his fingers, from the surface of Clara's delicate moist lips, even now, make him want to repeat his earlier tongue-lashing. Rory silently says to himself, "loving Clara this way is going to become a perennial favorite, and she made me feel so comfortable in doing it. And its still hard to believe she tasted so good."

Clara A. Feldon flinch a time or two as Rory's fingers slides over her gorgeous soft folds which is swelling more and more to his finger's warmth and pressure. Then with a move of her own, Clara lifts Rory's hand, singling out his middle finger, inserting it within her saturated vaginal opening, giving it the first playful twirl to get Rory going. Rory was surprised at the aggressiveness and liberation of Clara, saying as much to himself, "my – my, I love Clara's liberal nature ... the new generation I suppose." Rory lowered his roving fingers to a depth of one inch, slowly caressing her warm tender walls, pretty much the same as he had earlier with his surging tongue; to occasional moans, but after another inch or so, Clara tells him, "please stop on that spot Rory and just massage me ..." She is groaning and sighing instantly. Rory feels Clara A. Feldon's heat upon his fingers and proceed to lower his mouth over her firm breast, one to the other, manipulating her erect nipples with his tongue. Even without the loud breathing and moaning, Rory knows Clara is feeling pretty good. Her body is squirming and her gyrating behind is pressing her warm lubricated flesh against his fingers. Rory said to himself, "I will have to remember this spot." And no sooner than that, Clara A. Feldon started talking.

"Keep it there Rory ... keep it right there ... I feel like I'm going to ... keep it there Rory ... you are doing it right ... massage me a little harder Rory ... ooooh this is so good ...suck that titty harder Rory ... pull that nipple ... keep that finger going ...oh my...keep it going ... keep it going ...ooooh this is so damn good ... keep that finger moving ...oh my, oh my ... can you feel me ... can you feel me ... ooooh, oooooooh ... can you feel ... ooooh, oooooh, oooooh..."

Rory realized this climax was as big as the first one and all the others, and every bit as wet; his hand was totally saturated with Clara A. Feldon's sweet warm juices. And he was also every bit as horny as the first time.

"I know you are horny Rory," as if reading his mind, "but I'm almost done for tonight," grabbing his long hard hugeness, inserting it within her lovely smooth shaven vagina. "Here – go for what you know Rory – oooh, you are real nice size. Give it to me, honey ...give it to me. Easy Rory ...easy, I'm not going anywhere. Here, let me lay my legs across your shoulders; there, isn't that better. Give it to me honey...don't be afraid ... give it to me, I can take it ...give it all to me honey ... all of it Rory ... don't' hold back ... give it to me ... come on baby – come on – there you go – you're hitting it honey ...go on and get it baby ...get you one ... get it now baby. I can feel you honey ...I can feel you...I can feel it honey ... get it honey, get it, get it, get it."

And that was it for Rory as he squeezed her ball-shaped buttock with a last grasp of his palms before falling exhausted onto the bed. This was the first time during a series of lovemaking that Clara A. Feldon had ever gotten multiple orgasms, and for the first time she knew she was free; free of all the clutter in her brain of all that male apprehension. Rory had slid his long-broad tongue into the depths of her life and she was never going to throw that away, saying to herself, "Rory, you will never slide your teasing, tantalizing tongue into none other than my delicious hot zabaglione, my sweet chocolate pudding. What a smooth powerful tongue you have and I want it searching in my pudding every chance I get."

Rory was more than enamored with her loquaciousness; it was his first to hear such a pleasurable display of compelling sensate words. He even admired and was aroused enormously by the scintilating manner in which Clara A. Feldon's emotions flowed. It showed, he thought, the honesty of her heart. There was no legitimate comparison whatsoever with any prior lustful moments. Paradise it seems was upon him; Clara's rareness in womanhood silenced him with an impressionable passionate intoxication.

Monday morning finally came and Clara A. Feldon and Rory was up at their usual early work day hours, but a decision had been made between the two of them to take the day off. Too many vibrations were still going through their bodies as they showered together, gently washing the other's body parts with their soapy warm massaging-fingers.

"How long can I expect treatment like this from you Rory?"

"I was just thinking on the same lines Clara, and about yesterday, and about Saturday; this has really been wonderful. You really impressed Linnie Scott, being with me and all."

"Not half as much I bet as you impressed Helene. That girl is so nosey; wanting to know all about our lovemaking life."

"And what did you tell her Clara?"

"Well, I sort of stretched the truth a little bit Rory, telling her how good a lover you were. She is so inquisitive."

"Hmmm, what else?"

"Helene is pretty persistent Rory, inquiring about details, especially your long-fat tongue."

100

"And what did you tell her Clara about my long-fat tongue?" Rory was smiling, caressingly washing Clara's breast, simultaneously extending his tongue outward.

"Well, I sort of stretched the truth a little bit more Rory, telling Helene how good it was. She of course wanted to know more."

"More about what Clara?"

"Your tongue Rory, like I said … you know … if I let you ease it into my darkhollow – her word you know; your cherry blossom or my delicious hot zabaglione."

"And what did you tell her? Let me guess, (with a smile) you sort of stretched the truth a little bit more!"

"Uh huh, I hope you are not angry Rory; things were happening so fast, and it was afterall, your fault – the way you were wrapping your long tongue around everything. Even I became fascinated a little ahead of time."

"Oh, I see … coerced by Helene's loud mouth … and -"

"And I am extremely happy with you Rory, and I want this or I want us to last forever."

"Then you have answered your own question Clara, about my treatment. I am very much pleased."

Clara A. Feldon felt at ease as Rory fondle-lathered one of her gorgeous brown breast, then the other. And quickly as the warm shower rinsed the suds away, proceeded to caress each of her erect nipples in the same fashion inside his mouth; slithering his tongue over her lovely nipples and tenderly letting his lips suck gently inward. Rory had found Clara's breast to be super sensitive, clinging to them as he massage-lathered her round behind. Only soft moans could be heard from Clara, until she seized his middle finger, steering it slowly inside her anus for several inchy stimulating wiggles, then abrupt loud screams ensued. Rory felt the tight grip around his large lubricated finger loosen, surging another inch before the muzzling grip returned. His second sense, of course, told him there was more of Clara's sweetness to enjoy if he hurried. So Rory turned the water off, lifting Clara from the tub, only to have her bend on the tub's edge, arching her curvaceous behind upward, exposing her bald delicious zabaglione, within nurturing distance of his salivating tongue. Clara could feel Rory's long-fat tongue sliding upon and lunging into her before it actually dipped onto her moist swollen lips, teasingly so, and plunging onward through her inner folds. She felt his firm hands wrapped around her bottom, gently squeezing each bun as he thrust his wet tongue lovingly into her delicious zabaglione; tasting and promptly eating her incredibly sweet creamy flavorful wetness. Their fiery passion for each other was the same as last night. And Clara had apparently saved the best juices for Rory, as she heard him say, "Honey, this is even better than yesterday."

Clara responded positively by gripping and squeezing Rory's tongue with her great muscular action, later sending a stream of even sweeter juices into his mouth for his enjoyment pleasure. Yes, Rory had ended their shower in splendid fashion, simultaneously having his breakfast, drinking her succulent juices and licking her delicious zabaglione until it was sparkling clean. The morning had, begin for Rory, pretty much, as the night had ended; having an enjoyable appetizing time with Clara A. Feldon. We would have to say this couple is compatible for obvious reasons, as Clara directs Rory onto the commode, kneeling to her knees, accommodating herself for a nourishing treat.

With breakfast over, we now find them back in the bedroom. Both still naked, Clara sits upon the side of the bed, bowlegs gapped apart, facing Rory, seated to her front, smiling and exchanging admiring glances upon (what they think) each other's glamourous body. Rory was staring at her bald delicious brown pudding, thinking of the new generation and how considerate Clara had been of his needs; being willing to go beyond the ordinary. Unselfish. "Man," he said silently, "she is so smooth and velvety brown; I wonder what she see in an old guy like me." Clara A. Feldon looked toward Rory's waist, glancing upon his thighs and his drooping hugeness, then glancing, at the picture of her late father on the dresser. A lot of things occupied her mind, from how handsome Rory was, to how great a lover he was. But the one item of most concern, was finally divulged when she said:

"Rory, could I please sit on your lap!"

"Means by all means Clara, its all yours; put that gorgeous bottom of yours right there." Patting his large strong thighs with his large palms.

Placing her nude torso in his lap, Clara leaned backward into Rory's warm chest and his embracing arms, touching underneath her soft breast.

"This is something I have wanted to do all my life Rory; to sit snugly upon strong legs and have someone hold me lovingly. Will you hold and love me forever Rory ... will you -"

"Of course I will," Rory could detect a sentimental simmering in her voice. "Of course I will – I will always be here for you." He cannot see her moisture filled eyes, but feels a tear rolling across his arms. "I will always be here for you honey."

"Excuse ... me Rory ..." Rubbing her hands over her face and placing his hands over her warm breast. "Love me Rory ... please love me some more ..." Reaching and massaging his swelling hugeness within her warm palms.

Rory was surprised at how quick he was responding, feeling his hugeness nudging inside her thighs. She continued to stroke him gently as he ripened within her warm sensuous grasp.

"Let me just sit on you Rory." Simultaneously raising her buttocks enough to allow his hugeness to enter her and slowly easing down to encircle his throbbing knob. "Please be still honey ..."

Clara A. Feldon was now hovering, performing a masterful rhythm hugging sensational swirl upon Rory's huge-long penis. Slowly she guided his swollen knob, massaging and squeezing it so pleasurable until Rory could not help but climax immediately. She could feel him when he flinched, forcing his long shaft, piercing it deep inside her. Rory was fiercely biting her neck and massaging her swollen breast as she continued screwing him vigorously from her squat, resting her hands upon his knees, steadily, giving him a screwing like none other. He could not believe his penis would not subside, but seem to get even harder, as Clara rocked downward causing him to shove more of his shaft inside of her vagina and he felt like climaxing again.

"I can feel you honey ... grab my clit ...rub my clit honey ...rub my clit ... harder man harder ... don't be afraid honey...rub it harder. There, there ...rub it ... rub it good. Come on baby ... I feel it ...come on, come on ...I feel it... there you go ... get it baby ... go on and get it ...whew shit ... love it baby ... get you one more honey ... oh my Lord ...I'm gonna get one ... oh my ... I'm gonna get ..."

Rory could take no more, coming big time, crying out, sending Clara gasping for breath as she climaxed, screaming, profusely flooding hot juices down his shaft upon his swollen balls into the chair's cushion. Exhausted, Rory lifted Clara up into his arms and they both fell into bed. He said to himself, "I sure hope this is it for awhile or that forever might not be too far away."

After a moment's rest, Clara reminded Rory of a personal chore.

"Rory, remember, you have to pick up and fix my taillight cover today."

"I had forgotten about that Clara; it will be a breeze though. I'll have it on before noon, if I get started now."

"Good, that will give me time to clean up this dirty apartment and warm up some of mother Davanpourt's fine cooking. We have enough for at least two days, you know."

"Yeah, thanks to mother cooking enough for ten people."

Replacing the broken lens cover had not been as easy for Rory as he had figured. First, after a careless removal of the orange and red remnant, two of the four screws had fallen downward, where only a small round opening separated his large hands from reconciling the tiny screws to their respective position. Then after carefully holding the new lens cover, while sitting inside Clara's open trunk, another one of the screws fell.

After a few choice words and a glance outward, Rory noticed a curious looking young face peering directly at him.

"Hi there, young fella!"

"My name is Joshua!"

"Okay ... Joshua ... nice meeting you ... I am Rory!"

"Are you Mrs. Feldon husband?"

Rory could not help but smile, saying, "Not exactly ... why do you ask Joshua?"

"You working on her car."

"Oh I see ... well, I am just fixing her light Joshua."

"Are you Mrs. Feldon boyfriend?"

Rory's smile was even broader, saying, "Sort of ... how old are you Joshua?" Holding up one hand to Rory without saying a word, Rory guessed, saying, "five huh," and Joshua nodded.

"Are you Mrs. Feldon good boyfriend?" Moving closer to Rory and looking more serious.

"Well ... you could pretty much say that Joshua."

"My mama got a good boyfriend. Are you going to stay with her again tonight?"

Rory looked puzzled, saying, "I might ... we are sort of engaged Joshua."

"Engaged ... what's that?

"It's when two people meet before getting married."

Joshua looked at Rory without saying a word, as if satisfied; even satisfying Rory when he noticed the boy's small hands might be of some use.

"Joshua, how would you like to help me fix Mrs. Feldon's car?"

Joshua nodded his head moving closer.

"Good, I dropped three screws just like this one, behind the light. If I hold you, do you think you could reach through this hole and get them for me?"

Joshua smiled and nodded. He recovered the three screws, but had to do it, in part, at least five more times before Rory finally got them all fitted into place.

"Thank you my lil' helper." Patting Joshua on the head.

105

"My name is Joshua."

"Okay Joshua ... how about five dollars for your help." He nodded. Rory came out of his pocket with a ten being his smallest bill, giving it to Joshua, who had the bill and gone before Rory could say anything else; disappearing through a faded green door, matching the building's exterior surface, downstairs and across from Clara's unit. It was now one o'clock and Rory was starving as he slowly headed upstairs, wiping his hands, looking toward the closed door across the way. No one appeared.

"It's about time Rory; what took you so long ... the food has been warm for almost thirty minutes." Clara stood there, all gorgeous, smelling fresh, in a pastel-blue sheer waist-length top and matching bikini-bottom. "Hurry and wash up before your food gets cold."

Washing and seating himself across from Clara, saying, "I would have been sooner, but I had to get engaged to Mrs. Feldon." Smiling.

"I can tell, you have been talking to Josh."

"No – no ... Joshua, my dear ... this is better than yesterday."

Clara laughing. "That's Josh all right ... he has corrected me a time or two ... he is so proud of his name."

"Uh huh ... says he's five ..." Rory holding up his hand, displaying a mouth full of food.

"Five fingers huh ... well, he is really only four ... almost five Rory. I am surprised he talked to you ... normally he shies away from strangers."

"Probably had something to do with me working on Mrs. Feldon car; he even helped me out."

"He did, now isn't that sweet Rory."

"Uh huh ... even gave him ten dollars."

"He did not beg you for any money, did he Rory?"

"Oh no, he helped me a plenty ...I could not have made it without him ... he really earned the ten."

"So how did we get engaged so quickly Rory?" Smiling.

"Well Clara, I sort of felt guilty when Joshua inquired about me staying with you again tonight. I guess I was sort of thinking ahead, you know."

"Coerced by a little kid, and sort of stretched the truth, huh."

"You remember everything Clara."

"Yeah Rory ... well don't be surprised if I officially hold you to that unofficial proposal." Smiling.

"That would sure be something, wouldn't it!" Rory smiling and licking on his fingers.

"I did not heat any of mother Davanpourt's dessert Rory because I was not sure which kind you had a taste for."

"That's easy Clara, how about some of that delicious hot zabaglione." Laughing.

"You remember everything Rory ... matter of fact I did not think you were paying close attention."

"With you I pay close attention to everything... well – how about that delicious chocolate pudding of yours -"

"Rory, you are not serious, I know ... could we wait until tonight -" And before Clara finishes her surprised look, Rory has circled the table, lifting his dessert back to a soft dining bed. Clara lay backward engineering her nude body into one of her favorite positions, raising her gorgeous brown thighs parallel to her stomach, locking her arms around them, exposing the elevated gapped and delicious zabaglione. Thigh-tongued-thrust was her name for this scrumptious eating position.

Rory was amazed at Clara A. Feldon's versatility and athleticism and doubly impressed with the effort implored to maintain his enormous appetite of her delicious pudding. From his viewpoint, everything about her was overwhelmingly appetizing. Rory's mouth could not help but water, gazing upon her beautiful brown smooth cracked-buttocks, surrounding her large oval shaped luscious outer lips pulling further outward; opening her luscious cherry blossom flushed inner lips, exposing lubricant tempting pink walls, an inch in depth. The large opening was as magnificent as its clean shaven surroundings; "Obstruction free," thought Rory, as he prepared to lunge his

107

seemingly sensational eight inch fat tongue into the glistening gaping wide hole. But prior to this, Rory was in a kissing and licking mood and commence to kissing and slobbering all over Clara's delectable seamed buttocks, slashing his tongue with intricate movements, which touched and teased her rapidly swelling vibrating outer as well as inner vaginal lips.

Rory was taking his time because he remembered from yesterday, Clara loved having her large clitoris manipulated vigorously; so easing about her broad lips would surely create an itching for its appearance. Clara flinched as he kissed her vaginal lips repeatedly, sliding his warm wet tongue upon them; becoming more and more saturated with the presence of her flavorful juices. Occasionally during Rory's kissing and licking revolutions he covered her juicy flowing opening with his mouth, only to hear Clara begging for his long tongue to be thrust inside of her delicious vagina, which he obliged. And just like clockwork, her long swollen clitoris eased forward for their pleasure; for Rory to suck and manipulate, and Clara to have frenzy gyrating fits, screwing the living day lights out of Rory's mouth, and his tongue when he obliged her with his occasional deep surges.

Clara had now began to feel real good asking Rory to suck her clitoris harder and harder. She could not seem to get enough, begging for more and more as Rory's lips had a roaming good time slushing through and eating her wonderful sweetness. He could feel her on the verge of something big, but she hung on. *Pure ecstatic pleasure.* Rory reasoned Clara was trying to top yesterday's orgasms and he wanted very much to help her, because this meant her pudding would be ever so much sweeter. So he knew, hanging around, near, and on her delicate organ as she insisted was of supreme importance to them both; and he somehow guessed after several long grueling minutes, his middle finger sliding inside of her vagina might assist somewhat. At first there was no change, but then he apparently inched it upon a very hot spot and within seconds she had a magnificent orgasm. Amidst the screams, Rory eased his mouth

108

into Clara A. Feldon's delicious hot zabaglione and began to eat. And was it ever tasty, yes, much much sweeter than yesterday. An abundance of sweetness and good eating, lasting into the night, and bringing tuesday morning upon them. Clara has now ensnared Rory with the taste of her young tender candied breast and her flavorful fleshy succulent vulva, so neatly concealed between the borders of her irresistible mouthwatering round brown buttock and thighs. He happily devoured her delicacy while entangled in the net of her graceful bowlegs and gripping arms and palms. A lion roaming through the wilderness, no doubt would have been trapped and tamed the same; to dine and enjoy all future servings of this delicious meal. Rory roared his approval with licks, moans, and proficient dining techniques.

10

Clara A. Feldon decided again that today, **Tuesday,** was better as a non – work day, and Rory did likewise when he was unable or unwilling to unglue her mouth off his hugeness until total weakness was upon him after an extraordinary draining osculation. Clara, surprising enough was getting where she could not keep her mouth off Rory. On this day, at this moment she stopped him between the bath and bedroom doorway, leaning his back against the facing, while she fell upon her knees and took all he had had, cramming his hugeness deep inside her throat, miraculously massaging him to a weak-knee buckling orgasm. He ended up gasping for air and begging for mercy on the floor as she finished crowning his knob with her smooth mouth and tongue strokes. Rory was amazed, Clara had such powerful jaws, but he loved it, with his now weak and drained self, but he loved it. These two were enjoying being with each other; neither feeling bashful about tasting the sweet wetness generated on their behalf. In this short period of time Clara A. Feldon and Rory were growing ever conscious of the other's sexual pleasures and desires. *The great expectation.* Clara even went so far as to think she loved everything about Rory, and concluding with a gratifying grin that his long-broad tongue was superb. She was proud that he was aware of his tongue's wide ranging capabilities and his willingness to slide it through the folds of her delicious hot zabaglione at her digression. A hint or a glance at any one of her favorite exposing positions was all that was necessary for Rory to activate his saliva wet mouth-watering slithering tongue, sending it slashing wherever Clara wanted or directed it to go. Some and most times though, Rory's greediness took over when his eyes focused upon Clara's smooth velvety brown pudding, usually accompanied with palatable creamy moisture, running among its crevices. This eager disposition always propelled Rory to lick upon and between her tender folds and graciously eat Clara's delicious hot zabaglione. He had come to realize no eating was more enjoyable or appetizing. And ironically, Rory could not seem to get enough, wanting to eat Clara's creamy chocolate pudding repeatedly. He had never tasted anything before with such juicy rich flavor and soft texture. *Warm jubilant flowing ingredients.* His wide opened smiling mouth easily covered Clara's large lubricious outer lips, squeezing inward, forcing richer and richer succulent digestible portions through his throat downward into his waiting stomach.

It was extremely difficult to determine who was starved the most, Clara or Rory. If it mattered, and obviously it did not, from the way their lips were so firmly attached. Rory's broad lips mooched and kissed upon her outer and inner soft moist lips more ways than Clara ever imagined, always bringing forth the best in her. When she wasn't pulling his lips in deeper with her hands upon his head or her curvaceous bowlegs with an even tighter grip, she was squirming vigorously, pushing these luscious lips farther and farther forward as each nerve-shattering climax burst through. Rory always met the task, pressing tightly in his own right, careful to maintain their canals over the other for his dining pleasure. Hardly a difficult chore, once Clara commence to flood a steady torrent in his direction, fulfilling his hunger and satisfying some of her starvations. Rory loved eating Clara's delicious hot zabaglione, and from the brevity of their involvement, Clara loved providing him with an opportunity to eat it so lovingly. She knew that getting Rory to gaze into her gorgeous crimson folds, which purposely lay open on many such occasions, would have a magnetic effect. Of course, she admitted, it was really the sight of his broad lips, coupled with his long-thick tongue which usually made gaps between her thighs widen.

They were certainly enamoured by each other's sexuality; imaginative indeed, lips touching lips clasped together, each biting and getting biten, each providing the other with a stimulating sensual gratification. Yes, Rory crammed his tongue inside of Clara A. Feldon because she enticed him to do so, and yes, she gapped her legs apart for him to lick about, because he enticed her to do so. A perfect rhapsody of a feast or to be feasted upon; enjoying the creaminess of a delicious hot zabaglione. Being thrust upon and about and thrust within with powerful tongue surges, rimming deep pink walls, seem heavenly at times, as Rory and Clara is more than captivated by their bountiful resourcefulness. A sweet flavorful resource which Rory craves; loving to satisfy his appetite, and which Clara loves ... loves giving it up to him ... loves watching him eating and enjoying himself ... loves him for making her produce what he loves over and over again. *Sweet love.*

So, it goes without saying; Tuesday was going to be another one of those days where they stayed inside the house all day and obviously inside each other. Certainly there would be breaks and periods of relaxation, though only briefly, but enough for rejuvenation. And it seems those minutes took place while Clara showered, because here she is crawling onto the bed, lying upon her back, thighs extended and upward, with her large red clitoris already beckoning for Rory. *Swiftly.* Rory's lips however, stopped upon her mons pubis; he kissed her here repeatedly, even licking his broad tongue all over this area. He could smell Clara's sweet vaginal fragrance as she gave out soft moans. She loved Rory's patience as his wet tongue and lips thoroughly caressed her in this area and slowly eased downward pass her vagina to kiss and lick her inner thighs. Clara was steaming; this man she thought was magnificent in his lovemaking. Suddenly she could take no more teasing and pulled him onto her moist lips where he kissed her, oh so gently. Clara's body is so hot and she practically beg for more vigorous action, pulling Rory's head forward.

Rory's lips enclosed her clit and his tongue gave it those smooth gentle strokes; continuously, round and round, to and fro, over and under, gliding with ease from the moisture flowing profusely from his salivary glands. Soft, tender tongue strokes upon Clara's ever growing clit sliding freely within Rory's mouth, which also waited patiently for her sweet juices, surely to come in minutes if not seconds from such constant slippery tongue movements. This morning Rory's tongue had those warm slow-swift revolutions, touching the tip of her clit, sending stimulating tingles through her vagina, tightening her anus, exploding pleasurable pain into her large brown widely-gapped thighs; accommodating and virtually over powering Clara. Rory's vigorously moving head, now under the direction of Clara A. Feldon's palms placed lightly against his cheeks, encouraging the meticulous tongue roving as her final seconds expire, sending the first of many climatic juices his way. She now redirect his mouth and tongue revolutions into the pathway of this flood, where enjoyment is imminent for the both of them as her streaming hot fluid hits his palate, registering its sweetness, gushing onward down his throat into his stomach. Clara climax over and over, multiple orgasms, watching his long-broad tongue slashing upon her; craving herself, the lusciousness of what he's receiving, climaxing some more, tightening her hand grip on his head for a final episode, before they fell loosely upon the bed. Rory now, slowly licks and joyfully finish eating Clara's delicious zabaglione; sliding his tongue through her tender fleshy folds. Truly, breakfast was being served in bed.

"Rory, you are so good for me; where have you been all my life? Please do not answer; just keep that tongue of yours performing that pleasurable fluttering. You massaged my clit so good; I'm sorry I could not hang on longer, but your eating is so smooth and passionate."

It was only fitting that Clara A. Feldon did not expect Rory to answer, he was too busy licking inside her inner thighs. She felt his tongue searching all about her twitching tender folds; and wished to immediately send him some more sweet juices ... no doubt an evening meal treat. However, the sudden warmth of his tongue and breath so near her anus began to send new stimulating tingles into her. Clara wanted to tell Rory to experiment a little with that tongue search and, squirmed upward to give him a clue. Quickly feeling delicate soft flicking touches upon this pathway before her strength gave way to total exhaustion; and a mind set to explore this venture another time ... possibly for their evening meal. "It appears," thought Clara, "I have a real man that will stop at nothing to satisfy me ... and he reads me so well."

"Rory, you have made me so happy and I want you to know, I will do anything for you."

Kissing on her soft stomach, Rory said, "Thank you Clara; that means a lot to me." Sending his wet tongue sliding onto her navel. "After my Charllotte, you mean more than I thought any woman could. I have sweet taste whenever you are in my presence. Your heart-warming beauty sensitizes my taste buds, secreting flavored fluids inside my mouth and upon my tongue. Fluids, producing slippery wetness, moisturizing my lips when my tongue slither across them; inching slowly as if already upon your soft vaginal lips, receiving such juicy sweetness from within your delicate folds. Needless to say you exude excitement which begs for the harmonization of juices for ones appetizing pleasure. Even, thoughts of you Clara, produces electrifying

114

sensual effects upon my body parts, swelling them to gigantic proportions, in great anticipation of a hearty and tasteful reception. Given your enchantment however, I have no difficulty bowing to honor your gateway of life, caressing your succulent folds to your gratifying pleasure, digesting your delicious sweet juices. Partaking or eating any delicacies you provide Clara, is obviously a delight. Especially at your highest peak where your best is bound to come streaming into my mouth ... your juiciest ... your sweetest ... your most satisfying ... your most appetizing as it oozes out for my dining pleasure. Repetition and more repetition as you pull my head in deeper; wriggling your lovely hairless wonder in my face until I can hardly breathe ... giving and giving me more ...giving me everything you got. Making me lick and eat your delicious hot zabaglione, forceful and vigorously as you scream and cry. I always want to tell you this is the best, but I cannot talk because my mouth is full ... my throat is full ... my stomach is full; yet I am begging you to give me more. I feel like I too will have an orgasm and well ... most of the time, to be honest, I do."

"I really appreciate your honesty Rory and the poetry of your words; and speaking of eating, I am going to fix you a good meal today – any preferences?

"Not really ... you did say good ... that would be my only preference."

"I had better get going Rory, it is nearly eleven o'clock already."

After the sound of Clara A. Feldon in the shower, Rory could hear the clattering and rattling sounds of a kitchen being used. No inquiry was made of Clara as to what meal she was about to prepare, but his full stomach from eating earlier, told hin it did not matter. Clara was busily about the kitchen; for mother Davanpourt had told her Rory was a big eater and she had found as much herself. She was happy for this opportunity to show Rory there were other good cooks in the world besides his belated Charllotte and mother Davanpourt. Feeling in her heart, if she succeeded at further satisfying his stomach, Rory would definitely be eating all of her good stuff forever. Clara smiled as she thought of her thoughts of Rory's spectacular eating habits and how happy she was to be an active part in it. So far, she had been a hit on his consumption pleasures. Standing in the kitchen, Clara's groin tingled a bit underneath her soft blue cotton robe, when she thought how they had, since Sunday, made love virtually nonstop. After having her delicious hot zabaglione slashed thoroughly by this classic hunk of a man, giving him a tender breast of baked chicken seemed like an excellent choice of a different meat. Preparing it too with one of her creamy wine sauces also seemed like a grand idea. Knowing that the simplicity of things should not be totally ignored, Clara re-made her style, some of the canned french green beans, a golden gleaming squash casserole, along with a roman salad.

Rory never appeared while the cooking was going on, but he could smell the delectable aroma as it filtered into the bedroom, where he sat, attired in nothing but his birthday suit. Hanging in the bathroom was his freshly washed shorts and teeshirt, because going home had not been a priority since their torrid sexual encounters. Rory, however, was feeling comfortable and right at home, having made the bed, cleaned the bathroom – spotless, including picking up Clara's under-garments in both places. This was seemingly Clara's only weakness pertaining to neatness. She had this habit of letting her panties and bra drop and remain wherever they came off. And cleaning a bathroom was the one chore she absolutely hated. Rory solemnly thought of his Navy service to his country while observing the military picture of Clara's father on the dresser. He felt sadden she was not given an opportunity to know the handsome man.

"It will not be much longer Rory ... you mean you still do not have any clothes on ... oh, you have cleaned the room ..." Rory smiled and pointed toward the bathroom and she naturally kept walking.

"You did not have to do this Rory ... my, it is so clean in here ... and it smells good too. And you washed your underwear

... that is a woman's work ... why don't we go to your house and pick up some things after we eat?"

"Sounds good, but we don't have to ... they are clean now."

"And they are also wet Rory ... anyway I want to see how a good-looking bachelor live!"

Clara A. Feldon had never set foot in a man's house before; a hotel or two, yes. This caliber of a man was somewhat new to her, in more ways than one. She admitted to herself, Rory had spoiled her already, with that fantastic lovemaking he slithered upon her.

"That food sure smells good Clara."

"Uh huh, and it's probably ready ... you had better get ready yourself Rory."

"How? My clothes are wet."

"No problem ... wrap a towel or sheet around you Rory." Rory looked at Clara curiously like and started laughing.

"What's so funny?"

"I was just thinking, I could wear something of yours Clara ... a robe ... a blouse -"

"A bra ... a pair of my panties ... now you would look great in that get up Rory." Smiling herself.

Rory laughing even harder. "I can tell by the look on your face Clara, you would just love it. Now isn't that just too bad ... but if you had something my size, I would definitely style it for you." Still laughing.

"You would not be laughing so hard Rory if you were not so sure of yourself. I would give anything to see your laughing-hyena face, squeezing into something feminine."

"Well, I'm taking all bets Clara ... I would even wear it for the rest of the week." Laughing some more.

Clara sat quietly for awhile, taking all the garments in her closet through her mind. She was sure after a careful thought process, one of her larger robes would fit this tall dark handsome man. Then she started laughing.

"I will be right back Rory."

She returned with another blue robe, much like the one she was wearing, throwing it onto Rory's lap, saying, "Try this on laughing boy, this ought to shut you up!"

Rory picked the garment up, holding it in front of his face, saying, "Now, now Clara ... I can look at this and tell its too small." Giving her a fake smiling closed-lipped, puffed jaw, then laughing hard for real. "That's too bad too ... I was sort of looking forward to seeing that frown on your face disappear."

"Sure Rory ... you probably mean, seeing your laughter disappear."

"It would have been nice Clara, guess I'll have to wrap a sheet around me." Laughing.

"Hold it Rory, I will be right back." Disappearing again to the hallway closet, returning with a gift-wrapped package, handing it to Rory.

"Well now Clara, what did I do to deserve a gift."

"Open it and see, laughing boy!" A deep grin surfaced on her face.

Rory meticulously unwrapped and opened the package to one of the brightest red silk pieces of cloth he had seen lately. Matter of fact, when he sorted things out, he found there were two pieces – a sheer negligee and its string – nothingless bottom. Rory started laughing the moment he saw it, knowing it was his size.

"Now where did you get this fancy garment Clara?"

"It's a gift for a friend of mine who got married late last year; this present was for the bachelorette party which I was unable to attend. So you think it might fit, huh Rory?"

"From that smile on your face Clara, you know it fits ... she was pretty good size, huh?"

"Your size honey ... go on, try it on ... I am dying to see this."

"Clara, now you know I was just kidding." Smiling, half gazing at Clara and the garment at the same time.

"Yes, I know Rory ... kidding for the rest of the week ... remember? Go on honey, slip into your suggestive outfit and style it for me ... remember ... style hard for me honey."

"Okay Clara, but you are going to have to promise not to even breathe a sigh of this to anybody."

"I don't remember that being part of the deal Rory, but I will think about it." Clara had fallen to the floor laughing; more at Rory's changed expression than anything else.

Rory smiling, eased into the negligee and standing, eased into the bottom string that only partially covered his large penis; showing all of his pubic hair and his tremendous scrotum and its contents. He gave a rearward twist or two at Clara, showing a strap only halfway onto his behind. Needless to say, Clara was still rolling, her eyes in hilarious tears; they both were laughing hard as Rory pranced around for some more of his torso-shaking antics.

"Now honey, I can say you are appropriately dressed for dining."

Rory and Clara A. Feldon smiled and laughed all during the meal. She reminded him his final day for styling was Saturday. Rory could not believe how easily he had gotten himself into this ridiculous charade, but it did not appear to offset his large appetite. He ate as if there was nothing strange about his attire. This was indeed strong evidence to Clara that her cooking and food was excellent; Rory even had seconds and part of some more meat to finish out his bread, and part of some more trimmings to finish out his meat. "He eats my cooking," Clara said to herself, "as well as he eats my delicious hot zabaglione." Clara knew this man was hers for good now, promising herself to lighten up teasing him so much on his new wardrobe; preferring to use a new angle, geared toward sex appeal and how he really turned her on.

When Clara saw Rory stuffed, pushing his chair away from the table, she removed her robe and eased onto his lap. She felt his large penis rising immediately against her buttocks and within seconds his erect object had popped free. Holding and

119

admiring Rory's enticingly piece of flesh was the only natural thing for Clara, and she did just that, sliding upon her knees, easing his throbbing knob to her lips where multiple kisses transpired. Then she eased the glowing red knob and its beautiful ridges into her mouth and commence to tenderly suck it. She could hear Rory moaning as her wet tongue sensuously licked his much, stimulated knob, circling it over and over again as she continued sucking it. Rory's moans turned into groans, sensing readiness; so she removed her mouth and vigorously stroked his extremely hard shaft, upward and downward with her hand, and within seconds Rory had an orgasm. Using a table napkin for a receptacle, Clara enclosed Rory's large object as he swiftly lifted her in his arms and headed for the bedroom. She knew and welcomed what this meant as he lay her naked body upon the bed, where she spontaneously gapped her bowlegs as wide as she possibly could.

Rory crawled directly to her delicious hot zabaglione because he could smell its sweet aroma, knowing the goodness, inhaling deeply, spreading his tongue through his lips toward her already saturated swollen lips. His saliva drenched tongue softly touched the left side of her tender puffy folds, then the right, then the bottom, then he slowly dragged his tongue through the sumptuous mouth-watering groove, savoring the tasty flavor until he reach her inflamed clit, which awaited his smooth delicate strokes. His strokes this time around were ever so lightly. Exactly to the tune of a gliding tickling as the tip of his tongue did just that, encircling her clitoris. Giving it only enough touch to send sharp-streaking, sensational feelings throughout her twirling behind; up her spine to her mouth, forcing it open, sending saliva and joyous sighs over her parted lips. Clara's breathing was becoming intense as Rory's slithering tongue touches continue to ease over her clit. This pleasurable titillating clitoral massage was mind boggling to her, forcing her eyes to close, her arms to shiver in mid-air, her mouth to send out spurty hisses. She absolutely loved the way Rory kissed and caressed her large tender flesh.

This was the first time ever, Clara thought, that her clitoris had been played with so tenderly. Each of Rory's tiny teasing tender tongue touches brought her closer and closer to that gigantic climax which she wanted, had come to expect, yet did not want. Wanted because her orgasmic trip was always the ultimate; yet wanted to prolong because his tongue was gradually sending thrilling tantalizing tings over her body which she had never ever experienced. Clara felt Rory's caressing fingers upon her fleshy mound. Her head, her breast, and deep down in her vagina felt explosive. Even her lips, anus, thighs and ankles felt tight, to include her arms which still were suspended in mid-air. His calm caressing climax clearing clutches continued and so did Clara's twisting turning torso to the titillating tongue touching. Her movements and this fierce action, she thought, would have to cease if she was going to last several more minutes. Pushing his head away was her thought, but her mind delirium would not allow her arms to do so. This sensuous feeling was so overwhelming as Rory's tongue now made slippery sliding movements all around her sweet scented steamy slit, always returning to her red-glowing clitoris which seemed to meet him halfway.

Only seconds remained; Clara felt Rory's warm hands grip her buttocks, with one on each of her curvaceous cheeks, positioning his mouth directly over her luscious opening, thrusting his long-broad tongue inside. He knew better than she that the time had come, and there was no turning back. Sugary appetizing juices were already flowing, but nothing compared to the flood=gates his long tongue opened; enough to see his reflection, if he had the time to notice. His deep tongue revolutions, inside her delicious hot zabaglione was simply the beginning of a magnificent ending, releasing Rory's favorite tasteful treats into his mouth. She even heard a roar from the tremendous build up which flooded down his throat. She gasped for air as the intensity began to burst – burst – burst, with each of his ever expanding energetic eating movements. Rory was eating as he had at the table earlier, getting hungrier and eating more and more as she delivered spicy flavored juices for his dining pleasure. She was driven by his superb eating habits to produce an adventure. "A superb adventure ... a superb adventure," Clara said to herself, releasing more and more climatic juices his way. Rory was eating her delicious pudding at an extremely gratifying level. The heightening intensity of her orgasms, large multiple free flowing orgasms, powered her hands tightly around Rory's head and her brown thighs around his body, locking him in place, but not preventing any of his eating moves and tongue searching.

Even Clara could not move because his hand grip on her behind had tightened; a grip that forced his long-full tongue deeper and against her inner walls. The only thing that moved besides his wide-mouth and roving tongue was her constant stream of warm sweet-liquid. The more her floods came and the orgasms occurred, the less tense her body became and the more her body relaxed, until she lay flatly upon the large bed, telling Rory to continue his soft tongue licks upon her. She had experienced going to sleep like this and felt it was simply the ultimate. Each one of Rory's tender licks upon her succulent moist folds relaxed her exhaustive body more and more, but to the point of one final miniature jerking climax. The last thing Clara A. Feldon remembered was seeing Rory's large wide tongue cup a wad of her final goodness, pulling it slowly over his broad lips and into his mouth. Clara indeed would not have to worry about Rory going anywhere, because everything she served him today was eaten exceptionally well and he enjoyed it immensely. He felt it in his heart and said as much to himself before he finally dozed off; mouth still pressed upon her luscious lips, "I could eat Clara's delicious hot zabaglione every day."

11

During the night, things went well with Clara A. Feldon, extremely well when you consider her climatic dream. A nighttime occurrence for sure, but **Wednesday** was upon them, as it was actually three o'clock in the morning. She distinctly dreamed she clutched on Rory's head, which was comfortably positioned, between her gorgeous brown thighs, teasingly within striking distance of her delicious vagina. She playfully rubbed his head coaxing him to gently lick her. Talking in her sleep, words came forth saying, "come on Rory lick me, just lick me a little bit … I want to see how it feels." Well, this woke Rory up, especially the now stronger pulls on his head. Again Clara uttered, "Come on Rory lick me, lick me, lick me just a little …" Rory smiled openly, just when Clara in her inexplicable dream excitement pulled his mouth onto her gorgeous velvety voluptuous vulva. Gently rubbing his head again, she still talked to him, saying, "lick me Rory lick me." Rory of course now had no choice but to comply, so he commence to lovingly lick her delicious swollen vulva, to smoothly suck her luscious clit. Rory licked and sucked, licked and sucked, licked and sucked continuously, even though Clara had ceased giving out instructions, managing only squirms interspersed with moans, twirling her tender tasty flesh in his mouth.

Rory continued to caress and lick on this flavorful sweet meat until he felt Clara reach her peak and give way to reality. She began to have orgasm after orgasm; did she ever have orgasms, he thought, equal to any he had taken part in. *A beautiful dream,* Rory said to himself, "with such sweetness to consume." No sense in wasting a good dream, he thought, might as well try and accommodate us both. So Rory slowly and methodically continued licking his tongue up and down through Clara's large sweet juicy flowing slit. Who knows if Clara was out of her dream, and who cares is the attitude Rory took, as she flooded his mouth with some of her sweetest goodness to date. Rory's licking pace quickened a bit as Clara's moaning and gyrations speeded up. Suddenly after a fast flurry of her groin spirals, smearing Rory's face, Clara lay motionless and quiet. Rory however, was just getting started as he again eat and eat hearty of Clara's delicious hot zabaglione. Slashing his tongue through her tender puffed-up watering succulent lips, eating Clara's best, was indeed the right way, Rory thought, to start a Wednesday morning. He continued to eat as morning's light came through the windows. Rory's excitement grew when his eyes fell upon Clara's gorgeous reddened lips laying wide apart, still oozing her creamy juices his way. Small involuntary pulsating moves of her generous outer vaginal lips and the beauty to Rory of such a magnificent piece of artwork increased his appetite more. And within seconds he was licking and eating Clara's delicious brown pudding harder than ever, having no idea when he would ever get enough. One could tell, Rory was really enjoying himself the way his tongue was lapping through Clara's juicy folds and sliding it over her rounded lovely puffy lips, not allowing the slightest of her delicious dream delicacy to escape. Without a doubt he loved it and he ate like he loved it. Clara lay silently, but her oozing continued and so did Rory's frenzied eating. It was mid-morning before either of them stopped. Clara elevated her gapped thighs, feet flat drawn upward near her buttocks, with Rory licking and munching the last of her goodness, saying:

"Hi, you woke me up Rory ... you know ... I had the sweetest dream!"

"Uh huh, I know ... and I love the way you responded in it ... it was simply sweeter than you would ever imagine ... appetite wise, if you know what I mean."

"I do not remember exactly how it ended Rory, but I feel so good and relaxed right now. Would you like to love me; that licking was feeling pretty good just now."

"No – not now Clara, I just thought I would wake you up a little different this morning."

"Okay ... well how about some breakfast?"

"Maybe later Clara, I'm not real hungry right now."

"Do not forget Rory, we need to go by your place for some clothes later on."

Rory was surprised she mentioned nothing of him wearing the sexy negligee. Clara had not forgotten either, but knew better than to try and rob a man of his pride, even though it was in fun and he was taking it well. She knew, giving him his manly respect would be worth more in the long run than a few short-run laughs. And unless he brought it up, she promised herself she would never mention it again. Rory said nothing as his lips were rubbing her inner thighs.

"Rory, I love the soothing strokes of your tongue upon me; it makes me feel so good when you're eating my delicious hot zabaglione. The way you handle me makes me want to have it every day, even two or three times. Do you think you would be

125

up to the task at least once, maybe a little more, and could I possibly make out a schedule? You seem to enjoy it so much."

"Yes to everything Clara, I do not want to disappoint you at anything; I can handle it if you can stand it."

"Do not worry about me Rory; when you roll that skillful probing tongue over my ever waiting sensitive lips, they are always going to be saturated with sweet juices just for you. Great anticipation causes me, to automatically become moist and one touch of your mouth, lips, and tongue, starts a jubilant flooding that really rocks my entire body. It's draining, but each time it makes me want more. I hope I do not seem like a nymphomaniac to you."

"Maybe, after you get use to me Clara, you will slow down."

"I hope not, especially the way you fire me up. Your touches provoke me Rory and I honestly feel your tongue has cultivated the inside of my vaginal lips. When it is buried there I feel like the ultimate explosion is always inevitable."

"Two, three times a day is a lot you know, but whatever you feel up to Clara, I can definitely accommodate you."

"I love your positive attitude Rory. And in all fairness I do not want to make it seem like you are forced to love me so much, so let's just make it – lovemaking at available times."

"I will even agree to that Clara. Of course that could be all day at times; pretty much like the way this week is going, you know."

"I know Rory, that is why I suggested two to three times a day in the first place. I am enjoying myself so much; this has been the most pleasurable orgasmic week of my life. It was definitely a good decision to take the rest of it off."

"You are right there Clara; we would have been no good at work anyway. By weeks end we should be like normal people though."

"That could be true Rory, but with you I don't know; with you I am not even sore or anything. Like I said, your mouth, lips, and tongue, is so wonderful. And I just love the way you tenderly caress my clit and lick and eat my slit and lick and kiss my inner lips and - "

"Sounds like you are getting horny Clara."

"Yes - Yes."

"Just as I thought; we will never get to my place if you keep that up."

Without a doubt, Clara's mind, body, and soul, was now pruriently tuned.

"Okay Rory, I will be ready to go in no more than thirty minutes ... promise ... and I'll bet you are horny too."

Clara A. Feldon, Rory found, was not bashful about expressing herself, and he loved this about her; it made him want to kiss and lick and eat and all those other things she might have said. Clara was right, Rory enjoyed himself eating her delicious hot zabaglione, especially last night in her dream, because he climaxed himself while doing so. And to be honest he could hardly wait until the next time; that last orgasm had been an exhilarating ecstatic feeling that came when Clara fed him her very best. A first for sure and he was really as anxious to crawl back between her luscious thighs as she was for him to be there. Rory thought to himself, saying, "Well, if you eat something and it's good, and you enjoy eating it, why not eat it as often as you can." Smiling to himself and wondering how many more times today he would be eating Clara's delicious creamy chocolate pudding. It was ironic he thought, how they were becoming a great team so swiftly. Clara had put a new vitality in his life after his beloved Charllotte, and he to Clara subconsciously filled that loving father void. Each felt a closeness toward the other and probably felt that warmth between them when they met in that parking lot just this past Friday. Yes, six days and there was love among them for each other and to each other. Their lovemaking togetherness was the bonus of all bonuses. To Rory, Clara A. Feldon was no ordinary woman and he was surer than ever, she was the person for the new school's principal position.

When Rory drove into his community of fine homes and manicured lawns, Clara A. Feldon knew this was where she wanted to reside and said as much to him.

"Rory, this is a very nice area; I would enjoy living here."

Clara continued to admirably look around as Rory drove, placing her hand inside his inner thigh, gently rubbing upward until she reached his crouch. The approval expression on his face and the rising of his large penis under her massaging hand eliminated any need for words. Clara loved his enormous size, the feel of it in her hands when it popped through his unzipped pants and inside her cheeks when she leaned down upon it. Gliding, her watering mouth over his swollen throbbing knob produced sighs from Rory and a licking of his tongue across his dry lips. More sighs and more sensual sounds evolved as Clara commence to slowly move her tongue all over his crimson knob; and even more ecstatic sounds when she started her sucking; first, gently sucking his tender knob and proceeding gradually down his long shaft for some deep throat action. She loved having Rory's large tool clog the passage of her throat, easing it slowly to prevent gagging, but definitely trying to take it all. Rory could feel the warmth of her cheeks and throat about him as he cruised into his garage, closing the door behind him. Clara was in her groove now, throat massaging his large rod, pressing tightly around his shaft feeling his veins pulsate and his smooth knob penetrating deeper and deeper. Rory had pushed the bench seat back to give them more room. Clara, was loving him esophagusly and had become excited herself by the incoherent sounds Rory was making. He was wheezing and hissing and generating growling sounds she had never heard, but appreciated because it told his enjoyment pleasure.

It also made her want to continue doing what she was doing and she did exactly that as pre orgasm juices trickle from the slit in his knob. One taste of these sweet juices and Clara became hungry, her appetite began to sizzle; she moved her cheeks upward and concentrated upon his shining knob, caressing him with a soothing precision. Rory had grabbed onto the steering wheel and was having fits with each of Clara's mouth and tongue revolutions. This was the first time Clara had moved her mouth with such authority and her hunger increased. She wanted more of him, she wanted more than these pre-juices, so she sucked and licked on, enjoying his screams and his sweet flavor. She never knew he could taste so good, feeling some guilt for pulling her mouth away those other times. This craving upon her, now made her want to bite and eat this gorgeous piece of flesh, so she chewed on it with her lips, simultaneously flicking her tongue on it. Rory continued to scream making the sucking of him that much more pleasant and gratifying for Clara. She even felt, her vagina become wet, but she kept to her slow gentle sucking pace, which seemed most effective. Rory had not climaxed and was minutes away because Clara eased up when his intensity increased. She had been torn between draining his precious penis into her mouth or letting it flow outward as before; and deciding finally that the timing was right for changes. If Rory's pre juice was an indicator, she thought, she was going to love it. If his screaming and moaning meant what she knew to be real, he would love it. Happiness, she thought, is making sure your man is satisfied, so Clara started working on her final act. Licking and sucking his knob better than ever; she was smoother, holding it firmer inside her mouth, sucking with a tighter fit and a greater suction, pulling and working on his knob harder with her tongue.

Rory suddenly began to grunt and got still, except for his hand, which clasped the back of her head. Clara knew an orgasm was near and acted accordingly, sending his long-large shaft deep, into her throat for a final massage to pull his goodness forward with a force he had never experienced. Rory's brain and body all but locked up as Clara gradually slid her mouth outward with a powerful suction upon his shaft and finally his knob, pulling the exploding juices into her mouth. Rory all but passed out as she continued vigorously sucking and digesting his sweet creamy goodness. To her it was well worth the effort; it was different, she thought, but it was very tasty and filling; a unique flavor she would definitely consume again. It was worth it, she thought, if for no other reason than to sap Rory of his energy, as he lay motionless. She also knew what a husband and wife would do ... get it all ... get it all ... Clara admired his inflexible shaft and could hardly wait until next time.

It was hours later before Rory ever regained his composure. He gathered up enough energy however, to lift Clara and carry her across the threshold, showing her this is where she belonged. He could smell her aroma and headed straight for his bedroom, laying her in the bed and immediately pulling off her clothes. Clara's fleshy mound was wet, her tender folds glistened, and Rory's remaining energy seemed to be located in his long-broad tongue, which hung out of his mouth, sturdy and erect. Clara was more than ready. She pulled him down on her and their lips met; they were a perfect match for the other as their tongues touched. Clara A. Feldon's tongue, the beautiful engorged clit was completely encircled by smooth slow constant revolving movements perpetrated lavishly by Rory's artful tongue strokes; delicate caring strokes sending penetrating swishes upon her ever swelling long-large clit. Clara, for some reason was going for a real quick orgasm or orgasms. Rory's long-broad tongue manipulations thrashed this swollen object to and fro until Clara pulled his entire mouth over it; locking her hands tightly around his head, where he could not move it. Then she proceeded to twirl her behind, causing double revolutions and extraordinary thrills, making Rory massage her clitoris the exact sensual manner she chose, feeling the fine grainy surface of his warm tongue, and the quick orgasms she wanted slowly began.

This was one of Clara A. Feldon's escalating mandatory eruptions which she was solely in charge of, adjusting Rory's head, moving his mouth and tongue swishes to capture her already succulent sweet flooding juices. She was not going to even think of turning him a loose until gushes and gushes of her goodness streamed down his throat. It was a fairly quick process that they both enjoyed. Clara watched Rory hold her twirling buttocks, lapping everything in sight. His tongue surged into her vaginal opening to meet the onslaught of juices coming forth, virtually wallowing and swimming in this great tide at times. A tense strained expression covered Clara's face as she watched Rory utilize his artful tongue and mouth skills to perfection; his tongue and lips worked equally as well on her extremely tasteful lip's surface as it did within her delicious saturated inside. Watching Rory devour her rich-flavorful vagina was always worth several more orgasms than Clara anticipated. Today's late evening action was so powerful, and her juices so great that Rory could not possibly swallow it all, and it streamed over the edges of her sweet-mushy-gushing tunnel and down Clara's inner thighs upon the tan bedspread. Clara saw his tongue glisten with her sweet wetness as he pushed her away for a moment to catch his breath and eat some of her delicacy inside her thighs. Rory was really off into her now, after just having a large orgasm himself, eating like crazy, not wanting anything to escape that wide mouth and tongue of his. Even these few seconds of seeing Rory's also wet face sent additional chills, orgasms, and juices through Clara's body. That's when she again grabbed his head for a finale of giving Rory all she had. He loved this firm chokehold because he knew it would not be long before his mouth was again full of Clara A. Feldon's goodness; an influx he would truly love.

Clara twirled her saturated open vaginal lips with Rory's long-broad tongue inserted between them, eating her delicious hot zabaglione exactly the way she wanted it. He was trying to get it all. "Honey, you can't get it all … you can't get it all … you can't get it … oooooh honey … get it all … get it all honey … get it all …"The excitement of feeling and watching Rory eat sent more multiple small orgasms into his mouth and she finally lay still, only being able to now flinch as he enjoyed himself, continuously kissing and devouring her moisture filled delicious chocolate pudding. And though Clara A. Feldon had succumbed from umpteenth orgasms, she could still feel the touching of Rory's warm tongue gliding over her vulva's surface, in and out of every crevice. The feeling was so soothing, already serving its purpose; getting her ready for the next time, slowly rebuilding her juices, preparing another meal for Rory's delight. Rory loved Clara A. Feldon even more for letting him lick her completely clean and watching her flinches totally subside. Now her lovely crimson swollen folds lay here stretched outward with Rory's tongue pampering them. He was sure there would be no dreams tonight as he joyfully continued to receive small extraordinary bits of juices seeping from her foudroyant opening. *Talking crème de la crème.*

12

True, there were no intimate interruptions during the night, but here at six o'clock, this early **Thursday** morning, Clara A. Feldon was up and chattering intimate hungriness.

"Rory I really did enjoy you yesterday; you were so tasty, different but tasty; and you know, I have a craving for that unique flavor right now. I mean, after we have our baths and all. What I really want is for us to have each other for breakfast; I have often wanted to do that, you know, at the same time. It never dawned on me until yesterday that it probably could be doubly rewarding. I think I would really love that Rory; soixante-neuf, you know"

"Whatever you want Clara is fine with me."

And so it was, the age old "69" was implemented in Rory's bed with him lying flat on his back and Clara atop him in a comfortable inverted position. She was straddle Rory on her knees

133

leaning forward toward his genitals when she uttered some last minute instructions.

"Let us go slow Rory, I want my first time to be extremely enjoyable."

Rory nodded his head which had already moved into a position between her thighs with his tongue in a teasingly attack mode. His muscular hands clasped her buttocks on each side for steadiness, helping also to widen her vaginal opening. Looking up, into this lovely paradise seemed strange, but was just enough to cause an enormous erection, which Clara now held in her hand, glancing at it with a watering mouth. Rory commence squeezing her cheeks, watching excitingly, the delicious appeal of her vaginal lips moving in and out; the wetness already inside of her. A thought occurred to stimulate Clara so as to entice her to have sweet juices dripping into his open mouth. First, some tonguing effort had to be expended to encourage such a treat, he thought. With Clara's bottom swaying before him, he also looked admiringly into her beautiful round anus, which he greased caressingly with some baby oil, handily nearby. He noticed as he rubbed the oil, both Clara's anus and vagina quivered, and he could feel her tongue licking his knob, as her hands reached for the oil, applying a soothing application over his anus. Already the two of them had began to heat up and a few sensuous sighs followed, especially as they slowly played with each other's anus, seemingly following each other's lead; using their best finger to gently massage and then slowly ease it inward. These were sensuously provocative easy swirling touches, prior to entry, causing their elastic anus tightness to give way accordingly and pull their fingers in more, creating pre-juices in their respective sex organs.

It appeared Rory and Clara had connected perfectly, for each had something to eat if they so desired. Clara seized the first opportunity cradling his knob in her mouth, but quickly savoring his juice and backing off to again flick her tongue over his balls and up and down his long-hard shaft, clenching it with one hand while the other stayed put in Rory's ever stretching anus. Rory was having a difficult time preventing himself from having an orgasm, especially since he had started giving Clara's moist inner lips the benefit of his tongue. He was licking her slowly as had been suggested earlier; the spontaneity to go faster was the only thing that tortured him. Eating Clara's delicious hot zabaglione to him, was the absolute ultimate and he really wanted to get on with it, and with only a few trembling minutes more, the urgency in his tongue was surging deeper and deeper into her gorgeous pathway. Clara was moaning; she felt Rory's finger moving delightfully inside of her, she felt his long-broad tongue moving warmly inside of her, she felt the urgency to and without any more hesitation, had an explosive orgasm. Rory's mouth was unexpectedly flooded, but he was now use to her pouring her love into him. A rippling effect hit Clara as Rory was now vigorously eating her delicious hot chocolate pudding, sending her into an eating frenzy of her own upon his swollen throbbing knob, that too had an orgasm immediately. As both ate and ate heartily, thunderous bolts of orgasms occurred over and over and breakfast indeed was bountiful and nourishing. They ate and ate until each was joyfully exhaustingly drained. Clara lay still upon Rory, slowly losing grip upon his rapidly declining penis, but he held his mouth wide open beneath her torrid delicacy as the dripping of her sweet juices continued. He flicked his long tongue occasionally to speed up the process; Clara was happy for his slowness though, saying to Rory.

"Keep on licking me Rory, that feels so good."

After those words he heard nothing but breathless groans. Their breakfast had been a success, though Rory was still nibbling. Nibbling at the goodness Clara so willingly provided for him. And with him being in such a compromising position, looking lavishly upward upon her lovely luscious vaginal lips, relishing the last of her sweet juicy drops from a heaping breakfast, Clara again expressed the love of his living quarters.

"I love your bedroom Rory, it is perfect."

The bedroom they were in was very large and spacious and even from Clara's viewpoint, it was very clean and neat, obviously coinciding with Rory characteristics.

"Thanks Clara, how about a quick tour?"

And after giving her delicious hot chocolate pudding a few soothing tongue lashes, they were both standing on their feet. She looked at him dreamy-eyed, delivering a slithering wet tongue kiss between his lips, squeezing him tightly around his waist. Remembering last night, she uttered:

"Thanks for carrying me in; you are so gentle Rory, and express yourself well."

"Shall we began my dear!"

Rory held out his right hand and Clara grabbed it, in answer, with both hands. He graciously led the nude tour from room to room. Clara made a special mental note of the four bedrooms, the coziness of the large family room, the library's bright colors, and the plush sofas and chairs throughout the beautiful house. "Rory," she said to herself, "has never been loved on any of this luxurious furniture." She smiled at him, not saying anything as they continued. After viewing the laundry room and three-car garage, he appropriately ended the tour in the kitchen, as a giant thirst arose to both of them. Sipping on orange juice, they kissed each other intermittently and affectionately, leaning against the kitchen bar. Clara's mind though was back in one of the other rooms; she said to herself, "I can see my legs gapped to each side upon that L-shaped wrap-around sofa letting Rory pleasurize my delicious vagina."

"Your home is simply lovely Rory and it already has a nice feminine touch."

"Yes, I did some of it, but my late Charllotte gets most of that credit; of course, when you move in, you will be free to change whatever you want."

"Oh Rory, you are so caring and considerate, but there is nothing I would change immediately; maybe in time, we both might decide to redecorate."

Rory smiled, lifting her naked torso onto the bar as they continued to kiss, expressing himself further, caressing and kissing her soft breast, simultaneously easing Clara backward and his head downward where he began to eat on her delicious hot zabaglione. They had a perfect rapport for each other as Clara had began to itch in that area for that long-fat tongue of his. Clara A. Feldon knew she had made the right decision on not changing anything in the house for awhile; that was because most of their earlier time would be spent on more important things, like making love to each other, as was now evident. She loved nothing better than the way Rory expressed his appreciation, so meticulously, so thoroughly as his tongue and mouth massaged her vibrating vulva so tenderly. She could not help but generously have a quick orgasm with that kind of precious manipulation of her oversensitive scrumptious genital parts.

"My my, either I am getting better or you were really horny."

"Both Rory, plus I needed a good quick release to settle me down a bit; I would now like a nice warm bath."

And before Clara said anything else, Rory hoisted her into his strong arms whisking her to his master suite, placing her on the bed while he prepared her bath water, later gently placing her in it, where she soaked for awhile. Matter of fact, when she finally surfaced, wearing one of his shirts, Rory had showered, dressed and was preparing them lunch, a large ham and cheese club on sourdough bread.

"My my, that shirt looks to be a topmost fit; have a seat with those gorgeous legs; lunch is no more than five minutes away."

"Smells good Rory; what's on the menu?"

"Just a favorite quickie of mine; I hope you like it."

"If it's like the earlier quickie on that counter top, I know I will love it."

"Well now Clara, I cannot promise it to be that good."

"All of a sudden I feel starved Rory; I believe living off love has caught up with us."

"Speak for yourself Clara, I am still full of your sweet creamy pudding, but somehow there is a craven to place my head between your luscious thighs and immediately eat some more of your delicious hot zabaglione."

"No problem Rory, I will be ready in time; ham and cheese huh?"

"That, turkey, and some of my own special secret ingredients."

"This is real good Rory, and the peach halves, the syrup is so sweet and juicy."

"Uh huh, reminds me of something familiar."

"All right Rory!"

"Well, it's the truth, but okay."

"Oh, I did not mean anything negative Rory, the contrary; it's just that teasing me makes me horny before time, if you know what I mean. Even watching you eat, makes me horny; that is why I love watching you making love to me; such wonder tongue strokes. The crispiness of your slashes upon and inside of me is the ultimate. If we had not taken this week off, we would have truly missed out on some extraordinary loving, not to mention getting to know one another."

"Speaking of getting to know one another, I have been meaning to discuss that principal's job Ms. Clara A. Feldon!"

"Oh that sound; is this going to be one of those official sort of things Rory?"

"For a moment anyway. There are some important points we need to go over to maximize your chances for the position."

"Oh, I thought you had final say in the matter; I mean, I thought you were responsible for hiring someone Rory."

"Well, I am Clara … and I suppose I am responsible, but most of that responsibility goes to the naming of the individual; and the group or to be honest, Mr. Sauninger T. Metfield is the one person who we usually must please."

"So what are you saying Rory – what is the problem – my being a woman – is that it?"

"Uh huh, but don't worry; Linnie Scott and I figured it out. If you and I are real close, almost family, so to speak, because that is normally how such positions are filled, you would be a cinch or stand a much better chance anyway."

"So that is it Mr. Rory G. Davanpourt; you have been playing up to me, using me to win your egotistical contest!"

"Oh no Clara, you have it all wrong, my feelings for you are genuinely sound, but you know how men are."

"I am learning more and more every second Mr. Davanpourt!"

"And not only that Clara, but these men's wives are also very influential in their decisions."

"Wait a minute; a moment ago you said it was this Mr. Metfield who made the ultimate decision!"

"And that is true my dear; it is getting to that point that scares me also. You see they have sons and daughters; some of them have called me already to solidify their chances. Of course none of them, other than Linnie Scott knows about you."

"Oh, I see."

"Being a woman, based upon the past, I openly admit, has its drawbacks. So my first step Clara is to sell you, as sort of my fiancee and next to sell you as the right woman for the position."

"Hold it – wait a damn minute – what is this, "sort of fiancee," bullshit – you have been screwing, kissing, and licking, on me all week man – and that is the best word in your tired-ass vocabulary. I thought we had something special between us and here you are giving me some kind of double-talking happy-horse shit. The best damn way to sell me – for your information – is the best person for the job!"

"Forgive me Clara, my choice of language is awful and if I may temper it with a correction, I love you very much … and want us to be together forever … as my wife."

Clara A. Feldon who, had stopped eating, a long while ago was now all smiles. It appeared Rory's new choice of words had new meaning. She looked directly at those luscious broad lips of his with his tantalizing tongue moving inside and suddenly felt those movements slashing inside of her and him eating her delicious hot zabaglione. Easing upward, discarding his shirt from her gorgeous panting body brought an inadvertent tongue over his lips. Clara knew he was ready to eat some more, leading him to that large sofa she spotted on that wonderful tour, in the family room. He followed along like a little puppy, glaring at her nude shapely twisting behind. His appetite grew as they walked; they both knew what was in store; only details were being spared, that is until Clara pulled the sofa's cushions to the plush carpet. Sensuous perfume from Clara's delicious hot zabaglione, hit Rory's nostrils and his legs trembled from their weakness and his desire to not prolong his sumptuous appetite. Her firm breast found one, then the other in his mouth as they both slid to the floor; her swollen nipples were getting a royal sucking. It was only a matter of seconds before Clara would demand his downward move onto her delicious saturated vaginal opening. Rory's tongue was also very wet and he had already, began to swallow fast in anticipation of the sweet juices, which would ultimately pour into his mouth.

Clara's beautiful bowlegs were gapped wide as he kissed her stomach. Serious munching was on Rory's mind as he zipped across her navel, pulling a pillow under her bottom for the proper elevation, continuing a slow downward glide. Clara could feel his ravenous tongue and lips pursuing their favorite target; her large clit awaited and she started growling, wiggling her legs in and out, rubbing his head; having a wave of pleasure, pushed his mouth onto her swollen red tender and still rising clit. Rory gently caressed the long round sensitive flesh, sucking it to her satisfaction and swirling bottom. Inside of her, Clara could feel lingering eruptions and pushed his head downward onto her delicious hot zabaglione, where Rory could eat her creamy pudding and her soon to arrive, abundance of sweetness. Her watering vagina handled Rory's tongue probing well; seemingly it has expanded since their earlier action, for it covered his broad lips which hid themselves rewardingly. Nourishing. Clara's sweet creamy chocolate dessert was being eaten very well; so much to her liking that ecstatic whisperings came forth:

"Keep on eating Rory ... keep on eating."

And you would know Clara was not in a position to take much more of his eating indulges; her body intensified, quivered with delight and exploded. Rory pressed his mouth deeper inside of her large flavorful opening, meeting her tasteful creaminess halfway. He said to himself as he ate, "Clara taste so much sweeter this time around," and clutches her bottom tighter. This surging of his hunger lips brought pleasurable convulsions from Clara and jerking orgasms after orgasms. *Numerous orgasms.* She could feel the gyrating workings of his broad lips against her upper tender edible walls while his long-broad tongue simultaneously swirled against her lower tender edible walls. *Pleasurable ... ecstatic.* Clara said to herself, "I never would have believed a man could have such a versatile mouth; he eats better than perfect." She was frantic, but watched and held Rory's head in place for him to continue eating; somehow, she managed to scream loudly:

"Keep on eating Rory ... keep on eating."

Rory was enjoying himself so much; he stretched her bowlegs wider and did as ordered ... kept on eating ... kept on eating ... kept on eating, until she collapsed; his head still buried between her naked thighs and twitching-redden lips, and yet he kept on eating. They had come to know each other well in this, short period and she continued to twitch as he savored her last ounce. There was no pretending their enjoyment of each other. Clara felt him submerged deep inside of her deep juicy delicious vaginal cavity; he ate each time like there was no tomorrow like he could never get enough. Clara said to herself, "I'm bad, but I really believe Rory could live on me, live on what he's eating right now." Clara wanted to say something else vocally, but there was no energy. She just wanted to thank him for making her feel so good, so wonderful, but there was no energy. Indeed, they were a considerate compatible pair.

Reader's Personal Notes and Remarks:

13

Both Clara and Rory slept like logs; neither moving, from total exhaustion, but Clara was up and stirring early. She awoke happy, and why not, this was a special day. Noticing Rory was still soundly sleeping, she eased out of bed, through the bathroom and shower and was hurriedly back, wearing the sexiest bright red two piece lingerie (a sheer half top and a cover-nothing string bottom) that Rory had ever laid eyes on. His eyes lit up just as bright, looking at her fine naked body through the colorful silk material.

"Good morning sleepy head, happy anniversary."

"Huh!"

"Happy anniversary Rory ... this is **Friday** ... our first week together."

"Oh yeah, happy anniversary Clara ... you look gorgeous this morning and you smell so fresh and good. I guess you feel like celebrating, huh?"

"Uh huh; anyway you like!"

"First, let me just look at you ... your breast are so beautiful, standing out like they have starch in them."

Clara started laughing. "Starch ... Rory, that is so funny ... I would have never thought of that."

She was gleefully smiling as Rory pushed the soft cloth aside, caressing both breast with his hands, leaning forward, immediately placing his mouth over her swollen nipples, slowly one to the other, passing each time between on her smooth flesh. She loved the way Rory kissed and caressed his tongue between her breast; it shot energized tingles straight down her stomach to her vagina, signaling it to get ready for the same. The thought of his massive piece of flesh inside her was really unbearable and she hastened to get it there. It appeared as if the celebration had started. Clara was quickly becoming moist from his sensational sucking. Even her breast had responded by swelling up some more. A sweet aroma emanated from her pulsating delicious vagina, piercing the air and Rory's nostrils as he slid in that direction. Clara had hoped for this and was all smiles as his head passed her navel, sliding onto her pubic area. He smoothly desquamated the string strap or whatever and oddly said again:

"Let me just look at you."

Clara had no problem with that and said nothing, merely gapping her brown thighs wider to enhance his view.

"My oh my, you are really gorgeous Clara; I see why I cannot get enough of you. You are every bit as appetizing as you look ... so deep ... so breathtaking ... so mesmerizing."

Clara thought, "deep ... probably so ... I would have never thought of the other two though." Still silent, she stared in his direction as he stared inside of her sumptuous alluring lips.

"You look so good and inviting and your juices have already began to flow."

Clara said not a word, but gave out some sensual sighs when she saw his head and opened mouth bending toward and eventually touching her glossy irresistible lips. This of course was what she loved so much about Rory; translating into being

144

kind and caring. Clara could feel the heat from his smoldering lips clasped onto her tender outer delectable folds; she could also feel his tongue slither through her inner sweet fleshy lips. Rory was eating her delicious hot zabaglione precisely the way she loved it. Slow and easy rimming her inner walls – circular – horizontally – vertically; cupping the tip of his tongue like a dipper, pulling her flavorful juices onto it; savoring them into his palate before allowing her nurturing sweetness to seep down his throat. This too was the way he loved eating Clara's delicious hot pudding; there was not a better taste to anything he had ever eaten.

And this time as all the other times since his head had first found its way between her gorgeous brown thighs and his mouth onto her lovely wet lips, he was enjoying himself, graciously eating the servings Clara A. Feldon put before him. The amount of her sweet juices flowing down his esophagus was now abundant. Clara was doing everything she could to suppress her final episode, even biting her tongue to prevent screaming, which always caused multiple orgasms. Nothing however seemed to be working as Rory was pleasantly eating her delicious hot chocolate pudding, slicing his tongue through it like this was his last meal. His mouth and broad lips had dipped well below her surface folds, encircled tightly against her inner walls, providing a powerful fluid gushing which not only kept him eating vigorously, but pulled him in deeper and deeper.

Clara just loved the feel of Rory's entire mouth, nose, and part of his cheeks lodged inside of her large scarlet opening. She loved the gurgling sounds through his throat to keep pace with her tremendous flooding; she loved her long swollen clit bouncing against his forehead as he really got after it, twisting and moving his head. Eating hearty. Clara moaned loudly as Rory continued doing what he did so very well ... slicing and carving his long-broad tongue meticulously through her delicious hot pudding, awaiting her final orgasm, which lastly seemed to be near. Clara had began to squirm her behind, twirling her tender folds around his lips in rapid succession; the friction was becoming intense against her clit and she could feel Rory's tongue going rampart inside of her. He obviously knew the end was inevitable, squeezing her cheeks, gripping her round behind tighter, pulling it closer to prevent any spillage. Clara could feel her torso roasting all over as Rory's onslaught continued; his long-stiff tongue surged deeper and deeper and its broad sides touched new sensitive spots against her sensitive walls. This feeling was now ecstatically unbearable and Clara let go; she let go of her final orgasm, she let go of his head. Screams reverberated throughout the room, screams forced her mouth happily open; screams drowned the pleasurable sounds of Rory's licks and smacks, eating her delicious hot zabaglione as she exploded a final thunderous sweet liquidity into his jaws.

Clara exploded for some times it seems as different parts of her body jerked and bounced, responding favorably to Rory's fantastic eating habits. He had launched into a frantic mouth – tongue exercise upon and inside her sugary-soaked opening to further gratify his sexual prowess; he confided in her that he often climax himself while eating her delicious hot pudding. Ultimate gratification to him was clearing Clara's passageway of her sweet goodness as she lay sprawled and simmering, flinching sporadically to his numerous courtesy licks being inflicted; yes, this satisfied his appetite. Clara unconsciously groaned as her body revved downward from its ecstatic peak releasing more of her delicacy for Rory. He continued eating until there was nothing left; no flinching, no groaning. Silence stilled the room to occasional noises from Rory's full stomach and Clara A. Feldon's shift in body position.

When they woke up later that evening, masses of people were leaving work, starting their weekend; excursions, movies, happy hour, gathering at restaurants; and likewise, Rory and Clara A. Feldon agreed to patronize "The Steakhouse." Their taste buds were clamoring for a huge piece of red meat and baked potato stuffed with everything. They chit-chatted about a number of cute sensual things over dinner, which brought wide grins and smiles upon their faces, but the topic ultimately discussed and almost forgotten by Rory, was the task of satisfying his co-hearts on the board, with a proper principal selection. His mind of course had already settled on the gorgeous Clara A. Feldon, but there were details, which needed mentioning.

"Clara, have you thought of any teachers you would select if you become principal?"

"Huh!"

"I thought I mentioned it; the person chosen to be principal will be given the opportunity to select some of their teachers."

"Well, I know one guy who works with me now; his name is Ilique K. Fernfort. Talking about sharp, he is very sharp, and all the students love him."

"Well Clara, keep your eyes and mind open for others like him because they will be the ones to either make you or break you."

"Thanks Rory, I will keep that in mind."

"Ilique K. Fernfort!" Rory saying out loud, as if his mind had just recollected it.

"Uh huh, so you know him too Rory."

"I know of that family all too well; Ilique and his parents, Charles S. and Margaret Charwood Fernfort and his cousin Dulique C. Gildor and his parents, Alvin P. and Delores Charwood Gildor. The two gentlemen are two of my old buddies on the board, and the Charwood sisters are two of the tough wives I mentioned to you. There is going to be a big push to get Dulique in as principal; and he is qualified. I have had a call or two on his behalf, and I'm sure there will be other words and possibly pressure exerted before this thing becomes final."

"You really expect pressure from those people on something like merely choosing a principal Rory?"

"You bet I do Clara; this is not your everyday selection, primarily because of Sauninger T. Metfield; the school, if I failed to mention it before is named after his grandfather."

"You might have mentioned it Rory, but I have been so wrapped up in you, it probably didn't register."

"Understandably so, (a huge smile showing) and with such a personal name involved as his own, is another reason why it will be difficult for Metfield to accept a woman principal."

Clara A Feldon, for the first time realized the seriousness of Rory's job, and the difficulty he faced in getting a woman named as principal. "If Rory had explained things like this before, I would not have acted like an ass." Clara said to herself. It was more than being a part of the "good old boys network," she thought and said:

"Rory, I am so sorry for my outburst the other day; so I have to be a male for your buddies to select me, huh!"

"Now you see what I'm up against Clara. Sometimes change never happens and sometimes people just diehard in the process."

"I understand what you are saying Rory; do you think there is someway I could charm the "old farts," excuse my expression."

"It's applicable and I'm one of them; at least I use to be, before mother set my thinking right. Charm ... charm ... now that's something that just might work; we might have an opportunity to use it ... we'll see, but let's not ruin an entire evening discussing old Metfield's problem."

That bode very well with Clara because she had already started her antics. As they sat next to each other in a booth, Clara constantly rubbed her left hand upon Rory's throbbing penis. Both of them thought of the other as they ate, especially when eating the large potato all loaded with a dissolving mixture of creamy sour cream and butter. It looked and tasted so rich. Rory saw himself with his lips buried between her gorgeous brown thighs and Clara got hungrier and hungrier for his large tool inside of her as she crammed healthy bite sizes into her mouth. She even began to talk to him on that very subject:

"When we get home Rory, let's take a quick shower; I am so hungry for you."

"I could use a large bite of your delicious hot zabaglione myself."

148

As soon as they crawled into bed, Clara was kissing him all over; eager to have something upon and between her lips. Only moments passed when she slid beyond his waist and her soft palms gripped his shaft at its base next to his scrotum sac carrying those wonderful jewels. She pushed his legs apart, pouring baby oil on his now shiny jewels, spreading it as to prevent a baby's diaper rash, rubbing an abundant supply over his anus, where her third finger stopped for some serious massaging. Clara had learned, for quick effective results, a smooth finger concentrating in this sensitive opening did the job. She was not trying to be selfish because they both knew and understood the greatest enjoyment for them both, was when Rory ate her delicious hot zabaglione. And the quicker this point was reached the better. With her lips firmly around Rory's knob, she licked and caressed it with her tongue, slowly massaging and easing her finger sensually into his anus. It was tight, but as she licked and sucked on his throbbing knob and he gave out those loud groans, it opened widely. And of course, Clara, knew, an instant simultaneous orgasm was near.

It was amazing, Clara thought, how quickly she disposed of him. She was hungry for Rory and appreciated everything he gave her. Their true loving however, really started when it was Rory's turn; he admittedly, climaxed as much, eating her creamy pudding as she did – well almost as much. Clara said to herself, "I know what Rory prefers, but I love that strained sensual look on his face; he could not fake a nut if he wanted to, especially with his anus opening and tightening up against my finger as it is now doing." Rory's facial expression was exhilaration and exhaustion all rolled into one huge wide open mouth gasping for air and true to form, his anus opened widely to her smooth finger manipulation; the loud groans and it was over for poor Rory. Suddenly though, Clara's thoughts of Rory dissipated as he quickly recovered, crawled between her lovely thighs, wasting no time in eating her delicious hot zabaglione. He acted like a starved man, slashing his tongue all over it. Clara noticed he always ate her delicacy in an upbeat fashion after she sucked on

149

that knob of his. "Maybe it was," she said to herself, "the idea of him getting multiple orgasms that put extra excitement into him." Whatever it was, Clara was not complaining and was definitely enjoying his roving tongue.

Clara A. Feldon could tell Rory was eager to get after it, and immediately slid a pillow underneath her fine buttocks, where her smooth prodigious folds were arched for a full frontal view and their lips could make contact with ease. There was however some simple instructions given as she raised her knees upward and fell backward on the bed:

"Please go slow Rory; remember this is our anniversary."

Rory looked at Clara's large tender folds and became even more excited; it appeared to him that her folds were rounder and puffier, more sumptuous and delicious looking than ever before. Taking my time, he thought, will be a pleasure. He began to kiss her outer lips, slowly, circular, round and round, counter clockwise, up and down each side. Clara watched him attentively, glassy-eyed, giving off joyful sighs. Then Rory smoothly discontinued his kissing and eased his long-broad tongue onto her outer lips and did the same; slowly, circular, round and round, counter clockwise, up and down each side. Clara could feel his dynamic tongue revolutions causing sensational vaginal wetness; she felt it would burst before his mouth entered for relief. These slippery sensual movements upon her sensitive flesh were rapidly causing tremors to her whole body. Her entire vaginal area felt like it was on fire with his constant lavish licking. It would certainly be only minutes before Clara A. Feldon would have an orgasm. Additional heat steamed from Rory's tongue and breath as he slowly caressed every centimeter of Clara's throbbing-folds. The tip and flat side of his broad tongue even caused friction against her folds, stimulating her further. Rory was counting on a magnificent tidal wave of fresh sweet liquids to come rolling across his lips. His eyes were on her gorgeous wet slit as he maneuvered all around it. He wondered as he continued his precious licking, what Clara would think of him having an anniversary dinner of her every Friday night.

Clara's eyes became glassier as she watched; her mouth fell open, her sighs turned into hisses and burst of short breaths and sweet juices oozed through her ravishing slit. Rory was very deliberate, and noticing the glistening enticing juices, commence to criss-cross his tongue from fold to fold, lip to lip, crossing through her gapped saturated opening, capturing her sweet delicacy. Clara's eyes began to turn in their sockets; air was being sucked in through her wide opened mouth and nose simultaneously, her behind began to squirm, and she abruptly threw her beautiful bowlegs extremely wide. Rory was ecstatic, noticing her rosy-pink insides; her marvelous opening now gapped wide enough for his tongue, lips, mouth, nose, and cheeks. But it was his long-broad tongue which got the honors as he eased it into her large saturated opening; slowly, circular, round and round, counter clockwise, up and down each side. His mouth followed the same procedure as he was now having a good time eating her delicious hot zabaglione. And Clara did not let Rory down; she overheated and responded graciously by producing tons of the creamy sweetness he loved. She was now having screaming orgasms or orgasms with screams, or orgasms while screaming.

Clara still watched Rory eat, but it was little she saw as her eyes were open and shut as sensual pleasures streaked through her body; her mouth was still wide open gasping for air with intermittent groans between screams, as her large soaked opening gave Rory abundant juices. Rory still slowly ate her delicious hot pudding with his usual enjoyment; his hands held her continuous gyrating buttocks steady as his tongue surged deep inside of her luscious vagina, twisting and turning against her tender pinkish walls on its journey. His nose and forehead rubbed against her long-large clit until he now began to gently suck it. Clara's eyes were now completely closed and loud frantic screams came out of her mouth and multiple orgasms flooded her vaginal opening. Rory however, missed not an ounce as he alternated from her large swollen clit to her delicious hot zabaglione, where he ate everything. He did not take time to tell her how good and tasty she was, but said to himself, "I could definitely eat this every day," smacking his lips together while consuming a considerable large portion of her sweet creamy pudding.

Clara was very well pleased as she felt him pull her closer to his mouth and heard him swallow successfully. She was rapidly sending him lots of delicacies, but he coolly, slowly, ate it all. Rory continued his masterful soothing tongue strokes well after her gyrating and jerking was over; his head stayed lodged between her thighs during the night, with his lips inside her lips. He savored the last of her sweet juices as she moaned and groaned herself to sleep, happily feeling his mouth, lips, and tongue upon and inside her. Their first week's dinner anniversary had been wonderful, though in reality, it was not much different from the other wonderful times he gently ate her delicious hot succulent zabaglione. This was the week that was, truly wonderful.

14

Of course, now the day after the anniversary was here and Clara A. Feldon woke up cheerful this bright Saturday morning, nudging her nude buttocks backward against Rory's precious penis. His large firm fleshy tool, resting comfortably within the seams of her gorgeous round cheeks was throbbing, growing stiffer and stouter each second. Unable to resist such mammoth temptation, she arched her buttocks, quickly seizing his rod into her hand and ramming it inside of her delicate vaginal lips. She laughed aloud at the pleasurable sensation of his long-large shaft deep inside of her; the feeling, she thought was ideal as Rory really came alive, giving her a vicious pounding as he rocked backward and forward. Clara wanted more though; pushing Rory onto his back, and without missing a stroke, was atop him. Her buttock hovering in the air toward his face, and her vagina still clinging to his knob until she commence adjusting downward from a sitting position, rocking slowly upward and downward, twirling at the same time, resting her hands upon his legs. Clara felt good to be giving her all and taking all of Rory so early in the morning; it was pure ecstasy as she rode his rod, accelerating and decelerating at will to his delightful groans. She could feel his excitement inside of her as she rocked her gorgeous round buttocks before his face while he glared into the action of his confrontation of her steamy saturated vagina. Oddly enough, Clara A. Feldon wanted nothing for herself, promising satisfaction and more satisfaction to Rory, saying to herself, "I will ride this stud until he gives out," and within a few more seconds, that is exactly what happened as Rory screamed, grabbing her buttocks for a very powerful climax. She wanted to turn and see his face and that ecstatic frown he always made; his mouth wide open and his long tongue hanging out; "pretty much the same expression,"she said to herself, "that excite me so much when he is eating my delicious hot zabaglione, I bet." And with that in mind, began to really get horny, but knew her hour would come well before the day was over.

Last night and this morning, along with celebrating their week's anniversary, was Clara's way of officially welcoming Rory into his house with a new ravenous appetite; an appetite which in the future would only be gratified with his eating of her delicious hot zabaglione. She smiled as she felt him go limp. She smiled again when she thought of today being another one of those days where they spent it, off and on, getting to know each other sexually; yes, making love and getting to know each other's body tastefully. The irony of it all, Clara thought, as she rolled out of bed for the bathroom, Rory loves me as much as I love him; I hope nothing ever spoils our taste.

What is Saturday without time spent in a shopping mall; and today, Rory and Clara is doing just that, spending Rory's money, of course. In Hecht's he see plenty of items, which would look good on her gorgeous body, and does not hesitate to voice his opinion.

"Clara, I want you to feel free in selecting whatever you want."

"Thanks Rory, you are so nice; I will only get a few things for now."

"Suit yourself – now or later."

Clara knew she was not going home before Sunday and needed something to wear to church tomorrow. She knew people would be watching her, especially after seeing her with a man for the very first time last Sunday. And she wanted to look good; "no," she said to herself, "I want to look beautiful, stunning, if I can. It's a woman's right," after a thought crossed her mind about God not caring what you have on. Then she proceeded to select a stunning red suit; a waist length opened jacket with a body-hugging long flowing skirt. Rory's mouth flung apart when she paraded through the dressing room's doors. She dazzled him with seemingly a sensual walk and a fine white blouse, showing an appropriate bit of cleavage. His mouth just hung open, as if he was waiting on something to enter it.

"Well Rory, what do you think?"

"You look great – you look great – I love you so much!" A thought crossed his mind; if Clara will have me, I want her to be my wife.

"Is the skirt fitting okay behind, Rory?"

"Uh huh – you look great"

Rory's eyes were fixed upon her like this was the first time he had laid eyes on her. And to be honest, Clara had nothing like this in her closet. She knew what fine clothes looked like, but on her teacher's salary, it never seemed to be enough money left for them, after the basic essentials. Before they left the mall, she had two additional suits with accompanying accessories to match; the shoes, the bag, the jewelry, and a new image maker, some exclusive gloves. Good for Rory, she was just thinking about items for the next three Sunday's. He was pleased though, and smiled more at dinner than she had ever seen him ... just continuously pleasant. Clara realized she was being pampered by Rory and loved every moment of it. "If he will have me," she said to herself, "I will be his wife, and a good one."

155

It was around eight in the evening when they finally arrived home; back at Rory's home. He showered while Clara was still admiring and hanging up her new wardrobe. Smiles and smiles came across her face; even throughout her bathroom entry and exit. Her nude body looked so good and delicious to Rory as she walked into the bedroom, where he was comfortably tucked in for the night. She crawled beside him, looking into his face, admiring his handsome features in the well-lit room. It's no doubt, he had taken the place of her father; she now had a lap to sat on, someone to buy pretty things, someone to trust, someone to love.

"Maybe it's too early Rory, but I love you very much, and I also love the way you make love; talking about being gratified, I am totally gratified each and every time. I almost feel guilty wanting it so often."

"How well do I understand, because I get excited just know-ing that you enjoy it, and feel guilty wanting more myself, because you are so tasty."

And in these very moments, their lips met, feeling their bodies with passion. She found herself underneath him as he kissed and caressed her beautiful breast, ultimately finding his way between her gorgeous thighs. Clara could feel the love Rory had for her, she could feel his love as his smooth tongue moved repeatedly and rapidly through her slit, careful on each passage to touch her inflamed clit. Clara was immediately becoming hysterical, sending sweet creamy liquid oozing onto and around his lips, overflowing, crossing, the boundaries of Clara's gorgeous puffy folds. Rory consciously and cognizant, chased these goodies, inflicting spine-tingling tongue slashes against her crimson sensitive folds. Clara's sensual sounds were glaringly loud as he ate her delicious hot zabaglione; she squirmed slowly, not wanting their lips to get out of sync, not wanting their continuity to be broken.

Clara's thighs stood around her cheeks, waving in and out occasionally, touching his creamy wet jaws ever so slightly. Rory's sensitivity was aroused and he was deep into his work,

156

caressing simultaneously, both her inner and outer puffy layers. Clara responded to his chin nudging; gapping her legs wider as his depth pursuit grew more intense. She felt his long-broad tongue surging rampart inside her tasty vagina. She only saw the top of his head as she lay sprawled on the bed; his face was buried extremely deep in her delicious hot zabaglione as he ate vigorously. Clara could feel his enjoyment as he ate; her enjoyment was about to reach a high peak for the day. She could feel a new energy level burning inside her as Rory's tongue and broad lips manipulated beautifully; her large clit rubbed excitingly against his forehead. At any point from here forward, her bursts of delight would come crashing down; ecstatic fits would occur. Clara noticed how magnificent Rory's head movements were, as it bobbed and weaved in its strategically placed location; he was in a groove in more ways than one, knowing exactly what he was doing.

At times they had mutual explosions, but generally as beginning this moment, it was Clara A. Feldon whose nerve endings were shattered. Rory had now covered her gustable outer lips with his mouth and was meticulously kissing and licking them heartily. His tongue caressed this sensitive appetizing flesh gingerly, bringing Clara higher and higher each flicking, slithering movement. Clara's behind was forced deep into the mattress as her entire body tensed up; he followed, holding onto her, even surging deeper and massaging her inner folds with a slightly greater force. And suddenly, Clara's squirming and gasping became ferocious, but he never grabbed her buttocks nor did she reach and pull his head into her as she normally does. She merely arched her buttocks upward to meet Rory's challenge, and their synchronization was never interrupted. Neither was disappointed as she flooded with joy and he happily continued eating her delicious hot zabaglione, even as she fell helplessly relaxed. This relaxation lasted for only a few minutes as Rory slid his long-broad tongue over her swollen moisture layered flavorful folds. She felt his irresistible warmth and touch; suddenly reaching forward with her hands, pulling his head, lips, and tongue directly over her vibrant saturated generous opening. Rory was very much in the mood for Clara's directions and the sumptuous eating of her delicacy. She frantically squirmed as their lips clasped; producing multiple returns for his dining pleasure. Eating her creamy pudding was the ultimate display of his love for Clara A. Feldon, and she found him to be more than gratifying for his dutiful effort.

15

On Sunday, Rory again found himself along side Clara A. Feldon in her favorite church pew; she did not sang today, as her choir was off, singing only the first and third Sunday's of the month. The lil' old ladies, of course, were doing their talking again, but Clara nor Rory heard not a word, nor did it matter what was said, because Clara was clearly here this morning to thank God for Rory G. Davanpourt. At the appropriate time they marched to the altar; she kneeled upon her knees much longer than usual, thanking her Heavenly Father for the usual, but it was her thankful prayers for Rory that extended her stay. She even thanked God for their beautiful sexual encounters, and asked her God Almighty for a blessed future with Rory. They left church vowing to forever be with each other; had a sumptuous lunch, in the city and Rory at last, took Clara back to her apartment. Happily they departed with tender kisses; thinking aloud of preparing themselves for Monday and the routine of work. "A brand-new beginning," was uttered by Rory as he drove down the block. And Clara, walking toward the bedroom, said in a sighing whisper, "how difficult tomorrow will be for me, being away from Rory during the day."

After a solid week of strenuous lovemaking, Clara A. Feldon opted to turn in early, with a dreaded work day staring her in the face. Through the shower and later, sorting through bills which had to be paid, saw her hitting the bed for a restful night at only seven o'clock. Well, what should have been restful anyway, but she had trouble getting to sleep. The problem. She discovered after numerous squirms and turns, she missed Rory, or more accurately, Rory's head nestled between her thighs. She missed his long-broad tongue licking on her tender folds; she missed him caressingly eating her delicious hot zabaglione, which always caused her to slowly drift to sleep, happily, those prior few nights. Nearing midnight and truthfully, after her busy hands and fingers proved worthless; nowhere close to Rory's gratification techniques, she gave up. She thought of calling Rory for some consolation ... any kind, but decided to call Helene Scott instead.

"Hello Helene, I have been thinking about you – you are not in the bed, are you?"

"Hi Clara – girl you must be reading my mind; I was just thinking about you, before just now cutting off my lamp. Matter of fact, I called you several times during the week, but there was no answer. You know I want to meet that uncle of yours; where have you been – spending time with that luscious tongued Rory, I suppose?"

"You are so right Helene."

"Well, I don't blame you girl, cause I'm looking for a man like that; someone to lubricate my darkhollow. Clara, I envy you and that man you got, with those tools he displayed, and would give anything about now for one even halfway close. So when are you going to fix me up with that uncle of yours?"

" He might not be the answer for you Helene."

160

"Girl, I think you ought to let me decide that; still don't want me in your family, huh? Afraid of having me for your aunt, huh?" Both of them fell out laughing.

It was well into the night when Helene's phone rang, but she was alive and ready to chat; Clara was glad for it too.

"Girl, I have really been thinking about you and that Rory with his amazing feat of holding chips with his lips, while the inner workings of his mouth gradually made it disappear within. That action was so genuinely smooth, it momentarily stopped my breathing each time, and actually sent pulsating invitational vibrations inside my darkhollow. I am telling you now girl, if you ever get tired or fed up with Rory, please give me a call immediately."

"Helene, it is good to know you are impressed, and your wish-list will be kept in mind, but either you or Rory would be too old for anybody's good when I am tired of this hunk of man."

Clara was now able to speak confidently and very much favorably of Rory, after last Sunday evening and the week that was just magnificent. There was no more wondering or guessing as to the merits or his ability, and Clara A. Feldon was perfectly gratified and satisfied with Rory G. Davanpourt.

"That is good to know girl, anyway back to your uncle; you never really said, no, to hooking us up. What is the deal – can you do it or not?"

"I did promise to talk to you about that on last Saturday Helene, but for good reason, it slipped my mind and I had not thought about it since."

"Yeah, shows how much you think of your friends, girl; and you told me the man had money. What in the world are you waiting on? Why don't you just give me his number; tell him I'm calling and I'll take care of the rest."

"Helene, that is such a crude way of taking care of an introduction."

"Maybe for you girl; we are not in the dark ages anymore; either he likes what I am saying to him or he does not. Life, to me is about sampling what is here now and moving on."

"Okay Helene; if I do not call you back in an hour, it will be all right to call Henri. Let me warn him first, there is a vulture friend of mine who will not take no for an answer."

"Now, you are talking girl; nobody can be a loser in a deal like this."

There is something I must tell you Helene; he is a very private person and probably beyond a female challenge. Now do you still want to pursue my uncle?"

"Well, now that you put it like that – sure – why the hell not; when I am done, you will be real proud of that man, and me too, for that matter. I figured something corny anyway, when you told me he was forty-four and had never been married. I understand; in other words, women are not his preference. Well don't you worry about a thing girl, because if he looks good, when I finish with him, he'll be eating my darkhollow better than Rory is eating your za-bag. Difficult men attract me anyway, Clara. Some women think they can change a man, but me with my excellent ingredients, I know I can."

"I am proud of him now Helene as my best friend! Sometimes, I feel a divine intervention interfered with his hormonal makeup for my sake. Because, with my mother living out of town and me never knowing my father, Uncle Henri has provided that stability in my daily life as a father and mother. He has always been there – for – me - when I needed him." Clara's voice was breaking.

"Girl, I did not mean for you to get sentimental on me; you will still have a friend when I am done with the man."

"Sorry, Ms. Darkhollow; I forget your magical powers."

"Now, you talking girl; that is the kind of spirit he will be wallowing in. You make the call and let me impress upon this man just how important his life will become with me in it. Your Uncle Henri will regret, not having met me sooner. Do not worry about a thing girl, I will definitely keep you informed."

Staying informed seems to be the words for the week, thought Clara. Mother Davanpourt wanted to be kept informed ...and Rory was to call her after the meeting of their council. Then Clara, just now, almost informed Helene, against Rory's will, that she might become a principal.

16

Rory had returned his call to Edward C. Scott who was only interested in securing a position for his young daughter Bretanya. Also returned were the calls from Alfred K. Stuckworth and Albert K. Structworth, inquiring of employment and the availability of their highly qualified daughters; Janetqua Stuckworth and LaQueeta Structworth. These three men along with Linnie D. Scott was Rory's closest friends, so he made them aware of his plans to seek the principal's position for a woman. Their initial understanding, surprising to Rory, was pretty positive. "Rory, that is a great idea," stated Albert, "Janetqua will be glad to hear of the opportunity." Like words came from Alfred who was definitely for the advancement of his daughter LaQueeta to principal. Rory was looking for support for a female and had found it until Albert and Alfred realized Rory was not talking about their daughter. Finally, Rory appeased Albert with a promise, "I do not know what to tell you

164

Albert, but Janetqua will be at the top of my list for something good." Unfortunately, a similar promise did not get over so well with Alfred K. Stuckworth. His remarks exactly:

"I will fight you on this Rory; trying to bring in an outsider for such a prestigious position. You and I have been friends for over forty years and just when you get the opportunity to help me, I am given the shaft. I see now what our friendship is worth."

There was no deal to cut or talking any sense into Alfred during the two-hour colloquy. As a matter of fact, the more Rory talked, the more infuriated Alfred became. Rory sensed a division occurring among the fellows for the first time, and from the looks of it, for the first time, votes would have to be tallied. Also, from the looks of it, Rory was short in this department; having only Edward C. Scott, Linnie D. Scott, and Albert K. Structworth for sure. Four votes out of the ten-voters meant some heavy campaigning on somebody's part.

Today's meeting was to be a routine meeting of the school district's business, however word was out on Rory's unconventional mind-set. Prior to Rory's arrival, plenty of sibilation was going on. Alvin P. Gildor had his corner with his brother-in-law, Charles S. Fernfort, including Paul O. Wilhelm; looking out for their wives interest; Margaret Charwood Fernfort and Delores Charwood Gildor. Of their sons; Ilique K. Fernfort and Dulique C. Gildor, the Charwood sisters had instructed their husbands to support Dulique for the principal's position. Near the side of the room, close to the front door, stood Alfred K. Stuckworth trying to convince Willie B. Deinham, Rory's brother-in-law, for the spite of things, his daughter Janetqua Stuckworth, was the only choice if a woman was to be considered. Willie looked a bit uncomfortable, but owed Alfred a favor from contiguous events happening down through the years. Standing ablebodied in the center of the room, was much laughing going on among the Scotts and Albert K. Structworth. Their gaiety, of course, centered around; what brother Sauninger T. Metfield's reaction would be when it was disclosed; a woman might be considered for his old grandaddy's school. This was as cheerful as this bunch had been in years. "There is nothing like a good laugh," Edward C. Scott was heard to say. Linnie D. Scott voiced no opinion; only holding his side from the stitches his two comic friends kept him in. Albert joyfully wondered who was going to give Sauninger mouth to mouth resuscitation when he passed out. Edward happily suggested shoving his old stogy deeper into his mouth.

It was now eight-forty five or so, which was the normal time of the old men's gatherings; though the formal time for the meetings were not until ten o'clock in the morning. All, usually arrived early, mingling and chatting with each other concerning families; mostly, wives ingenuity dominated; followed by children's intellectualism; and onto triviallzation of summer vacations and the like. Sauninger T. Metfield, for some reason was late, of which his wife, Charmayne Strutley Metfield was just now inquiring:

"Saunin, you have your meeting this morning, do you not?"

"Sure thing Charmayne, but for once, I will have breakfast at home; those early morning doughnuts and jellyrolls have been fatiguing the balance of my day."

"Oh, finally you are taking my advice on the calories Saunin; I will fix you a turkey omelette with whole wheat toast. Plus a glass of low-fat milk and orange juice should add to your nutrition; not to mention your health and longevity."

This was another of Charmayne's opportunities to impress Sauninger T. Metfield, her devoted husband of thirty-five years, the importance of eating healthy related to feeling healthy. Charmayne was only fifty-six and much concerned with her older husband's bad habits. Eating, she had told him and exercise was just part of being physically fit; the no smoking of his favorite cigars was the other part. There had been mini-tirades from Charmayne over his smoking; which she constantly reminded him was only a copycat style of his grandfather, Ordon T. Metfield. Charmayne was still very much a beautiful woman that Sauninger prided himself, especially when they went into the public together. Her shapely body and smooth walnut complexioned face always made him walk the much taller. Of course, it also made him puff harder on those old cigars; a direct relation to puffing his chest out. Sauninger had gone to the altar at the ripe age of thirty-nine, in accepting the twenty-one year old Charmayne; the prettiest girl in the world. There had been a lot of promises made to Charmayne about her eventually using the college degree she earned. Ironically, two boys and one girl, Renatra, later; Sauninger T. Metfield had not kept his part of the bargain. This had a lot to do with Charmayne being an educated mother to his children and housewife, but very little to do with him staying the tall slim handsome man she cherished. Standing wonderfully-robed in the kitchen, after all those years, she again reminded Sauninger of her desires.

"Saunin, I want you to lose some of that weight and stop smoking."

"How about breaking one bad habit at a time Charmayne; I will eat this gorgeous looking healthy breakfast for starters."

Sauninger had come to rely upon the cigar for relaxation and stability; and today he really needed it. News had seeped to him that Rory G. Davanpourt was going to try and get a woman installed as principal at the new Ordon T. Metfield Junior High. Sauninger wanted to tell Charmayne he was late this morning because of his frustrated thoughts of Rory and what he was trying to pull. Rory wanted to tell Charmayne, no woman was worthy of such a position at his grandfather's school. He knew she would understand little of what he was saying; as she surely would have, if he tried to explain why he had failed to tell her, his real name should be Sauninger T. Meadlarkin. Sauninger was unswervingly gloating in the Metfield name because of the educational status and community throning it had bestowed upon himself, for confidence-justification.

"Okay Saunin, but promise me you will try harder."

"I will try harder Charmayne; dear, I must run."

Sauinger T. Metfield arrived at the meeting exactly on the hour. Katherine was clearing out the empty boxes of the sugary sweets and making a new commercial pot of coffee. Usually one full pot at the start of a meeting would suffice. Katherine was not permitted in the room once order was called. This morning was no exception as everyone, noting Metfield's presence, quietly left their unusual clannish positions for seats around the dark oak boardroom table. Everyone, except Rory G. Davanpourt who deliberately stayed away from the doughnut session, as he called it. Afterall, he had no wife, or kids; nor was he in any mood for discussing socially; his principal's position, again and again, prior to the meeting. The meeting itself, he decided would be the proper initial forum. Another early attack on the merits of his selection, like that by Alfred K. Stuckworth was certainly preventable. As Rory entered the room, Sauninger T. Metfield was seated and lighting up his large cigar; this tradition being the signal, the meeting was officially called to order. Ordon T. Metfield was again peering upon this room of distinguished gentlemen.

Rory wanted to tell Sauninger, for once; his cigar was stifling and ruining the clean air, decent people had to breathe. No one had ever challenged Sauninger in this regard; primarily because of respect for his grandfather, Ordon T. Metfield. Even if Rory had not known of the division this morning; he would have noted something because of the tension strained-eyes and galvanized steel-stares upon each board member's stone face. All such faces froze upon him when Sauninger spoke:

"This morning for the sake of saving time, we will omit the reading of the minutes and proceed with what is on everybody's mind. Rory, will you bring us up to date on the status of the new school's principal position."

Rory expected as much; for Sauninger was known for being pretty direct, especially when he felt uneasy. You could have heard, "a rat pee on cotton," it was so quiet right now. Sauninger's eyelids had an extra degree of puffiness and the previous white, was now an extra degree of redness. The only difference between Sauninger and a dragon at this point was; Sauninger was blowing tons of smoke instead of fire. Everyone sensed Sauninger's discomfort; waiting for Rory to tell them what they all knew already; what had been circulating through the, "grapevines."

"Gentlemen, my choice for the prestigious position is a highly qualified Ms. Clara A. Feldon, who even have substantial doctorate hours; which make this candidate a real plum for our children's educational future." He does not know how plum came out, but he let it go.

Rory tried desperately to stay away from mentioning the female gender as much as possible; to soften the, already, word of mouth news. Slowly descending to his seat, Rory noticed Sauninger's eyes narrowed into a beaded point of concentration. His double chin; one of the body parts, his Charmayne wanted to speak against, but lacked the exact words, or maybe courage, was more pronounced as the groove had deepened. The tightness of Sauninger" lips added poutness to the lower chin's half, creating a cigarless Sauninger T. Metfield. Never before had Sauninger squashed the old stogy. It was as if he had not believed what his perfectly good ears had heard.

"Are you telling me, errr ... us that you have selected a female for the principal's position at Ordon T. Metfield Junior High School, Mr. Davanpourt?"

"That indeed, I am Sauninger; I have selected a well qualified person for this position."

"My personal opinion tells me a female; no matter her qualifications cannot handle such a difficult position; Rory, have you given this matter considerable deliberation?"

"Sauninger, you asked for my input, and I am here to tell you and all the others, this candidate has the stamina to make us and the entire community proud of us."

"I was hoping it did not come to this Rory, but I feel we have no alternative, but to solicit other candidates from our other distinguished members."

"Gentlemen; is there anyone else here who would like to submit a name?" This action proceeded as if it had been pre-arranged; Charles S. Fernfort stood quickly, saying:

169

"I nominate my nephew, Mr. Dulique C. Gildor for this position."

There was a chorus of seconds, in the windowless room. Sauninger re-lit his cigar and commenced puffing. A glint of a grin circled his lips. Then before the roaring completely faded away, Willie B. Deinham nominated Janetqua Stuckworth. In a later expression, both superfluous and hesitantly, Willie B. Deinham stated:

"If a woman must be considered, she should be reflected upon from one of our own flesh and blood; Alfred K. Stuckworth's daughter is a very fine and capable lady, and a credit to us all."

"Thank you for those kind and gracious remarks Willie. Gentlemen, it appears that we have enough to vote on. Can we get a motion!"

"Sure Sauninger, I make a motion that the nomination be closed on the following names." Yelled Paul O. Wilhelm as he jumped to his feet.

Most of the noise seemed to be coming from the Charwood group, who felt pretty good about Dulique C. Gildor's chances. If the Charwood sisters, Margaret Fernfort and Delores Gildor had been there, they certainly would be all smiles. Paul O. Wilhelm was all smiles and did sit down. It was stated by, this confident group that a hand count would be the most expedient. Starting with the last name, Sauninger T. Metfield shouted out:

"Who all is in favor of Janetqua Stuckworth; give me your hands!"

Only two loyalist hands; the nominator and the father were raised. Sauninger continued to smile as he asked for a shore of hands for Dulique C. Gildor. Talking about a partial buildup, Sauninger yelled:

"Would all the distinguished gentlemen in favor of our favorite son, please lift your hands proudly above your head." Sauninger's hand was the first to hit the sky; followed simultaneously by Paul O. Wilhelm, Alvin P. Gildor, and Charles S. Fernfort. Sauninger, now standing, looked around; each passing, waving his right arm in the air, pointing with his index finger at the raised hands; counting silently with mouth open to four. One – two – three – four. The count each time totaled a surprising four on his lips. A glimpse of granddaddy's portrait, hanging next to him seemed to even turn the frozen smile on his face downward. Sauninger tried not to show his displeasure, but the rest of the members not only saw the disheartened man's eyes cast upon the boardroom's table, they also felt a bit of thunder roar out of his muscular stature, as he slumped into his chair. Most of the front of Sauninger's shirt had deserted the inside of his trousers; causing his intumescence stomach to look much, much larger. Sauninger was looking at Davanpourt with those shining chilly eyes; the coolness of which caused illusory puffs of white frosty smoke to stream into the atmosphere. Rory G. Davanpourt felt the algidity, but chose to ignore it; preferring, to concentrate on an initial monumental victory. Not to be completely out done, Sauninger T. Merfield continued conducting the meeting.

"Well gentlemen, it looks like we have a tie, unless there are some abstaining votes." Before Sauninger could say anything else, the four remaining menbers; the Scotts, Albert K. Structworth, and Rory, jubilantly lifted their hands.

The members then agreed to give the second place finisher, the Assistant Principal's position, when they took another vote next month; and the meeting was adjoined.

"Rory, could I see you a few minutes before you leave?"

"Sure Sauninger."

"Man, do you honestly feel you can belittle our group in this manner and get away with it! Why don't you withdraw this woman's name and let us be in accord as usual. There is no reason why we should not all be happy with our appointments. A controversy or a woman, Rory, is not in our best interest or the community's best interest. So why don't you back off! I feel you have proved your point, that a woman can get appointed; and I concede that, but let's get real; that is a future woman's right for Ordon T. Metfield Junior High."

"In all that you said Sauninger, you are right about one thing!"

"What is that?"

"That, this is a future woman's right, like this future school's opening. Sauninger, we must think in terms of what is just, right, and long overdue."

"What has gotten into you Rory? You have never been a trailblazer before!"

"That is precisely my point Sauninger; at our ages, maybe we should blaze a few trails; deviate from the old status quo, and give women – partners in marriage, a chance to face equal opportunity and responsibility. Factor in your earth's remaining years, and make a just decision for a lifetime Sauninger."

Sauninger looked at Rory, wanting to say, "don't get sentimental and philosophical on me," but the words would not flow from his opened mouth. He could only walk away.

Linnie D. Scott, who had waited around; standing outside, saw a bewildered look on Sauninger's face as he passed him without a word and drove away.

"What was that all about Rory?"

"Well, we sort of stated our positions; and I in essence asked Metfield to search his heart, Linnie."

"You must have asked him to search more than that. The man looked straight through me, and never said a mumbling word. If it works, we are talking about a miracle; because you know as well as I do, Metfield can be very stubborn. What do you say, we talk about this over lunch Rory."

"Sounds fine Linnie."

17

Sauninger T. Metfield, left the meeting heading straight for home, when depression seem to grab his aching head and body. There was no way he could let his Charmayne see him in this dolorous state; especially since it was of his own making. So driving around or better still, up and down Seventh Street NW, was the likely thing to do. This street always provided good therapy to Metfield, because it was where he once lived; lived in the sense of being there everyday, in his younger days of rambunctiousness. Cruising near the boarded-up Howard Theater, off 7th, around the corner on T Street, gave him memories of seeing some of the world's greatest entertainers: Sarah Vaughn, Lena Horne, Moms Mabley, Charlie Parker, and Duke Ellington, just to name a few. Even Diana Ross and the Supremes performed there. Oh, the girls in that place were really something, he thought, dressed to kill. Metfield could not count the times he purchased booze in the Log Cabin Liquor Store and shot pool for four bits a game, up and down Seventh Street. Metfield remembered learning the game of pool or hustling as he and his boys called it, while leaving Shaw Junior High School in the evening. Pleasant memories came to mind as he cruised by the old school's site; now Asbury Dwellings, a housing for elderly and handicapped citizens. Metfield thought how rapidly time moves along; it seemed like only yesterday, he ran in and out of the school building. And now here it was, rehabilitated; ready for his use again as an elderly old man.

Everything was going fine in Sauninger's Seventh heaven until he reached the area where the Starlight Club was located. Today, however, the building had been razed and the spot was vacant. Suddenly, the stench from his cigar was stifling to himself and Metfield cracked his window. There had been fond memories in this club, because it is where he met and later courted his sweet young Charmayne. Metfield still refers to that night as his lucky one. The three young ladies: Bonnie, Kathy, and Charmayne were celebrating Charmayne's twenty-first birthday, he later found out. Being in the club, however, was not construed as lucky for Metfield; this was where he habitually hung out after work, and practically "after" everything else, he could think of. Anyway, Metfield's attention was drawn to the gorgeous young ladies by their harmonious laughter; they were having a good time. The noise incidently was not abnormal to the other noisy sounds, but a glance in their direction by Metfield, focused his eyes upon the prettiest girl he had ever seen. From that time on, Charmayne was in his sight. He wanted to send them a round, and later, ease into an introduction, but that seemed like a much too old-fashioned way. And besides, it was more expensive. After all, he thought, I am only interested in one of the women.

Now the club was getting stuffy, as was his auto; and Metfield lowered his window about halfway. Metfield did not smoke in those days and generally hated the suffocating cigarette smoke as the evenings and nights wore on. Anyway, Metfield decided on a bold approach, at least for him. He would just walk over and introduce himself, and well, hope for the best. He could never remember a time, he had been more nervous. And as he neared their table, he was so scared, but nothing else really mattered, but that pretty girl. He meant nothing. Metfield found himself standing next to Charmayne. Each; Bonnie, Kathy, and then Charmayne, quit talking as they became aware of his presence. When the silence and stares hit Metfield, he knew what he did next, had to be good. Nervousness showed in his voice; "excuse me – my name is – Sauninger T. – Sauninger T. Metfield – and you are – the prettiest girl I have ever seen." He was looking right into Charmayne's bright light brown eyes. The other ladies laughed saying, "Sauninger T and pretty girl," but Charmayne only smiled; she later said, the sincereness was in his eyes. Sauninger spoke again, feeling a bit more relaxed; "I do not mean to trouble you, Miss, but could I have your phone number and call you later." The other two ladies, surprisingly, turned to each other and starting talking; leaving Charmayne to fend for herself. She politely told Sauninger, she would give him her name and number, only if he would not write it down at their table. That was fair enough, he told her. And as we see now, Sauninger remembered; remembered enough to form a lifetime relationship.

Sauninger noticed the old theater as he continued to cruise, Seventh Street. The cigar smoke was much stronger; he let the window all the way down, and tossed the old stogy into the street. Sauninger remembered; he never smoked when he and Charmayne stole kisses in the theater. Maybe, he would quit smoking like Charmayne wanted him to. Charmayne's beautiful face appeared before him as the smoke cleared itself. Sauninger then noticed a freshness about him; a sunny shade-tree lined Seventh Street, and a gorgeous cloudless day. He thought of how he had paused in his introduction, years earlier; "My name is Sauninger T., before going on to Sauninger T. Metfield." The lie lived on; it was with him daily. What would Charmayne think when she found out; that she too was living a lie; all because of him. To hell with it, Metfield thought; their lives had been a success because of it. Their two boys, Sauninger T. Metfield, Jr. and Ordon T. Metfield II had been a success because of it, and their daughter, Renatra Metfield, would be a success, because of it. The Metfield name, he often assured himself, was not that of a farmer; it was a name which stood for something; which meant being a, somebody, instead of a no-body.

Charmayne had lunch prepared for Sauninger when he arrived home. A wholesome meal indeed, but Charmayne's mouth fell open when her husband bowed over the food before taking a bite. An unusual move Sauninger never before made; and today, there too, was no blessing for a wonderful prepared meal or a blessing to the cook; he simply asked God to forgive him for the lie. Sauninger was disturbed when he saw Charmayne's beautiful face, and still, "the prettiest girl he had ever seen," living a lie with him. He wondered how long it had been since they had gone to a movie; or even made love. As Sauninger looked into Charmayne's face, he felt a mild body tingling. Charmayne in her thirty-five years of being with Sauninger knew, things had not gone all well, at the board meeting; but asking what was wrong was out of the question. She knew Sauninger would become belligerent if she so much as hinted that she knew something was wrong with his school business. She felt that he felt he was a much superior being; speaking double that for a woman. No doubt, that Metfield name, propping up his ego. Charmayne would wait for him to start the conversation; everything had to be his idea, for the most part. Sauninger stared at his beautiful wife, finally asking her:

"Charmayne, how long has it been, since we have been to a movie?"

"Several years Saun." Charmayne either called him Saunin or Saun; whichever came to mind.

"When I finish eating; how about us catching a matinee?"

"That would be fine Saun – that will be fine – what do you care to see?"

"Oh, it does not matter Charmayne."

176

"Okay, I will look in the newspaper, to see what is showing." And it did matter. Charmayne knew her husband well enough, to know of that particular mood swing. She knew it had to be a love-movie. Her body now began to tingle. And as expected, after the movie, they prepared for bed early, and made love. Charmayne felt wonderful as Sauninger held her tender spots within his grasping lips. She thought, of the day they first made love; and how Sauninger had held her body firmly to his lips. That had been after a love story at the movie. The movie routine was not regular in these days, but it still was a sound indicator for expressive nibbling. Charmayne now felt powerful. Making love to Sauninger was the only time she felt strong enough to use her power, and she always took charge; pulling his lips away from her breast, onto what was the more urgency; the wetness between her thighs were clamoring for his powerful tongue. Charmayne made Sauninger linger in this area until she was more than gratified. Making him eat and eat hearty. She never knew how long it would be before the feeling hit him again.

Charmayne heard Sauninger choking on her steady flow, months and months of buildup, but she would not release his head. She had the power now, as she smiled, locking her powerful thighs around Sauninger's head; making his swishing tongue split seams and surge deep; only loosening the grip when the loud gurgling noises completely ceased. Charmayne loved their togetherness at these moments, but did use the union to get a little sweet revenge. And Charmayne, in her opinion, had a reason to be upset with Sauninger. After graduating from Benedict College and marrying Sauninger, was relegated to being in her words, "a kitchen woman." This she opposed, because as Charmayne put it, "her mother had been a kitchen woman for those people," and had seen fit to raise her daughter different, so she would not fall into that situation under any circumstances. Charmayne faithfully promised her mother, she would get a real job with that education. However, Sauninger talked her into staying home until their two planned children were of age; whatever that meant. Well, two boys of age, and after ten years she saw a surprising lovely Renatra, unplanned, added to the mix. Now, some twenty-three years later, to cut a long story short, Charmayne is still in the kitchen. Her course in history, she thought, had been derailed.

Suddenly, Charmayne was hit with a brainstorm; the thought of testing her power. If she was able to take charge and use her power while Sauninger greedily maneuvered through her love creases and crevices; why wasn't she able to dictate, at this moment, what she desired later.

"Saun, I want you to stop smoking that stinking cigar; it will no longer be tolerated by me in this house. From now on, when you think of smoking, you will think of where you are right now." Pulling his head forward to concentrate on an engorged mini-cigar sized protruding object nearby. "From now on Saun, you will hold this sensitive red extension between your lips. Do I make myself clear, and do you understand. And furthermore, you will start telling me what goes on with your daily personal and work activities; is that clear?"

Sauninger nodded as his lips clung to the fiery object while his tongue manipulated it to Charmayne's satisfaction. Charmayne never felt more powerful than right now further tightening her thigh grip as the gurgling noises started again. Sauninger even felt himself being under her control, as when she made him remember her phone number years ago. He felt himself loving her dominance each time her curvaceous thighs moved inward against his cheeks. He also felt under her control as Charmayne was screaming with pure delight; the more his tongue wiggled inside of her. Charmayne smiled at Sauninger as she removed her shapely strong thighs from around his head and watched him pull his wet puffy lips away. Only time would tell if her power had been effective. Again, she wondered what had happened at the meeting today, as Sauninger smiled back, in her direction, saying:

"That was real good Charmayne. You were really in charge. Speaking of being in charge; do you think a woman could be an outstanding principal?"

178

"I suppose so Saun; why?"

"Something came up at the meeting today. Rory Davanpourt submitted a woman's name for the principal of our new junior high school." Sauninger had never even told his wife, the new school was to be named after his grandfather, Ordon T. Metfield.

"There are some good women principal's already Saunin. I know of at least two elementary schools with them." Charmayne's knowledge of what was going on in the world surprised him. He wanted to say, "yeah, but they are not good enough to be principal of Ordon T. Metfield Junior High School." He also wanted to say, "no woman will ever be principal of my grand-father's namesake. Metfield schools should set a different prece-dent. A higher standard."

"I suppose you are right Charmayne."

"Well Saunin, what are you going to do?"

Sauninger's face, hardened as his puffy lips seemed to rise a bit more. His large stomach appeared to suck in, as his clenched fist pounded several times in mid-air; before answering in a fulminating voice:

"I don't know Charmayne; I just don't know!"

Charmayne could not imagine what had upset him so, but decided, now was not a good time to inquire. After all, his head was no longer in a compromising position. Prior to the mood swing, Charmayne was feeling real good about her vocal love commands. One question from her, in over thirty years, concern-ing Sauninger's business affairs, Charmayne thought, was a major accomplishment. Maybe he was beginning to soften and see his wife as a co-partner, in all affairs. Or maybe, Char-mayne's new power tactics had a tremendous crossover affect and would command a positive response involving any of their relationship. First things first, she thought, I will be happy to find that just one demand worked. It would be so good if she could pass to her daughter, Renatra, what her mother had passed along: "Get a real job with that education." Renatra would be out of college soon, so time was running out for such a profound statement to be made; especially since she had no related occupation. Charmayne, unexpectedly feeling depressed, turned over on her side, falling asleep. Sauninger looked at his beautiful wife's smooth naked buttocks in admiration; and wondered how she ever got the idea, that women could make good principals. His admiration spoke to him loud and clear; women, he thought, the possessors of soft delicate breast, round smooth bottoms, cultured warm thighs and legs; composing a curvaceous awe-inspiring shape, had no place, other than home. "Charmayne would even attest to that," he said to himself, " she has been my helpmate for over thirty years and is very happy; never grumbling or asking to take a position away from the men." Sauninger wanted to believe Charmayne was happy or at least content in being a housewife, mother, and cook, during their long years of marriage. The only unanswered question was how to get Rory G. Davanpourt and the majority of the, board to think like him in his decision of choosing the best MAN for the job.

18

Rory G. Davanpourt and Linnie D. Scott left the meeting for Linnie's favorite restaurant; Sandy's place.

"Linnie, is this a new place you are taking me to; I do not recall anything by that name."

"It is new in terms of owners and menu, but it is still a soul food eatery. About six months ago, a close friend and myself bought the defunct Beulah's kitchen; and have made major renovations, not only structurally, but also the menu. I kept it a secret until now; we got it up and running two weeks ago. There has been no grand opening yet, so I hadn't forgotten about you."

"Well, how is it doing Linnie?"

"Not bad in my opinion. Sandy, my partner, an experienced chef has been sort of disappointed."

"Why is that Linnie?"

"She feels, there should be lines formed outside the door for both the lunch and dinner meals. So far, the dinner crowds are outperforming the mid-day gathering."

"Have you been advertising Linnie?"

"We did radio and newspaper for this week. The first week we let word of mouth spread the opening, other than a large ad in the community weekly. Working out the bugs, were important to me, and I really did not favor large swarms of people immediately. Like I said Rory, I am pleased; the response has not been great, but it has been very – very good. Only time will tell. Celebration time arrives when it comes to getting a repeat of the same crowds daily."

"Have you had a response questionnaire made available to your customers Linnie?"

"No, do you think I should? I have been sort of asking around as they eat and when they finish; as to the service and the food."

"Have you made a note of the negatives Linnie?"

"Well – no – Rory, but that is because I have not heard any!"

"That is precisely my point Linnie. In most instances, people will refuse to tell you a negative, opting to write it down instead or just never show back, thinking you really don't care what their views are."

"I had not thought of a written survey; I will discuss it with Sandy."

Rory G. Davanpourt was introduced to Sandra Vaugghan, who led the both of them to a rearward table, near the kitchen entrance; where the three of them sat down. "So this is the Rory, you have been talking about, eh Lin. He is a very handsome man. You must be special Rory; Lin talks about you all the time. He wanted to get your opinion about the menu as soon as we finalized it, two months ago, and I talked him out of it. So it is so good to see you here; ready to try it out?"

"Sandy, maybe you should explain the menu; I have not told Rory of it yet."

"Just like a man, leaving all the details to the women folk. Very well; Rory, my experience around food stretch many years.

182

It seems, closer to my age of forty-one. When I heard of this popular restaurant going out of business due to mis-management; a special opportunity presented itself to me. That was to make my dream come true of making a soul food restaurant succeed without all the "fat" if you will; while still retaining its soul flavor. I have experiented with certain foods for years, with much success, I might add. Of course, only Lin and a few other close friends and relatives were partial guinea pigs. And due to that partially, I was never sure if they were telling an unbiased truth; especially when they told me, there was hardly any difference in the taste. This idea meant so much to me, because more and more people are becoming health conscious; and we as a people, because of our high percentage of high blood pressure, should also."

"One thing about Rory, Sandy, he will definitely let you know the truth, even if it hurts your feeling."

"Ah – come on Linnie, you make me sound awful; I have merely found in my many years on this planet, there is just no substitute for honesty."

"See honey, I told you; that is his nice way of saying – brace yourself." Rory laughed without saying anything.

"That was very well put Rory; I have the feeling you are the perfect guinea; please excuse my expression. The food served you today will be on Lin – well, on the house. I do hope you are hungry."

"I am hungry and getting hungrier, just thinking about it Sandy."

"Do you try and eat healthy these days Rory?"

"Sure, he does Sandy; what kind of question is that. Look how big and strong Rory looks. Tell her Rory, how your sweet lady have you eating healthy as mine."

"I try to eat as I should."

"That did not really answer the question Rory. Does she prepare healthy food or just good food – there is a difference – you know."

Rory thought for a moment, figuring quickly; Linnie must have thought he and Clara A. Feldon had been together for quite some time. And of course, his only recollection of eating or being served by Clara took place, ironically, in her bedroom. And he gave the only logical answer.

"I can truthfully say Sandy, her food certainly looks healthy, and without a doubt, it is definitely good. As a matter of fact I could eat it everyday, if given the opportunity."

"Men – you guys probably don't know healthy food when you see or taste it – as long as you are eating something and swallowing something that taste good."

"That is probably correct Sandy, because Clara's stuff sure is good; she will never have any trouble getting me to eat it." Rory's mind had leaped completely away from the restaurant and onto Clara's delicious folds.

His mind strayed back to Clara A. Feldon and how they had talked to each other since their meeting only a few days ago. Rory had not seen Clara since Sunday, three weeks ago, but each and every night, there had been long conversations on the phone. Both agreed by their communication and past experience, hot and heavy relationships always faded out after a while. However, it had been a while in their lives since any thing of that nature occurred. Each opinion, expressed forth rightly, told the other, maturity or a lack of maturity was generally the reason for such fadings. Clara, of course, was a bit stronger in her belief, of the relationship lasting. Time after time during the absent weeks, she used phrases like: Never being this happy; happier than I have ever been; being yours forever; and my love for you lasting forever. Those were strong words, Rory thought, and told her as much; primarily of his concern, their age difference. He asked Clara to look far down the road into that "forever" she was so certain of. She stunned Rory with the remarks; "A flower's blossom may last a moment, a day, a season; whatever the duration, it makes its recipient happier because of its presence. A definite time of longevity is not promised either of us, at any age. Therefore, age should not

184

matter, if we are happy. We will enjoy and be happy in the other's presence, forever." Rory smiled to himself, thinking; God had made only one Clara A. Feldon and sent them literally, crashing together.

"Linnie, while Sandy is getting the food, I need to make a quick phone call to mother. Is there - "

"Sure, go through those doors, there is one in our small cubby office."

Rory called his mother, mostly to inform her, he would be by later, rather than shortly after the board meeting. And to please, not go to the trouble of preparing anything edible, because he was dining with Linnie D. Scott in his new restaurant. Mother Davanpourt graciously accepted the news, but told Rory to bring her a blank-thank-you card; informing him, the gift by Clara on that Sunday was a beautiful decorative, white and blue plate, inscribed with "HARBOR PLACE, BALTIMORE, MARY-LAND." Mother Davanpourt described Clara A. Feldon in the next breath as, "that child is the most gorgeous - thoughtful young lady, I have ever known and I like her a lot." Rory remembered, she had said the same thing about his beloved Charllotte after their first acquaintance. She had been right about Charllotte. Rory now knew, this was his mother's way of saying, "boy, that girl is good for you; I want her in your life."

On Rory's slow walking return to the table, he thought seriously of Clara A. Feldon in that vein – we are talking about partners until "death do us part". A smile crossed his face as he asked himself this question, "how can a mother know a girl so quickly?"

"Man, that food sure does look and smell good."

"Thanks Rory; Sandy will bring yours right out; I had her to hold it until you got off the phone – sorry I couldn't wait buddy. I sure hope you like it; I plan on retiring into this restaurant, if things go well. Serving good food to good people is something worthwhile in my opinion. It is what I call enjoyable work."

185

"That is what I would like to do Linnie; retire into an enjoyable money maker. What kind of time limit are you looking at?"

"Within a year or so; I am sixty-four already. The divorce set me back a ways; a little bit more than I ever imagined. Sandy tells me, if we take care of business, the business will take care of us. Oh, I might as well tell you now Rory; Sandy and I are more than food cooking partners."

"Hey – everybody needs somebody Linnie."

"Hello Rory, you're back – 'bout ready for the meal of your life."

"You bet Sandy, bring it on before I grab Linnie's plate." While Sandy head out, Rory smile and talk to Linnie, saying, "Man, Sandy is one good looking woman; sounds like you have a complete package – chef, good looks, and businesswoman."

"Yeah Rory, Sandy is really something; her head is screwed on right. Certainly not like that first woman of mine; all she knew how to do was spend money. I still cannot believe we stayed together for nearly thirty years. Man, we were no more compatible than an ant and a grasshopper."

"Could have fooled me; you always looked real happy together – ."

"Move those elbows Rory, lunch is now being served."

Sandy returned to the table with Rory's food: Moderate helpings of collard greens, black-eyed peas, and candied yams; each in its own dish, rounded out the cooked vegetables. This was Monday's special, along with the golden pieces of fried chicken. Rory also had a choice between a green salad or fruit salad; and of course, the sprouts of green onions, and cornbread was standard. This was to be followed up later with the dessert of the day – peach cobbler. Rory looked at the delicious food and imediately shifted his eyes about the table; the table to the side, and the table behind him. Sandy and Linnie began to laugh, because they knew what he was looking for.

"Looking for the salt Rory?"

"Uh huh, I need some salt, folks."

186

"No Rory, you want some salt; Sandy had to convince me of the same thing. You mean you are going to dump tons of salt on your food before you even taste it. We have, or Sandy has found that most foods are tastier and healthier with their natural flavor or very little salt, which we add, if necessary during the cooking process. Ninety-five percent of our foods have no salt added."

"Yes Rory, why don't you taste your food!"

"Okay folks, but I promise you, I am going to need me some salt."

"Just taste the food Rory."

"All right Linnie, all right!"

Sandy and Linnie look at each other and then straight at Rory as he taste, first the collards, the peas, and the chicken. He smacked and saturated his tongue with each item. Then a broad smile surfaced on those large-thick lips of his.

"Hey, this is pretty good; I don't need no salt!"

"We are glad Rory, because we don't have no salt. If you had been paying close attention upon entering, you would have noticed the, "NO SMOKING and NO SALT BEYOND THIS POINT," sign. Plus Man, the menu which you did not see, warns the customers of no salt shakers."

"I certainly missed those signs Linnie."

"I found, Rory, it did no good to cook healthy if people loaded their food with unnecessary salt. We, Black folks, are killing ourselves with a consumption of entirely too much salt. And I want to do my part in trying to correct that."

"Sandy, this is really good; no salt huh! Any complaints so far?"

"There has been a few, but each, like yourself, accepted it pretty well, especially after they tasted the food. Also, on each table, you will find a small container filled with take-home plastic cards of information on high blood pressure and hypertension. So the, no salt, has gone over quite well. Most admit, they poured the salt on, out of habit."

"That is what I have always done Sandy; simply shook the shaker until I decided to stop. And in a lot of cases, I would shake some more salt on, for good measure, during the course of the meal. Talking about a bad habit; I suppose salt abuse is my worse."

"It is really abuse of the body Rory. You will also find that Sandy has eliminated the pork-fat from the collards and peas; and use only vegetable oil in frying that chicken. There are, of course, some of Sandy's secret ingredients added, to give it the real flavor. Just think man, we might live as long as your mother."

"Yeah Linnie, her secret is probably due to stress-free days, which we cannot seem to find. And speaking of mother, I must be going – got to get by and see her."

Rory, surprisingly, skipped the peach cobbler, promising Sandy, he was going to be one of their regular customers.

19

"Hello mother, here is your card."

"Thanks son; do you expect to see Clara within the next two days?"

"I suppose so. How does later on sound; why?"

"Because I was going to send this card to her, by you – that is why. You sure don't smell much like smoke today; was that Metfield there?"

"He sure was, but come to think of it, he did not smoke as much. I suppose there was too much to think about. Sauninger T. Metfield was none too pleased at the idea of a woman principal. Mother, let me tell you; after the meeting, he even privately asked me to withdraw Clara A. Feldon's name."

"I know you are not going to do that – are you?"

"No mother – no way. We voted today and there was a four all tie between Clara and Dulique C. Gildor. The fellows agreed to let the runner-up be the assistant principal; so Clara is automatically in, one way or the other. Metfield's greatest fear is, Clara A. Feldon just might win."

"Isn't there ten people son; what about the other two votes?"

"That is what I am talking about; Willie B. Deinham voted along with Alfred K. Stuckworth, for his daughter, Janetqua, to be principal. Either one or both of those votes, with a little persuasion, could come to our side. Hopefully, the entire episode will be solved when we meet again."

"It seems to me, there still could be trouble son; what happens if it ends up five all?"

"It's simple mother; by our rules, Metfield makes the selection himself."

"Now son, there is nothing democratic about that procedure; that gives Metfield two votes."

"I know mother, but that is what we have agreed to. Metfield has the ultimate power."

"I was afraid of that. When will you meet again?"

"There is no real urgency – probably next month – as far as this matter is concerned."

"Is there anyway you can find out, how the voting will go before then son?"

"Sure mother, I will just ask Willie B. Deinham and Alfred K. Stuckworth, which way they will be voting. It is no big deal as far as I am concerned; Clara A. Feldon is in – number one – or number two, because I am definitely not withdrawing her name."

"Well son, it matters to me. I want Clara A. Feldon to win; this is our best opportunity to win."

"What do you mean mother; the odds are not in her favor if the vote remains tied. Metfield is sure to go with Dulique C. Gildor in that case; and really, he is not a bad choice."

"Listen son; I said I want Clara to get that position!"

"Okay mother – okay; I will let you know how the other two fellows are voting as soon as I find out."

Mother Davanpourt had her arms folded across her bosom, all the while she and Rory sat at the kitchen table. Rory's sweet tooth acted up as he devoured teacake after teacake, with a large glass of milk. Mother Davanpourt's expression even told Rory, she was extremely serious about either Clara A. Feldon or a woman getting the top post. She seemed just as eager for a woman to win as Metfield did for a man to win. Only when mother Davanpourt, felt she clearly understood the outcome of the board's position, did she start scribbling in the Clara A. Feldon's, Thank-you card. The plate Clara gave mother Davanpourt hung on her living room wall, between the two windows, facing the front of the house. That told Rory how much she felt toward Clara. Not many items hung on those four walls except family portraits. A picture of he and his beloved Charllotte was slightly to the left of the new arrival. Rory wondered what would happen if his mother had a picture of Clara and himself; though he felt pretty sure of the answer in his head. His affirmation of delivering the card to Clara A. Feldon solidified that answer.

"Son, you make sure Clara get this card."

"Don't worry mother, she will get it; I am on my way over to her place right now." And he was on his way, smiling as he bid his mother goodbye.

Clara met Rory at the door with a warm smile, giving him a huge hug and kiss. It had been almost a month since "the week that was." She tiptoed to his lips with her bowlegs happy and wiggly like. Rory embraced her tightly, lifting her somewhat to get a better angle at balancing themselves upright. Soaking in the bathtub for an hour had prepared Clara A. Feldon for Rory's arrival and sensual touches. He could smell the freshness of Clara's sweet natural body scent through the pink silken tight-fitted pajama top and bottom; outlining the firmness of her breast and the roundness of her behind. His large-broad palms irresistibly slid loosely upon her buttocks, cupping her cheeks lightly as he pulled his head back, to look into her cheerful face.

"You are so beautiful – you know that."

"Thanks Rory, I miss you so much; I really miss seeing you. How long are we going to sanely be able to survive with the absentees such as this. And I'm aware of what we agreed upon, before you answer."

"We'll work it out Clara; don't you worry about a thing."

He had his fingers to his lips for reposefulness. That was another thing Clara loved about Rory; his calmness in expressing and handling what appeared to her, difficult situations. She could do nothing here, but smile and kiss him as they again embraced.

"You are so sweet Rory."

"Uh huh, and look what I brought you from mother."

"Oh, a thank-you card; mother Davanpourt is so thoughtful. I see now Rory, you get your sweetness, honestly."

Clara held her head down and focused upon the words which read:

My Dearest Clara

I am looking forward to many more visits from you with Rory. He is happier now than I have seen him in years. And of course I'm attributing those blessings to you. That principal's position he is working on, though, concerns me very much, especially after talking to him today. You will be successful at getting this job; maybe after much ado, but you will be successful.

This is not what the card is for, but that was just on my mind. Thanks very much for the plate; it is already making my wall look adorable.

Love,

Mother Davanpourt

Clara finished reading the card, looked at Rory, then back at the card, as if it held the answer to her puzzlement.

"Is there something wrong Clara?"

192

"Yes, what happened at the meeting today?"

"Mother must have mentioned something huh; she was more than concerned when I told her of Sauninger T. Metfield asking me to withdraw your name -."

"He what!"

"Just be calm honey. That is correct Clara, but that will never happen; so don't even worry about that."

"That guy is dangerous, isn't he?"

"Well, let's hope not Clara."

"He sounds like he would do something real stupid to get his way Rory."

"Oh, I wouldn't go so far as to say that Clara. You're really in, one way or the other."

"What's that now!"

"Well Clara, we voted today, and it ended in a four all tie. We decided the runner-up would automatically be the assistant principal, so you're in, one way or the other. Of course, that upset mother, because she feels Metfield is going to pull something to eliminate you – just because you're you – a woman."

"Call it a woman's instinct Rory, but I feel the same thing after hearing what he asked you to do. If you were one of those weak men, I've ocassionally run into, my name would have already been withdrawn."

"There's no question of that."

"So where do we stand now Rory – I mean, what's going to happen now – tie and all?"

"We will vote again next month, hoping the other two members will vote the same way, breaking the gridlock. Otherwise, we're worse than where we started, because a final tie gives Sauninger T. Metfield the right to make the decision himself."

"And in that case?"

"And in that case Clara, Dulique Gildor will certainly be the principal. But, I'm going to do everything to lobby Willie B. Deinham and Alfred K. Stuckworth over to my side."

"Rory, I love what you're doing, and not because of my selfishness for the position. You do not know how good it makes me feel to be in the presence of a strong man."

"You can count on me Clara to do what I feel is right." And with that said, Clara was pulling him into her bedroom. The picture of the other man in her life was still there. Uncle Henri. Clara glanced his way, but never saw him for the attention she was now receiving from Rory. He quickly assisted in the removal of her pajama top and bottom; baring all. It was obvious, he was anxious to satisfy his lady.

Clara wanted and needed Rory to pickup where he left off, the last time they were together. And before Rory could come up with, anything on his own, she pulled him upon her, and pushed his mouth directly over her delicious hot zabaglione, for him to eat with delight. Rory placed those soft kisses upon her tender lips; first softly circular kissing her outer lips, then roving around her tender outer lips. She loved for him to do this until they gradually, rose round and puffy, enticingly meeting his amorous broad lips. Clara loved it even further when his moisturized tongue eased onto the same sensitive swollen lips and began licking them, also softly, but thoroughly. And she loved it, still more, when her excitement eased her clitoris out, causing his broad nose to inadvertently caress this gorgeous red delicacy as their lips glided upon each other. Finally, Rory's nostrils caught her sweet scent and his tongue caught her sweet juices oozing forth. Clara ecstatically loved this, twirling her behind upon his long tongue as he slid it within her inner lips, and more ecstatically when he rotated outward, sucking her clit. Rory knew how Clara A. Feldon wanted to be loved and he enjoyed doing so. He had told her, he could eat her delicious hot zabaglione all night. And she had told him, she had no problem with that.

Yes, Clara A. Feldon was lying here in sensual amazement, thinking how she had accidently stumpled onto a man or accidently ran into a man with a sumptuous appetite. She had met a man who ate with pleasure, with her in mind; a man who

194

ate for pleasure with her in mind. Yes, to both of these gratifications. His powerful broad lips had latched onto her round puffy lips with an extraordinary tenderness, and his long firm tongue had an uncomparable smoothness. When he ate, his mouth provided an additional lubricant that made her provide an additional lubricant, that prevented any irritation whatsoever. Yes, Rory was smooth as smooth could be, thanks in part to Clara's largeness. Clara locked her hands loosely behind his head to keep Rory on course; to keep him from backing away when she needed that extra pressure to her clit and that extra surge of his tongue into her delicious hot zabaglione.

Clara could feel this huge orgasm coming and wanted to stop it, but it was too late. Rory had too much going on inside of her, for her to do nothing, but gasp for air and try to hold on. She knew, after darn near a month, she was not going to last long.

"Damn, Rory – damn…"

And that was it for the big one. Rory continued as if he never heard a thing, because he knew Clara A. Feldon loved his soothing lips upon her as he finished eating her delicious hot zabaglione. Rory was in no hurry as he lovingly held her delicacy to his mouth, eating slower and slower, enjoying it more and more. This is the sweetness he had longed for the entire three plus weeks. It seemed if he could not ever get enough of Clara. Rory said to himself, then out loud, "I love eating your creamy pudding honey … I love eating your pudding … keep it flowing baby … keep it flowing." Rory's actions spoke for themselves as his broad lips devoured whatever crossed them.

Rory's superb lovemaking felt even better now than it did last month, and Clara was surer than ever; spending the rest of her days with him was what she wanted out of life. He could hold her in his hands … better than a father … he made her melt with warmness … better than a father. And Rory – well, he enjoyed all of her love and affection … better than a father. He was definitely soothing right now, as her moisture filled puffy lips responded graciously to the attention given them by those broad lips of his. Clara had found a man that loved her through and through. As his tongue slashed in and against her tender folds, she suddenly felt rejuvenated enough for a final orgasm for the evening. In one week, Rory had spoiled her by remaining tightly between her curvaceous bowlegs, fully satisfying himself while she dozed with a gratified smile on her face. His eating lasted into the night before he was ever completely gratified. Continuous eating to make up for the lost time, for the both of them. This was really the first time since their great lovemaking sessions that Clara A. Feldon had slept so soundly.

20

Meanwhile, news was traveling fast among the circles of the board members and their immediate families. Ilique K. Fernfort, a co-worker of Clara A. Feldon and the first cousin of Dulique C. Gildor found himself in a win-win situation. He obviously approached both about being one of the new teachers for the new junior high school. Even without the close contact, Ilique's cheery disposition and positive outlook on life made him a shoo-in. There was no one close to Ilique in his bright approach to living each day, making him an ally and friend to everyone nearby. So, to him, it mattered not, who was principal. His status was certain either way, in his opinion, "a classroom door with his name above it, was as good as gold." Congratulations had gone out earlier to his cousin Dulique, and today, congratulatory remarks were extended to his co-worker as she strolled into his room during lunch.

"Clara, you are going to make a fine principal."

"Hold on Ilique, I do not have the position yet. Do you know something I should know?"

"No – not really – just this unequivocal feeling I have."

"Well now – isn't that something Ilique; I guess, being a math teacher make things that precise, huh?"

"Sometimes."

"Of course, you have a positive attitude toward everything I know Ilique. You probably told your cousin the same thing, didn't you?"

"Sure Clara, that is my nature, but my feeling is very strong in your direction – you're the man."

"A strong feeling huh! Just between you and me Ilique, I hope you are right. Surface wise, I say it does not matter, but deep down, I really want the top position. I want it, to prove that women can perform as well as men, if given their just due and opportunity. Maybe, I should think as positive as you that I will get it."

"Maybe you should Clara; afterall, there is absolutely nothing wrong with having faith and believing. Didn't you go to church on Sunday? Wasn't that reinforced from your pulpit?"

We might be talking about two different things Ilique – positive – faith/believing!"

"I don't think so Clara; you gotta believe! That is really where the positive reassurance comes from. Check it out, and you'll find, forces working against you and barriers in your way, will flatten themselves out. If you think back Clara, to the last thing you conquered, it no doubt was done, by your believing."

"Well Ilique, I do not know about that; does hoping and wishing count toward being positive?"

"It might."

Clara A. Feldon immediately thought of Rory G. Davanpourt and how she had wished for his lucious – lucky – lips to be upon her; and it had happened. But this was different altogether, she thought. Coaxing a man into an infatuated affair had little to do with having faith, believing, and thinking positive. Any woman, she thought, could persuade a man to drop his pants in her bedroom and have him kissing either or both sets of her lips in no time. Saying to herself. "Impulse signals rivets in their eyeballs, especially when a nude thigh captivate them. Of course, keeping one of them captivated was the key and what really mattered; something, any smart woman should have no problem accomplishing." Clara thought, getting the other person to believe in you, might just be more important.

"Listen Ilique – would you say – getting others to believe in you, has any less merit?"

"Certainly not, that is truly part of the big picture; definitely a carryover though, from the positiveness displayed toward them."

"Let me see if I understand you Ilique; are you saying, one's perception of your positive attitude make them believe in you?"

"Exactly."

Clara A. Feldon, feeling more confident, rose from the stool near the blackboard, and strolled out of his room; throwing one curvaceous bowleg into the other, as one short step was taken directly in front of each red pump. Ilique thought, Clara's walk alone, might be enough to solidify the top position, as her red skirt had a wonderful rearward motion ... certainly enough for a positive attitude perception.

During the week, Clara had a surprise call from Janetqua Stuckworth. This only meant that Rory or somebody had convinced her father, Alfred K. Stuckworth to vote her way the next time around. And if that wasn't enough to give Clara A. Feldon a positive outlook, LaQueeta Structworth's call, wanting to come on board with her at the new school, definitely did so. Into the next week, Rory called; well, they talked almost every day, but he wanted to come over and share his excitement. He had gotten around to meeting with Willie B. Deinham and Alfred K. Stuckworth, who had assured him, their vote would go to his candidate for principal. But Clara A. Feldon in her sketicism and strength to keep their agreement said:

"Not tonight Rory, you know our once a month agreement; one of us must be strong – you know."

"Yeah – I know Clara, but I thought with the good news and all -."

"It definitely sounds like good news Rory, but I still have a funny feeling about Metfield."

"Why are women so much alike Clara? Mother feels the same way, saying she just does not trust Metfield to do what is right."

"We have those instincts Rory, you men just don't have, plus mother Davanpourt personally knows Metfield."

"I know him too Clara."

"Yes, but if you remember Rory, the day of the Sunday dinner, of her sentimentality when Metfield's name came up. She knows him a little bit better, or at least something about him; that is the impression I got."

"Well, she has never mentioned anything of the sort to me Clara; and if she has a secret, that's her right. You could be imagining things – you know. As far as I'm concerned, you're our new principal, and I'm certain the board meeting in two weeks will bear that out. If you'd rather wait until then to celebrate – that's fine – I'll just want you that much more. I am so hungry for your love Clara."

"I hope you be that way for me forever Rory; it feels so good to know you're there for me. It also feels wonderful to know I'm saving my sweet self for the man I love and the man that truly loves me through and through. Before we get too mushy, making me want to also break our agreement, I can certainly say you have taught me what real loving is. Just promise you'll always love me."

"That goes without saying Clara, but I'll say it anyway. I love you very much and can hardly wait until we marry and live under one roof. Then, I am going to be munching on your delicious hot zabaglione all the time – day and night."

"Say goodnight Rory; you're about to get me worked up. But could you make it morning, noon, and all night long." They laugh and say their goodnights.

Jewel E. Dearman

Later in the week, Clara also had a call from Helene Scott, but it pertained to positions at her Uncle Henri's place, rather than a position at the new junior high school.

"Clara, your Uncle Henri asked me what his favorite niece said of him?"

"I have been intending to call you Helene; how are things going?"

"Girl, like I told you; if I couldn't change him, nobody could. All he needed was the right teacher. Girl, I know you don't want a blow by blow report, but you would be real proud of that man. He is a good pupil, learns fast, very studious, and loves his homework; matter of fact, Henri is eagerly tearing into his assignment and eating it up."

Helene was one fast worker. She had Henri doing things he never anticipated; things he never thought of, but now enjoyed. In just a few weeks, Henri no longer used bending-wrist mannerisms, and the only time he used "girl" was in talking to Helene. Matter of fact, she loved to hear him call her girl, especially when he was bowing into her. Henri had a very deep masculine voice, but it reached an extremely high soprano pitch when he said "girl," causing excessive excitement between Helene's parted thighs. The word triggered her sensual senses, simultaneously opening a flood=gate, which always made Henri happier and much more active. Helene would feel the smooth, rigorous rhythm of his tongue, thereby creating more stimulus and sweet juices for him. Helene firmly held his head to the task while Henri repeatedly told her. "Girl, this is real good." She prided herself on teaching him this great common courtesy and he was now thanking her daily for it. There were even days where Henri, somewhat, took advantage of Helene by bowing down to her sweet darkhollow, six and seven times a day. Somewhat, because Helene rarely ever complained. They both agreed, it was indeed good therapy for Henri. He vowed to never return to his days of old; even, changing his up and coming trip to Uganda with his former friend Charles, to take only Helene.

201

Helene would spare these minor details to Clara for the time being; as Clara wanted no parts of them anyway.

"Splendid; say no more Helene, I believe I get the picture. Now what did you tell Henri, I said of him?"

"Nothing more than what you actually told me Clara; that you looked upon him as a father figure, and hoped one day, he would meet a strong influential woman."

"And looks like he has met that strong influential woman in you Helene; I really want to thank you."

"Girl, I'm the one that should be doing the thanking."

"No, I really mean it Helene; thanks for telling him what I have never been able to say to him."

"You did not have to say it Clara because he knew your actions said it best."

Clara thought of her Uncle Henri and that father figure; then she thought of Rory. Suddenly, she realized, Rory had become that father and more. He had the maturity, the understanding, and she could sit in his lap.

"Oh, while you're on the phone Helene, I have some exciting news to tell you. Rory made your father and me promise not to say anything until it was definite -."

"What is it girl, hurry and spit it out."

"Okay Helene – real quick like – I am in the running for the principal's position at the new Metfield Junior High School."

"Girl, I understand you're a shoo-in."

"You mean – you know already Helene."

"Well yeah – daddy told me – you know men can't keep secrets like we can Clara."

"You got that right."

"I am happy for you Clara, but I'm also happy for me, because I am so unhappy at this school where I am. Put me down as one of you prized teachers right now."

"You got it girl, but I still have my reservations on the disposition of that Sauninger T. Metfield."

"Daddy says, he will be out voted in the next board meeting; so you're in Clara. For my sake, you had better get it, because I cannot last at this school much longer; they are not utilizing my skills correctly."

"Why don't you tell them about it Helene?"

"I did Clara, but he is a real dumb-ass; even told him how to do it, by just switching myself and another teacher around. She would be happy and I would be happy; utilizing our proper education and skills. Sometimes, men can be real pains in the rear; especially when you're not screwing them."

"You mean, it's one of those things huh."

"Well, he hasn't said it, but that's the way I see it; he wants me to give it up, before he gives. Wouldn't be so bad, but he's married, and I don't do married men, because after they get a taste of my action, they get real crazy Clara."

"You are something else Helene."

"Girl, I'm telling you the truth; after a man crawl between these big juicy thighs of mine, they be wanting to stay all night. And it's just not worth it, to have one of us sisters looking for her man, at your place, at three and four in the morning."

"That has happened to you?"

"No – not me – but it happened to a friend of mine Clara, who was dating this married guy. She opened the door and let the wife in though."

"You're kidding Helene!"

"No I'm not. She had no choice after this heifer threatened to blow the windows and tires off her BMW. She left with dignity in that ride of hers though, telling them both, they had two hours to get their business squared away. Girlfriend took no chances though, and spent the rest of the night in a hotel."

"Helene – that sounds like you."

"Yea it was girl; couldn't fool you huh?"

"Not when you called the name of your ride Helene."

"Well, that's when I learned my lesson; I will never – ever go that way again Clara. If he ain't free – he ain't for me; free meaning - not married. Those other jokers better watch out though, especially if I think they're teachable."

"But, how would you know that Helene?"

"Just by talking to them Clara, usually over the phone, because most brothers are shy in the intimate department; so they respond to my questions better when they're not looking me in the eye. Most, I find are game, but you and I know, most of them either can't cut it or can't pass the taste test."

"Yeah, but when you find a good one, watch out girl."

"Clara, you got it going on, I know it. I figured you had a good man in that Rory; are you guys thinking about marriage?"

"Uh Huh! Going to wait until we are absolutely sure though, Helene."

"Sounds like you're pretty sure now Clara."

"I am in certain areas Helene, if you know what I mean."

"Still a little hesitant about the age difference huh?"

"No, not really; age itself does not matter, but I would like a child, and I sometimes wonder if he still got that in him Helene."

"That is your least problem Clara; just ask him."

"I know that is what you would do Helene, but my personality is not like that."

"You got to learn to open up around your man about everything Clara."

"Let's hope time solves my problem Helene."

"It will – if you get off the pill Clara."

"I don't know about that Helene; wouldn't that destroy his confidence in me?"

"It could Clara, but I doubt it; not if he loves you, plus you wouldn't have to ask any embarrassing questions. And even if he can't produce girl, you can always adopt or use some of those other expensive procedures on the market, dealing with other people's sperm."

"Helene, you are hilarious, but you make sense."

"Thank you girl; you just don't forget me when you get that principal's job; now I gotta go."

"Don't worry girl – you got it – if I got it; see ya."

Clara A. Feldon hung up the phone, looking at Uncle Henri on her dresser, thinking about Rory, and what Helene had said, while she lay on her back, in her cozy bed. Helene had made sense about her getting off birth control, and she was definitely considering doing so. Her mind kept saying, "why not, he loves me; the worse that can happen is having a baby by the man you love." The more Clara A. Feldon listened to her mind, the more she felt, getting pregnant, was the right thing to do. Tonight, she reasoned, would even be the time to do it; afterall, with them getting together only once a month, it would probably be a while before anything happened anyway. Then her thoughts could not help but fall upon her new position of principal at Metfield Junior High, and some of the people she would be hiring.

So far her list was short; consisting of Imelda Tregil, her twenty-three year old cousin, Ilique K. Fernfort, Janetqua Stuckworth, LaQueeta Structworth, and of course, Helene Scott. She even smiled at herself for thinking positive for a change.

Things were quiet for the rest of the week; even the next two weeks. Rory called her the Wednesday night prior to the board meeting the next day; mostly to make sure of her availability for dinner that Thursday evening. He had already made reservations at one of the area's finest fancy restaurants. Yes, celebrating his lovely lady's new position was high on his agenda; so was getting another taste of her sweet love. What a memorable night, tomorrow, will be, he told her.

21

Today, Thursday; the morning of their big important board meeting, Linnie D. Scott and Rory G. Davanpourt decided they would ride together. Linnie, who lived near his friend, did the honors by driving his automobile. They felt real good about the business at hand, so a fairly lively conversation took place enroute.

"Rory, it is going to be interesting to see Metfield's reaction when he find out he's outnumbered this morning."

"Yeah Linnie, I can see him now, puffing on that huge cigar, like a Chattanooga choo – choo train."

"When the bad news hits him Rory, he's not going to know whether to stand up or sit down; should cut down on some of his ranting and raving though."

"Yeah it should, when he gets the surprise of his life, Linnie."

"You know Rory, this will be the first time I can remember, things hadn't gone Metfield's way."

206

"You're right Linnie, definitely the first time, but when it's all said and done, it's really time for a female principal. I'd be the first to admit though, it sounded sort of farfetched when mother brought it up. More than that, I thought it was real crazy; then the more I thought, the more it grew on me as a brillant idea."

"Mother Davanpourt gets the credit alright Rory, but don't sell yourself short, because you had the fortitude to run with a good idea. And let's not forget, it was you who convinced Willie B. Deinham and Albert K. Structworth to vote our way."

"Shucks, that was the easy part Linnie; I just needed to know who to talk to. In the case of Deinham, it was his wife, Maybelle Deinham, my dear sister-in-law. We have always been and still remain close, even though my beloved Charllotte is gone. So it was out of respect to her sister and a little for me, that she probably got her husband to see things our way. In the case of Structworth, it was somewhat easier, I merely told him, his daughter, LaQueeta, would probably be next, and she already had my vote locked in."

"That was good strategy Rory, and like I said earlier, don't sell yourself short; you did a magnificent job and deserve your share of the credit. You are to be commended; it makes me feel good to be your friend. And from what I saw in Clara A. Feldon, she is going to make a fine principal. By the way, how is she taking all of this?"

"Well Linnie, I told her about Sauninger T. Metfield, and she's just like mother; believing he will be up to something shady. She even turned me down on a dinner celebration until tonight."

They have a good point there, Rory, but we got Metfield this time."

When Rory and Linnie entered the room for the meeting, Katherine Kelton, the maid/server had the huge commercial pot of coffee ready. And for some reason, there was an unusual supply of goodies; five boxes of donuts, all types, and one box of jellyrolls. Katherine was also unusually jovial; it was apparent, she had heard of some good news. She had raised two daughters, and she and her husband were spending all of their hard-earned dollars to keep them in college. The smile and cheerful disposition Katherine, possessed, somehow appeared to have a female victory glow. As she traveled to and fro to the outer room, Katherine could be seen munching on some of the glazed donuts.

The men were clattering, exchanging greetings; moving about to get the goodies and coffee, and returning to their small favorite groups – more or less. The meeting started at ten today; and here at nine-thirty, everyone was already present, except Sauninger T. Metfield. No one really missed him, from the sound of the loud talking and laughter going on, but it was obvious, he wasn't there.

He was still at home, finishing up a fine breakfast, prepared by his lovely wife, Charmayne, who noticed that her Saun was not very talkative this morning. He was not grumpy either, but silence stirred, other than the clearing of his throat every now and then, and the obvious sound of his fork, touching his plate to get at that delicious ham and cheese omelet. His mood was really happy, but it showed now, only in his inside. His outside expression was that of someone thinking, because that is exactly what he was doing. Thinking of how he had won or was going to win his battle today, over what appeared to be overwhelming odds.

Metfield had also contacted Willie B. Deinham and Albert K. Structworth, about getting their vote, and the most he got out of them was, "still thinking about it," and "not leaning any particular way right now." He had already admitted to himself; those were not exactly the right phrases to be in your corner. Being the mastermind that he was, Sauninger T. Metfield knew not to bring up, what was brewing on his mind to his sweet Charmayne, for fear of an early morning reprisal. Men folks business, he thought, should be taken care of by men folk. And it's not like Charmayne was sitting there watching his every impression anyway; there was a harmonizing clock-thermometer ticking above her head. She was, however, still preoccupied in her thoughts of somehow getting back to work. A real career. It seems now, those were her daily thoughts, but she still had not told her Saun. Being a housewife, looking at these four walls and going to those funky women club meetings were just about to tear her apart. Then when the kitchen wallclock neared ten to the hour, and she could stand the ticking no longer, she reminded Saun that he would be late.

"Saunin, you are going to be late for your meeting if you do not hurry." A courteous, house-wifey duty.

At this point, Metfield smiled; a beautiful smile that even made Charmayne smile. She still had an effect upon him, from when they made love after last month's meeting. And wouldn't you know it, those were the precise thoughts on his mind.

"I suppose I should hurry Charm; this is one of our most important meetings. If I feel as good after the meeting as I do now, maybe we can catch another movie or something."

Charmayne knew what this meant; the something of loving on her. Usually, she was always in the mood for the slashing of his very active tongue; it was generally her Saun, who was too tired or whatever. She kissed him; one of those wet ones, and he was on his way.

When Sauninger T. Metfield, arrived at the meeting. There were very few donuts left, but plenty of coffee remained, because Katherine made sure of that. He loved him some hot coffee – all black – with that cigar. After a few sips, and the wiping of his mouth, with the back of his hand, he lit up; signaling the start of the meeting. And as before, when Charm's charm, hit him from their last love session, he quickly squashed it; preferring to chew on it.

"Well gentlemen, due to the controversy of our business at hand today, I have elected to use rule number eighty-seven, which clearly states that, "the chairman can make any and all decisions to avoid such controversy." In that light, though difficult it is, I am withdrawing Rory T. Davanpourt's candidate, and going with one of lesser confusion. It's really the only way to prevent us from being torn apart. I will, however, study it for a month."

"What the hell are you talking about Metfield; you know damn well, I have the votes to get Clara A. Feldon selected as our principal."

"See, it's that type of outburst, Mr. Davanpourt, that will further cause more controversy. If there's nothing more gentlemen, I need a motion for adjournment."

One of his three loyal sidekicks quickly gave him that motion and another seconded it; and just like that – one – two – boom – the meeting was over, and Sauninger T. Metfield was on his way home to his lovely wife. The whole charade as Linnie called it, took every bit of five minutes.

"Rory, this is the biggest charade I've seen in years; there is no way we can let Metfield get away with this kind of ridiculous action."

"I understand what you're saying Linnie, but he's right, in the usuage of rule eighty seven. In the back of my mind, I thought about it myself, when mother and Clara were so skeptical. Not in my wildest dreams did I think Metfield would use it though. He certainly pulled one out of his hat this time; he even pulled Clara out of the running."

"Why in the hell did we allow that rule in, anyway Rory?"

"If you remember Linnie, it was there from years ago, and for some reason, we left it there; probably figuring it would be of some constructive use, by a sensible person."

"Is there anything legally to be done in this case Rory?"

"You bet your sweet black bottom." Chimed in Paul O. Wilhelm, "and I'm going to get my attorney daughters, Analicia and Felecia, to look into this mess. I was on Metfield's side, but he has gone too far, in denying an individual her basic and fundamental rights. Just think, out of loyalty, I was standing with that crazy idiot."

Katherine was now in the room. She had heard the stunned silencer remarks; then, an up-roar, when everyone realized what had just happened. Discombobulation. She told herself, this was not her concern, but since she listened in on all the meetings, it was difficult to keep her remarks to herself.

"Why that dirty low bastard." Not knowing she was halfway right. "He can't throw that poor girl out without even giving her a chance. Sorry gentlemen, but I heard the whole thing, and I know this is none of my business – somebody gotta do something!"

"We are going to do something Mrs. Katherine, and this is your fight – you have girls in college – you should take this personally."

"Well, let me know if I can be of assistance Mr. Wilhelm – wait until I tell my husband about that dirty lowdown piece of scum." Katherine's voice trailed off as she headed back into the outer room.

Two of Metfield's loyal supporters in, Alvin P. Gildor and Charles S. Fernfort hightailed it out of there. They were brother-in-laws; husbands of the fame Charwood sisters, Delores Charwood Gildor and Margaret Charwood Fernfort. Incidentally, the ones doing the motion and second. They hustled out of there to their wives for some new directions, since things had changed significantly, since they left home. Rory, being the leader that he is, could see they needed a new setting to cool some tempers, so he calmly said:

"Why don't we head over to Linnie's place – Sandy's; they have a separate dining room where we can just sit and talk, and iron through this mess."

Linnie called ahead to inform Sandy of the entourage headed her way; he knew she was in the midst of getting food prepared for lunch and would be busy. It was now just ten-twenty five. By the time they arrived, Sandy told Linnie, their mouths should water for some of her exquisite lunch appetizers. Linnie immediately felt warm, as in lovingly warm. That is what he loved about Sandy; she was his business partner and lover, but she was extremely supportive. No, "What" or bitching about what all she had to do; just a simple, "bring them on Lin." Now you can see why Linnie does some of his best eating of her fine delicacy in their restaurant's kitchen. When Rory, Linnie, and the gang; Paul O. Wilhelm, Albert K. Structworth, Alfred K. Stuckworth, Edward C. Scott, and Willie B. Deinham arived, the dining room was quickly noticed as intimately cozy, with its red and gold patterned, velvet wall covering.

A long large rectangular cherry-wood table, centered under two grandiose candle-styled chandeliers, was more than adequate to seat this distinguished group of gentlemen.

Sandy had some of that soft appetizing lunchtime music going, and the room smelled, of freshly cut red roses, which adorned the table in two fine ivory-colored vases. An aroma, a real saliva brewing aroma, poured through the open door. Whatever the appetizer was made of, it was quickly consumed as fast as Linnie and Sandy served them. It was understood, they were on the house. A menu was passed around for those who opted to hang around for lunch. Everyone remained; as any superb chef figures, it is virtually impossible to refuse a good meal. And after Sandy's golden brown flavorful peach cobbler, they were too full to murmur short phrases, let alone, discuss in detail the happenings of the day, and old Metfield. So, one by one, they excused themselves until only Rory and Linnie were left; and Rory would have too, had he not been riding with Linnie. A few major points, however, were accomplished at today's luncheon. One; they would meet here again, before the next month's board meeting. Two; they would definitely come back and eat on a regular basis. Three; next time, they would discuss business before eating. Practically everyone noticed there were no salt shakers, but quickly forgot about them, when Linnie made them taste their food.

"Well, where do we go from here Rory?"

"Take me by mother's, I'll have Clara pick me up."

"I mean – with the funky decision – Metfield made this morning."

"Oh – that had almost slipped my mind Linnie."

"You look sleepy Rory; sounds like it had completely slipped your mind."

"You're right on both counts Linnie. Man – that food was good and filling. Oh – I don't know; we'll talk about it later. And Linnie, please fix me two of those lunches to go; there will be no going out to celebrate tonight. Plus, mother and Clara need to know why I'm doubly miserable." Rory was trying to keep his humor in the midst of all this turmoil.

With that done, Linnie dropped Rory off. Of course, while Rory was being driven to his mother's, Metfield was still driving. All this time, he was still driving, up and down Georgia Avenue. One would think, he should have been happy; afterall, there was a smirk kind of a smile on his face, when he left the short board meeting. The short meeting, where in one sentence, more or less, he had gotten rid of the female candidate for the principal's position; the short meeting ... and that is part of why, there's no happy smile. He wondered what he would tell Charmayne Metfield, his lovely and loving wife, if for some reason, she inquired of why such a short meeting; especially since it was so important. Metfield knew she was happily waiting for the movies and their infrequent love feast, and he did not want to spoil that. He did not want her unhappy for any reason ... she was his cornerstone. How could he explain to her, he was turning his back on women ... that he had done what he had done.

Sauninger T. Metfield drove up and down Georgia Avenue to clear his head. Georgia Avenue; a roadway where he normally made his best decisions; where he always had great thoughts of his wife – of women. The same thoughts, as before, cluttered his brain, where a pretty woman ruled his life ... controlled his brain ... made him commit her phone number to memory. Happy times – when woman first became king – or made man feel like king. He wondered what the king would tell him, when he told her what he had done. What would she do – how would she react – would she give him another number to remember. He was afraid to face her now. Fear. Metfield needed something to help him think. A cigar; however, the king – she made him put it out, no sooner than it was lit. His window went down and he tossed it out onto Georgia Avenue. The smoke; it made him nauseated until all four windows were down, and the air around him was the same as that on the Avenue. Bread. Relaxation hit him like a ton of dough; that being the wonderful aroma of Wonder bread, from the bakery, tickling his nostrils. Yes, Georgia Avenue relaxed and cleared his head; he remembered drinking those cold grapette pops as he loitered in Doc Jones Drugstore. Those were definitely the good old days, he thought, as he passed his alma mater, Howard University.

Sauninger T. Metfield glanced at his watch and smiled; became happy again, because it was time for the meeting to be over, and he no longer needed an excuse for an early arrival home. He was king again. He saw them going to the movies and later making love – lying between Charmayne's smooth thighs, as she directed his bobbing and weaving head and lips upon her tender lips; giving instructions for him to quit smoking and to allow her career to began. His fears were gone. He was ready to hold Charmayne in his hands, further conquering his fears; to completely lick his fears, so he headed home.

On the other side of town, Rory G. Davanpourt had entered his mother's house; handed her, the two dinners, told her Metfield had deleted his candidate, that he was exhausted, and would talk later. She politely pointed toward his bedroom, which was never relinguished in all these years. Then, with malice in her heart and anger showing on her face, as clenched teeth, parted lips, and beady-starry eyes dominated; mother Davanpourt sat down to think. She thought of her brother, Rafeal Meadlarkin who had died a war hero. And no doubt had died with a broken heart, because he had been denied his true love, in Leslie Mae Brontlier. She too had died of a broken heart, due to a tired and grief stricken body caused by suffering, for being made to marry someone she did not love, and who was not the father of her child. Mother Davanpourt thought of the child, Sauninger T. Metfield, her nephew, her brother's child; who by right should be Sauninger T. Meadlarkin. She thought of her two great nephews and great niece in sweet Renatra, whom she had herself been denied the right to love. Then she lowered her knees to the floor, crisscrossed her hands and fingers together under her chin, tightly to her bosom, looking heavenly upward; asking God to forgive her for the malice, to forgive her for the anger, to forgive her for what she thought of doing. She asked God to point her in the right direction; "just set the record straight, Oh Lord."

A little later, Clara A. Feldon arrived, and they now sit at the kitchen table, trying to eat that delicious meal, Rory had brought them. Clara could see the anguish in the wrinkles on mother Davanpourt's brow as they talked.

"I know Rory feels bad mother Davanpourt; he was so sure of me being named the new principal today. I can see why he was so exhausted; he must be awfully disappointed."

"He is not any more disappointed than I am Clara. I even warned him about Metfield."

"What do you mean, warned him? You sound if you know Metfield personally."

"I do Clara." She looked sincerely and directly at Clara; knowing she would now divulge the secret between she and the late Leslie Mae Brontlier. She knew Clara was honest and trustworthy.

"So that is what you meant a few weeks ago, when you told Rory to leave Sauninger T. Metfield to you."

"I knew it was something I liked about you Clara; you not only heard my comments, but remembered them. That's more than I can say for Rory."

"Well, you know how men sometimes get wrapped up into their own genius ideas and refuse to listen. So, how is it mother Davanpourt, that you know Metfield, so personally?"

"You see Clara, Sauninger T. Metfield is my nephew, but Rory does not know that. I have never told him because of various circumstances. Someday though, the truth will come to the surface and somebody is going to be hurt real bad. I can tell you this; that Sauninger is so hung-up on being a hot shot Metfield."

"You mean – Metfield is not his real name – mother Davanpourt!"

"Right Clara; years and years ago, Sauninger's mother was allowed or made to marry a man, Benjamin Metfield. A man she neither wanted nor loved. This however, presented two problems; one, the girl, Leslie Mae Brontlier was in love with my brother; two, she was pregnant with my brother's child. I can still remember Rafael, worrying about what mama and daddy was going to say, when they found out; as if it was just yesterday."

"Oh my, that sounds complicated mother Davanpourt, but of course your parents and Leslie's parents did not know all of that."

"Sure they did Clara; they even cut a deal to keep it a secret. Thomas Brontlier and my father, Willie Meadlarkin agreed to five hundred dollars; can you believe that! I had never been so disappointed in my father; it took me decades to forgive him. That was one of the saddest days ever; my brother was simply devastated – Leslie was too, for that matter. I can still remember crying something terrible." And her eyes watered for some more of those tears. After Clara A. Feldon provided some tissue and rubbed her back, mother Davanpourt quickly recovered, because she knew, she had to get it all out. Her story ... her sadness.

"But why – Mother Davanpourt – why would two grown men do such a thing?"

"A number of reasons Clara, but you must remember, they were farmers, and they thought, they knew what was best for their kid's future. I want to show you something." Mother Davanpourt left the room and returned with the letter from Leslie Mae Brontlier. After Clara finished reading it and finding out what happened to the poor girl, she was in tears. She recovered to ask more questions though.

"Well, whatever happened to Benjamin Metfield; is he still alive?"

"Oh, the forgotten person – to answer your question Clara – just barely. Poor Benjamin is over there in the Veterans Hospital; his mind, useless to himself … useless to the world. They probably think he's in a bad way, because of the war, but it's really all for what happened to Leslie Mae."

"Does Metfield know where he is mother Davanpourt?"

"I'm sure he does Clara, but knowing Metfield, he has probably told everybody his father is dead." And that is exactly what Metfield had told his immediate family. He was right about his real father, but he was lying through his teeth for the Metfield glory.

"That man is so pitiful, mother Davanpourt."

"Indeed, he is Clara. Rory does not know any of this yet – bless his heart – so - ."

"I follow you – well, what are you going to do, mother Davanpourt?"

"I have asked the Lord for direction Clara."

"Enough said, mother Davanpourt; I am going to wake Rory up, we need to be heading for home."

On their way to Rory's place, he sat silent as he drove her car. Clara could see the hurt in his face; she could feel the hurt in his body. This was one of the darkest moments in his life; the darkest since his beloved Charllotte said goodbye.

"This is not the end of the world Rory. You know – I was pessimistic at first, but now, I truly believe things will be all right."

"You are just saying that to make me feel better Clara." The smile upon her face was as genuine as he had ever seen it though. "And you know what, its beginning to work. I love you so much." He lays his hand upon her exposed gorgeous thigh.

"You are just saying that to put me in a lovemaking mood Rory; and you know what, its beginning to work."

They both laugh, because they both know what's going to happen when they get home and rinse the Metfield filth from their body and mind. Clara had some sweet mischievous something on her mind that had been there since she was first at

Rory's place. And it happened again; she led Rory to that L-shaped wrap-around sofa. The invitation of that corner always drove her to a new excitement. It was hard to control what was racing across her brain. She threw a large pillow on the floor in the angle of the sofa, sitting on it and raising her curvaceous legs high – wide, comfortably sprawled apart, atop the sofa's seat. A perfect right angle of her gorgeous nude thighs exposed a sumptuous delicacy. Her vagina was gapped wider and more beautiful than a large cup of delicious creamy tomato soup. This was by far her best acrobatic maneuver. Clara's delicious hot zabaglione was gapped wider than Rory had ever seen it; her long-rounded folds, her deep luscious pink sides glistened from its own sweet moisture. The adrenlin flowing into Rory's body as the saliva flowed over his tongue; told him this eating was going to be mindboggling. By then she had scooted her arched buttocks forward; his mouth had already touched her and began to do wonderful things.

Rory's tongue was lodged in her flavorful opening, slowly twisting and turning to Clara's enjoyment. He was eating her delicious hot chocolate pudding exactly the manner in which she absolutely loved it. Rory held her bottom in his strong hands with a delicate firm grip, snugly and tightly to his broad lips that slitherly covered her tender folds. Her behind squirmed a little, but squirmed it did, pressing forward, tighter to his wide wet lips; the feeling, the movements of Rory's tongue was astonishing. Clara could feel its tip touching every sensitive nerve as he ate slice after slice of her delicious hot pudding; moving his head from side to side, with her watchful eyes happily looking on. Her long clit was out, and as he moved his face, he played with it with his nose, just as Clara loved it; real smooth, never missing an important stroke with his tongue.

Clara loved Rory's concentration; he knew how to make her climax. He knew how to make Clara get multiple orgasms. Even when his teeth accidently nicked her as it did now, it was ecstatic; Clara merely wanted Rory to tear into her and eat the whole thing ... become greedy ... get real aggressive ... suck that juice out of her with a mighty force ... bite her tender folds ... chew her delicate clit. Rory however, knew best; he ate hearty, but he ate smoothly, slowly grinding it out, slashing his tongue upon the right spot inside her lovely pink walls, and caressing her clit with the same soothing smoothness. Rory was eating her delicious hot chocolate pudding real good right now, and Clara A. Feldon really had no complaints, for she was too busy having orgasms. She bawled a pleasurable hum as she felt a warm object slowly going from threshing inside her delicacy to gently massaging around her swollen clit. Each time Rory made the transition and all in between, Clara could not help but come and come ... orgasm after orgasm.

Pure sheer delight. Yes, as always, Rory was enjoying eating Clara A. Feldon's delicious hot zabaglione, as was evident from his face; his lips, nose, and entire face were covered with her creamy sweetness. Clara had been watching, but the constant orgasms had forced her peepers shut and her mouth open to loud hissing sounds. She vaguely heard Rory utter the word "missing," but Rory was not missing anything at the moment, and was eating everything close to his mouth. Clara could feel her final orgasm coming as Rory's tongue slid smoothly about; probing, wriggling, swirling, inside her saturated passage and against her moist inner folds. Electrifying stings burst through her vulva, bringing with it juicy sweet liquids; Rory had opened her flood=gate and was ecstatic himself with the abundant succulent creamy nourishment. Clara screamed pleasurable quivering, toebuckling, buttock fluttering rejoices, and it was over, except for her generosity to Rory. He was now eating her delicious hot zabaglione with the thoroughness she loved; slow and slower. Clara could hear and feel nothing but the lapping from his long-broad tongue as she happily dozed off.

When Sauninger T. Metfield finally did arrive home, he had logged about one hundred fifty miles of cruising Georgia Avenue, but his mind was quite a bit clearer; and he too was in the mood for love. Charmayne was eager to give out some more directives, and she did, while holding his head to her innermost sensitive lips; twisting and twirling as his tongue and lips landed ravishing touches and kisses. She said to him during their mutual synchronization of lucious lips, "Saunin, I am going to work to pursue a career other than these household chores." She repeated it numerous times, over and over, as Saunin enjoyed the loveliness of his sweet Charm, and better still, the sweetness of his lovely Charm. All during their exchange he devoured her every word as happily as he devoured deeply into her love. Charmayne locked her well-constructed proportioned thighs around him until she felt his cheeks responding with, "yes dear, yes dear." The more he cried out, the tighter she held him; to make sure it all sank into his inner self with meaning as well as passion. Charmayne held Saunin tightly until they both had "yes dears," coming.

Shortly after they finished making love, the phone rang; Charmayne handed him the phone after answering it.

"Hello Sauninger T. Meadlarkin, this is Rachel Meadlarkin Davanpourt. I heard about the meeting today. Our interest would be mutually shared if Ms. Clara A. Feldon spoke before your group, prior to her selection as principal."

"I understand Mrs. Davanpourt – that – that is a wonderful idea." Getting himself together and speaking stronger. "Thanks, for your tremendous input." And with those remarks, their conversation ended.

"Who was that Saun?"

"Oh, that was Rory's mother, giving me some additional input on the female candidate for the principal's position and some ideas for fairly selecting her."

"So there is a woman in the running; I didn't think you guys had gotten that far Saun."

"Oh sure, we're very advanced in that area Charm; been leaning that way for some times now."

"Saunin, I am so proud of you; what is her real chances though?"

"As far as I'm concerned, she's in Charm, but we'll probably have a challenge or two from the guys. So, to smooth things out, I will have her speak at our next board meeting."

"That is a great idea Saunin."

What Charm didn't know, Saunin was full of great ideas; most of which would surprise her. He was startled at the call from mother Davanpourt, but pleased to hear their secret was still intact; especially with a good future response on his part. The thought of Charmayne finding out the truth did make him nervous at times. In reality, he was scared to death, because so much was at stake, in his opinion. Because in the real big reality, Sauninger T. Metfield had no backbone, other than the Metfield name; and he was riding it for all the glory he could.

What was also surprising, this action filled day, was when Rory answered his phone moments later, and his mother asked to speak to Clara.

"Sure mother, hold on – telephone honey."

"Clara, this is mother Davanpourt; I want you to prepare to speak before the guys at their next board meeting. Tell Rory to expect a call from Metfield to that effect; also tell him you're optimistic about your chances now. Between you and I, you're in – most definitely. Sleep tight my child."

"Thank you very much mother Davanpourt." She hangs up and Rory is looking at her with wide glaring eyes.

"What was that all about Clara?"

"Mother Davanpourt said for you not to worry about me; for me to prepare to speak at the next board meeting; that you would receive a call from Metfield to that effect."

"Really!"

"Uh huh; you know Rory – I feel real optimistic about my chances now – I am a pretty persuasive speaker – you know."

"You're persuasive even when not speaking Clara."

"We are definitely talking about two different things Rory."

"I know." Sending sensuous eyes directly into hers. "I wonder what brought all this on – and how did mother get involved. I have a feeling she knows that rascal – do you

222

remember that statement she made several weeks ago — something about taking care of Metfield. She is so funny about some things; it's impossible to pry anything from her if she's set on not telling it. Did she tell you anything just then Clara?"

"No – no more than what I just told you; Rory, what was that you were missing earlier?"

"Huh?"

"When you were busily caressing me, you talked of missing something."

"Oh yeah, I was just talking to myself Clara; curious huh?"

"Well, why shouldn't I be Rory ... after all ... I was the open subject, if you can recall that far back."

Rory smiled at Clara and laughed aloud when her expression turned sourly serious. "Seems like I do remember a very beautiful and tasty right angle. It was nothing bad though."

"So tell me then – or is it that personal?"

"No, not really Clara – it's a long story – but for you. A simple sentence should suffice. I enjoy eating your delicious hot zabaglione. And to elaborate, I have been missing out on some real good stuff."

"Oh, okay ... see you in the morning honey ... by the way, I'm calling in to be off tomorrow – you know what that means ... good stuff huh – thanks Rory, I enjoy it the same as you. I could go on and on about how good you make me feel. In a few words, you are incredible."

And Clara A. Feldon curl up, feeling Rory's large hard shaft pressing against her buttocks; ever the more conscious of this hunk of a man and her duty to keep him pleased – keep him hungry. They both knew she would be rejuvenated by morning, and no doubt, full of that good stuff. Tonight, Clara told herself, would be the night she weaned Rory of resting his head comfortably between her lubricative thighs all night, caressing her slit and its adjoining tender twitching folds, with his long-broad slippery tongue. She discovered, early on, this smooth delicate post activity was what gave her the most trouble once she was back home alone. Trying to sleep with her fingers where Rory's

223

roving warm tongue had been, proved ineffective. It was no question, Rory had spoiled her to something magnificent; to something she had loved immediately, something that solved the irritability of having those mini-post orgasms, while completely rejuvenating her body for the next gigantic orgasm. Rory loved it too because of the tasty sweet honey flavored juices. He however never pressed the issue, but was always willing to accommodate his favorite lady.

Anyway, for ten minutes, Clara A. Feldon's abstinence went extremely well; then it dawned on her. "Why should I deny myself something I truly love." She would not wean herself just yet. And within seconds she eased onto her back, simultaneously easing his head downward and between her sumptuous thighs onto her lovely puffy twitching lips. So it appears that Rory's ritual is safe and his eating techniques would continue being exceptionally productive. Yes, Rory loved Clara A. Feldon's calm moans, groans, and sighs throughout the night, as she produced choice flavorful nutrients to their gratification.

23

Word had gotten around prior to this morning's board meeting what was going to happen. Sauninger T. Metfield had told Rory to invite his candidate to speak before the board. So Rory had Clara A. Feldon, at their scheduled ten o'clock meeting at nine; to meet the guys, so to speak. Do a little politicking. In her black suit and white blouse, Clara was stunningly beautiful. And her mid-thigh length skirt gave a definitive portrayal; she was a female. Rory saw to her making the rounds, talking to the distinguished gentlemen, collectively and one on one; however he found them. Linnie D. Scott tagged along with them. Clara was more gorgeous than Linnie had remembered her, and he was all smiles and fascinated how professionally she handled herself. Speaking of smiles, each of the seasoned gentlemen had a huge smile upon their face no sooner than they were introduced. None of them could keep their eyes off her; her gorgeous shapely figure, her beautiful thighs and bowlegs. Only an imprint of her firm breast showed, but that did not keep these matured gentlemen from casting their eyes in that direction, and no doubt using their vivid imagination. All this admirable looking, and within minutes of seemingly meeting everyone, Clara A. Feldon found herself encircled, along with Rory and Linnie of course, who stood on her sides. Even Sauninger T. Metfield would have been impressed, but he was still at home with his lovely Charmayne.

For some unknown reason, Metfield was finishing up breakfast in bed, under the direction of Charmayne who lay squirming from the results. His cheeks were full of her creamy delicious servings as he murmured, "yes dear – yes dear," to her directive. Charmayne was constantly telling Saunin while he ate her wonderfully prepared breakfast, "you will make sure the woman is selected." She smiled as she removed her thighs from around his head and hurried him off to the meeting.

The crowd quieted and took their respective seat around the table, as soon as Sauninger T. Metfield entered the room, lit-up and quickly extinguished his cigar. His breakfast no doubt had put him in a good mood for tolerating females as principals. He glanced at the picture on the wall of Ordon T. Metfield, and seemed to beg forgiveness. Then he looked about the room, at no one in particular, saying:

"I have decided on Ms. Clara A. Feldon as the new principal for the prestigious Ordon T. Metfield Junior High School. I want you to know ma'am, I will be watching you closely. If there is nothing more, this meeting is adjourned."

All those words were spoken without ever looking in Clara's direction. Her mouth as well as everyone else's, including his two diehard supporters, fell open. Metfield bit into his cigar, hastily leaving the room. On his way to the meeting, he had decided against prolonging his agony. Now that he was on his way home, he decided to mull over what had just transpired. Well, not directly home, he was driving around again; again down Georgia Avenue, but this time he headed for Rock Creek Park. Metfield needed a serene setting where he could think. He and Charmayne used to come here when their daughter, Renatra, was small; now she was about to graduate from college. Oddly enough, he thought, the trees and the bushes still looked the same; and the mammoth park still had a peaceful effect upon him. In a nice shady spot, he sat in his car and wondered about a lot of things, both past, present, and future. A lot of things, but all related. He wondered why some people live so long, notably, Mrs. Rachel Meadlarkin Davanpourt. He told himself, she would never expose him, if he never riled her. No way could he ever exist, being anything but a Metfield; the thought of anything different suddenly gave him a headache.

While Sauninger T. Metfield was in the park, consoling himself and searching his soul, Rory G. Davanpourt and the whole gang were celebrating. Even Metfield's staunchest supporters in Alvin P. Gildor and Charles S. Fernfort were laughing and piling congratulatory compliments upon Clara A. Feldon. Their sons were automatically in; Dulique C. Gildor, as assistant principal and of course, Ilique K. Fernfort, who was also Clara's coworker and friend at Dunbar High, as one of the teachers. Katherine had managed to slip in a word about her daughter, Sherri Kelton who was graduating soon, Linnie D. Scott, to be on the safe side, mentioned that his Helene was really looking forward to the school's opening. Rory had cautioned Clara, of names possibly being thrown about by his close associates and friends. Clara could not have forgotten their names, even if she had not been taking notes, because each son or daughter's name was proudly written upon their business cards and carefully placed in her hand.

Yes, everyone was indeed in a good mood, and you would know it, in all their excitement, they did get hungry. Linnie had forewarned his Sandy, they, more than likely would be by for lunch. Rory again, made the suggestion.

"I don't know about you guys, but I'm getting a little hungry; why don't we continue this celebration at Sandy's. The tab is on me."

Rory did not have to volunteer his money; they would have gone anyway, but he wanted to get Clara up and running on a good note. He knew, down the road, their assistance could be needed. Plus, he owed Clara a meal out. Before their hearty appetites were satisfied, she told Rory, she wanted to go by and personally thank mother Davanpourt for all she had done. During the course of the fine healthy lunch, Clara A. Feldon told the group, some of the words written down in her prepared speech, which never left her leather case. Metfield had not wanted to hear any of her verbiage, and that is the way it was.

Mother Davanpourt thanked Clara for her appreciative hug and kiss, giving hers in return. She also thanked Clara for the wholesome food brought her from Sandy's. There were no tears shed this time, but there were some long silent moments interspersed as they talked. One could tell, each of the ladies had much on their mind. Much that each knew would be said later. This however, was a time to celebrate and be jovial, if possible. Rory walked around the kitchen with his chest stuck out, waiting on his women; tea, water, even reheating the baked chicken, carrots, and peas, for his mother. Mother Davanpourt ate slowly, folding her arms across her bosom from time to time, looking at Clara. She smiled while doing so, and her eyes sparlked. It was easy to see; Clara's youth and beauty reminded her of something and someone, a long time ago. Clara understood part of it and smiled in return. One day, Rory would know the secret between them, but today was not that day. One secret was divulged though, when Clara removed an eight by ten picture, and presented it to mother Davanpourt. It was of she and Rory together; the one taken by Helene when they were in Baltimore. Talking about a pleasant surprise that really brightened her day, this picture was the wonder of wonders. Mother Davanpourt knew it was going on her living room wall, and she said so:

"I know just the spot on my wall in there." Nodding toward the living room with her head, but holding the picture tightly to her bosom, as if someone was going to snatch it from her.

Jewel E. Dearman

It was good Clara waited until most of her food was consumed, because mother Davanpourt ate nothing else afterward. Her facial expressions; the eyeball gleams, the puffy cheeks from grinning, told Clara, she was now that daughter in her world, and said as much.

"You are going to make me a fine daughter, child."

Even Rory smiled widely, because he knew what his mother was saying; Clara was going to make him a fine wife. It had been a month since they made love and he could hardly wait until he got Clara home. He thought, their discipline monthly love-ins weren't so bad, especially since tonight was the night. Rory sensed the same horniness in Clara and said to his mother.

"Mother, Clara and I have a lot to do; we better be going."

It was only 2:30 in the evening, but mother Davanpourt also had had a full day, with all the good events happening, so she did not mind. She thanked Clara for the picture, still holding it to her bosom, promising the next time she came over, it would be hanging on her wall. Clara did not mind that she received no hug in leaving; mother Davanpourt kissed her cheeks, clutching the picture. Clara understood; never had she given a present before that had been so tightly gripped. It made her very happy to be able to make someone very happy. Clara A. Feldon promised herself, she would remain happy through the night, when Rory held her half as snugly.

Clara had a surprise for Rory as they emerged from a shower and entered the bedroom. She kneeled to her knees and fell forward on her hands like a dog, arching her buttocks upward, with her thighs widened just enough to expose the pretty pink flesh of her luscious moist vaginal opening. Rory, alert, quickly was on his hands and knees moving slowly toward her voluptuous round behind. Her gorgeous folds were gapped perfect for the entry of Rory's large nose as he eased it inside of her a little ways and proceeded to slide it up and down, within the slippery wet groove. Clara felt the warmness of his nose, flinching, moving backward as each of his downward strokes slightly touched the area where her clitoris was hidden. Clara was loving the fullness

229

of his broad nose; filling to capacity the space of her slit. Rory's large nose was moving about and inside her lovely creamy pudding as vigorous and wonderful as his mouth and tongue. As he slowly moved around her tender folds, she felt a tremendous itching deep inside her juicy cavity. Never before had Clara been loved exclusively by a nose, and in her words, "Rory, this is fantastic – it's working – it's working." "Rory's nose knows," she said to herself, "this man is incredible, I cannot believe he is going to make me ... with his nose. Damn, this is fantastic and I cannot last another second."

"Rory – Rory – Rory."

Clara's mouth watered as she called his name and anticipated the inevitable and Rory's mouth watered as the inevitable commence to happen. Suddenly, Rory's tongue moved outward onto her precious lips, licking about them slowly, thrusting it between them as he felt sweet juices appear. Clara joyfully felt and heard Rory's smooth lapping sounds; the constant flicking of his long-broad tongue was making her feel so good as another orgasm was near. She loved the way Rory licked inside her folds; sliding onto her outer lips and smoothly back inside. Clara again talked to herself. "I love the way Rory brings me to my peak; he eats my zabaglione like he is loving it ... he eats it like it is so good ... this man's mouth and tongue and nose is so wonderful." Then a vocal crashing; "love me Rory, love me Rory, love – me – Rory." And she was furiously having an enormous orgasm. Rory gripped Clara's bouncing buttocks, continuing his smooth tongue lashes until she was completely gratified and his appetite was more than satisfied.

Metfield had told Clara A. Feldon, he would be watching her; and at today's celebration/orientation for the new junior high school and staff, he focused his eyes upon her, off and on, but each time, his stare toward her grew more intense. Metfield still could not believe, a woman was going to run the school bearing the name of his late honorable grandfather, Ordon T. Metfield. "If it had not been for that Rachel Meadlarkin," he said to himself, "I could have had my way." The more Metfield seemingly frowned, the more mother Davanpourt smiled. She had made Rory bring her to this affair; she told him, "I would not miss this for anything in the world." She was mingling well in the crowd, focusing a great deal, if not all of her time on her great niece, Renatra Metfield. This made Sauninger T. Metfield nervous, because in his opinion, "there is no telling what might slip out of this old lady's mouth to his daughter."

Metfield smiled however, when he saw Janetqua Stuckworth, because she unknowingly, was in his scheme of things for watching Clara A. Feldon and the going on's at his namesake school. Renatra would too, totally without her knowledge, be his other lookout. To think Metfield would even think of using his daughter, for his dirty deeds, was an intolerable form of treachery. Anyway, it was now time for him to say a word or two, and the crowd quieted down as he approached a lectern, located in the upper center of the administration's large gathering room.

"Ladies and gentlemen, this is truly a fine day in our lives, and I might happily add, a historical one. It gives me great pleasure to wish Ms. Clara A. Feldon all the luck in the world; she'll need it." There was a loud roar of laughter in the room. Metfield was not being facetious, but it came across to the crowd that way, they eagerly awaited his next joke. "It has always been my intention to give qualified women their just due." Looking squarely at his wife, Charmayne, who smiled proudly. "And one day, there will be others; Janetqua is prepared and could easily be next." The crowd, mostly women, gave Metfield a thunderous clapping applause; deservingly so for those kind remarks. What would they have done if they could have looked into Metfield's treacherous heart? "It is good for the world, change is occurring; too slow in my opinion. I will, however do what I can. Thank you for coming and stay as long as you please."

More thunderous applause as Metfield disappeared among them. People near him was shaking his hand and patting him on the back. He made his way toward Janetqua, shaking her hand saying:

"Ah, Janetqua, it could happen soon, you know." Slipping a business card into her palm. "Give me a call." He paused no longer than he had to; moving ostensibly cheerful among the crowd.

Mother Davanpourt saw some traits of her brother in sweet Renatra; this was a glorious day for her. Present at this event were the wives of each board member, and it was obvious by their jovial behavior, they were pleased with Metfield's speech. The school opened the following September, with no hullabaloo.

Janetqua Stuckworth and LaQueeta Structkworth were ecstatic about being part of the same staff. It would give them an opportunity to be together for the first time on a daily basis and really enhance their chances at pursuing that family tree matter. Aggressive as the plump, but extremely shapely and attractive LaQueeta was, she considered this assignment an honor. Janetqua, on the other hand, looked at it as a mere stepping stone to greener pastures – much greener pastures; especially after she called up Sauninger T. Metfield. He told her what he expected of her in the way of looking out for him; in other words, anything of an adverse nature on Clara A. Feldon, and the school. Metfield stressed to Janetqua, "your rewards will be great and swift in coming."

Dulique C. Gildor, had of course, been chosen as the assistant principal. He was an unassuming sort of fellow; no real ambitious plans. His mother, Delores Charwood Gildor did all of the ambitiousness for him. And the gorgeous Helene Scott, Clara's new friend, was in, as was her cousin, Imelda Tregil. Sherri Kelton, Katherine's daughter was also included. Then, without an explanation, there was Renatra Metfield, sporting her lovely freckles and Ilique K. Fernfort.

Jewel E. Dearman

PART TWO

24

Clara A. Feldon stopped by later in the morning to commend Ilique for his unconstrained participation. Leaning inside his classroom, clasping onto the door's facing, she cheerfully uttered.

"Hi there Ilique, it is so nice of you to help out with everything around here! You are the only man we can really depend on."

"Oh, it was nothing Clara, consider it a pleasure; I mean folding up the chairs weren't that bad."

"Yes, but it was so many of them, and all the other guys merely walked out and left you there; full well knowing they were not going to walk into the closet and fold themselves."

"Well, in their defense, it is Pop Belder's duty"

Mr. Robert Belder or Pop Belder as everyone called him, was the school's aging janitor. Ilique respected Pop Belder; always thinking when he saw him moving slowly about, of the opportunities, which were never, afforded the gray-haired old man in his day. It was obvious from his stooping upper-back, Pop Belder had carried his share of the load. Ilique has promised himself, if there was anything which, could be done; not conflicting with Pop Belder's pride, then he was about the task. Information emanating from their discussions was a beautiful source of wisdom for Ilique.

"That makes it extra special of you to do it Ilique."

"Like I said, it was nothing – you are looking nice today Clara!" Ilique reached out, touching Clara's belt loop, protruding the left side of her waist, in completing his complimentary remarks. Their eyes met briefly, as Clara looked downward and abruptly backed away.

Yes, Clara Arletra Feldon was the new principal of the new Ordon T. Metfield Junior High School, and she had helped hand pick, most of the teachers. Ilique Kraven Fernfort had met Clara's qualifications, because of his being one of the best math teachers in the school district. At least that is the reason given, but that was a whole year ago. Clara and Ilique were friendly co-workers at Dunbar High, when Clara was vaulted to the ranks of the hierarchy.

From all indicators to Ilique, Clara was partial to him, like a secret admirer sort of thing, but shied away anytime he even hinted at an approach. It was like Clara wanted him to know, but to just leave it be; displaying the actions of a turtle when disturbed, withdrawing its head into a safe haven of a protective sanctuary.

"Thanks for the compliment Ilique; this outfit is not very appealing to me. It has never been one of my favorites."

"Oh, it's not so much as the outfit; you would look good in anything. I am sure – last year's fashions are racing for the opportunity to adorn your gorgeous frame."

"I don't know about that Ilique."

"That is right Clara; garments are of little importance, but you see, that's because I'm partial."

By now Clara had moved some four feet away. There was no answer upon her expressionless face.

"Did you hear me Clara; I am partial!"

There still was no answer. Only a blank look was exhibited as she turned and slowly walked away. The curvaceous bowlegged Clara A. Feldon did lend something special to her clothes. Not particularly provocative, but appealing. This had been a good morning for Ilique as he smiled, thinking; why doesn't she just admit it, she is in love with me.

But life is never that simple; Clara was engaged to Rory G. Davanpourt. No ring was present, so poor Ilique had no way of knowing the real truth as opposed to some hear say. Clara, an attractive brown, oval-face beauty, had been in the district only six months before she was discovered – so to speak – by Mr. Rory G. Davanpourt, in a big way. But that was all of nearly two years ago. And though their engagement is not widely known in her school circles; they have been seeing each other on a very regular basis. Ilique, no doubt had seen signs, but was consumed in his own wishful thinking.

Ilique continued to smile, ignoring the waiting students. He could sense he and Clara A. Feldon getting closer and closer together. The strictly – professional image, thought Ilique, was evidently how Clara wanted to be portrayed among the teacher-student body. He however expected her to ease this stance soon. Ilique had often told Clara, she looked nice, and the perfume she was wearing smelled good, but never before had he told her of his being "partial." Why, this morning had he muttered those crossover words. He had no right to use personal language in a professional conversation; had been Clara A. Feldon's de-meanor. Ilique now envisioned Clara's face as the "partial" penetrated her comprehension. He remembered how stunned Clara had appeared; as if she had received the bad news of a close love one's departure. Had he said the wrong thing or was the timing bad, he wondered. "That is it," Ilique screamed inside, "the timing was bad; Clara was stunned that I know of

236

her secret advances." There could be no other answer as he continued to analyze the situation.

Though amorous words had never been spoken, there had been many occasions, Ilique thought, where she had been affectionate toward him. To be exact, it had been happening every Tuesday morning, the past two months, at the principal-teachers meeting. This, meeting, had been started by Clara A. Feldon as a means of exchanging sound educational ideas and improving teacher relations. It was Clara's opinion that, "a cohesive unit worked more smoothly and efficient; all in the spirit of, good educational methods, for an original intent. Bond together for the essential declaration of dedicating their human resources to the tiny minds trusted in their care." Clara A. Feldon's primary concern was obviously to her little ones; of which these meetings kept her staff focused. However, it's at the meeting's end, which send conflicting messages to Ilique.

At the end of each meeting the group stood in a circle holding each other's hands while, a departing word of encouragement was administered by whomever felt inspirational. Well, to cut a long story short; Clara A. Feldon always managed to be standing next to Ilique. Clara's antics started by simply squeezing Ilique's hand, which later turned into rubbing several of her fingers over his hand as it was being held. Until now, Ilique never reacted, at least, not noticeably. In the excitement, however, this morning Ilique responded by digging a finger into the center of Clara's tender palm. After a few seconds of circular finger movements, Clara tightened her hand around Ilique's fingers as if an orgasm had just taken place. As each session ended, including this morning, Clara merely walked away without saying a word to him. It is not clear to Ilique whether the secret admiration started the meetings or the meetings started the secret admiring. And Ilique's thinking is; unless one is doing a research paper, it probably does not matter. Who is to say where love always began between two fervid creatures.

Anyway, Ilique never heard any of the inspirational messages. His inspiration came from the lovemaking generated

237

through their hand and finger movements. Clara had more than communicated her message and upon this morning's end, Ilique had more than received it. With this being the case, Ilique thought, why hadn't there been some verbal exchange to move to the next intimate level; what stood in their way? Decretion certainly was not a hindrance. Since moving to Washington, D.C., Clara A. Feldon had her own apartment, and Ilique who was a native of the city, was buying a home in nearby Ft. Washington, Maryland.

Every conceivable question of why had also perplexed Ilique. The conclusion as he figured it; Clara was the initiator and it was up to him to take charge, be the aggressor and move their relations faster and farther. That is why, at Ilique's next available opportunity; being this morning, he had come forward with his "partial" statement. It was meant to be another, breaking of the ice, exchange. But from the looks of Clara A. Feldon's chilled expression, there might have been an artic freeze. Ilique remembers Clara's light-brown eyes fixed in a non-blink setting. Her eyes were even wider than normal as Clara made the turn to walk away. Clara's lips had tightened and her throat protruded forward in the turn. It was as if she was trying to swallow and there was no saliva – only dry – hot parched air. Taking charge of a situation had never before brought such an adverse reaction to Ilique K. Fernfort. For now, what was done was done, and there were no apologetic bones in his body for it. Ilique thought, I will face up to whatever is proliferated as punishment. And without even Ilique's understanding of it – a silly giggle crossed his face – more suited to an embarrassment. Ilique expected any minute to be called into the principal's office. After all, that was the usual procedure when there was a problem at a school. There was a sound on the intercom – but it was only Renatra Metfield, down the hall, wanting to know the date of a math seminar. The sound had temporarily caused Ilique's muscles to twitch a bit. One of his students, Tashanesha Berry, standing nearby noticed his sudden jerk, inquiring:

"Mr. Fernfort, are you all right?"

238

"Oh, no problem Tashanesha, I am okay."

"You know Mr. Fernfort, that intercom makes me jump that way too. I think it is the unexpected hissing sound before the voice comes through."

"I think so Miss Berry."

Tashanesha returned to her seat, but Ilique could not help but think how noticeably his response had been to the intercom. He had not felt – well – that nervous; and of all things, he must not allow his personal aggravations to stand in the way of his instructiveness or his teacher/pupil relations. He must make sure the students be about their work as assigned.

It was approaching noon and lunchtime and there was no sound from Clara A. Feldon. Then it dawned on Ilique – Mail! So he headed for the front office to his mailbox. It was full of mail; large envelopes, small envelopes, small white one, large brown ones; a newspaper, newsletters, and all types of pamplets. Ilique grabbed the stack of mail, flipping quickly through each piece.

"Good morning, Mr. Fernfort, where is Tasha? Is she out ill today?"

"Oh, good morning Mrs. Englehoff! Oh – no, we sort of broke the ritual today; lesson before play, you know."

"Thanks goodness, she is okay; Tasha is the sweetest most mannerable girl at this school. I look forward to seeing and chating with her everyday. Please tell her hello for me."

Was Ilique losing it; he had forgotten that Tashanesha, and probably his pet of the bunch, picked up the mail, just prior to lunch everyday. Mrs. Terri Englehoff, the principal's secretary and the elder statesperson at the school also loved Tasha, as she called her. She also loved to figure things out before they happened or as they unfurled in her mind; according to what she saw or heard. Some people called her Mrs. Quidnunc. But being the sweet lil' old lady of some sixty plus years and a former teacher, maybe the words, informative and enthusiasm, are more appropriate.

239

Ilique continue to flip through the mail as he walked slowly toward his classroom. He was looking for an inter-office envelope from the principal – Clara A. Feldon. Ilique kept flipping – suddenly there it was – the envelope – a large white one with the red string that wraps around the circular red-button like tab. Those strings are always a nuisance, thought Ilique; when they are not cutting your fingers, they are always too long to quickly get at what's inside. Maybe the contents would explain the reason for Clara A. Feldon's cold expression earlier that morning. There was no reason to apologize, so Ilique did not expect that type of a note; but maybe, there was a note telling him the reason for their hand – love affair. Anxious to see inside, Ilique bypassed unraveling the string, which held the envelope shut; tearing it open. The other mail dropped, scattering pieces across the floor in a most disorderly fashion. Ilique looked as though he stood in the middle of a garbage bin; unorganized paper spread non-symmetrically would have litter implications. Ilique however, did not lose his concentration, noticing a smaller envelope inside. A name "ILIQUE' was written across the face of this envelope. This was it, he thought, as he ripped the left end off. Grasping the envelope with his right hand, he reached inside with the other. There, the note was within his fingers; he began to be relieved. "Now," he said to himself, "we are getting somewhere; from this point on, Clara and I will be able to talk and communicate like normal people. There will be no more secrets." Ilique hastily opened the folded piece of paper, but it was only a receipt from where he had bought a church raffle-ticket from Clara.

Talking about disappointed. Maybe there was another envelope. Ilique began to pick up the fallen mail. He stooped, reaching and looking over each piece carefully before moving to the next. Nothing, there was nothing. Ilique sat at his desk thumbing through the stack again, thinking somehow, two envelopes could be stuck together; but again – Nothing.

The bell rang for lunch. Ilique would see Clara A. Feldon there. She would be there, in the cafeteria, as usual with her cheerful self and positive demeanor that generally flowed into the students and other teachers. She would be there, smiling, sacrificing her own inner feelings to encourage others. Even if there were no exchange of words, thought Ilique, there would have to be an exchange of secretive lovable glances. Any movements of Clara's dark-purple eyelids or blink of her delicate light-brown gleaming eyes in his direction, would be enough to harmonize his mind for the day.

Ilique seated himself next to Renatra Metfield at the teachers lunch table; exchanging greetings with the others as he did so. Renatra struck up a conversation about their up and coming, seminar. Ilique was doing more looking toward the door, than listening to Renatra, as Clara A. Feldon had not yet made it. Ilique pretended to really be busy eating, keeping his mouth full at all times, glancing and nodding at Renatra every now and then, to eliminate totally ignoring her. He looked briefly at LaQueeta Structworth, a smiling pertinacious teacher like himself, and no doubt, like Renatra, an admirer. But all in all, his eyes stayed on the door for Clara's entry, but there was no Clara in sight. Then some-thing pierced his ears:

"Oh Ilique, by the way, Clara told me to tell you, she was skipping lunch today."

"What! I mean – what did you say Renatra?"

"Clara told me to tell you and the others, she had to work on a report and was unable to come to lunch. You were late getting here, the others know already; I almost forgot to tell you. Of course, that is not as important as our math seminar – Ilique – you have not heard a word I have said. Are you okay; you have been awfully quiet, and why were you constantly looking out that door?"

"No Renatra, I have heard every word. I am interested in what you're saying; Clara A. Feldon will not be here today. See, I heard you all the time."

"That was near the last thing I said Ilique K. Fernfort; what about the seminar – you never answered my question, whether you were looking forward to it."

"My mouth was full of food Renatra; didn't you see me nod?"

"That is part of the problem too Ilique, you were nodding to everything; even to LaQueeta when she asked you to tutor her "slow George" this evening. I was hoping we could have finished our conversation on the seminar." Renatra's tone had changed because of the encroachment of a shapely able-bodied co-worker. Speaking and rolling her eyes in LaQueeta's direction was amusing to the latter. Renatra never had any problem stressing her point or commanding her position vocally. LaQueeta, on the other hand, was not very talkative and smiled, as her character only allowed that type of combative display. Never a harsh word would LaQueeta speak, even when confronted as now; only a direct word generally, after that smile, to accomplish her goal.

Ilique suddenly directed his attention to LaQueeta who was still smiling, and gingerly toweling her long tan fingers. Lunch was over and apparently a lot had been accomplished by some as she spoke.

"I will expect you at three-thirty Ilique!"

Back in the classroom for the evening, Ilique again started listening for the intercom to speak; waiting for Clara A. Feldon to call him to the office. He also wondered if Renatra knew of their hand-love affair. She must know, he thought, but he had even more questions: Why would Clara tell Renatra to tell "Ilique and the others" she was not coming to lunch? Why was Clara specific on "tell Ilique? These questions haunted Ilique all evening, because the intercom never did sound; it never did call his name. Clara A. Feldon never called him to the office. Later, the bell rang; the day was over. "To heck with it," Ilique murmured to himself, "tomorrow will be a new day."

It was time for slow George's tutoring session. We must clarify "slow George's" name. It has nothing to do with his learning ability, though it once could have; he was already sixteen and still in the seventh grade. The slow part merely applies to George's movements; he moves slow and easy about

242

everything. He is never in a hurry; not late mind you, just last. Last to enter the classroom; last to enter the lunchroom. Last to turn in his homework; last to leave the school because of his need for tutoring. Most of the time the tutoring is done by LaQueeta; his lovely broad-eyebrowed teacher. Her thick black hair molded a shadow over her gray-eyes, turning them of that darkened shade. She was really a very beautiful woman despite her excess weight. LaQueeta had convinced Ilique to share in the tutoring because in her opinion, "slow George needed the male positive role model image. Sometimes George was there after school, while all too often, there was no George. Ilique never questioned the lovely LaQueeta about missed appointments; for there was always a subject or two they usually discussed – intellectual discussions. Devious persuasive illusions, for now, had no way of entering Ilique's thoughts. To do so would mean the interferance of pleasant thoughts of Clara A. Feldon.

Tomorrow came; so did next week. And now next month and Clara said nothing to Ilique. Oh, the meetings went on as usual; the inspirational talks as well as the inspirational hand-lovemaking. Clara acted if though nothing ever happens. There was one small difference noted by Ilique. He noticed that Clara A. Feldon never put herself in a position to converse with him now. She conveyed the usual "good mornings" and all that, but nothing more. On several occasions when Ilique tried to strike up a conversation, Clara either said, "I have work to do" or "I must go." Now – other than that – the principal was normal.

Ilique K. Fernfort, a timid twenty-four year old, did not know quite what to think. And – action – that was even further down on his agenda. If he could just talk to her, he thought. Ilique was not schooled in the ways of the world and was the first to admit it. The significance of that being, there had only been one girl, Analicia Wilhelm. Well, that is, if you don't count Mrs. Lydia McQuire, a favorite college professor, who called Ilique her "little boy friend." Of course, her greatest display of affection was the patting and rubbing of her hand on his head, in the manner one would pat and rub a favorite puppy. Oh, her hands

243

often touched his shoulders and there were the pats on his back. And there was one time where she kissed him on one cheek; but without more deliberation, one gets the picture – my little pet.

Ilique's greatest asset though, was his willingness and eagerness to learn. He caught on extremely fast and really solved problems quickly. Of course, to date, we are only talking about math problems. Ilique was not just smart, he was blessed with a great degree of common sense; which is sometimes a rarity in these whizz-kids. His status for right now is – puzzled, but inquisitive. His project for now has become Clara A. Feldon. Ilique reasoned in his mind that he was going to latch onto Clara (other than by hand) and see what the problem was. For a starting point, he knew a couple of things about Clara; one, she was no mummy and two, she was no marionette – obviously a woman with feelings who could not be manipulated or dangled. Such intrepid reasoning led him to another conclusion; she was like a drowning person – she would not let go of his hand. Ilique's thoughts soared … people cry out for help in different ways. Some are very vocal, while others say nothing and grab onto whatever is available – a raft – a leaf – a hand. Ilique K. Fernfort's analytical thoughts satisfied his ego, but it seems as if the sensation generated through the hand-lovemaking has created some lightheadedness.

Ilique projected himself into the future with Clara A. Feldon, the same as had been with his family – a mother, a father, a girl and a boy. Clara's hesitancy, though troublesome, really created no real, bending out of shape, for him, because in his opinion, no one else gave him any real attention. Well, there was Renatra Metfield and LaQueeta Structworth, but their attention he reasoned, was purely from a professional point of view. Ilique constantly looked forward to the teacher meetings with his self-telepathic vision of Clara A. Feldon.

Though Ilique had a lot going for him, in the sense that he had the three essential "C" ingredients from the ladies point of view – career – car – crib; he was not the most handsome fellow in the world – nor close to it. He was small, about five feet-five, with bugle-eyes. Eyes, that seemed rounder because they popped outward. But he was a sharp dresser; was he ever sharp. We are talking about a different suit for most of the month; none of that sport-jacket stuff. Just expensive well-tailored suits, with a nice exclusive collection of ties and shoes, that blended very well. There was no particular colors that Ilique favored, as they all blended well with his charcoal complexion, especially those deep-rich sort of colors. He had this one double-breasted green combination, which truly suckered Renatra and LaQueeta in. When he wore that pea-green suit with his bright burgundy, blue, gold and pea-green decorative tie, accented with a matching handkerchief in that jacket pocket, showing only enough to tease; it looked like he had just been stamped and shipped out of the Denver mint. And with his olive colored glasses and expensive alligator green shoes on, Ilique looked darn good, head – to – toe.

The students called him Mr. Clean (behind his back) which he had over-heard and adored. This nickname was partially due to his excellent taste in clothes, but also in response to his hair, which was kept cut real close – not shaven – just close. Close enough to show off that toothpick size and length part, which angled across the left-front corner of his head. The students loved and respected Mr. Clean and responded to his challenge. He was a hard instructor as the students put it, but a good hard – kind, patient, and fair. In other words, Mr. Clean made sure you got your lesson and got it right. Plus, he was never too busy to give them additional time – tutoring his own when needed. Yes, the principal, Clara A. Feldon knew what she was doing when she selected Ilique Kraven Fernfort.

And Tashanesha Berry, his pet student, though he was no fairer to her in class and homework, just relayed a message to him from Mrs. Englehoff. "Please stop by the office as soon as possible." The class went to lunch and Ilique went to the office. His entrance found Mrs. Englehoff in a rather subdued state. There were no tears, but her eyes were reddened as if the flowing had only momentarily ceased. She rushed to Ilique to obtain some fortitude and physical support. With handkerchief a waving across her nostrils, as if a sinus condition existed, Mrs Englehoff managed to speak.

"Ilique, it's about Clara; she has gone for the day. My heart goes out to her, the poor child; I wish I could have exchanged places with her. Oh, what will she do now; she'll need all of our help ..."

Mrs. Englehoff was talking fast and uncontrollable. It was apparent she knew her story, but was not conveying it very well to Ilique. And he was just standing there as a prop against her feckless body; listening to the lengthy wailing. Blue veins rose in her neck as an unduly stress level appeared from within. This moderately large woman was assuming more grief than a non-relative should. But love transcends relative-family lines and the pain as well as the joy, goes with it; for when a new family is created, it bonds the more – tighter. Finally, Ilique, tired from the weight of an, oxen, upon his frail body, led Mrs. Englehoff to a chair. Ilique, patient as always realized, eventually there would be a breakthrough of the Englehoff stumbling block. Seated firmly, she gazed upward into Ilique's perplexity and said.

"Clara's uncle just passed; what is she going to do. He was like a father to her. During his several months of illness, Clara has really worried herself; now this."

25

Upon hearing of the passing of Clara A. Feldon's uncle, Ilique felt, was the perfect opportunity to invade her personal world. This could be the break he was trying to create. Afterall, people were often soft or vunerable during these times. Clara would have her guard down. Sympathy has a way of opening doors, closed for decades. And one must learn to utilize personal tragedies to build pleasant future relations; known here as penetrating her innermost verbal communication barrier. To Ilique, Clara, no doubt would approve of such strategy for one of her lost pupils or one of her chosen teachers, who was having difficulty with life. Yes, there would be a period of carrying food to the family's home. And if the above failed, though hesitant, Ilique thought, he would show up at the wake or funeral itself, if necessary.

The uncle's address turned out to be in the northwest section of the city; one of those newly renovated, stone and brick rowhouses. The large single-paned windows had been changed to four-panes for each tall oblong-half. Each half now had a large pane covering the bottom two-thirds and three smaller horizontal panes at the top one-third. Each smaller pane on the upper window was stained. The stone and brick had been sand-blasted to its original beautiful rustic-burnt-orange splendor. The windows and door's trimming had been repainted with an antique beige, burgundy, and green. No description could now explain the beauty of this magnificent three-story structure. (Well, three stories, if you count the steps, which pass to the basement, as a story.) English Ivy, now covered the small ground area, left of the massive steps leading up to the shining front gold-door knob. The oversized burgundy door was also fitted with a one-foot golden handle; making it appear to have been ornament from a castle or the door itself, from a sixteenth century chateau. Italian, white stone vases were mounted centrally on each side of the steps. Little women, either eating grapes or pulling at its vine was carved romantically around each thirty-inch tall vase. The flowers therein had quenched the September evening's, sunrays for the full purple and red blossoms. There was a peacefulness about the place, as one could only hear distant automobile horns, from a nearby traffic thoroughfare.

Ilique, now had an eerie feeling as he climbed the steps, carrying two twelve packs of seven-up, and a small potted violet geranium. Somehow, the thought of being impressive and penetrating the personal wall seemed insignificant. He rang the bell and the door flung open immediately. Several distinguished looking people – three or four or as many as Ilique's bulging-eyes could focus on, had crowded the doorway; after apparently paying their respects. Ilique squeezed to one side and was hardly noticed as they said their customary, "now Henrietta, if we can be of help, don't hesitate to call." Alone, now standing before Ilique was this lean, but shapely elegant woman. A white full-throated bubble-sleeved blouse covered her well-endowed chest. The long red skirt had also truly captured the body that dwelled within; enhancing moreso, a similar glowing complexion with dark-red hair to match. Stunning, simply stunning. Ilique was startled to find a woman with a striking resemblance to that of Clara A. Feldon, but devastatingly far more beautiful, and the fragrance coming from her body was even more invigorating. Ilique stood there in awe. Picture him with those bugle-eyes on the next level outward and his mouth standing half-open, only because it was frozen in place when the magnificent, Henrietta-lightingbolt struck.

"Well, don't just stand there young man; come on in!"

The exquisite sumptuous-figure motioned her arms backward, simultaneously turning her smooth tan hands in an upward begging-position, with the grace of a hypnotist. It was none too soon, breaking the temporary spell cast upon Ilique Kraven Fernfort.

"Good evening ma'am, my name is Ilique K. Fernfort; is Clara A. Feldon here?"

"Slow down young man – I mean Mr. Fernfort. My name is Henrietta Feldon; Clara's mother. My, aren't these flowers beautiful and one of my favorite colors; please set them on the table by the window. Here, let me have that soda."

Off to the kitchen Henrietta strolled, carrying the two twelve packs as if they were luggage for a late flight; taking those minuscule quick steps, yelling back at Ilique, to please have a seat. This he did, into a comfortable wing chair, opposite the sofa, and directly facing the coffee table in between; upon which set three empty cups and one glass. Also present was a crystal bowl of green and white mints. Several small chairs were nearby, in a circular position; all appearing to have been pulled out of place. No doubt, by the entourage that almost knocked Ilique off the steps, only moments earlier. Ilique looked around the high-ceiling living room until his eyes focused on the dark-glittering wood-sculptured molding, zipping around the wall into the ceiling corners. It appeared that each side had a six-inch border; and after a closer look – herds of jungle animals rampaging. As it turned out, only two species of the African wilder-

249

ness were present – zebras and elephants. And the glitter, well, that was inlaid ivory representing the tusk of the elephants and the delicate artistic white stripes of the zebras. By far, thought Ilique, the most powerful display of thunderous herds upon ebony wood. It left nothing to the imagination as to how beauty and strength exist in the motherland.

"Well Ilique, I see you are admiring one of my brother's pride and joys of life!"

Henrietta reentered the room and sank her shapely flowing skirt into the sofa, gazing helplessly into Ilique's revolving face. He appeared to be returning from a far away trip, as their attention drew to one another. Henrietta, continued, to speak on the subject of her loved one.

"He loved to travel, especially to Africa; Nigeria and Uganda were his favorites. The border in this room is from wood shipped back from one of those trips. It took Henri; that was his name, nearly seven years to finish that woodwork. He called it the piece that gave his life "patience". Especially the zebras; they became challenging when he found out, no two had the same stripes. And elephants – represent just plain good luck. Yes, Henri use to tell me, "Henrietta, put a zebra and an elephant in your life – patience for good luck will come to you." I am sure going to miss Henri; we were apart, but we kept in touch all the time. We were twins you know."

Henrietta became sentimental and began to cry. Ilique was young, but knew when to hold a woman. He had seen a few scenes like this on television. Before the rolling tears could touch Henrietta's lovely rosy cheeks, Ilique had bolted to the sofa; sitting with his right hand patting her back. A handkerchief, in his left hand was gently wiping the sadness away from her beautiful light-golden brown eyes. Ilique became excited as he noted that Henrietta was even more gorgeous close up. Then the sorrow was gone and a delicate smile came through; the same as sunshine, after a thunderstorm. She was now as radiant as ever. Henrietta looked at this moment to be no more than twenty-five to Ilique, but knowing she was the proud mother of Clara A. Feldon, short-circuited that falsity.

As Ilique gently stroked Henrietta's back, cheery eyes fell upon him and she commence to tell how Henri had dreamed of leaving the Northwest rowhouse for that "Detached House" somewhere. His dream was to move from the crowded congested conditions of the city, to that home standing, all alone. Henrietta began to cry again, murmuring "his dream never came true." But Henrietta was wrong, thought Ilique, his dream had come true; Henri was for all pratical purposes, assuming his soul was right with the Lord, now living in that large "Detached Home" in the sky. Ilique looked Henrietta directly in her wet reddish-eyes and said.

"Henrietta, I think his dream came true; I really do believe Henri's dream came true."

With those words of reassurance, the most beautiful smile slowly emerged from Henrietta's solferino lips. Her cheeks rounded, throwing forward a more radiant glow, if this is possible. Ilique thought, she is one more digestible looking lady. Henrietta was indeed that; a sensuous forty-four year old, whose red hair had none of the wisdom strands showing. Also, there were no time lines in that honey-tan face; and as Henrietta now held Ilique's left hand within her soft palms, there were no sign of wrinkles on the back of her hands. A young daughter for sure, and a mother with unconquerable youth, thought Ilique. Their eyes met again; this time there were no tears; there was no waterfall crackling between them. Henrietta's soft lips quivered as Ilique's lips felt swollen and extremely dry. A beam, sealed their sights together, their bodies tense; when abruptly, Henrietta said.

"What are you dreaming of Ilique – I mean what is your life's greatest dream?"

There was no question, presently, what Ilique's dream was, but the break in silence had suddenly woke him up.

"Oh, I don't know – the way you put it – life's greatest dream; that calls for some thought, because of the extraordinary connotation."

In reality, Ilique needed no time to think; his love and only dream had been to capture the heart of Clara A. Feldon, well until seconds ago. Henrietta still held Ilique's hand, but had turned to look across the room. Ilique stared at the side profile, thinking, what a pretty ear. It was no doubt the prettiest ear, he had ever seen. The diamond-studded lobe glittered upon each circular line, pulling them seemingly in its direction; flowing smoothly and being disturbed only by the variation of twinkles. It was apparent, thought Ilique, that Clara A. Feldon had not told her mother about their hand-loving sessions. "Should I tell her," echoed a brain wave, "that my life's greatest dream is to penetrate your daughter's world." A likely story indeed, but a foolish move while holding her mother's hand, in confusion, echoed back. Ilique was now feeling the identical vibes – like mother – like daughter. Of course, the sensitivity he felt with Clara's foreplay, he also felt with the slightest touch of Henrietta's hands. As Ilique got back to speaking, Henrietta focused her eyes downward upon the African statute upon the coffee table. She was listening attentively.

"Your brother, Henrietta, might have had his dreams, but this house, to me, is a dream come true. It is so warm and personal; much like, that of a love affair. I suppose, if I had a dream, it could be as such."

"You will have one, one day Ilique; just wait and see. Thanks for the comfort today."

Henrietta smiles; pat Ilique's hand, pulling slightly away from the attachment and turning her thoughts to Clara. "Ilique, did you find out about Henri from Clara?"

"No Henrietta, I didn't; I sort of found out about this through the school's office."

"Clara should have been back by now! She and that Rory Davanpourt went to her place to pick up a few things; she is supposed to spend the night with me. Running around with a man old enough to be her grandfather. Have you met that man Ilique?"

"No, I have not Henrietta; only in hearing I dare say. It appears, not to meet with your approval though." That bit of information about Rory Davanpourt was news to Ilique, but his expression never changed.

"You are so right; he is using her for his - excuse me Ilique – sexual fantasy! It burns me up every time I think about that cradle-robber! I wonder if he has any daughters!"

Henrietta's mournful moments were now being energized upon the sad state of Clara A. Feldon's choice of men. Men, since the beginning have always had a restless desire for a fresher bouquet. But, here too, young women are more than enamored by the delicate precision of being plucked from the stem. They become a symbol of having their greatest fantasy realized. Many times, unusual plenteous gratuities surface, making the elderly gentlemen a piece de resistance. Clara A. Feldon was certainly no different, having obtained such distinguished position at her tender age. There had been no seniority waiting line scrutinies or applicant weed out committee because there had been a Mr. Rory Davanpourt to bring her forward, thought Ilique.

"What do you think of my daughter Ilique?"

Without hesitation Ilique spoke. "Well, I feel Clara A. Feldon is the best principal this school district has ever had, and should rise to even greater heights in the educational arena before she decides, she is through."

"Very well put Ilique, but that is not quite the answer to my question. Professionally, I am real proud of Clara, but you're a young man and all, and the question was directed at you from a social viewpoint. Excuse my bluntness this time Ilique, but have you ever considered asking her out or taking her over to your place for a little recreation? I hope, Ilique, that I do not have to be more specific."

Ilique's bugle-eyes beaded on Henrietta, cautious as not to blurt out words of exuberance upon being included in mother's

253

plan. He had known all along, the implication of the original question. But because of the conflicting signals being received from Clara, there was not an easy way of answering, without exposing Clara's hand manipulation and possibly jeopardizing a secret which he saw leading to an immediate intimate setting. Whatever Henrietta said to Clara of her own free will was one thing, but Ilique felt his strategy would be quicker and smoother. Because if there is one thing Ilique knew; it was the conflict sometimes exhibited between mother and daughter – like what is best for you – daughter. Daughters are susceptible to rebellions when told who to – and not to – date. Mother's choices, rarely becomes daughter's prince charming. Henrietta wanted to deliver Clara's chastity belt to Ilique and was not interested in any of his non-essential garrulity. Ilique finally answered, but what left his lips was of no use to Henrietta; looking intently at his watch.

"It is getting late Henrietta, I really must be going; tell Clara I came by."

Henrietta nodded her head in approval, and takes Ilique's arm to lead him to the door. Upon his exit, Henrietta leans forward, kissing Ilique on the cheek. Again, that captivating fragrance flows through his nostrils.

"Thanks so much for coming by Ilique; I hope to see you again!" Gently squeezing his hand, slowly letting it loose.

"Sure thing Henrietta, here is my number, give me a call for anything."

Ilique's drive to Ft. Washington, Maryland was full of Feldon's thoughts – Clara A. Feldon – Henrietta Feldon; moreso Henrietta. On the immediate, what had she meant by, "I hope to see you again." Ilique was trying to grasp the tone in its usage, but felt he understood the grasp of her hand. It sounded stupid to be going through all of this; "I could be her son," he uttered out loud. As Ilique reaches home, something tells him to call Henrietta. Well, it is proper etiquette to call one on your arrival home from their house, especially when it is late – and it was eleven o'clock – well, almost eleven.

"Hello Henrietta, I just called to say I made it home safely, and to see if you are okay."

"Oh Ilique, you are so thoughtful; I will never forget your kindness. Thanks again for everything. I was just unrobing for bed; it has been a long and challenging day."

"It has been that Henrietta; goodnight."

"Goodnight Ilique."

Ilique was really in a frenzy now. Henrietta's voice over the phone was anything but business like. It was soothing and friendly, damn near inviting. Even with "goodnight Ilique" that trailed into a whisper. This day was indeed challenging. Ilique could not wait to continue his thought process under the covers. He yanked the spread off the bed, tossing it toward a distant chair. A neat folding of the spread is traditional. Ilique hurriedly jumped into bed, and lay on his back with his eyes closed. Through his mind went a number of things; nothing stood out more than the next; other than a number of Henrietta things. Why had the day been so challenging to Henrietta; maybe he should have asked her, as he smiled. Could it have had anything to do with me, Ilique thought.

Ilique's insides were warming to a sensational feeling and got even warmer, when he thought of her unrobing. Why had she mentioned - unrobing? What color was the robe? Or was she merely referring to removing the last stitch of clothing from her gorgeous body. What color was her bra? What color was the panty? All of a sudden, Ilique's mind had lapsed into colors. What Color? What Color? He loved Colors especially the bright ones. Excitement was sprinting through Ilique's limbs as he moved all around the kingsized bed. "I hope to see you again." Sprang into his mind. Those words by Henrietta now applied to him, and he wanted, so much to see her again. He could still feel her soft hand firmly pressing his. Ilique lay awake in a confused state of mind – the mother – the daughter; they were so much alike, yet so different.

Though his heart was still set on Clara, it troubled Ilique to be getting mixed vibes from her; and now mixed vibes between the mother and the daughter. It was not fun to be getting the feelings of when he got his first bike. Those were true-heart touchings for something he had really wanted; the red one with the light upon the handlebar. Ilique wanted the bike so bad, he could taste the white-walled tires. "I want nothing more than that bike," he remembers telling his mom. He persisted and she finally gave in. Ilique could only wonder, if being an adult was the same as growing up as a child. He meant, talking females into something you really wanted; if that was the case, a difficult task might lie ahead. At least mom talked and listened, but Clara A. Feldon does neither, except for school business.

Ilique was really one of those guys who saw a lovely lady and for no genuine reason, fell in love, generally holding his thoughts on that one, before moving on. His thoughts moved back to Henrietta; she for the moment was his red bike; he could taste her. She, in her edible glow, gave him an overwhelming hungriness for her digestible looking body. And he said to himself, "If I could just get enough courage to ask her." No thoughts came as to why he wanted to do such a thing, but the taste was there ... a swelling occurred in his tongue and he wanted it upon her. His mind sought refuge within her arms and his thoughts explored her unrobed body, but his dreams took over for the night, and Ilique found himself smiling upon Analicia; the first girl in his life, and his first love affair. The dream simply tells him how he remembers. Young and old males alike have a tendency to do this; go back in time for research; something to help them seize a new and exciting piece of flesh.

26

Ilique, was suddenly, awakened by the phone ringing. "Good morning Ilique, you are sure sleeping sound; I was about to hang up."

"Hello Henrietta, I was in a deep sleep, what time is it?"

"It is a little after six; I am sorry if I woke you up, but I was trying to catch you before you left for work. I did not sleep well last night; Clara called, but never came over, and sleeping in strange houses alone is a bit uncomfortable. To get straight to the point, would you come by after work? I will have some food prepared for you; Ilique, I did not have anyone else to call." Henrietta's voice, to Ilique was so soft, so sweet; he gave her his only possible answer.

"Oh sure Henrietta, it will be about six, this is my tutoring day."

Ilique thought, after dreaming about Analicia, this was quite a way of waking up. He could imagine Henrietta being afraid in unfamiliar surroundings. That was the extent of his thoughts on anyone, as it was past time for his toiletries.

On the way to school though, Ilique put it all together on Clara. Henri, her uncle was like a father and naturally, with him being sick, she was upset. That is when all the hand jive was taking place. To think, he almost made a fool out of himself, thinking Clara A. Feldon loved him. She had a man in Rory G. Davanpourt. This is really a cheerful day for Ilique, because all of his conflicts are cleared up; and he can now concentrate on Henrietta, his new found love of yesterday. Ilique was even nice to Renatra and LaQueeta in the lunchroom. He could now hear what they were jabbering about.

"Hello Ilique, how is Clara doing – I mean – is she holding up okay? Here, I brought you some of your favorite cake."

"Oh I suppose she is doing okay Renatra; ump, this smells good – you girls are always giving me stuff – thanks."

"Yeah, and one day, you'll love to appreciate it!"

"Did you, not go by there, yesterday?"

"I appreciate it now, and yes I did Renatra, but I talked to Henrietta – I mean – Mrs. Feldon; Clara's mother." He is really cramming her cake into his mouth.

"Do you mean Clara was not there?"

"That is what I am saying LaQueeta; maybe she came after I left."

"And what time was that Ilique?"

"Yeah Ilique, I am curious, what time was that?" Echo's Renatra.

"Well er… it was early, about ten or so; what are you two so curious about anyway?"

Neither one of them, say anything and pretend to be eating for a change. Obviously, something is going on, thought Ilique, but he is part of their chattering or hotline group; so he decided to teach them a lesson.

"Maybe Clara was with Mr. Davanpourt."

Renatra and LaQueeta's ears perked up now like two stubborn jackass.

258

"You say, she was with old man Davanpourt, Ilique!"

"No LaQueeta, I said, maybe!"

"For the life of me girl, I do not see what she see in that old man. I mean, he looks good and all that, but I would think he is a bit over the hill."

"I would not know about that Renatra; Clara A. Feldon and I are not on that type of communicative level."

"Oh; what type of level are you on Ilique?" He gives Renatra an odd look. "Forget that question Ilique; it is not that important to me, to know what is going on in Clara A. Feldon's bedroom. I have too much to worry about for myself."

"Girl, you got that right!" Both women are now looking at Ilique; realization of their own, orgasm frequency, finally comes to mind.

"Ilique, you will be present for the tutoring session this evening, won't you?"

"Sure thing LaQueeta, I will be there! Thanks again for the carrot cake Renatra."

Renatra could only look; she was without words. LaQueeta had eased one in on her; she had Ilique for the evening. The freckles in her face changed colors as she excused herself from the table.

During the evening's tutoring session, slow George did not show up. Ilique thought nothing of it, because it happens all the time. Slow George's quest to imbibe book learning was still not a primary priority. LaQueeta was talking to Ilique as usual; the normal school chit-chat, but his mind was focused on his after school visit to see Henrietta. LaQueeta was tall, carrying a noticeable shapely broad behind, with a real cute pudgy styled face and tawny complexion. Ilique was really unaware of her presence, and rightfully so, for she had left the room. But upon her return, Ilique though busy with some papers, smelled a familiar scent.

"What is that perfume you are wearing LaQueeta?"

"It is a new fragrance I purchased last Saturday, called Titilation. Do you like it?"

"I sure do." Like it, he loved it; it was the same fragrance he smelled on Henrietta last night. "It's about six, I must be going LaQueeta!"

LaQueeta was all smiles; for once she had gotten Ilique to notice her, other than as an unexciting, school teacher.

Ilique thought about calling Henrietta prior to going over. He figured there might be something she wanted – like something to drink – beer, wine, or another alcoholic beverage. Ilique was quite new at this and was fearful of not knowing how to inquire. After much deliberation, striding down the corridor toward the office, he decided upon giving Henrietta a call.

"Hello Henrietta, is there – is there anything I need to bring – like er… some wine – or something?"

"No Ilique, I do not drank any of that stuff, but if you do, bring whatever you like. Dinner is almost ready, will you be long?"

"I am leaving the school right now!"

"Oh Ilique, there is something I need you to bring; I need a box of tampons – small will be fine."

"Okay!" Ilique's answer was short and assuring; pretty much as if this was a daily purchase. Then it dawned on him what had been said – a box of tampons. There was no need to be nervous, but Ilique wondered how he was going to look carrying a box of tampons to the check out counter. While in the supermarket, he figured to get a lot of other items, and the tampons would not be noticed as much. So he grabs the shopping cart and commence pushing it through the store. Aisle by aisle, Ilique find items he needs; milk, cereal, bacon, sausage, bisquit, grape jelly, eggs, and orange juice. There, his breakfast for the next couple of weeks is all set. Ilique now wheels around for the tampon's section; discovering the item, he put it in the baby section of the cart, covering the tampons with the box of cereal.

On toward the checkout counter, Ilique stroll, with a masterful achieving smile across his face. His bulging eyes are shining with a confident brillance. That is until he thought he saw someone he knew. His original mind had told him there was little fear in the sight of someone knowing him. However, about four registers over there stood Analicia. She was as lovely as ever and probably more so, than Ilique would have remembered her from their college days. Busily watching her, item amounts, one after the other, flash onto the register screen. Analicia would never have seen Ilique, even if she had looked across and beyond the grocery checkers in front of her. That is because, fortunate for Ilique, he was standing to her right, directly facing her back. Of course, the urgency did exist for his checker to hurry or they just might meet exiting the supermarket. The checker rang item after item, finally giving him a total.

"That will be thirty seven dollars and twenty cent sir!"

Iliique, who had been fumbling in all his pockets, realizes he has no money – well – that is not quite right; he does have a ten dollar bill, which he displays to the checker.

"No problem sir, it happens all the time; is there anything you really need?"

Ilique is reluctant to say, as he is also aware of the female shoppers behind him. Smiling at the checker, he utters:

"The box ... how much is the box?"

"The cereal sir?"

"No ma"am – the other one!" Nervously speaking, wanting to hurry.

"Oh, the sanitary napkins sir; you have just enough to cover them."

Ilique wanted to say, "I am so sorry," to the checker, but the embarrassment was hitting him so hard. His armpit was soaking wet and large pellets of perspiration, had formed across his forehead and was beginning to run along his temple. The checker handed Ilique the change with a beautiful smile, but he could only recognize it as one making fun of him.

"Will that be paper or plastic sir?"

Ilique had hurriedly picked up the box, responding likewise.

"This is fine ma'am"

The checker gave him another beautiful smile as he scurried to leave the supermarket, holding the tampon box along side his leg. It was at this time as Analicia slowly returned her check-book to her purse, waiting for the bagboy to complete bagging the groceries, she caught a glimpse of a recognizable figure hurriedly approaching the store's exit. Analicia would have, but it was too late for hollering to Ilique. "If the bagger hurry," she said to herself, "I can still catch him in the parking lot."

It was not until Ilique reached his auto that he noticed no sack around the box of tampons. He sat under the steering wheel for a moment – not moving – trying to compose himself. Then Ilique thought out loud. "I need a bag." It would be smart to simply return to the store, make a new purchase and get a bag, but with no money, that was impossible, thought Ilique. Or he could just go back and ask the smiling check out lady for a bag; that was a terrible thought, thought Ilique – Analicia will see me with these doggone tampons. The daily paper – a man was getting a newspaper from the vending stand – that is it, thought Ilique, I can carry the tampons in Henrietta's house, stuck inside the newspaper; I must hurry – too late – gotta go.

The bright red ford, carrying the familiar looking man, was disappearing through the parking exit onto the street, as Analicia stepped outside. Again, she wanted to holler, with the word – Ilique, fixed upon her lips, but again it was too late. "I'll be darn" still left her lips for missing an ex-boyfriend. A bitter – sweet taste was swallowed as, "Well, I'll Be Darn" left her lips with a powerfully bit more sting.

Ilique did manage to get the tampons in the house, concealed within the daily newspaper, he got several blocks away. Henrietta never noticed her tampons were not in a bag, however she did notice one thing.

"Ilique, you got me the wrong size – these are large tampons!"

"I remember now Henrietta, you did say small; my mind was going in so many directions in that supermarket – I completely forgot."

"Did you have a hard time locating them in the store Ilique?"

"Yes, I believe you could say I had a hard time Henrietta! I can return them later if you like."

"No, it is too late for that, I need one now, so I will have to make do. One large one is not going to kill me. It will be a bit uncomfortable, but it will serve the purpose. I am almost done anyway. Ilique, you did not, by some chance, think I was large, did you?" Giving out a hearty laugh for the first time.

"Oh no Henrietta, it never dawned on me, you were large – I mean – I never thought about your size."

Henrietta is really laughing now. Meanwhile, Ilique is just standing there, looking sort of funny. Henrietta, still smiling, finally manage, another remark:

"Please excuse me Ilique, but you seem a bit nervous about the whole thing; I really did need that laugh though. I hope you won't think hard of me."

"I will be okay Henrietta; I mean it is okay. To be honest, that was my first time doing that, and it sort of threw me for a loop." Ilique explained to Henrietta, how he tried to conceal the tampon box in the shopping cart; to no money, to trying to get out of there before Analicia saw him; to forgetting the bag. Now, they are both laughing real loud. Nonetheless, it was a good way to start an evening; for now they are both relaxed as relaxed can be.

"Ilique, can we keep this as our private joke?"

"I would not have it any other way Henrietta; you got one on me! Whatever you are cooking sure smells good."

"Oh, it is ready Ilique. Let me tell you about it, to see if your mouth water. You are going to think you are dining in a first class restaurant. I went overboard a little, but you made me feel so comfortable yesterday. And after the laugh today, I will say you deserve the best ... First the salad ..."

"What ... no appetizer Henrietta!" Ilique smiles.

"I thought of that Ilique, but there is a possibility, we might be appetizing enough."

For the first time this evening, Henrietta displayed a sensuous smile with equally suggestive eyes. And for the first time, Ilique noticed the low cut seductive purple dress, showing a goodly amount of cleavage; with the remaining few inches, covering a mere tenth of her gorgeous tan thighs. This partial garment was far more glamourous than the red one last night, thought, Ilique. Ilique thought again – this is a Real Woman.

"I tried to find some candles Ilique, but I guess Henri was not very romantic or into delicious evening meals. So we will have to settle for the overhead beams."

"No problem Henrietta; I sincerely believe your beauty should never be concealed, but I'll pick some up tomorrow."

"Thank you Ilique and that is quite a compliment. I hope there are more where that one came from. It has been a while since I heard such a genuine compliment. I do not mean to get too sentimental, but I needed something to give me a big uplifting. Meeting someone as nice as you, to share the evening's meal with, is really perfect timing."

"Well, you know what they say Henrietta, timing is everything."

"As long as you do not feel inconvenienced, Ilique. Now, I believe, I was about to tell you about this evening's meal before you so politely interrupted me. First, the salad ..."

All during the meal Ilique could feel a warmness from the tender hearted, sumptuous looking beauty before him. The meal, he thought, was delicious, but for some unknown reason, Henrietta looked delicious enough to devour. Her beautiful smooth skin glowed like a hot shiny biscuit just leaving the oven, and her lips seemed as inviting as his favorite cream cone on a hot summer day. The nipple imprint of her obvious braless breast made Ilique's mouth pucker, and saliva poured into his mouth each trip, she bounced and rolled her twirling rump to the kitchen for an item. Her lovely thighs blended into her buttocks like a flavorful turkey-drumstick. To Ilique, this woman just seemed like something digestible; and that is when he came to his conclusion, and said as much to Henrietta.

"You are one delicious looking lady!"

"Thanks Iliique, that is a very powerful compliment. I'm willing to fix dinner again tomorrow; would you like that?" No, change that to Thursday; there are some things Clara and I must do tomorrow. Henrietta could see the gleam in Ilique's eyes, knowing he only had one answer. Also knowing after the funeral on Saturday, she should be returning home shortly thereafter, and time was definitely of the essence. "Afterall," she said to herself, "it has been a while since a man of any type has crawled between my thighs, and what this darling hinted at is what I truly love."

"Sure, you bet Henrietta – be glad to! You're a doll!"

"Thanks again Ilique – you are full of compliments tonight – certainly the mark of a real caring gentleman. Is there anything special, you would like for dinner thursday?"

"No, not especially – you're so beautiful – your presence is all that's necessary; you're really my gourmet dish."

"I love your dining attitude and appetizing spirit Ilique; I truly look forward to being a ravishing part of that. You speak bold and decisive and I love that – a man I would bend over backwards to please. If Thursday goes well, maybe you could spend Thursday and Friday all night; would you like that." Henrietta was really hoping for great things on Thursday; she was speaking as soft and sensuous as she had at any point.

"Oh – yes ma'am – I would love that!"

"Your eagerness and freshness is about to overwhelm me Ilique; if not for certain formalities and etiquette, I would ask you to stay tonight." She knew mother nature was the real barrier and in her horniness said as much to herself; then thought, making a horny man wait opens his senses wider – his nose, his mind, his mouth ....

"That's all right, I believe I understand Henrietta."

"Good; well, it is getting late Ilique, and I want to look good while you're dining Thursday."

"Thanks so much for that wonderful meal; it was great and your cake was superb doll."

When he departs, Henrietta gives him a kiss – a real woman sexy kiss; a kiss where her tongue smoothly ease in and out of his mouth in a sensuous teasing fashion. Never before had Ilique experienced anything like this, which made him all the more, wanting to devour this woman; it had really sunk in. So, on his way home and all through the night, he thought of what he needed to tell her. That is why he now, sit at his desk, at school, composing this long letter to give her over their next dinner.

Hello Doll:

Thanks again for the meal and the delicious cake; it was very good. As you cut me a piece, the sweet aroma alone, was enough to prepare my taste buds for something, extra worthy. (Worth waiting on for sure.) If you noticed, I held it with both hands – gently – as to not lose an ounce. It was so moist and creamy. I could taste the richness and sweetness of each ingredient as it passed over my tongue. Juices from the carrots flowed into my mouth causing a like spontaneous reaction from my saliva glands as juices flowed outward.

Of course the most gratifying part is your unselfishness to serve fine dessert. You probably did not notice, but I was constantly licking my lips and swallowing as fast as one could. The piece was larger than I expected, and several times, as you noticed, it was all on my nose. That tells you something as to how good it was, and I did see you smiling as I dug into it.

You are almost as good at cooking as I am at eating (Smile). I look forward to eating your sweets again real soon. To sum up the enjoyment of eating your cake; I licked my fingers clean. Now that is what you truly call delicious dessert, and good eating. Here's hoping that licking and eating every crumb, left you with complete satisfaction and a yearning to serve me fine delicacies over and over again.

Doll, now that we are on the subject of eating; and I did not want to be too bold, starting a letter, but from the first day I set eyes on you, I wanted to taste you. And, as well as you look, you

266

deserve to be pampered as such. I have never felt this way about anyone, and do not feel bad telling you how I feel toward you. Hinting at wanting to love you orally and beyond, by using your cake as an example, was really too much of a brainteaser for me. In reality, I thought; I should be able to tell you what is really on my mind. The closest I came to it the other day, was when I told you – you were my gourmet dish – and that is what your vagina would mean to me. If I may dramatize a bit: That means the setting of your finest table and making sure the gourmet dish is eaten properly. First, the dish must be close enough to the nostrils to allow the sweet aroma to penetrate – activating my taste buds, tongue, and salivary glands, while eating gently and slowly. At the slightest touch by my tongue, your gourmet dish will be bubbling with hot juices and commence to run over the sides. But because you are so sweet, I will put away all the goodies your gourmet dish can produce. I feel it will be moistier and creamier than the cake.

With your assistance Doll, you will direct my tongue to the right spot at the right time. Tasting and eating your gourmet dish is going to be a delight. If you are half as good as you look, I will probably never be the same, in terms of conventional sex. Your appearance is so great upon me that my mouth waters everytime you are in my sight. To see one and want to devour them is like thinking and eating an apple or other delicious food; you look that appetizing. You look as appetizing as you are beautiful and that makes you special. You are not only special, but a sweet lady, Extraordinaire – sweeter within, I am sure to find. To dine at your table will be an initiatory festive event. Certainly, a piece de resistance, in my opinion.

Like the cake, I will hold your gourmet dish with both hands and feast to your gratification. There must be a hundred ways, but consuming it one way is good enough for me; I just want to eat what appears to be sweet delicious stuff and good sustenance. So, I hope you will agree and consent to me tasting, nibbling, eating and whatever else my mouth and tongue can do to your sweet gourmet dish. The way I envision savoring it, it is definitely going to be enjoyable to us both. I am going to love you until your sweet juices stop flowing or until you tell me, you have had enough. Doll, I am going to eat your gourmet dish real good; and too, like the cake, you will probably have my nose inside of it. (Smile)

Doll, please let me know if you are disappointed that I want to sank my tongue into your gourmet dish. I am in no hurry to eat your wonderful dish, but wanted you to know. I promise, if that is possible, with my inexperience, this will be your most pleasurable sexual experience. I will dine upon your gourmet dish until you are perfectly happy. You deserve nothing less. When I finish, you will have no doubt that I love you.

Love Always,
Ilique

By the time Ilique finished this letter, his mind was racing in so many different directions; one of which, was how much Henrietta reminded him of being an exciting sophisticated lady and how Opera would be impressive. And it occurred to him from browsing the weekender, Leontyne Price was in town for tomorrow's Opera. He quickly ran to the office, making two calls; one for reservations and the other for Henrietta's approval.

"Ilique, that is so wonderful; just what I need to get me through this period, but what about dinner?"

"If it's okay Henrietta, we could eat out earlier."

"You are capturing my heart Ilique and that means a lot."

And he whispers into the phone, "Thanks doll – gotta go – see you Thursday evening – bye-bye."

Sometimes later that morning, Ilique realized he had misplaced his letter, but with lunchtime fast approaching, he heads to the cafeteria. Earlier, however, Renatra thought so much, seductively of the letter while sitting at her desk, she was sensuously busy, moving her amber-colored thighs inward and outward. So much so, that she could actually feel Ilique's tongue lapping her sweet wetness as it oozed into, luckily, the hideaway of her cotton panties. Such an instantaneous and intense release, Renatra thought, that she neither tried to prevent or felt remorseful of its occurrence. "Afterall," she said to herself, "what's underwear for if not to assist one in the comforts of a day." She smiled as her rapidly motioned thighs squeezed the last liquid spontaneity onto Ilique's hungry-quivering-beckoning awaiting open lips; then, she too headed for lunch via the ladies room.

27

"Hi Ilique."

Renatra was all smiles as she takes a seat next to Ilique in the cafeteria. A conspicuous smile, but Ilique never noticed anything unusual. He knew Renatra was interested, but because they always talked, the friendliness of a good co-worker relationship was as far as their bond was likely anytime soon. And it had nothing to do with Renatra personally; she was definitely attractive, freckles and all. Before now, it was Clara A. Feldon who had his eye, and today, Ilique's heart, mind, and body was consumed into Henrietta; leaving no time to pursue another adventure. Renatra's elbow nudges Ilique in the side to gain his unwavering attention, before speaking these words:

"I got your romantic – er ... erotic letter this morning Ilique. That is by far the most exciting letter I have ever received. As far as responding, will you give me time to re-read it and clear my mind. There are features within its contents, which literally took me by surprise. Do not get me wrong Ilique, it has nothing to do with my expectations of your sexual capability, but with my limitations in life, so far. Each line was a provocative wonder that stirred me to a point of release. We are fortunate to have desk instead of tables."

Renatra's panties were still wet and her emotions were rising again, as she rubbed mustard on the hot dog; slowly slid it into her mouth, all the time, looking at Ilique with revealing eyes — which put them together — alone.

Ilique had listened to Renatra, and it did not take a genuis to figure out what had happened. He had accidently put Henrietta's letter in Renatra's folder. And while she was celebrating and chanting anticipations to his ear, he had decided the best thing to do, was to tell Renatra the truth; the letter was not intended for her. So, without any warning, out comes:

"Renatra, in all fairness to your beauty, the letter was a mistake — I mean it was not suppose to be sent to you — could I please have it back?"

Renatra looked at Ilique in disbelief. "A mistake — are you playing with me! How could you make such a stupid mistake?"

No more bites would be taken from the tasteless hot dog, as Renatra dropped it to her plate and abruptly left the table. Renatra had looked forward to this new experience, even though she pretended to think it over. Now, her day was completely shot; her panties were wet, her eyes were wet, and her feelings were shattered. Several things presently occupied her mind: How she had made a fool out of herself. How could she fall for such a dumb letter anyway and how could Ilique be so insentive, to not at least, lie to her. Renatra thought, Ilique could have told me, he sometimes thought of me that way, or ... or anything other than — a mistake. If she had known he was no more than a tyro in such matters, she would have deemed any remark by Ilique, pertaining to such loving to be a very stupid mistake.

Renatra, however, was done for the day and reported to the office as being ill; telling Mrs. Englehoff that her stomach became upset while eating the hot dog.

"Renatra, you young people will eat anything; that is not wholesome food and should be banned from the menu. Weiners are made out of the worse of everything. I tell you - ."

"Yes, Mrs. Englehoff, please excuse me, I must go – I feel terrible!"

Renatra arrived home and immediately crawled into bed. She needed rest; she needed to relax, and she needed time to think. Renatra's first thought was to get even with Ilique for such a trick; her only thought was to get even with Ilique for such a trick. She had not heard him apologize or say he was sorry. The only words still ringing in her ears were; it was a mistake. Renatra would demand an apology from Ilique.

Renatra calmed herself down as her unappareled body sank into a relaxing mode. With her eyes closed, a tingling feeling of enchantment prompted her hands to move across her breast and down her stomach. In an instant, Renatra sprang to her feet, removing the letter from her purse. She had to read the letter over. Crawling back into bed, she lay sprawled on her back, reading each line closely and slowly. Renatra's body began to swell. How could this be happening to me, Renatra thought; the letter is not even meant for me. But her mind was consumed in the letter and she continued to read. She no longer felt angry at Ilique. How could she, when her fingers had lost grip of the letter and found their way onto her opened thighs. She imagined Ilique's warm breath on her legs as she moved her right hand into her soft curly pubic hair, thrusting the other rapidly onto her right breast; then onto the other as she could not decide which was the most sensitive.

Renatra knew what she was doing and was not ashame. How could she, when she felt Ilique's lips meet the lips of her gourmet dish. Her right hand moved onto this identical spot and began to slowly caress it. The constant massaging of her breast had created some moisture as she noticed each nipple hardening within her manipulative fingers. Renatra continued to gently caress the outside of her moist vagina until she felt Ilique's tongue slide inside. She could see him eating her gourmet dish as her fingers lunged deep inside. The more Ilique ate, the more Rentra twisted her fingers. She moved her derriere in a circular motion, pressing firmly against her constant roving fingers. Renatra no longer felt ill as her left hand fell onto her clitoris. Ilique was still eating; she felt his warm tongue as she began lovingly squeezing her clit. Renatra knew it would not be long, as all her fingers caressed like a massaging machine. This was Renatra's first attempt at self-pleasure using her fingers. At her desk earlier, she had merely worked her legs inward and outward until it happened; and now she wanted more as she felt Ilique's tongue all over her tender folds and clitoris. She could feel him eating her gourmet dish more and more as her fingers championed the cause. And then it happened, Ilique's tongue had licked a vunerable spot once too often, and Renatra's fingers and hands were full of fluid. She had done it and it had felt good; Ilique had eaten her gourmet dish, and she had enjoyed it. Renatra thought, if only the letter had been for her, as she fell asleep, with a smile across her face.

The next morning though, as the sun cheerfully danced into the bedroom, Renatra awakened with a frown, and an attitude. She felt used and again had thoughts of getting even with Ilique. Renatra, thought, as she dressed for school; there is no way, I am going to go around playing with myself, when I could have the real thing. What would my friends think, if they knew I played with myself last night. Renatra continued; why wouldn't Ilique want to eat my sweet stuff, I look as good as the next person. She had a warm interest in Ilique before now, but suddenly his stock had risen to be a hot commodity. Renatra even wrote Ilique a note, inserting it in his mailbox as she arrived at school.

Tashanesha picked Ilique's mail up as usual, laying it on his desk, as he gathered his work material for the day. There was no hurry to peruse the morning's mail; so Ilique casually moved about his other daily rituals, until some forty-five minutes later. The letter was clearly identifiable as being from Renatra, so there were no surprises as to its sender. Ilique never thought of its contents because it was not unusual to receive mail from

Renatra. The note inside simply read: Ilique, I accept your offer and will be available tonight or at least by Saturday for discussing it. Please call me, I will be home. Ilique smiled to himself saying, "This chick is crazy as hell – she actually does not think I am going to ... I told her the letter was a mistake; why can't she settle for that."

Ilique saw Renatra at lunch; she smiled at him from a distant, appearing to deliberately avoid coming nearby. Renatra's yesterday had been bitter-sweet, and she was not about to have a similar today; especially the bitter part. Renatra had thought it over; somehow, she would get even with Ilique, and make him apologize to her, while he was eating her gourmet dish. She would make him eat until she got tired; and would turn him away into the streets without a climax. Their session would not be about love or lovemaking; it would be about getting even and teaching Ilique a lesson. Those were Renatra's surface feelings and she, no doubt felt she would be able to get a good dose of revenge. She was not dating anyone, and in her opinion, had nothing to lose.

Ilique later dressed and headed for Henrietta's, giving little thought to Renatra, other than to maybe call her the next day. Ilique had reconstructed the original letter and handed it to Henrietta as he entered the house. She was already dressed for the opera.

"A letter – for me – Ilique; I hope it is a love letter – I love, love letters. I am starving now; will it be okay if I open it a little later, when I'm more relaxed?" She winked at Ilique as if she already knows of its contents. Henrietta took the letter, kissed it, and patted it across the front of her long blue-flowing dress, as they headed for the restaurant.

"Sure Henrietta, there is no hurry."

There was never any rushing into anything with Henrietta. She felt in order for a relationship to be right, it had to run smooth and easy; much like an automobile, and never exceeding the speed limit. So as they entered the restaurant and was seated, she calmly said to Ilique:

"Ilique, why don't I open your letter for dessert."

"That will work." Ilique smiled.

All during the meal, he had wondered what Henrietta's reaction would be when she read the letter. He was hoping it would cause the same kind of readiness response as in Renatra. Then it was time, the meal was at its end. Ilique looked on curiously as Henrietta slowly opened the letter and began to read. At first, there was a serious look upon her face; then a slight gleeful expression appeared on her tightly closed lips. As Henrietta read, her cheeks grew fuller and fuller, as the grin upon her lips widened. Ilique could tell she was being amused as she began to make expressions with her lips – puckering to twisting them round and round. Then Henrietta began to make noises vocally; in succession they went something like this: Hmmm, well – well, I say, whoa, umm – huh, I see; all the time never taking her eyes off the letter. Henrietta also never laughed out loud and continued to only smile; finishing the letter pretty much the same as she started it – with a serious look upon her face.

"Okay – can we discuss this after the opera Ilique?" Again, her voice was calm; much lower though, almost a whisper.

During the first part of the opera, there were no tell-tell signs from Henrietta as to what was on her mind, about the letter, that is. She was immensely involved with that operatic voice of Leontyne Price; her performance was magnificent. Ilique had thought a time or two what the discussion would be about, but even he got caught up in Leontyne's excellent performance. Nearing the end though, Henrietta commence to rub the inside of Ilique's thigh, slowly and gradually upward until her hand rested atop his swollen rod. Then she sort of held on as his throbbing took place under her warm hand. Her mouth began to water; she thought and said to herself, "I look forward to getting this generous piece of flesh inside of me. Ilique was beginning to feel good about her thoughts on the letter, but he said nothing. Matter of fact, only small talk was made between them until he had her seated in the living room of Henri's house. Then she again spoke softly.

275

"So you want to caress me within your cheeks, huh. What do you know about that sort of thing Ilique?"

"Well, nothing really; no more than what the fellows say. But maybe you could teach me about it. I would like to know enough to write a book of savoir-faire as it pertains to cunnilingus; for all the naïve guys and my ignorant friends."

Henrietta could see the young man was serious, and she was not about to laugh as she did about the tampons. She guessed correctly that Ilique threw the book in about cunnilingus, to save face, if his remarks were offensive to her. She however, immediately appreciated his honest aggressive style, and the least she could do was to teach him what she absolutely loved, or knew about such an important subject; one that she would be proud to help him master. Her body parts suddenly began to swell and vibrate with great anticipation. Henrietta, sensually thought, let me see how serious he really is.

"Ilique, you called it a gourmet dish; wouldn't it be appropriate if I actually served you from the dining room table?"

"Well Henrietta, I had not ventured that far in my thinking; just what did you have in mind?"

"It is really simple Ilique; I will place my gourmet dish, as you call it, at the proper place setting and you will merely pull up a chair to my dish and dine in a normal fashion."

Ilique looked at Henrietta with his head to one side and his mouth open, as if he, either did not believe Henrietta, or still did not understand just where she was coming from.

"Okay Ilique, I can see you are confused. Apparently, you did not think, when you mentioned me as your gourmet dish. And you even mentioned setting the table. So what I am saying is; I am going to place my dish on the dining room table and you will simply dine on it from that same seat you ate from the other night. Come, let me show you."

Henrietta took Ilique's left hand and led him into the dining room. As soon as she was there, and without saying a word, she removed a chair at the end of the table and sat upon the table. No sooner on the table, Henrietta layed backward, pulling the blue dress over her breathtaking, golden naked thighs; propping her feet on the table's edge. Ilique was just standing there. Her gourmet dish was far more delicious looking than he had imagined and written about in his letter. Those bulging eyes of his looked as if they would leave their sockets any minute. Fatigueness clamored in his legs; he was motionless until Henrietta spoke.

"Well Ilique, don't just stand there; pull up a chair! Afterall, this was your idea. It was you who wanted to plant such wonderful kisses upon me. So have a seat and pull the chair up to the table."

Ilique, unconsciously followed Henrietta's clear instructions. Though he had written in his letter, what was to be done to a gourmet dish, it was now different. Henrietta's dish was so close; close enough in fact, that Ilique could feel a rising heat upon his nose. He could also see a long precious slit, but closed his eyes before discovering any depth. Ilique was terrified at such gorgeous beauty before him; he found at this moment that her lovely red hair was none of that dyed stuff. A pleasant aroma rose with the heat, and Ilique's tongue moved about, inside his mouth. A vision surfaced in his brain to place the gourmet dish into both hands. Henrietta, though, had her own vision as she draped her legs across Ilique's shoulders, pulling him abruptly forward. She eagerly assumed he knew the basic eating techniques and she could teach him the rest later. Ilique's eyes opened, but he could see nothing; it was dark – real dark, however, he could feel a plush wiry mesh in his face. Ilique could also hear Henrietta's soft voice telling him to kiss her, but he was too numb.

It was not as easy as Ilique had imagined. There was even a wetness on his chin. The distinct sweet aroma of Henrietta's gourmet dish now consumed his nostrils, opening each, wider with every breath. Ilique's salivary glands activated and he could taste Henrietta's dish; his tongue swished around inside his jaws, but his mouth would not open. Ilique was fearful. He wanted so much to take Henrietta's dish in both hands and commence to eat, but his actions were frozen. Henrietta's sweet aroma told Ilique that it was tasty and good; and the wetness told him, it was ready to be devoured, but Ilique could no longer move. He was fearful of what to do. Henrietta sensed his tension and whispered to Ilique:

"Take your time Ilique – kiss me – kiss me gently; open your mouth and let your tongue touch me."

Henrietta pulled Ilique's lips upon her gourmet dish and spoke softly:

"Open your mouth darling – take your time – slide your tongue into my juicy dish. Come on darling, open up – do it –

please do it. Do not be afraid darling – take your time – eat it – come on darling. Eat it now Ilique – please Ilique – I cannot take much more; please eat it now. Don't let me down honey, please don't let me down; eat the dish now."

Henrietta's gourmet dish was piping hot. And rightly so; afterall, it had been nine years since a man had eaten it. Needless to say, she was overdue for such a treat.

Ilique heard every word, but he was still frozen in time. It was too late now anyway. Henrietta was overcome with passion, and with a forceful desperation, pulled Ilique's broad nose inside her steaming vagina. She moved his head to her satisfaction. Ilique could hear Henrietta murmuring something, but could not make out what, because her hands came tightly across his ears. It was a vise grip he had never experienced before. Henrietta was making lots of sounds; sounds which got louder and louder as she continued to rotate Ilique's hard effective nose inside her gourmet dish. Ilique could feel some long protruding object along top of his nose, but he could not move. He could also feel a hot wetness across his lips as Henrietta screamed – releasing her hands from his head.

Ilique pulled back and focused his eyes upon Henrietta's gourmet dish. He was curious as what to expect, as he rubbed his shirtsleeve across his nose and mouth. He could see that Henrietta's gourmet dish was large; much larger than his mouth, and her clitoris hung long. Ilique wanted to wrap his lips around the delicate red organ. He watched in amazement as the long object slowly disappeared. Henrietta's dish was also moving; it was moving as to tell Ilique to do something, like – eat me now – at least consume my sweet hot juices, as it oozed out onto the tablecloth.

Ilique had not eaten Henrietta's gourmet dish, because he was afraid, nay he was scared to death. Ilique thought, I have failed Henrietta; what will she think of me now. He noticed the table-cloth was saturated and the oozing was still slowly coming down. He wondered what would happen if he touched her with his tongue. The secretion looked so good and he wondered how it tasted. Ilique moved in closer to Henrietta's gourmet dish and opened his mouth; his tongue slid slowly through his lips as the oozing continued. Ilique wanted so much to stop the oozing and taste this delicious looking stuff. He also wanted to eat Henrietta's gourmet dish, but he was still too frightened.

"Henrietta, I am so sorry, I feel so stupid; to let you down after all that talk. This will be a day most memorable in my life and no doubt the first chapter in my book."

"Why is that Ilique?"

"Look at me Henrietta, I am a nervous wreck. I know I am not shaking or anything like that, yet that is part of the problem, I am not moving; my faculties are inoperative. So the first thing I should tell the fellows is to keep their composure on their initial oral genital contact."

Henrietta is aware of a man's pride and is willing to go along with Ilique, especially since she is going to greatly benefit from her teaching. "There are also two extremely important sentences to add, Ilique. One is to learn about the female body, especially the sensitive areas and the sensitive spots. Sensitive areas are innumerable; the lips, ears, neck, breast, stomach, arms, legs, toes, thighs, and many others; each generally depending upon the individual. The sensitive spot, of all sensitive spots, however is different and is the spot to make the woman come on home. That spot for me is my clitoris; the object you probably felt, rubbing against your nose. Mine, as you noticed is extremely long – probably close to three inches – which is rare; rare indeed. Most are much shorter and smaller; you will even have to search for some of them. It is imperative that a cunnilinguist learn about the clitoris and all the other parts of the vulva."

"What do you mean – other parts – Henrietta? I heard a lot about the clitoris and as far as what the fellows say; that is the spot."

"Well – yes and no Ilique; that is where most men make their mistake. They head straight for the clitoris and expect the woman to respond; she responds, but in almost every case, it's a turnoff. And while the word is of Greek origin and means "key" you should be careful. Bear in mind that you will rarely if ever totally satisfy a woman in such a direct manner, and you will be far ahead of the competition if you do not try. For your benefit and mine, of course; take me, I can be satisfied with your lips on my nipples and your fingers manipulating my clitoris. I said satisfied, but not totally satisfied or gratified. To totally satisfy a woman, you need to combine the sensitive areas with the clitoris and all the other parts of the vulva. In essence, we are talking about gratification."

"I believe a moment ago, you were going to tell me about this vulva Henrietta; what is that?"

"The vulva is the external sex organs consisting not only of the clitoris, but the labia majora, the labia minora, the mons pubis, and the vestibule, Ilique."

"How in the heck is a guy suppose to remember all of that Henrietta?"

"It is not difficult at all Ilique; it is probably what you and the fellows are erroneously calling the vagina or the gourmet dish. Remember these parts, to be around the vagina itself, and must be stimulated also. So before you dive onto the clitoris or into the vagina, think enough of the entire area and give it a kiss – a bunch of kisses. Now that you know where to kiss Ilique, it is very important to know how to kiss. And please, never get carried away with one area – unless instructed to do so; which brings me to your other important sentence or paragraph."

"This is pretty interesting stuff Henrietta; you mean a fellow needs to know more?"

"Sure Ilique; it is equally important for a fellow to follow instructions from his lady. But before you can follow instructions, you guys are going to have to learn to listen. The easiest way to gratify a woman Ilique, during an oral intercourse is to listen. Guys don't listen, because of a number of reasons; most of which pertain to – thinking you are in charge of something. And in reality, is just messing up. Let us take a live example; when I told you to use your tongue – you were suppose to use it.

On the other hand, when a woman tells you to stop doing a particular thing, you should stop and move on."

"Move on to what?"

"In practically all cases Ilique, a woman will instruct you on what to do, once you go down on her; especially if she has doubts about your experience, but you must be paying attention. And please don't be offended even if you think you are the best eater in town, because each woman is different, and what pleases one does not please the other. Remember, if they like you eating their dish, and some don't, but those that do will let you know if you're doing it right. Generally, she will move your head with her hands to the proper location, at the time, she wants it. Then she will instruct you what to do – like use your lips, open your mouth, or use your tongue. So Ilique, it is extremely important to be listening. Most important; never crawl between a woman's thighs thinking you know everything. That is a very serious mistake."

"Well, it looks like I am going to have to include more than, having a lot of nerves and keeping your cool in my first chapter Henrietta."

"I believe so Ilique; much more."

"Will you help me compile the rest of the chapters Henrietta?"

"Sure, on one condition; you must write me a love letter every time you want to have an affair with me. I was truly charged up by this letter today; or turned on, whatever the case." Henrietta was more than glad to go along with Ilique's chapters; in the process she was definitely going to add a few of her own. She still felt his nose and longed for his tongue, which she knew for certain, to be hours if not minutes away. Afterall there were lots of sweet juices currently at his disposal throughout her saturated vulva, if his nerves suddenly improved.

"I am glad something good came out of it Henrietta, because otherwise, I failed you totally."

282

"Not totally Ilique, I did get some benefit out of it; and you did learn something. Matter of fact, this is a good time for you to learn about a good clean-up."

"Clean-up, Henrietta?" He nervously looked inside her vaginal opening, noticing the flow of sweet juices. His tongue excitedly crossed his lips, involuntarily.

"Yes Ilique; you will notice that I am still oozing out. Personally, I am never fully gratified until a good cleanup is done. For now though, just focus your eyes on it and we'll get you involved later – tomorrow night if you feel up to it."

"Yeah – maybe then, I'll respond better." Ilique thought, if she nudged me I believe I could clean that delicious looking vagina right now.

"You did fine Ilique; these things take time – a great deal of practice."

He thought of Analicia and how this first encounter with oral sex was far worse than their first attempt at making love.

Ilique had had the Wednesday of his life; by the time he got home he was so horny. He could still see the sumptuous wetness oozing out of Henrietta's vaginal opening; how good it looked. That and other manifestations of uneasiness finally got the best of him and he now lay in the bed, like Renatra, taking himself into his own hands. He found some vaseline in his cabinet and pretended his tightly gripped hand, sliding up and down his rod and over his swollen knob was indeed Henrietta's vagina. Suddenly he had a small bit of sympathy for Renatra and promised to at least be more understanding.

Thursday morning, bright and early, Renatra was far ahead of Ilique, having deposited a letter on his desk. It was the first thing he saw when he arrived shortly thereafter. He quickly went back out the door looking both ways down the hall, as if he would catch a glimpse of Renatra. Men sometimes do thing that only make sense to themselves; now, if she wasn't there when he walked in, how could she possibly be in the hallway when he immediately ran out again. Renatra had used her own monogramed stationery, and that alone was impressive to Ilique. Inside it read:

Hi Ilique:

I know this is far short of expectations, but we are both in the same category. Though your letter did create some stress and suffering, you can make it worth while; a tongue inspection, either now or in the near future would be very welcomed and reliful. In the cafeteria today and from here on, everytime I walk by, my fine oscillating derriere will make you wonder whether the inside walls of my fruitbowl (not gourmet dish) is moving as freely. Your Henrietta might have a gourmet dish but my fruitbowl is sure to make you forget about it. As I was saying, when I walk by today, you'll see. With each step, your tongue will move within your mouth as it will surely move within my fruitbowl. Eating my juicy fruitbowl will be such a pleasure when I make you slide your delicate tongue inside of it. Your tongue will move as I dictate – licking rapidly and smoothly as I flood your mouth with good warm juices.

I do not want to hear anything else about your mistake. Why don't you just chill and leave that up to me. Now if you are afraid I am going to make you eat my fruitbowl good, that is a legitimate concern.(Smile). Yes, with you sliding your tongue in and around my slit, it is going to produce lots of Good-Ness. I will make you eat until I am good and wet and continue until I am good and dry. I will make you eat my fruitbowl in ways that you have never eaten one before. I admit, having that much power over another person's tongue is not good, but you will suffer real good under my dominance, as I make your tongue lick the sweetest juices ever.

One fact for sure Ilique; you will eat my fruitbowl real good – drinking the flavorful thick juices I produce. Every bite you take at lunch today will taste of me. Another fact; when you finish, your tongue will be no good – that is until the next time –

I make you eat my tasty fruitbowl. And a fact that is good – you will love eating my juicy fruitbowl – doing so until both our gratification; on a regular basis, and that is good.

So the only thing not good, is me not letting you eat my fruitbowl on a regularly scheduled basis or daily if you are up to the task. I wanted to be brief in my first letter to you Ilique, but it seems like my pen would not stop writing. Remember when we are having lunch today, every bite you take will be out of my fruitbowl. And when you return to your classroom, every belch or food particle between your teeth will remind you of me. And finally Ilique, as you lie down tonight, slide your tongue across your lips, and think of your tongue doing the same thing to my slit. Then think of the excitement when I tell you to lick it real good. And as the juices began to flow, think of how I will pull your head into my fruitbowl, telling you to eat vigorously. You will eat until I scream and flood your mouth with sweet juices. You will do as I say, only because, my fruitbowl is real good and is real good eating. You will regret not having eaten it sooner.

Lovingly yours,
Renatra

P.S. Attached here is a bouquet of my pubic hair.

Ilique folded the fruit scented letter; carefully putting it in his inside jacket's pocket. Prior to doing so though, he lowered his nose closer to the pink bouqueted soft pubic hair, to verify the origin of the sweet fruit smelling fragrance. Ilique thought, she is not only bold, but arrogant as hell – make me eat her fruitbowl or out of her fruitbowl – whatever – isn't that the darnest thing you ever heard of. Subconsciously though, Renatra had already affected Ilique; his swollen tongue leveled a wetness across his dry lips and swallowed a mouth full of saliva.

29

Lunch was more than three hours away, but Ilique became curious as to what Renatra was wearing today. Would she have on that tight yellow dress, she looked so good in.

"Mr. Fernfort, do you have any mail to go out?"

"Oh, no thank you Tashanesha."

That was a thought pondered Ilique, telling himself, "maybe I should write Renatra, telling her to lighten up, and to pursue something more definite. She would be quite upset if she knew I knew absolutely nothing about eating a woman's vagina." At lunch, Ilique noticed Renatra prior to the arrival of her good friend LaQueeta and headed in her direction.

"Hello Renatra, I got your letter this morning; fruitbowl huh."

"Hi Ilique, I expected to hear from you last night!"

"Oh, I am sorry Renatra; also I want to apologize for the way I acted the other day. You deserve the treatment so well exemplified in your make up; that of a truly lovely fine lady, in every respect. This is not to fill your head with pretty petty nothings, but to express an observation and to say, just keep on being you. I hold you in my greatest esteem."

"That is real nice of you Ilique, because I get too good a vibes around you, for you to be as tense as you were the other day. I hope this means, we are going to be friends and work things out."

"Renatra, I am no good, especially at what you are thinking. Contrary to the letter, I know very little of oral eroticism. So, I guess, what is being said is; I am no good and will be unable to accommodate you in that endearment."

"No Ilique, I guessed what was being said, the moment you opened your mouth this morning, with all that sugar and spice garbage. You can be nice when you want to, but no way are you going to sweet talk me out of what I want, and what you are going to give me. So I suggest you save some of that lip service for my fruitbowl. If I have to teach you myself, I will; If I have to turn you in as an incompetent instructor, I will, the choice is yours."

"Are you kidding me Renatra; writing a letter has nothing to do with being incompetent!"

"It might Ilique, when you are doing it on the school's time; not to mention its contents."

"Renatra, I do not like the idea of being threatened. Goodbye!"

Ilique had tried unsuccessfully; a method of apologetic and complimentary sugar-coatness to soften Renatra's original overtures. However, she was not succumbing to his shrewdness. Ilique's letter had caused a transformation in Renatra's mind and body, and there was, "no way" Ilique was going to escape. When he returned to his desk, he remembered that Henrietta wanted another letter from him tonight, and he felt there was no better time to do it than right now.

Hello Doll:

I should say I really enjoyed myself last night, and to a certain extent I did. Especially the learning part, and the fact of learning even more from you in the days to come. Tonight is the night, hopefully, I can crawl between your gorgeous thighs and allow you to teach me to be the man you want me to be, or that I aspire to be. I see now that it is more to orally caressing a woman than what meets the eye; even a good looking juicy woman like you, but tonight my mouth, lips, and tongue is hankering to do well, with your help of course. Just sitting here at my desk, thinking about your ultimate swollen clitoris, is really all the encouragement I need.

I promise to kiss your puffy tender lips gently. I will kiss them ever so slightly – touching the nakedness softly, until it throbs and warm up, sending sweet juices through a beautiful tiny slit. I smell an aroma and must rub my nose in the liquid. The tiny slit opens wider upon impact and my nostrils become saturated. My mouth flies open and I began to gently lick every ounce of sweetness there is. My tongue has cleared the surface and my appetite is just beginning as I plunge it deeper into the slit, which is now gapped wide open and flowing freely. This is good eating and you are loving every moment of it. You are screwing my tongue and pulling my head in deeper and deeper.

There is a never-ending flow of hot juices streaming down my throat. I am getting full, but cannot stop as I tighten both hands around your buttocks and pull forward. You throw your legs open wider and it appears my whole face is in your gourmet dish, as juices flood all before my eyes. You are flowing faster and I am licking and swallowing equally fast. This is good drinking from your fountain of love. I am so happy I chose you, and you allowed me to eat and drink your pleasantries tonight. I will be forever grateful. It appears you're never going to stop flowing and that makes me feel even better.

I can tell you are getting happy, because you keep telling me to eat. You are holding on to my head and directing the swishing of my tongue, which is hitting all sides with success, as your screams indicate. I honestly don't see how you are taking it, but you are still flowing – even heavier – I believe. I am lovingly and tenderly sucking your clitoris and eating your gourmet dish real good and still steady gulping down every ounce. I hold on even tighter to your buttocks as you wrap your legs around my head, pulling me even tighter within your vagina. Talking about going down, I am way down inside of you, and we are both, loving every minute of it. How long will it last – I hope forever. Henrietta, I am so fortunate you let me eat your succulent gourmet dish tonight.

Your Hungry Love,
Ilique

Soon, the day was over and Ilique found himself with Henrietta. She had prepared a delicious meal for him; it had now been consumed. She is reading his interesting letter; she read with intrigue; wonderment came unto her. Henrietta looked up from time to time as she read; then finished, she laid the letter on the table, patting it under her fingers.

"I love this letter Ilique, this seems to be a well thought-out request; you make it sound as if you already know what to do. Moisture is forming just thinking about that active tongue of yours."

"Well, you know what they say about talk Henrietta, "cheap and uneventful." Tell me, how will I know when I'm doing it right?"

Henrietta looked at Ilique and said, "you'll know. Your mouth will be flooded with hot juices and I'll scream, just like you mentioned here. Are you sure you haven't made love to me before?" She smiles and winks her eye at the bashful looking Ilique. "However, don't you stop – continue to eat my dish until

289

you have drained me dry and licked it completely clean. In other words, as long as I flow I want you to eat – just don't get carried away and sank your teeth into me."

"Ummm – ump, it can get that good huh?"

"To be honest with you Ilique, mine probably will."

"I can't wait Henrietta; how else will I know if I'm doing it right?"

"Oh, besides screaming; I'll let you know your eating is good by simply telling you so, and also by pulling you in closer and deeper. Sometimes I'll smother you because I will lock my hands and thighs around your head, but somehow, and I do not know how, you keep right on eating. Never stop eating my dish unless I tell you so. If you love my vagina and I know you will, you'll quickly get the hang of it." Again winking at Ilique.

"That's what I'm hoping too Henrietta."

"I really expect you to do quite well, and after tonight, want to eat my dish every chance you get! There is not a lot of things I brag on Ilique, but I know my stuff is good."

Ilique looked at Henrietta, saying, "when do we get started!"

"Not so fast Ilique, you are just horny now and ready to screw. I am not here to teach you about screwing – just eating. As long as you are with me, screwing is secondary. With me you will become a professional cunnilinguist."

"Think so; professional huh!"

"Put another way; an expert connoisseur of eating my vagina. Let me see your tongue Ilique."

Ilique stuck out his tongue. "Is that as far as it will reach, and it is so small!"

Ilique nodded his head saying yes, almost apologetically.

"Don't look so gloomy Ilique; just kidding. It is narrow, but it appears to be very long. You'll be fine if you have good tongue mobilization and lip modulation."

"What is that?"

"Well, tongue mobilization is having control of your tongue. You must learn to move your tongue like that of a lizard. This is extremely important when you tackle the clitoris; not mine though, because it is at least three inches long. You will merely grasp my clitoris with your lips and suck it gently. However, most women have short ones, so the tongue mobilization is extremely important. Just encircle the clitoris inside your lips and let the tongue action take control – manipulating it on that clit with movements, you probably didn't even know you had. This also works wonders around the outside of the vagina, or especially in my case, licking underneath my clitoris. There is so much to do in that area with a versatile mouth, tongue, and lips – you'll see."

"Sounds good to me; I believe I'm going to love it!"

"Either you have it or you don't Ilique – most men don't – and as result, never master the art of cunnilingus. I do not want you to fall in the trap with most brothers who think inserting their long tongue inside a vagina is good; excuse me, good pussy eating; shit that is nothing but a turn off, causing many sisters to fake an orgasm."

"Well Henrietta, what about this lip modulation?"

"Sure Ilique, that is very important. As you have probably guessed already, women have different size vaginas. When the vagina is large and sloppy, juicy to you, you simply put your whole mouth inside, including your nose, and let your tongue swim around while you vigorously ease the hot juices downward; also try and find that hot spot inside. For me I have one located inside at the top of my vagina. If the vagina is small, you place your lips outside, inserting only your tongue to roam about, still swallowing and enjoying the good sweet liquid. And for practically all women, they love for their tender folds to be massaged; they will show you what they like best; whether it's with your mouth, lips or tongue, or all three. It is simple when you get the hang of it and your woman clues you in on what she loves. Now Ilique, that I have said all of that, one method alone is not good pussy eating."

"It's not!" Ilique looked rather puzzled.

"No, it is not; you must master, tongue mobilization and lip modulation in synchronization."

"Now I am really confused Henrietta!"

"Oh, it is nothing Ilique, but combining the two, with its myriad of combinations, and doing them at the same time. You will have to virtually cover the whole area at the same time, caressing the clitoris and the vagina, inside and out, and those wonderful lips and the entire genital area. Even as the hot juices flow, you will not desert one for the other, unless instructed to do so. If you are doing it right, she will leave you alone, but always listen for her directions. Keep one thing in mine; you are eating primarily for the woman's gratification. The juices will flood out, but you will learn to swallow fast without strangling yourself while gliding from the vaginal opening, across the lips, to the clitoris and back. If you are smart though, you will bring a small towel to the table with you to absorb some of the overflow; it's sometimes neater and shows professional consumptive cunnilinguist etiquette."

"I hope I can remember all of this Henrietta."

"Don't worry about it Ilique; if you love it, you will do it right. And whatever you do, don't get in a hurry; eating a gourmet dish is supposed to be smooth and enjoyable. And another important fact to remember is to never blow into a vagina; that could create problems for your mate. If you need air, come up for a second and dive back in. There are some short cuts to good cunnilingus Ilique, but I will school you on those later."

"Boy, this sounds like a real job!"

"It is Ilique, it really is, but when you master the art of being a cunnaphile, one who loves vulvas, your mate will always be gratified, because the tongue, unlike the penis, always remain firm and ready to go. And personally, this is all I want or need."

Ilique looked Henrietta straight in the eyes and said without batting an eyelid. "Henrietta, I am ready to eat your gourmet dish – let the training began – Now!"

The young man's bashfulness had quickly faded and he was ready to indulge in the unknown. However, it appeared as if he had the right teacher in Henrietta. Henrietta was also ready, because it had been several years since she had a man to roam his tongue around on her vagina; nine years to be exact. The last relationship of about three months had been with Keith; introduced by her girlfriend, Barbara Seawel. Before that, it was a year with Raymond who introduced himself in the supermarket. In all, there had been eight sexual affairs since the demise of her husband over twenty years ago. None had been bad relations, just non-complimentary for one reason or the other, and of course, only one had attacked her sweet vagina with his tongue. He too had since passed on, so she knew what she wanted.

"I believe you are on to something Ilique, wanting to explore my vagina with your mouth. That is because women's vaginal openings are so much larger than any penis; the match in most cases is never a perfect fit, and we do not get orgasms as much with such penetration. That is why oral foreplay is extremely important; and with me, like I said, that is practically the only thing I love; foreplay and all the way, is my way. When I teach you how I want it done, you'll even love it. And if you learn how to caress me right, just the thought or the fact of your mouth nearing my pubic area will give me an orgasm."

30

Even now, Henrietta was not looking for a man. Staying busy and self-gratification when absolutely necessary was more than sustainable. Absenteeism or celibacy was never Henrietta's intentions; it was simply, moving on – doing what one wanted to do – enjoying life without the "got to have a man hassle." Though the scarcity to non-existent supply of black men in and out of Correa, Maine might have had a little to do with it. The real truth was, there were just no desirous tongues available. She was stunned when Ilique mentioned loving her in this fashion, but excitingly happy. She swore to herself to teach him right, because she wanted it done right. Henrietta thought, as she could feel a sensual burning inside her wet vagina; "he wants teaching, I'll give him teaching, I'll give him good teaching."

Finally, she raised her dress showing a pantyless bottom. Her vagina was already soaking wet and running from all the anticipation, but Henrietta knew it was not time – not just yet. Ilique looked at her wet vagina with his tongue hanging out. He knew the timing was right and slid to his knees in front of the gapped open luscious vagina. He could smell the sweet aroma; it penetrated his nostrils, causing his salivary glands to flow. Ilique knew nothing about being an expert cunnilinguist, but he felt he could eat the dripping wet vagina before him – real good, based upon what Henrietta had told him and his personal instincts. As he grabbed her buttocks and began to go down on her, Henrietta placed her finger within her juices and rubbed the moisture across his lips; stopping Ilique in his leaning position. She then rubbed two fingers through her wet vagina and made Ilique lick one, then the other; he did so with ease. Then Henrietta placed two of his fingers inside her vagina and had him repeat the same licking ceremony. She then whispered to Ilique.

"What do you think – is it good?"

Ilique's bashfulness returned as he stuttered. "Er – well – I think so!"

Henrietta laughed out loud. "You think so!"

"Well Henrietta – I mean – there was not enough of it there on my fingers to really tell. But I think it was good – should I know by rubbing my fingers in it, whether it was good or not – I am sort of at a loss for the right words."

"Oh Ilique, you are doing fine; so what would you do next to determine if it is good?"

"I would probably stick my tongue in your – in your self and sample some more."

"Come on Ilique, don't be shy. You are too damn proper; for once get nasty for me – say, stick my tongue in your pussy – tell me with confidence – I am going to eat your pussy real good!"

Ilique, hesitating, never quite saying anything.

"Come on Ilique, say it!"

"Henrietta, I am going to eat your – eat your – eat your - ."

"That was real sad Ilique, but you will get better; never be afraid to tell your mate what goodness is coming her way. After all, you are the one writing the book. I want you to get so good

295

that you can talk a woman's mind into an orgasm, including myself. Okay, proceed with sticking your tongue in."

In a rapid fashion, Ilique put his tongue into Henrietta's gourmet dish and out again, making a smacking sound.

"Well Ilique, can you tell?"

"No Henrietta, I am afraid I cannot tell whether it is good or not."

"Ilique, you are doing fine; what you tasted was merely a little lubricant to help glide your tongue along. The good stuff will be made as you commence to use your tongue. The other things that make it good, is how your mate is enjoying what you do. It's a psychological thing really; the better you slice that tongue of yours, the more she creams and screams, the better she loves it, the better you will love it. But, more on that later; let us take a bath for now, so you can create your own juices. Remember to always have your woman bathe before eating her vagina."

"Why is that Henrietta ... what if you're in a hurry and just can't wait?"

She smiled. "Because I said so Ilique ... women sweat in this area as they move around, thereby creating – let's call it salt; and you just don't want no salt in your honey – it is as simple as that."

After the bath, Henrietta proceeded to show Ilique the vital areas and further explain their functions. They both sat nude in the center of her huge bed while doing so; he listened attentively. She did this to assure him of a good gourmet dish eating session, and herself of a very excellent orgasm. She told him to caress her breast real good, even showing him how, and to kiss her all over before even attempting to head for her creamy vagina. This, of course, she was hesitant in saying, but Ilique was being taught how to do it right. Henrietta was so hot, after only a few moments on her breast, she quickly pushed his head downward between her gorgeous thighs. Then suddenly, she began to talk to him.

Jewel E. Dearman

"Eat the gourmet dish baby –eat the dish – let your tongue do its thing baby –oooh – there you go – ooooh - ."

Ilique was doing as Henrietta was instructing him to do. She was lying there, watching him, as any good instructor should. Ilique had not known what to expect. His tongue quickly inflated as the warm sweetness touched. Surprised by Henrietta's excellent flavor, he pulled her gourmet dish in closer as to be more comfortable. Henrietta applauded this move and continued to talk to Ilique.

"Take your time Ilique – there, that is good – you are doing just fine."

Ilique loved getting these compliments, but after getting a second chance, he knew he had to take charge or at least do something to impress Henrietta. Then he remembered something about those funny named sensitive areas around the vagina, and decided to go for it. Again, not knowing what to expect launched a tongue attack. Henrietta, still watching, merely said:

"Take your time Ilique – move slower – move slower – that is much better – that is good – you are doing real good – keep on moving!"

Ilique's tongue was getting real tired with all this slow moving. He wanted to get on with it. Man, he thought, this is hard work. Even his lips and jaws had began to hurt and his throat was dry, because her initial sweet liquid was gone. Ilique was getting worried about this listening part, as Henrietta continued softly:

"This is good Ilique – this is real good – take it in your hands – take it in your hands – Ilique, take it in your hands!"

Suddenly, Ilique had heard a new command as Henrietta raised her buttocks a little for his hands to slide under them. Though tired, Ilique continued his slow tongue movements, but did feel more in control with his hands holding Henrietta's labia majora and her labia minora onto his swollen lips. There, he thought, those words are coming back. Henrietta's lips and his lips was a perfect match as he remembered to continue giving them a bunch of kisses. Then Ilique, again felt the object atop his nose. This was his opportunity to take charge, Ilique thought, and make Henrietta real proud of him. So he eased the object into his mouth and began swishing his tongue upon and around it, while gently sucking it as it grew longer and larger. This was a unique object, which activated Ilique's salivary glands, providing a necessary lubricant for its firm softness. He could hear Henrietta breathing loud, as she vigorously moved her derriere round and round. Her delicious clitoris continued to grow, even becoming firmer, while retaining its softness.

The louder Henrietta breathed, the more Ilique sucked this object. Then the moaning and screaming started. Henrietta's buttocks were gyrating in Ilique's hands, but he held on; continuing to massage the object with his tongue. Henrietta had thrown her arms outward and was holding onto the covering on the bed. Then the motion stopped; even the moaning and screaming had ceased, and the bedroom was quiet, except for a few sensual sighs.

Ilique remembered what Henrietta had told him about the cleanup, and proceeded to do so. This is when he really noticed her red hair. Oh, there was a strand or two of gray but it was real. Even before, when he was so nervous, he had thought, why had this gorgeous sister dyed her hair, and red of all colors. She was indeed a natural. The oozing had started, so it was vestibule time and the harvesting of his work. Ilique's tongue, mouth and throat were busy, as Henrietta merely lay there and quivered.

Ilique had eaten his first gourmet dish and found it to be more tiring than he ever could have envisioned. Matter of fact and in his words; "This is darn hard."

"Henrietta, you are going to make a good instructor. Those lessons about the vulva and its many sensitive areas, is going to take some time though."

"You were damn good just now Ilique, and the cleanup was magnificent. I am going to sleep so good tonight. You really did take it serious and appeared to be enjoying yourself."

"Oh yes; that was the best part Henrietta. That warm juice of yours is real good stuff. It made me forget how tired I was. It is too bad, one has to work so hard to get a supply of that wonderful sweet juice. I never would have imagined, caressing your vulva, to be that difficult; my poor jaws and tongue are still aching. I know one thing, you're one bushy lady, I still feel I have a lot to learn."

"You will learn Ilique, because you are interested in satisfying your woman. Most guys make the mistake of satisfying themselves, and hope the woman is satisfied. Oh, and you know, I can shave all that hair off.

"Henrietta, I would never let you do that; I got extra excited treading through that thick patch. Pretty soon, I'll be able to make a pathway with my mouth."

"Do what you like Ilique; I noticed you had no problem just now. Matter of fact you were great; you either learn some kind of fast or you're a natural. This was one of the most gratifying orgasms I've ever gotten. Eating like that gives you the right to crawl between these thighs of mine anytime you like. How about trying it again tomorrow?"

These remarks left Ilique feeling pretty good; he wanted to pat himself on the back. Henrietta had given him a great compliment, and the large grin on his face showed his appreciation. His short term definition of Henrietta's gourmet dish was one filled with all the goodies a man wanted to eat.

"I would definitely love that, sore jaws and all." He knew Henrietta would get a kick out of that remark. They both laughed and wrapped their nude bodies together; Ilique, of course spent the night and went directly to school from there.

31

On Friday, prior to Ilique's arrival in the cafeteria, his two lunch friends were holding a private woman's talk; that is, after they got on the same airwave.

"Girl, have you ever had a man to go down on you?"

"Uh huh; have you ever checked into your genealogy Renatra?" LaQueeta was looking over some rather interesting developments, she and Janetqua had discovered about their families.

"Look LaQueeta, I don't mean to be rude, but could we talk about that family tree shit later; this is really important to me."

"Okay Renatra, what's the importance?"

"Have you ever had a man to go down on you?"

"Sure Renatra; you mean eata sweeta LaQueeta!"

"You know it. Well, what did you think of it – Miss eata sweeta LaQueeta?"

"It was okay Renatra; I can either take it or leave it."

"Why is that LaQueeta? I understand it can be real nice."

"I suppose it can Renatra, if it is done right; the ones I had did not really know what they were doing."

"Why did you say that LaQueeta; I mean, how would you know if it is done right?"

"Get real girl – you would know! On every ocassion I was left hanging. So, if that is all the brother can do Renatra, I would rather leave it. Just between me and you, though it's certainly no secret, I have been taking care of myself."

"I know where you're coming from girl, I did that the other day myself. Of course, LaQueeta, I did have an excuse because of a mild case of depression."

"It worked though, didn't it?"

"Of course it did LaQueeta, but I would still rather have the real thing."

"Me too Renatra, but on second thought, I have gotten so good here lately, I'm not so sure. Plus, I can self-pleasure every day, even twice or three times, if I really need it. I know because last Saturday, I did it three times."

"Really LaQueeta, you must have been some kind of horny!"

"Not really, I just woke up feeling good about myself. So the first thing that morning while admiring my gorgeous body, upon those colorful sheets, my graceful hands sort of took charge Renatra. Once my fingers squeezed my nipples and my sensitivity reacted, especially that slippery slit between my exposed thighs, I wanted to make myself feel good or extra good, just for me."

"You felt so good, you did it twice more huh?"

"It wasn't planned Renatra, but I should have known it was coming. Speaking of coming, I found that early morning self-pleasuring is fantastic; it gets your day off to a fast and go-getter type start. It always makes me more productive; you know,

301

clearing any male nuisance out of my system. Anyway, I should have known it was coming when I did not put any clothes on after a hearty breakfast and shower. Walking around the house nude, always turn me on, but not in the way it did Saturday. So after all that vacuuming and exhausting house cleaning, I found myself resting on the sofa, and again feeling real tingly like. Now, after the tremendous orgasm I had gotten earlier, I know I did not need another so soon, but my mind told me I deserved it, and it was okay if I really wanted it. So I lay back on that sofa and manipulated my swollen clit until I came again."

"Funked up your sofa huh?"

"Call it what you want girl; it worked – that much I can tell you. Look at it this way Renatra, I'm never frustrated by not having a man around."

"Yeah, but what about the penetration of a man girl?"

"Oh Renatra, I can tell you're a rookie at self-pleasuring. I can use one hand on my vulva better than a man can use his penis. That's because I can insert my fingers and caress my clit as it should be. Most men you know, just hit and miss, even if they have their tongue roving around ... but then, that is another story."

"So I have heard LaQueeta, and I hope you are going to tell me about that later, but what happened to cause you to self-pleasure yourself a third time?"

"That one Renatra, unlike the second one, was planned. It really answers your question about penetration. Like I said earlier, I felt good about myself Saturday, and continued to do so when I crawled into bed that night. And I honestly wanted a humongous orgasm to send me tumbling into dreamland. Well, I have a large penis shaped vibrator for that deep penetration that you referred to. It's battery operated, but I never use it that way, because it always seems superficial, plus it irritates me somewhat. For the fullness and depth in my vagina, is the only time I really use it. Especially so, when I want to use both hands; the other massaging the hell out of that clitoris. Talking about a guaranteed orgasm girl, you cannot help but get off."

"Really!"

"Really Renatra, that baby oil-greased penis gets you ready even if you're ice cold. And once you learn how to manipulate it inside, you hit some pretty good spots – anytime – all the time. That free hand to caress your clit is the clincher though. You know, most men won't let you manipulate your clit when they're socking it to you; it makes them feel inferior I believe."

"I have never tried to do that anyway LaQueeta; does it work?"

"Well, it helps to assure you of an orgasm Renatra, especially if your man can last long enough. Of course with the vibrator, you don't have that problem of maintaining erectness."

"Hmmm – sounds like I need me one of those; where did you get yours LaQueeta?"

"A boyfriend of mine picked me one up; well I really have eight – different sizes and texture – you know Renatra – nothing like a little variety girl."

"Sounds like you're ready girl!"

"I am Renatra; if I never get another man, I have missed absolutely nothing; and you can't get pregnant or any of that other crazy shit going around these days."

"You think I can get your friend to pick me one up LaQueeta?"

"Ah – Renatra, I was shy like you at first. He got the first one and I went and picked the others out myself. We can go and get them ourselves girl."

"Oh, I don't know about that LaQueeta."

"Scared huh?"

"Well – shy is the word – right!" And they both laugh.

"The clitoral action is really the key though, when it's all said and done Renatra."

"Okay, that gets us back to what I asked you about a fellow going down on you."

"There's a bunch of ifs, but it can work Renatra. Why do you ask; do you have someone who wants to do you?"

"Not really – well maybe - ."

"What do you mean, maybe, Renatra?"

"Well, there is this one guy who I think, I can make do it."

"Now girl, that does not even make any sense. Why in the world would you make a man go down on you Renatra. First of all, you are going to have to make him want you."

"I know that LaQueeta, but what if I want him and tell him that is what he is going to do; this might even be new for him."

"Renatra, you are crazy – make a brother do that – either he wants to or he is not putting his face anywhere near that hot box. Why let some rookie do you anyway; you stand a chance of getting someone who is really inexperienced. Then you are going to be left hanging, like I was. It is just not worth it – you will be totally frustrated."

"It will be worth it LaQueeta, if I make him do it right! And you said I would know. I will not let him remove his head until I am fully satisfied, and he is happy. I will make him digest my wonderful stuff and he will love doing it."

"Renatra, that sounds well and good, but if the brother does not know what he is doing, it will be very annoying. You will want him to take his no-show somewhere else, plus you don't want nobody experimenting on you. Do you know if this person has any experience?"

"Well, I think so LaQueeta."

"What do you mean Renatra – think so! Most brothers would never admit that to a sister unless he thought she kept secrets. On the other hand, if he guessed you to be appetizing, he would also probably tell you. Has this brother told you or even hinted that you might be appetizing, or asked to eat that hot box of yours?"

Renatra could never tell her friend LaQueeta Structworth that Ilique had sent her this erotic letter by mistake. Not yet anyway. Renatra had told LaQueeta, she was going to make the poor brother go down, and not come up, until she was ready for him to do so. She had not told LaQueeta it was their well-dressed co-worker – Ilique, who she was going to make crawl on his hands and knees, and cater to her every desire. Not yet anyway.

Renatra could not tell on Ilique, because a congenial method had not been worked out. The initial idea of threatening Ilique had not been taken very kindly; he was truly upset.

Tact and diplomacy was not exactly Renatra's forte, especially when she felt she had the upper hand. The next move, in that conniving brain of hers was to fight fire with fire. Renatra thought: If Ilique can make me horny; have me doing self-exercises, and craving for a tongue swishing, simply by writing a letter, then I should be able to do the same. She continued; I will write Ilique again and again, giving him a taste of my erotic letters, until he is burning inside. I will show him who is in charge of his body and mind. When I am done, he will wish he had made love to me the first time I requested it. No, I will never be lenient with Ilique. I will not only make him go down on me; I am going to tell him that he will digest me and love it. Further, I will punish his face with my fruitbowl. Renatra, it seems, had her game plan in place. This should prove very interesting.

"No, not yet LaQueeta, but I am seriously working on it. I tell you, I am going to make him digest me."

"Girl, I like the way you operate; so you are going to make the brother digest you. That is the funniest thing I have ever heard. Renatra, you are crazy, but please let me know if it works. I may have been going about the men I meet the wrong way. So when can I expect the first update?"

"Any day now – I mean – any month now LaQueeta."

"Any month! Girl – you are going to grow cobwebs. Renatra, what are you going to tell the brother – stick your head in here man and do what I tell you to do."

"You got it girl – Oh, I will be a little more sophisticated or tactful, if he lets me; otherwise I will merely tell him to get on his knees and rim the thing out. I will make the brother follow my instructions, whether he is experienced or not. I know what makes me feel good and he does not, so he will follow my directions LaQueeta. I will make this brother use his tongue, for what it was made for – eating good stuff."

"Girl, you are tough – please keep me informed – I got to know what the verdict is. Just one more question Renatra; do I know this brother?"

"It is a great possibility LaQueeta, but I will keep you well informed."

"Renatra, I wish I had your nerves, but that could blow up in your face if it does not work."

"To be honest LaQueeta, it is not taking nerves, it is taking – being horny. I am so horny, I do not know what to do. I have tried that regular stuff, but I need a little growth in my life."

"That is certainly growth Renatra, if you can find a brother to do it right. But to demand a brother to dine in your hot box is like shooting for the moon."

"You are probably right LaQueeta, but I know what I want, and I know who I want to do it. And he will dine there; I will see to it. I will not only make the brother go down on me, but I will make him tell me, he loves it. I will demand that he swallow every ounce of my production. I understand, if you give him good stuff, you can hook him forever; and make him do anything at anytime. Of course, I will just use him for digesting my fruitbowl. I also understand, no other woman can take him from you, if your stuff is good. This brother will be sniffing close to me, like he is on a leash."

"Renatra, I understand, if you do not hook him the first time, all that good psychology is just that – good psychology – with no man period. And another thing girl, if it works in reverse, your sweet ass could be following him around."

"That does not worry me LaQueeta; once this brother digest me, he will be eating out of the palms of my hands, or better still – under the palms of my hands – anytime I want him to."

"Girl, you are truly crazy – eating under your palms – that is cute. Tone it down girl, here comes our friend Ilique. If your system works Renatra, I want to try it out on him, so you keep me posted."

Ilique took his reserved seat, after a "good morning ladies," sitting down beside LaQueeta and opposite Renatra, who seemed to be in a pleasant enough mood, asking:

"Well, how is Clara A. Feldon holding up Ilique?"

"I don't know Renatra; I haven't seen her."

"Well, how about Henrietta?"

"She is doing pretty good Renatra; it comes and goes. She was holding up pretty good last night."

"Yeah – I bet it comes and goes Ilique; that is what – your second – third – fourth day going by there. Is there something going on that we should know about?"

"It seems to me LaQueeta, your mind has already answered that question. I am just trying to be a friend; Clara has been spending most of her time with Rory Davanpourt."

"They do have a thing going on, don't they!"

"I heard they were engaged LaQueeta, but she is not wearing any rings."

"She had better marry him soon Renatra, before the old buzzard kick the bucket."

The women were laughing while Ilique just sat and listened. His nostrils captured an intoxicating fragrance and he wondered if it came from LaQueeta, or if it was another awe-inspiring aroma residing on Renatra's soft pubic hair.

"Ilique, we really must be going." They slowly walked away, still chatting and laughing.

Ilique watched; especially Renatra, as her body hugging skirt gave a new meaning to a nice ass. And like she said in her letter, a thought crossed his mind as his tongue inadvertently moved within his mouth, onto a juicy fruitbowl.

32

"LaQueeta, I am so sorry for ignoring your family stuff earlier, but as you saw, my body was reeling; now what was it that you were saying?

"Well, I – or Janetqua and I – just found out we are sisters instead of cousins; well, half sisters anyway – and we're still cousins."

"Damn LaQueeta, sounds like a lot of hanky-panky has been going on. You sure as hell is taking it calm girl; if something like that happened to me, I'd be pretty upset."

"Yeah, well we were a few weeks ago Renatra, when we first stumbled on to something screwy. Of course, finding out that we were sisters eased some of the pain, that neither of our fathers is really our father."

"And how did something like that happen?"

"Both our moms got pregnant by the same guy, who was killed in the war. It seems, according to our moms, the guy, and a soldier at the time, along with themselves were out to having a good time in those days. They were two cousins running loose, they say. Later, they married two nice guys who raised us as their own daughters; so you see Renatra, it turned out pretty well."

"I would still be pretty upset LaQueeta; I mean, after all the years. If something like that happened to me, I don't know if I would ever be the same, and definitely not as forgiving as you seem to be."

"Have you ever thought about looking into your family tree Renatra?"

"No, not really; I've got plenty of time for that."

"As a word to the wise Renatra, the sooner the better; it's so much easier – what I'm saying – while your relatives are still living."

"I see what you mean LaQueeta."

"And I would be glad to help you Renatra; it is really a pretty simple procedure if you know what you are doing. The key, like I said, is to start while most of your kin is still around."

"Later for that LaQueeta; I have something else to do right now ... talk to you later girl."

Renatra pretty much knew the way Ilique now looked at her, she had stirred up his curiosity. Another short letter to keep the pressure on and start him to craving for me, thought Renatra, is what he deserves. And when she left LaQueeta, she quickly wrote and placed this letter on his desk. Ilique found and read it, as soon as he came from lunch.

Hi Ilique:

I love the way you have been watching me lately. It is getting closer and closer to the moment that I will be watching. Think. I will be watching as you lift and spread my thighs to eat my fruitbowl. It will be big and gapped wide open for your entire mouth to enter, and you will do just that. You will really get after it. Ilique, you will love me watching you eat my fruitbowl and tell me so. I will watch as you lick up my juices and produce more as you do so. Think of me doing that, as you read, and tonight, you should self-pleasure yourself, as your mouth fill with saliva. Have fun in doing so; think of me as I climax and tighten my thighs around your head, watching you all the way, as you really get after it.

Sometimes Ilique, I feel you are a bit bashful. Well, do not be bashful, because when I stick my fruitbowl in your face and tell you to eat, you will only be able to think of how good it is. And there is no question it will be good. So you see, there is nothing to worry about, but lots of hot tasty juices saturating your mouth, and a real good feeling on your part. When I finish watching you eat my fruitbowl, you will only have to worry about one thing; when I will let you eat it again.

Lovingly yours
Renatra

Again attached to the letter was a fruit scented pubic hair bouquet. This time, the soft curly black hair was wrapped in a bright red ribbon. Ilique read the letter carefully, getting somewhat hungry, even though he had just finished lunch. He grasped the beautifully red tied lock of curly hair in his hand and immediately did what all men would do; he put it before his nose and took a deep breath. The aroma hitting his nostrils was sweet, unreconizable to him, but it was an edible type fragrance. The feel of the soft pubic hair on the tip of his nose, admittantly so, teased Ilique. And before he was truly aware of what he was doing, he was rubbing it back and forth across his top lip, through his moustache, touching his nose on each pass. He stared outward, at nothing, as if he was hypnotized as visions of Renatra's swaying body loomed before him. He wondered what she was really like ... was she like Henrietta ... if her taste was as sweet. Suddenly, his real senses reappeared and he quickly put the curly lock in his shirt pocket, saying to himself. "There is no way, I am going to crawl between Renatra's fine thighs ...

there is absolutely no way I will allow her to wrap those gorgeous legs around my head ... and roll my lips in her soft pubic hair."

Renatra sat at her desk wondering what was going on in the head of Ilique, but somehow, the genealogy thing crept into her head. So, when school was out, and a brief stop off at home, she drove to her parent's home. Sauninger T. Metfield, her father, was not yet in, but her mother was. Their discussion on the family tree was very wholesome.

"Renatra, I think that is a wonderful idea; you can continue mine where I left off."

"Mama, you mean you already have something on your side of the family!"

"That's right; well don't sound so surprised ... you young-sters think you're the only ones with good ideas. Of course, you might have to start from scratch on your father's side of the family; nothing has been done there for sure."

"Why is that mama?"

"Your father is much too busy with other things Renatra; that school business is all that matters to him. You can see that for yourself, and I wish that were not the case. Besides a movie, here and there, we never even go anywhere."

"Mama, that is partly your fault, but I don't want to get – what's for dinner?" Renatra suddenly remembered there was nothing at her apartment to eat.

"You can stay for dinner Renatra; your father hardly ever makes it in time these days. And that's my fault too, I suppose?"

"Mama, I did not mean to cause a disturbance, but I find things work a lot better when you tell men what you want. Just tell them point blank what you expect and what they must do."

"Oh really, Renatra, you have so much to learn about men; that only work half the time, then you're back to square one."

The mother and daughter dinner was pleasant, because and especially because, Sauninger T. Metfield did not make it home in time.

Meanwhile, Ilique had become super horny; so he knew after the wake tonight, he and Henrietta would have to make love. And speaking of Henri's wake, Helene Scott was there. Helene had changed Henri's life the short time they were together. She smelled sweet and tangy, like the spoilage of an apple, left uneaten. She however, tasted sweeter than the sweetest of apples and was juicer than the best of them. One bite, and the juices struck the palate of one's tongue with such sugary force, that it was virtually impossible to remove one's head. This is what Henri had found out as his tongue eased its way into Helene's darkhollow. The twangy-sweet flavor was unlike anything he had ever experienced. For sure, Henri knew his life would be different from that point on. He said to himself at the time. "If this is what I have been missing in women, life's viewpoint is worth a second look – a sweet darkhollow to peep into justifies giving myself a chance." At least he was able to make the transition and enjoy Helene before he passed on. Anyway, before the wake ended, Ilique agreed to be with Henrietta and Helene at the funeral. Meanwhile, it was time for Ilique to go and get some more of Henrietta's instructions.

"Well Ilique, are you ready for some more knowledge on us women?" Henrietta lay in the bed with a sheer negligee on, but she had willingly pulled it up, to uncover her gorgeous body.

"About as ready as a man can be."

"I am looking forward to it myself Ilique, after last night. There are some things you must understand; there is a difference between nursing a vulva and eating a vulva."

"Huh, sounds the same to me Henrietta!"

"To nurse Ilique, is to start the flow using tongue manipulation and titilation of our precious puffy folds; to include licking the area around the clitoris. And merely opening your mouth to drank when the warm sweet juices commence to flow, letting them glide down your throat slowly, as you savior every ounce. Whereas eating a vulva is continuous tongue manipulation and titilation of the outer lips with a mighty-gentle force, with constant vigorous smooth tongue surges inside the juicy vaginal opening. Eating a vulva calls for your lips and mouth to dive into the juices, meeting them head-on, as they are produced. It calls for getting your nose wet; it calls for your face to be smeared with juices if you don't eat fast enough. This is not to mean you go about it haphazardly, because eating your favorite lady the way she supposed to be eaten is an art. You will be able to master it well when I am done with you."

"Do you really think so Henrietta?"

"You bet your sweet lips Ilique, and we'll have fun doing it. Nursing a vulva is harder than eating, because of the patience involved. It takes real discipline and patience to lick a vulva, foregoing the temptation to dive in; while waiting on a trickle, then a flood of juices to enter your mouth for delightful nutrition. In many instances, a woman will not let you nurse her vulva because she cannot withstand the pressure. She will pull your face into her succulent overheated vagina, and you are forced to eat. My job as I see it Ilique, is to teach you how to eat my delicious pussy, excuse me, and have patience if I can, when I teach you how to nurse this delicious vulva of mine."

"I believe I am ready Henrietta!"

"Settle down Ilique, we'll go over a few things first; just a few of my personal good eating tips. Remember every woman is different. I am going to put my finger in me and stir it, then let you taste it ... there, what does that taste like?"

"I suppose I could get use to doing that Henrietta."

"Well, that is not exactly what I wanted to hear Ilique, but let's see if you can do it ... okay put your finger in here, stir it around a bit, then put it in your mouth, making sure it register on your tongue. I know this sounds freaky to you, but sometimes I get a little freaky when I make love."

"Okay Henrietta, here goes; stir it around a little bit huh!"

"Yes ... oooh ... that feels good ... I think you touched something ... oooh ... just keep rubbing in that same spot ... oooh, that's real good ... oooh, that is wonderful ... keep doing what you're doing honey ... oooh – ooooh – ooooooh ...I believe I'm going to ... oh my – oh my ... rub it harder honey

... rub it harder ... rub it harder ... rub it harder ... oh my ... ooooooh – ooooooh – ooooooh ...."

Ilique obviously had hit Henrietta's hot spot she had told him about the other night. She now lay back on the bed and her lovely vagina was wide open, showing a pretty pink color, with sweet smelling juices oozing out. Ilique was astonished at how easy things went when one listened and followed instructions. An urging told him, this was no time for rolling his fingers across his tongue, with such a delicious looking delicacy before him. So he eased his mouth closer, wiping clean her swollen outer lips with his swishing tongue ... the oozing continued ... he could hear Henrietta moaning ... and more juices came ... and he continued slashing his tongue onto her ... and the oozing continued as did Henrietta's moaning, except it was louder. Then instinctively, Ilique eased his mouth directly over Henrietta's gourmet dish, sliding his tongue inside, allowing all of her delicious sweet juices to flow inside of him. He had never tasted anything this good before; to him she tasted like cotton candy. Even his lips stuck in her sticky-thick wiry mesh, felt like cotton candy. But Henrietta was better and sweeter, much better – much sweeter ... and he got carried away with eating ... the sweet flavor had him going ... Henrietta screams ... more sweet flavor crossing his tongue ... more screams from Henrietta. Finally, after a long while, the oozing and screams stopped. And Ilique noticed her gourmet dish to be the most gorgeous thing he had ever seen; her lips lay wide open, displaying beautiful puffy folds of reddish flesh, and a spectacular three inch-plus long round object, lying in the center of it all. Ilique amazingly watched, as the precious red object slowly withdrew itself inside Henrietta's fine shapely body. Henrietta began to talk, as the fascinating object disappeared.

"Are you sure you have not done this many – many times before you met me? Ilique – Ilique - ."

"Huh!"

"Are you sure you have not eaten a woman's vulva or done anything like this before?"

"Uh huh … that clitoris of yours is a master piece."

"Thank you Ilique, and you never even got to it today; you are simply wonderful. You are really a fast learner and you're so young. I do not mean anything by that age remark, other than I am pleasantly surprised."

"Well Henrietta, what you taught me really works; and you were so right about a vagina tasting better and better when your mate loved and reacted well to what you were doing. Because the more you moaned and screamed, the better you tasted; the more you flooded, the more you got sweeter and better. Your reaction was phenominal, making your gourmet dish taste like something I could eat everyday."

"Thanks Ilique, that is by far the best compliment I have ever received." And she curls up and falls asleep.

33

"She caught him by his robe and said, "Come to bed with me," But he escaped and ran outside, leaving his robe in her hand." Genesis 39:12

During the funeral, Ilique found himself at all times between Helene Scott and Henrietta Feldon. For a person who had little to no experience at consoling a crying lady, he all of a sudden was having to pamper and hold two of them. It was a good thing Rory G. Davanpourt had given him three small packs of kleenex, along with an eight-set package of soft white hankerchiefs. Because in Henri's journey homeward, through the church, the gravesite, the limousine ride to and fro, Ilique had practically used it all. He had returned the squeezes to their hands and bodies; had rubbed their faces of moisture, both sweat and tears. He had also provided a shoulder for each to lean on. By the end of it all, they were a wholesome threesome, heading back to Henri's house, or now Helene Scott's, who had received it during the reading of Henri's will. Henrietta received the bulk

316

of his wealth; money, furniture, clothes, jewelry. Clara received his extremely valuable portfolio of marketable securities along with his shiny new Lincoln – Mark something. Anyway, the three of them were sitting around talking and resting ... well, Henrietta and Helene were doing the talking; Ilique was just resting.

"Henrietta, you can stay here as long as you like; I have another six months remaining on my apartment lease, which I intend to honor."

"That is awfully nice of you Helene; maybe in that time, I can decide which pieces of furniture you can have ... the two bedrooms for sure!"

"That's good news Henrietta, but what about Clara? I do not want to come between you two."

"Oh, it's okay Helene, I offered it to her, but she wanted you to have first choice, especially since most of the furniture was bought for this house."

"Oh ... I see!"

"Well don't look and sound so gloomy Helene, it is very nice furniture, you know!"

It's not that Henrietta, I just don't want any rejects or hand me downs."

"Well, I be damn; I guess you call Henri's house a reject also!"

"No I don't Henrietta ... that was given to me out of love – ."

"Well at least you could be tactful about it Helene!"

"Tact and diplomacy is not one of my strong suits Henrietta."

Just as Henrietta opened her mouth for an obvious thunderous reply, there was God's thunder and lighting present, and no more electricity. They now sat in the dark. It was dark because of night, but it was darker because of the storm; it had begun to rain extremely hard. The noise outside and the dark inside would have been frightening to the women if it had not been for their comforter – Ilique.

"There's some candles on the dining room table ladies ... be right back."

317

Ilique had been looking from one to the other, thinking how beautiful they looked, freely expressing themselves. Now, they were quiet. He quickly returned carrying two flames, placing one on a table by each lady; he also fully lit one of the two candlelabrums. Thanks to Henrietta for this addition; she obviously intended their use for she and Ilique. The six flames flickered, as did the faint light upon Henrietta and Helene. Ilique could still see their beauty; their eyes became luminous and the outline of their faces imagined a radiance through the eyes of Ilique.

"You women are really beautiful."

"Is it because we are quiet Ilique?"

"No Henrietta."

"Or is it because you can hardly see us?"

"A little of both Helene." They all laughed.

"What do you think happened ... I need to be getting out of here for home!"

"Helene, I know you are not thinking about risking your life in this stormy weather; you too Ilique! It's after nine already and tomorrow is Sunday, in case either of you are looking for a work excuse. You can spend the night here."

"Henrietta, I really appreciate the offer but -."

"There's no buts Helene, you'll have your own bedroom ... give me one of those candles Ilique; let's get it ready."

When Henrietta and Helene entered the bedroom, they heard a dripping sound, before laying eyes on rapid drops of water falling near the center of the bed.

"My Lord, Henrietta look at all that water!"

"Quick Ilique, bring us a large pot from the kitchen!"

"What," was Ilique's answer as he stood in the doorway. "Oh my ... it's raining in here!"

"Will you please get a pot man, before the bed is ruined!"

"Coming up Henrietta ... man this is awful."

"Well, there goes my "own bedroom" Henrietta ... look out Mr. Sofa."

318

"I won't have you sleeping on the sofa ... that king sized bed is big enough for the three of us. Of course, I will sleep in the middle Helene."

"Scared of me huh! Well, you should know now Henrietta, I am an opportunist."

"To be honest Helene, I had not thought of what's probably on your mind ... there should not be any of that going on."

"Well, for all of our sakes Henrietta, I suggest we all take a nice bath before retiring."

"It has been a long day hasn't it ... you would certainly need one, I'm sure Helene."

"Are you two at it again ... this huge chitlin pot should work."

"I do not believe my brother cooked any of those things ... maybe one of his close friends."

"Well, don't look at me Henrietta ... I did not even know that pot was in there."

"You two must learn to get along, since it looks like you will be sleeping in the same bed ... the sofa is mine."

"I have already solved that equation Ilique; Helene will sleep with us."

"Yes Ilique ... Miss Trustworthy here is putting herself in the middle of us."

"Henrietta, you mean -."

"Oh, I trust you Ilique ... it's little Miss Hot Stuff here, where I have my doubts ... I can feel heat coming off her body now."

"Anybody can see that -."

"Hold it ladies; nobody is going to get any rest if you two don't simmer down."

Ilique was the first to shower and hit the bed. Later, Helene and Henrietta crawled in; Henrietta in the middle wearing a gown, and Helene along side her, wearing panties and a shirt, compliments of Henri. Ilique was sound asleep when they came to bed; each of the ladies quickly fell asleep. Hours into the night, nature called Henrietta to the bathroom to urinate. And when she returned she crawled into bed on the outside of Ilique, pushing him against Helene. Well, all of this movement woke up Helene, and she realized immediately what had happened.

Ilique's body felt good to Helene, lying against hers, and a different kind of nature began to surface ... her darkhollow became saturated. Who knows what the initial plans were ... if she had any, but the sound of Henrietta snoring had a sensual effect upon her breast and inner thighs. Helene slid her panties off and eased her soft hands inside of Ilique's shorts, for some slow and effective massaging upon his dormant penis. Ilique ... sure as she knew he would, slowly responded, rising and penetrating through the short's opening, just as Helene turned on her side and nudged backward into him. Her buttocks curved and protruded favorably into Ilique's mid-section, where her busy hands made sure his throbbing penis found its mark. Then she reached backward, grabbing his behind to steady it, while she slowly twirled her darkhollow. She was quiet, even as she reached her peak, and so was Ilique, because he did not want to wake Helene. Ilique even climaxed in the excitement; knowing Henrietta was teaching him a thriller; making love without Helene's awareness. He really powered his rod into this extremely wet and warm delicacy, as this was the first time Henrietta had wanted to make love this way. Both gratified; Helene slid her panties back on and peacefully went to sleep.

When morning came, Henrietta crawled out of bed, thinking nothing, but fixing the three of them a large breakfast. The aroma of food finally woke up Ilique and later Helene, as they still lay in bed. There was a smile on their faces ... well, until Ilique noticed who was on his right side. Helene still smiled, even winking at him.

"How long have you been over there Helene?"

"Most of the night Ilique, why?"

"I was just curious, that's all ... why are you smiling like that? Do you normally wake up this happy?"

"Not unless I have reason to Ilique ... how about you?"

320

"I want to ask you a question, but I think I already know the answer ... you are one dirty bitch!"

"Remember Ilique, you helped me be dirty ... anyway, I wouldn't call that good sperm of yours dirty if I was you ... that's selling yourself short. If you had not been in such a hurry, I would have let you suck my nipples." Showing him both her lovely breast.

"Like I said Helene, you are one dirty bitch!"

"Now that's a fine way of talking brother, after you just got the best piece of pussy you ever had. Hey ... you're not so bad yourself, so put a smile on that sour looking face."

"Who would have ever figured you Helene for such a thing ... and you are supposed to be grieving too."

"What does grieving have to do with it ... the man is gone ... his screwing days are over. And for your information Ilique, I am now in the market for a new man."

"Yeah, but that don't give you the right to go doing what you deliberately did last night Helene."

"The right ... well, I be damn ... look who's talking – right ... you got the biggest nut of your career last night ... had the biggest smile on your face this morning, and you're talking this "right" shit Ilique!"

"Yeah, but it's all your fault."

"Look Ilique ... I accept my responsibility for what happened, but don't you try to wiggle out of your responsibility. Anyway, let that be a lesson for your young ass, for screwing around in the dark."

"Young ... you're no older than I am Helene."

"Yeah, but I have experience on my side; you're still wet behind the ears Ilique. Don't let dating an older woman go to your head and give you a false sense of experience. You're good honey, but you're not there yet ... hang in there though, and either Henrietta or better still, I might be able to teach you something."

"You can't teach me anything Helene, but how to be a dirty rotten whore." Ilique thought of Joseph in the bible and

Potiphar's wife, (Genesis 39) and how he was going to have to steer himself clear of Helene. He feared it was too late since their flesh had already met, but thought a sincere prayer might prevent him from considerable seduction in the future.

"Listen Ilique, I will say this only once; that is the second or third time you called me a slimy dirty name. Let it be your last time or you will be sorry you ever laid eyes on me."

"You can't tell me what to call a slut like you Helene, and for your information, I am already sorry I laid eyes on you."

"Remember, I warned you Ilique!"

"Is that suppose to be some kind of serious threat or something -."

"Hurry guys and get up, breakfast is almost ready … what are you two mumbling about?"

"You wouldn't believe it Henrietta … Ilique is reading me my rights on our beautiful secret love affair last night."

"The way he was snoring Helene, I'm sure it was beautiful … Clara called, she will be over, later this morning … hurry up you two."

When they assembled at the kitchen table, the first words after the prayer was by Henrietta.

"Now, what was all this talk about making love last night … who loved who?"

"Well Henrietta, I told Ilique I made love to him last night, and that is why he had such a big smile on his face this morning."

"Good loving will make a man smile … Ilique is entitled to all the good loving he can get … and he should have enjoyed it, if it was good."

"That is what I was trying to tell the boy Henrietta, but he insisted on calling me a bunch of dirty names unbecoming to a lady."

"That seems totally out of character for Ilique … good loving is always worth smiling over – dream or real. Come on Ilique, cheer up; if Helene loved you, she loved you … worse things could happen to you, you know."

322

"That is what I tried to tell the boy Henrietta ... my loving is probably only second to what he is getting from you."

"I love your modesty Helene, but you are probably telling the truth."

"Maybe another storm will come today and I could love him again tonight Henrietta; how about that Ilique?"

"Why don't you just drop it Helene!"

Ilique could not believe his ears; that Helene was the cunningness little bitch he had ever seen. He said to himself, "she admitted loving me to Henrietta and then built up Henrietta's ego on loving me, by taking a back seat. The question is; is Henrietta naïve enough not to believe her or did she really believe that whore tricked me into loving her. In time, I will ask her."

"There's the doorbell, that must be Clara." Henrietta ran to the door.

"Don't you ever mention loving me again Helene or I'm going to lower the boom on your ass."

"Look who is trying to talk tough again ... you lowered the boom on my ass last night, if you can remember Ilique."

"You know what I mean Helene ... do you think you're getting away with something ... do you think you're pulling the wool over Henrietta's eyes?"

"You have a lot to learn about women Ilique ... Henrietta knows I am telling the truth ... she knows I'm an opportunist, because I told her. Now, she might be in denial a bit because I was able to pull off screwing you so easy, but she knows I made love to you. And if you ask her, she will probably tell you she knows it; the only reason Henrietta will not admit the truth to you is, she let her ego get in the way of letting a younger woman get the best of her. But believe me man, woman to woman – she knows I got a piece of her man's meat. You should calm down a bit Ilique. Henrietta is not disturbed with me giving you a good screwing, so why should you be so upset; after the fact. You seemed to forget, you were smiling pretty good when you woke up."

"Don't tell me Helene what I shouldn't be ... you tricked me and you know it."

"Look Ilique, I made you screw me because I was horny, and the opportunity presented itself to me. Now why don't you just leave it alone or my earlier warning might go into effect."

34

Clara came inside, still looking a bit solemn.

"Hi girl; hello Ilique!"

"Hello Clara, are you okay; you took it pretty hard yester-day."

"Yeah Helene, we all took it pretty hard, but after some good loving from Rory and a good nights rest, I feel much better this morning."

"I know exactly what you mean girl."

"She knows too ... she loved Ilique right through the storm Clara."

"Yeah mother, I heard about that storm this morning; Rory told me I never even twitched. It was bad huh?"

"Sure was Clara, the roof sprang a leak in the bedroom, and we all had to sleep together."

"The roof is leaking mother; that is awful."

"Oh, Helene, I almost forgot, I will get with the insurance company and get the roof taken care of. You sure don't want to move into a house with a problem as serious as that."

"You got that right Henrietta; though we weathered the storm pretty good last night. Thanks to Ilique and all his assistance. He is really great at smoothing over a stormy crisis. I was never ever afraid, even when the lights went out. Ilique lit candles Clara and helped with the leak. I was moved by his wonderful assistance throughout the storm - the night - his passionate help throughout this ordeal has penetrated me ... my heart. Your mother is indeed fortunate to have him in her life."

"That girl is incredible," Ilique said to himself, "she actually thrives, living her life on the edge."

"Well, every woman needs a strong man in their life Helene."

Those words seemed to have touched Helene and she started crying. Ilique thought of them as fake tears for sympathy, and made no effort to hold her as he did yesterday. Clara embraced her until she regained her composure.

"Well, Clara, Henrietta, I must be getting home. I know you two need to be alone; and thank you Clara."

"Do you need Ilique to see you home Helene?"

Helene looked at Henrietta, then at Ilique, but their stern expressions did not change, so she cooly said. "No Clara, I too need to be alone; Ilique has already helped me more than he'll ever know. Could you walk me to my car?"

"Sure Helene, be glad to; are you sure you're going to be okay girl?"

As soon as they were outside the door, Helene started crying again.

"Are you sure you don't need Ilique to see you home Helene?"

"No Clara, he's now part of my problem; I made Ilique love me last night."

"You what! Does my mother know about it?"

"I tried to tell her Clara. I know she heard me, but I don't know if she really believed me. I am so sorry; will you please tell her, I am sorry. Everything seems to be happening so fast ... my head is turning over and over ... I don't know what came over me. I just needed someone to hold me ... to love me ... to screw me ... and Ilique was there, with his throbbing shaft. It's not his fault, he actually thought I was Henrietta. Make her believe that, will you?"

"Girl, I think you had better be going ... how could you?"

"You're the only true friend I have Clara, please forgive me."

"Just leave Helene!"

Clara was crying as she came back into the house.

"Now what's wrong with you Clara; you were doing so well a moment ago ... we will all, miss Henri."

"Mother, it's not that at all."

"I guess I better be going Henrietta – Clara."

"No, you're not going anywhere Ilique; this concerns you too, so you can just have a seat. Mother, tell me what happened last night when you three so gracefully slept together? Helene told me she made Ilique make love to her; is that true?"

"Probably so Clara, she told me the same thing and I believe her."

"Well, you are certainly calm about it mother; seems like you should be mad as hell!"

"I am, at least I was, but I'm over it now. I feel bad for Ilique, but I was going to discuss that with him later, because he is entitled to an apology from me."

"Mother, what the hell are you talking about? Helene is the one that should be apologizing."

"Well, that's true too Clara."

"Look mother – what happened – I want some answers before I get mad and fire Helene right now. Come on, let's hear it!"

"Okay, have a seat, before you have a baby. After the lights went out and the storm seemed so bad, I insisted on Helene and Ilique spending the night. Then the roof sprang a leak, wetting up her bed, and I told them, there was room enough for all of us in the king-sized bed. Prior to that, Helene offered to sleep on the sofa; and later Ilique offered to sleep on the sofa, but I insisted on the bed, with a comment that I should sleep in the middle. Sometimes during the night I went to the restroom and without thinking, crawled back in beside Ilique on the other side, leaving Helene next to him. Ilique can fill you in on the rest."

"Henrietta, I was going to talk to you about this later. Anyway Clara, I felt someone rubbing on me and naturally I thought it was Henrietta wanting to do something different, you know; making love next to another person, without them knowing about it. It seemed especially that way, when her body – well Helene's body eased to the side, backing up to me, welding her behind into my penis, pulling me in. The rest is easy to figure out."

"Well I be damn ... the girl is a tramp mother."

"Oh, don't be so hard on Helene, it is all my fault Clara."

"Mother, you are beginning to sound like that slut that just left; she said it was all her fault!"

"There is enough blame to go around Clara, but I challenged Helene and lost."

"Mother, this is beginning to sound crazy-crazy; what are you talking about?"

"Well, when Helene and I first started talking about the three of us sleeping in the same bed, she told me she was an opportunist; meaning she would screw Ilique if she got the chance. I could not pass up a good challenge; how was I to know, I would go to the restroom and come back to the wrong position. Even she would not know that. So you see, it's all my fault Clara."

"That still does not give her the right to screw your man in your own damn bed mother."

"But I invited her into my bed Clara and in essence told her to screw Ilique, if she could. I have no trouble believing what happened is my fault."

"I still disagree mother – and what about you Ilique – can't you tell one damn pussy from the other?"

"Now Clara, you leave Ilique alone; there is no way he could tell. We have never made love that way."

"Oh, this is really getting personal; well Ilique, maybe you should have stuck your damn tongue in, for a test before you got started."

"I resent that Clara!"

"Okay, I apologize mother; maybe I should just drop this."

"It would be a good idea, and do not break up your friendship with Helene because of it; this also is not job related."

"I will have to think about it mother ... I will have to think about that."

"There should be nothing to think about Clara; nothing that happened here has anything to do with your school."

"I am not so sure Henrietta. In the course of my telling Helene how dirty she was, I pissed her off, and she threatened me with something."

"Like what Ilique?"

"I am not sure Clara; and I can't remember exactly what she said, but it was to the tune of doing something to me."

"Even if she did something to you Ilique, that would be no reason for Clara to fire the poor girl."

"Mother, don't go having sympathy for Helene; she might do something to Ilique which might affect what happens at school. And S. T. Metfield is watching me some kind of close."

"I think you are trying to read more into this than there actually is Clara. Ilique just got him an extra piece and that's all there is to it. It's all my fault and I think we should forgive the poor girl and drop the whole thing. This was a great loss for her too, you know."

"Okay mother, but I am still going to watch Helene."

"Suit yourself Clara, but don't make yourself miserable worrying about nothing. Ilique is a big boy and can take care of himself."

"He can mother as long as you don't go around giving him girls to screw."

"I have heard enough of that Clara; I thought we agreed to drop that screwing incident. If anyone should be upset, it's Ilique, and I don't see him carrying on like a maniac."

"Not now anyway, but what about later mother."

"Everyday is different Clara; that should be dealt with at that time and not any sooner. I will make up favorably for Ilique for me putting him in such an awkward position, and I'm sure he will make up for me, what he did. I honestly feel the experience was good for him; it should definitely help us in our sexual relationship."

"Mother, I can't believe you said that!"

"I'm human just like you are Clara, and I need a healthy sex life just like you. Matter of fact, I'm getting horny just thinking about some of Ilique's rearward action."

"Whoa – I think I had better be going on that mother; it seems if you two have some business to take care of."

"Okay Clara; I love you … and tell Rory hello for me."

"See ya mother – and watch yourself Ilique – this lady is hot." They all laugh.

"Hold on, I'll see you out Clara."

They held hands just like a loving mother and daughter when they passed through the front door to the outside, and beyond to the curb, where a conversation of some sort would take place, before Clara got in her car.

"Mother – do you think you are going to be all right with Ilique – you know, he is about my age."

"I am not blind honey; I am going to teach him the same as I taught you how to teach that old geyser, you got."

"From the sounds of it, inside a moment ago, you are already doing a pretty good job."

"It's working out pretty good Clara, because he wants to learn; even wants to write a book about oral sex.. What I love about Ilique is, he catches on extremely fast and does not forget anything he has been taught. The key though is having a mate who is willing to listen to you and cooperate with you. Age is a small factor, yes, but most young men are willing to listen to an older mature woman without being intimidated ... as most older men are willing to listen to a young mature woman, without intimidation. I am sure you have Rory eating you all over that house of his."

"Mother!"

"Well!"

"Okay – it's true – it's working just like you taught me; cook those good meals for your man ... tell him how you expect to be loved ... sit back and enjoy yourself while he eats. It's still give and take, but what I love about Rory the most is, he takes charge on doing exactly what I prefer. I have never been happier; we have even talked about marriage. What do you think about that mother?"

"Well now, that's another whole topic; we will talk about it later though."

"It sounds like you are happy too mother."

"I am Clara, and so far, it's working out. Of course, I have been without so long, anything would probably work out. You can see why I'm not getting upset about last night; I truly believe Ilique is worth my patience."

"So you're not worried about a younger woman, huh?"

"Definitely not Clara. When I'm finished teaching Ilique, I will not be worried about any woman. Sounds stupid, but I am going to encourage him to have some other relationships, probably while I'm gone. It's the long term I am looking at. This young guy, believe me, has some real potential, and I really want it for me. And just between us honey, the man is good; I haven't had orgasms this numerous and powerful since your father was alive."

"Sounds like marriage talk to me mother."

"Honey, you have marriage on the brain; we are no where near that point, but we'll see. I'll talk to you about that later too. Tell Rory hello; we both must get back to our men ... see ya."

When Henrietta reentered the house, she told Ilique she was preparing a real down-home meal, and he was welcome to stay. Obviously he agreed to the nice gesture, and within moments, after a nice soothing bath, they were back into that bed where she slept so soundly, only hours earlier. Henrietta knew she had to keep herself on the front part of Ilique's brain, as well as on the tip of his tongue. He loved entering that succulent gourmet dish of hers, but for now, Henrietta had other ideas. She eased his penis inside her mouth until it disappeared, resting comfortably in her mid-throat. Then her cheek muscles began massaging the long rigid shaft, pressing and squeezing the whole circumference, until she felt him throbbing against the walls of her throat. Simultaneously, spreading baby oil between his upper thigh, she lightly slid her soft warm hand over his greasy scrotum sac, feeling and cupping her palm gently over the precious jewels inside. Ilique could feel her warmness. His mouth had already began gasping for air; delirium was about to set in. Then Henrietta slowly walked her center finger in sensual pressing tiny circles toward his anus, staying on the seam or ridge underneath the sac between the two. She worked this area several minutes to and fro, touching and gently squeezing his balls, every other time and slightly touching and patting his slippery anus, every other time. Doing so until she heard him moan.

As Ilique's moaning grew, Henrietta moved her middle finger directly to his oil saturated anus and began massaging it; still cheek massaging his penis, feeling those tremendous throbs and small juice trickles. Gradually the warmth of her mouth and finger massages upon his anus turned his moans into groans and more groans. She, steadily massaged his anus to a small involuntary opening and slowly glided her roving finger inside. Now screams began and she eased her finger deeper and deeper, circling it a bit as his anus suddenly involuntarily became wider. Ilique did not know what was happening; only that his mind and body appeared to have exploded at the same time. Henrietta was now slowly moving her finger up and down Ilique's responsive cylinder, to his extremely loud exasperating screams, until her throat was filled with his creamy sweet semen, and a few jerks signifying the end. She knew he was done for the evening;

knowing no man could come through this action without hours and hours of recuperation.

Henrietta smiled as she watched Ilique snore with his soft penis lying flabbily upon the sheets. She instantly knew she had gone about lovemaking all wrong, saying out loud to herself, "he should have eaten my gourmet dish first; I should have made him eat it first, but he deserved a good zapping." Henrietta called this procedure, her sapping-zapping-knockout special. This in her opinion, along with teaching Ilique, fine dining techniques upon her gourmet dish, was why she was not worried about Helene or any other woman – young or old – taking the man she had set sight upon. Ilique slept through the night, and was awakened with a nice meaty breakfast before heading for school.

35

Ilique arrived early for school, as usual, and was quickly approached by Pops Belder, the janitor, while rushing down the hall.

"Ilique, we need to talk; there is something I think you should know."

"All right Pops, but will this take long, and could it possibly wait until tomorrow?"

"Well, it possibly could, but I didn't bring a dinner today, and that sir, might cause some more problems."

"Could it wait until after school Pops?"

"It could Ilique, but the Mrs. is not going to like it; which is going to cause some more problems."

"What is all this about problems and more problems Pops?"

"Can you slow down sir; I'm not use to walking and talking at this pace together."

"This is a hectic day for me Pops, and every second counts."

Pops Belder stops in his tracks at this remark, raising his winded voice. "It's Tashanesha sir!"

Ilique, not ready for the halting, has covered about ten steps before the name sinks in. Now he becomes aware, his walking companion, Pops Belder is behind him, now leaning against the wall with his arms folded tightly across his chest.

"Tashanesha! My Tashanesha!" Ilique looks straight at Pops; Pops nods his head in an up and down motion, never unfolding his arms. He walks slowly back to Pops, saying again.

"Tashanesha! My Tashanesha! What's this about my Tashanesha? Is she all right? Nothing has happened to her, has it Pops?"

"Calm down Ilique; Tashanesha is all right, but she does have a problem or two. In a nutshell, she's pregnant and homeless."

"We need to talk Pops; why didn't you tell me this earlier! Please forgive me Pops, but not another word of this until we are in the conference room."

Ilique turns and is now walking briskly in the opposite direction.

"Do we have to walk so fast sir; we do not want another problem."

"Oh, I'm sorry Pops Belder."

Slowing down to Pops careful strides, they astonishingly look at each other, as the lockers, drift by, one by one. Though they moved much slower, the floor tile speed by, as Ilique hangs his head downward. Questions were forming in his swelling head. Why hadn't his favorite student and pet told him? Why hadn't he noted any changes in Tashanesha? Had there been any behavorial changes and he failed to catch them? Thought after thought occurred to Ilique. He spoke to himself."If I had not been so rapped up in myself on loving Henrietta, I would have noticed. I have not been very observant of my classroom lately. My responsibility to my students has eroded."

All of a sudden, Ilique was hard on himself. And the worry of neclect was not totally correct. It was true, Ilique had developed a delicious love fest in Henrietta, but his classroom had not suffered; especially, not in terms of assignments and workloads. Oh, there might have been a time where he daydream a minute or two longer about Henrietta, but nothing to the detriment of his student's education. The concealment award goes to Tashanesha. "She is always in his face," as the other girls say. It is often pretty difficult to notice something when it is right in your eyes; like the old saying of "not being able to see the forest for the trees."

Ilique has forgotten about whatever else was so important. It is amazing how some things take precedent over other "hectic" things. Priortizing one's schedule, is not always simple, but becomes exceptionally easy when we know what is at stake. Once they reached the conference room, Ilique waited patiently to hear Pops talk.

"Well sir, it all started last Saturday, but for me, it started last Monday. I mean – Tashanesha said she was kicked out of her house on that Saturday. I told her not to tell me about the past, because at my age, the present is all I care to handle. Anyway, I discovered her Monday night, hiding in your room. She started crying and asked me not to tell you or Miss. Clara A. Feldon. I admit Ilique, I was not thinking too clearly among her tears and all. So I simmered her down with the promise of dinner, which I went out and bought. I mean, she had to eat – for the evening meal. She said, she was in the school's breakfast and lunch program, and wasn't really that hungry, but I knew better. A child's mind is just no good sir, without supper! On Tuesday I brought extra chicken from home. On Wednesday I brought an extra helping of a meatloaf casserole. Man, that child can sure put away the grub."

"Well sir, things were working out fine until the Mrs. inquired as to what was happening to the leftovers from the night before. Her very words when I told her of Tashanesha, was, "Are you crazy or out of your mind or what!" We then talked it over and decided the best thing was to tell you; and you would do what had to be done. We know Miss. Feldon is the principal, but thought you should know first, being the child's teacher. I feel bad telling on the child after making a promise and all, but I feel real relieved right now. You will tell Miss. Feldon for us, won't you! Please don't be too hard on the girl Ilique; she seems to have had a rough go of it. And remember, she has to have a big supper, if you take her tonight."

"Wait a minute Pops, where has tashanesha been staying?"

"The Mrs. made me bring her home, when I told her of Miss. Feldon's uncle, and the interruption and all; before that I don't know. Tashanesha is really a nice kid; we have become quite attached to her, but her situation needs to be made right. It's hard ... for me ... to understand how a mother could put out a sweet child like that."

"Don't worry about it Pops; we'll take care of it."

"You know Ilique, there is only one thing that puzzled me about that child; she can eat, but I can't understand why she hardly touched my Mrs. chicken. And the Mrs. can really get down with some fried chicken, you see."

"Huh! Well thanks Pops – you don't know how much I appreciate what you and the Mrs. done."

On that note, Pops Belder was on his way to the exit. If one looked hard enough, you could see part of that stoop in Pops back straightend out. A load had definitely been lifted from his shoulders. Ilique headed to his classroom, where he knew Tashanesha would be; coming in early, with Pops and all. He could see the grief on the child's face as he entered the door.

Ilique and Tashanesha were tight, but this morning they were real tight-real close; not an inch of space was between them. Janetqua saw them from a distance, as she accidently nosed down the hall. She saw them embraced in each other's arm; Ilique was rubbing Tashanesha's back gingerly. Janetqua's sharp cornered mouth fell open. She sought not to disturb this union, this secret, she thought; a grown teacher screwing around with one of his students; a thirteen year old. Janetqua now understood why this young girl's breast had become full and sensuous; why her body had suddenly rounded out into shapely curves. This child, she thought, with jealous detestation, is finer than I have

337

ever been. "Ilique, the dog," Janetqua said to herself, "was loving on this poor girl, the way loose words thereabout, had him loving Renatra and LaQueeta. Janetqua could not wait to tell her friend Sherri Kelton, her latest discovery; running down the hallway, entering Sherri's room.

"Sherri, wait until you hear what I just found out; you are not going to believe your ears."

"What is it Janetqua; slow down, you are talking much too fast. Catch your breath; have you been running or something?"

"Okay, Sherri, but you better sit down!"

"No Janetqua, I think you are the one who needs to sat down."

"Okay Sherri, I warned you." And without pausing. "Ilique is screwing Tashanesha."

"He is what!"

"Yes Sherri, I just found out. They were hugging and kissing on each other in his room, only moments ago; and probably, still doing so. Ilique had his hands holding her behind, as if more than that was about to take place. I know he thought his door was completely closed; that girl should never be at school this early."

"Janetqua, are you sure you are right; that is serious. Are you sure it was not Renatra; they are about the same size, you know."

"I am telling you what I saw Sherri; my eyes would not lie to me."

"I cannot believe it; I cannot believe it Janetqua!"

"Well, you better start believing it, because it is the truth Sherri."

"That is incredible; that dirty bastard; that poor innicent girl!"

"What do you mean Sherri - poor innocent girl – she did not look like she was suffering to me."

"And we were just talking the other day, how that young girl was looking so fine Janetqua. Ilique and Tashanesha; I still cannot believe it."

"What are you going to do Sherri?

"I don't know; this is dangerous stuff. Clara A. Feldon should know about this Janetqua."

"She is not going to do anything; you forget, Ilique is going with her mother."

"That is true, but she still should know; this is her school, you know. I think you should tell her what you saw Janetqua."

"You are out of your mind Sherri; I am not telling that heifer anything. If she cannot control things in her school, that is her problem. She will find out soon enough, I'm sure."

Janetqua was not going to tell Clara A. Feldon because this was news for Sauninger T. Metfield. She wasted no time, calling him later that morning, and telling him the same thing, she had told Sherri. Metfield thanked her for the information, telling her what a fine job she was doing.

36

In the meantime, Ilique had calmed Tashanesha down, and they went to Clara A. Feldon's office. Clara took matters into her own hands, volunteering her place as a temporary residence for the child. The baby, Tashanesha told them, belonged to "slow George," but he did not know she was pregnant yet. At least, the right person knew the truth in this situation, but by lunch, Ilique was getting another rap laid on him from Renatra to LaQueeta.

"You mean – Mr. Frog man and you Renatra – is really -."

"Yeah girl, we got it going on, and with that action of his, he really got it going on. When he zap my clit with that frog tongue of his, I feel like I'm heaven bound. He has that sticky-wicky action."

"I never would have figured Ilique for that Renatra, but I guess it does make sense. Sticky-wicky huh – sounds interesting."

"Yeah girl, and that's not all; I have an orgasm in record time when he merely flick his tantalizing tongue upon my vaginal lips. I tell you, Mr. Frog-man has a technique that really works LaQueeta."

"It's really good huh?"

"Uh huh – and something else LaQueeta – Ilique acts if though he really loves his work. This sounds awful girl, but I wish you could try him. Anyway I gotta go – see you later."

LaQueeta was more curious than ever now, and decided she would put additional pressure on Ilique to pay more attention to her. She had become lubricated, listening to Renatra tell of how his tongue worked wonders between a girl's thighs. LaQueeta said to herself, "Renatra suggested in passing, she wished I could try him ... but would probably die if she knew I had some of his sticky-wicky. Listening to her talk has made me horny for Frogman and his tongue ... and one way or the other, I'm going to have him licking on my large tender folds. My conscious would be clear too, if I could make it seem like his idea ... well at least I wouldn't feel so bad facing Renatra later on. And if I had him only one time, I would not feel so bad, regardless." LaQueeta was naturally still there when Ilique arrived.

"It is so good to see you Ilique; man you had women hanging all over you at the funeral. Do you find me attractive?

"Sure LaQueeta; why?"

"Oh, I just wondered; I am glad you're tutoring slow George. Can I expect you as usual this week?

"Oh, speaking of slow George, he really needs tutoring now; Clara and I just found out, he has Tashanesha pregnant."

"Then that explains it; that is why her breast is looking so full. So you questioned her about it huh?"

"No, I hadn't exactly noticed all that LaQueeta; she told Pop Belder and he informed me. So that's how you tell huh?"

"That is one of the ways, especially with a girl that young. If you spend some time watching something other than Henrietta, you might just notice a lot of things about women. Better still, talk to me more, and I will educate you on the subject; gotta go Ilique – my time is up."

LaQueeta did not wait or even pause for a reply to her remarks. It had only been made to plant herself on his mind. She also purposely did not mention his contact with their friend Renatra, because that, in her opinion, might scare Ilique away from her. And as she walked away, he did notice her stout shapely body for a change; he had already noticed her large full breast, bulging in her white blouse, before she stood up. Funny, he thought, how he had never noticed LaQueeta's gorgeous body before. He noticed, moreso, out of the conclusion, that he was not very observant, but he did notice.

No sooner than Ilique returned from lunch, he got a call over the intercom from Clara A. Feldon, to meet with her on his first offperiod. Earlier, just prior to lunch, she knew the minute her eyes saw the large brown envelope, it contained trouble. The letter inside, from Sauninger T. Metfield, especially about Tashanesha so quickly, was a surprise though. She, had frowned something terrible as she read these lines:

Dear Ms. Clara A. Feldon:

It has come to my attention, one of your students at the Ordon T. Metfield Junior High school is pregnant, and one of your chosen teachers is responsible. While I do not intend to belittle your ability, this is a direct reflection on your ability to lead a school the caliber of an Ordon T. Metfield. And unless you can show justification to the contrary; disciplinary action will be forth coming from my office.

This is a serious matter Ms, Feldon, and your immediate attention is warranted. I expect to hear your corrective action within forty-eight hours.

Sincerely,
Sauninger T. Metfield

342

Metfield had sealed this envelope with a smile, knowing it would not be long before a male, Dulique C. Gildor would be in charge of the renowned Ordon T. Metfield Junior High. Clara read the letter with the disgust that she had for S.T. Metfield, as she recently, come to call him. She was still fuming when Ilique arrived.

"There is a snitch in this school Ilique; did you notice anyone when you were comforting Tashanesha this morning?"

"It wasn't exactly the time Clara, that you would look around to see if something else is happening!"

"Okay – okay, but you see what I am saying; this response from S.T. arrived as if he was here himself."

"Well, what are you going to do Clara; you know you can't just keep Tashanesha as a runaway, especially with S.T. on your trail."

"Yeah, I thought of that; I will talk the entire situation over with Rory tonight. And please do not mention anything about this to mother; I do not want her to be worrying about me and my problems."

"For tonight and maybe for the week you're safe Clara."

"Why is that?"

"Let's just say, your mother knows a fellow's normal reactions, once he's filled with her love."

"Oh really." Clara wanted to give out a hearty laugh; knowing after the Helene affair, her mother had put something extra on poor young Ilique. Things she had taught her. She did exchange a smile with Ilique as he left for home.

And speaking of home; as Pops Belder headed for home tonight, he could not help but think about Tashanesha, especially as he refueled his car "at the corner." High intensity street lamps lit up the area; it looked if though it was daylight. The women's restroom door constantly opened as passersby's, both men and women, convenienced themselves. Water ran from the doorway of the men's toilet. Surely, thought Pops, that toilet recently malfunctioned and is not an every day occurrence. His curiousity peaked though when he saw, at times, a man and woman

343

entering together. Public accomodations here had assumed a new connotation. Nightbugs swarmed from the lights and crawled swiftly to avoid taking on the inevitable dead – cockroach look. A strutting pair of three-inch heels, swinging on the arms of a corner Casanova, appeared to be the nightcrawlers only enemies though. Occupants of the four corner benches were stretched out, it looks, for the night. Other vagrants merely sat or lay nearby upon the red-bricked sidewalks.

The liquor store across the street was closed, but the loitering and drinking had not ceased. Bottles and cans were clutched by, their dark hands as laughter rang about. There was no sadness here. Voices talked above voices – above voices – above – voices – chatter which quickly blended into the light evening air, as did the thick smoke from their cigarettes. Scents of Winston, Chesterfields, Pall Mall, Lucky Strike, Camel, and the like, filled the air, but from where Pops Belder stood, there were only fumes of gasoline. Pop's thought; where was Tashanesha standing, on those nights, before he and the Mrs. took her in. He focused his eyes across to the other corner, where there was a long line of patrons at the chicken carryout. No one appeared to be leaving, so a brand-new batch of fried thighs, wings, and breasts were probably sizzling in that hot grease. There was no doubt, some gizzards too, because that is what Pops always ordered.

It now dawned on Pops Belder, where Tashanesha was, some of the time, and why she had no taste for chicken on that Monday night. A frown crossed his face slowly and dissappeared with a smile as his taste buds began to act up. Maybe, he would surprise the Mrs. with her favorite order of wings and large peppers. Somehow, the chicken just did not taste right without those hot jalapeno peppers; even the gizzard basket. The timing would be right when he left the grocery store on the diagonal corner. His instructed list called for milk, eggs, bread, and bacon, "if he wanted breakfast the next morning." Pops Belder said hello to the all night security guard as he left the grocer. Nearby, sprawled near the shopping carts were two

344

homeless-helpless type people. They were not in the way of the customers, so the guard let them lie. What a caring guard thought Pops; he wondered if the same guard had watched over Tashanesha, feeding her batches and batches of that hot fried chicken. The world is not all bad he thought, there are still a few that really care.

37

And as time moved on, a week or so later; and after another unsuccessful encounter with Ilique, LaQueeta was determined and hornier than ever to meet with him this evening; obviously, a tutoring session to Ilique. From all indications of their phone conversations, she thought his jitters were over, and she would finally have him caressing her body in the same manner as Renatra's. Somehow, LaQueeta had assumed Ilique to be nervous around her lately. She could feel his long froggy-sticky tongue upon her as she slid out of her panties; her nude breast brushed against the venetian blinds when she looked through the window, to make sure his car was still on the parking lot. This was not eactly how LaQueeta wanted to have Ilique, but it was better than nothing; she would have him at her place later, when he was not so skittish.

"Just think," LaQueeta said to herself, "a man that is afraid of loving me, all because of loving my friend. If it had not been for her, I would have had that sucker, no harm intended, sliding his head between my luscious thighs a long time ago. I really hate doing this to Renatra, but I'm entitled to his kisses too; after all she knew, down deep, that I wanted Ilique as bad as she did. And she should not have deliberately told me how he was licking and eating on her. When I have had enough of that sucker, I will tell her all about it; damn, I'm getting wet already." LaQueeta glanced at her watch, noting half past the hour, and quickly rolled the fold-up cot from the closet; opening and pouncing on it, lying seductively upon her back, legs gapped widely, facing the door. One of her hands massaged her breast as she patiently waited Ilique's entrance.

The knock on the door sent a clear loud yell from her:

"Come on in Ilique, make yourself comfortable." Her eyes were closed.

"Girl – what the hell are you doing?"

"What are you doing here – Renatra?"

"Trying to deliver a damn message from Ilique; he told me to tell you, something came up. Are you and that rascal sneaking around on me LaQueeta?"

"This is the first time ever," Renatra's mind spoke instantly, "that I have peered into a crimson creamy cavity of another woman; and wow, LaQueeta's rosy red wet lips are damn near intriguing – almost excitable – almost kissable ..." She smiled caressingly at the sight of LaQueeta's nudity.

"No Renatra, it's not as bad as it looks; obviously he had never planned to show up, after promising me an extra tutoring session for slow George. I was desperate to make him love me the way, you say, he has been loving you. You will have to forgive me, but your talk made me so horny for some of his froggy-tongue action. So, this evening I was pretending a session for slow George, when it was to really trick Ilique into loving me."

Renatra started laughing at LaQueeta's puzzled stare.

"Get your clothes on LaQueeta; I will tell you about that damn Ilique over a drink. It appears we both need one. Meet you on the parking lot; I have to get something from my classroom."

In the restaurant, no sooner than the first round of drinks arrived, Renatra confessed.

"Girl, I have been lying to you, big time."

"What do you mean Renatra?"

"Well, I lied about the whole thing; I made all those sexual episodes up LaQueeta."

"Girl, you mean that sucker has not been licking on you!"

"That is what I'm telling you LaQueeta, and I tried everything, short of forcing it down his throat."

"As I was about to do huh?"

"You got it girl, and I have been leaning in that direction, here lately. Nothing I tried worked. Well, I did get a couple of rocks talking to him on the telephone; and to be honest, a few more, reading his sexy letter over and over again. A little self-gratification, if you know what I mean LaQueeta. I did not think the frogman would be such a tough nut to crack."

"It must be that old broad he's seeing; probably sucking the life out of the poor boy. I have heard Renatra that older women can make a young man do anything she wants. I wonder what Clara's mother is doing to him."

"Whatever it is LaQueeta, it seems to be working."

"What did he say when he told you he couldn't meet me Renatra?"

"Said he was going home, something came up."

"Let's call his house and see what's going on Renatra."

"Girl, that is stupid to do something like that ... let's do it!"

"There's no answer; I bet he is over to that old lady's house Renatra."

"Yeah, and we don't have her number ... that Ilique is a lucky bastard tonight LaQueeta."

"Especially the way he stood me up ... had me lying around – with my legs all sprawled apart on some raggedy old cot."

"You were gapped open real good ... I could see clear up to your stomach, LaQueeta ... he definitely missed out on not being there."

"And he missed out on something good ... girl, I was already wet."

"And think what Ilique has missed, by not taking me up on any of my offers LaQueeta."

"Either we're doing something wrong Renatra or there is some real truth to that myth about older women and young men."

"Hell, he's a boy compared to Henrietta; she's got to be in her upper forties LaQueeta."

"Renatra, I would give anything to know what she is doing to that poor soul."

"I don't see why LaQueeta; after all, I was the one who made up all those good love stories."

"You are right; they were believable stories too Renatra ... had me horny as I have ever been ... you and your lying ass!"

"All I can say LaQueeta, you're lucky I'm experiment shy or I would have your rosy red wet lips crawling up the wall by now ... that old cot would not have been big enough for you."

"Girl, I wouldn't let those three or four drinks load your ass with more than it can carry ... I can handle whatever your mind thought of dishing out Renatra."

"Well, I'm not drunk enough to not know a challenge when I hear one LaQueeta."

"Girl, you don't know nothing ... just all lip service, like that Ilique thing. If I didn't think you were kidding, I would take you up on it and show you a few things ... Lord knows I'm horny enough."

"Tell you what LaQueeta, let's take a cold shower together and see if we still feel that way afterward ... I'm curious to know if you can compensate for my lies on Ilique."

"Oh I don't know Renatra; you're a novice and I know it ... what the heck ... what do we have to lose – our virginity!"

They both laughed, leaving the restaurants's bar, and ended up in the showers at Renatra's apartment. The lukewarm shower did not dissuade either of their minds as they stood facing each other, washing the other's breast for starters ... still not really into what was really happening; at least Renatra wasn't. Their soft hands felt extremely good lathering each other's breast ... so much in fact, their nipples hardened and their breast began to swell. For the first time tonight their eyes met and they embraced, rubbing the other's round buttocks. Warm water vibrated against their faces as their fingers meticulously massaged each other's twirling buttocks. Their throbbing vaginas had already responded to their own wetness. Their bodies felt good clamped together, tingling all over.

"Come on Renatra, let's finish showering and get in the bed before we fall and kill ourselves."

When they crawled into bed, they continued to embrace, not rushing anything, just caressing the other's body with their soft hands, and kissing the other on the side of their necks. Then they alternated, kissing each other's breast and finally allowing their tongues to touch as their lips met. They were amazed at how smooth they operated with each other and how exciting their bodies were becoming. Renatra eventually emerged on top, whispering to LaQueeta:

"Are you ready to climb that wall girl?"

She said nothing, but Renatra knew she was ready by the loud sighs she made; plus she could smell LaQueeta's sweet aroma. It reminded her of earlier, when she came through the door and saw LaQueeta's luscious vaginal opening staring her in the mouth. It never dawned on her at that moment, this lovely hunk of flesh with these large folds would be hers to caress; even now the thought seemed unthinkable.

It's several weeks later, and during that time, things had been going well for Clara A. Feldon and Ordon T. Metfield Junior High. Tashanesha was now living with her new guardian, Clara;

and slow George had been made aware of his new responsibility. So, between Ilique doing the tutoring – real father type tutoring and Clara's new mothering duties, there was not much for Sauninger T. Metfield to meddle her about. Well, that was until this morning, when a new brown envelope found itself in Clara A. Feldon's hands. The letter inside was bold and direct.

Dear Clara A. Feldon:
Helene Scott is pregnant by your chosen teacher, Ilique K. Fernfort. Under no conditions will I tolerate teachers getting teachers pregnant at the great Ordon T. Metfield Junior High School. Your job is terminated immediately if this supposedly reliable information, which has just come to my attention, is true.

Sincerely,
Sauninger T. Metfield

By pure coincidence, late yesterday, Janetqua caught helpless in the restroom stall in dire need of a sanitary napkin, asked the party outside:

"Whoever is there, please get me a napkin from that wall machine?"

"Janetqua, is that you girl?"

"Hey Helene, I was in a tight when I ran in here without my purse; let me borrow one from you."

"Sorry girl, I'll have no need of those for awhile."

"Helene, I did not know you were pregnant!"

"Nobody does girl; it's no secret though."

"Who is the lucky guy Helene; anybody I know?"

"That's the secret part Janetqua, but between you and me, it's Ilique."

"I thought that was Clara's mother's stuff Helene."

"It is girl, but you know, things happen."

"I'd say, they do indeed Helene."

"Yeah, keep that under your hat girl."

"Don't worry about it Helene, it's safe with me."

And Janetqua probably meant what she said at the time, but her mind during the night turned and churned on thoughts which could help her move up; so the first thing this morning, she called Sauninger T. Metfield with the information.

"Are you sure that is correct Janetqua; Helene is really pregnant by this guy, Ilique?"

"I heard it from the horse's mouth Mr. Metfield; you bet it's correct!"

Well, without saying, Clara A. Feldon was in shock; called Helene who quickly verified it to be true. Then she called Ilique, who knew nothing about it. Then she called her mother.

"Mother, that Helene is pregnant with Ilique's baby!"

"Don't sound so excited Clara."

"This is serious; Metfield just threatened to fire me. Do you think Helene is lying?"

"Probably so; you and I both know, Helene loves excitement and living on the edge of things. I understand your predicament honey; stall for time. Tell Metfield, she is pregnant, but it's not Ilique's."

"But if it turns out to be a lie mother – do you realize – I'll be fired!"

"You were going to be fired anyway – remember – without real proof. That Helene is up to something, I'm telling you. This is probably part of that threat to Ilique, remember?"

"Oh yeah; mother I had completely forgotten about that."

"That's the trouble with you youngsters; your minds are too short."

"Well, it has been over a month mother; I wish you weren't leaving town just now."

"Me too, but Ilique really needs the air, if I'm going to hang onto him for the long term. It will probably hurt him when he finds out, but I'll make him understand tonight."

And so it was, later on that night, Henrietta explained her position to Ilique.

Jewel E. Dearman

"Ilique, if we are going to have any kind of a meaningful relationship, you are going to need space for growth. My leaving has nothing to do with Helene; that in my opinion is part of your growth. And because of your age, this will be good for us both, if we are to have something between us in the future. I am leaving Ilique because I do not live here; hopefully it will be temporary. That however is up to you after your growth period. This is not goodbye, but goodluck; use some of the things I taught you. It should even help you with your book. Remember, if you still feel the same after your growth period, I'll be there. If it's meant to be Ilique, it will happen. You have my number and address, but please do not use them as a crutch; I will not allow that."

Ilique seemed if though he understood as they quietly and slowly removed each garment and their nude bodies appeared. Moments of kissing her breast and she gently nudged his head downward, onto her waiting gourmet dish. He slid his tongue round and round the tightly squeezed oblong puffiness before gently touching its center, then pity-patting it with the tip of his tongue, until it gapped open – contracting, pulling the stiff object inside. Henrietta wanted to savor this moment, so she pulled Ilique back to her breast for some more of his mouth and tongue manipulation of her sensitive nipples. She wanted tonight to be one of multiple orgasms and she wanted them to come slowly and continuous, like many of their others.

Ilique heard Henrietta gasping as he slid his fingers through the wetness of her soft folds, pressing and gently rubbing her swollen clit. Suddenly she thrust her head backward into the pillow, arching her buttocks upward, sending his hand sailing; pulling his mouth downward, where his protruding tongue eased gracefully into her extremely wet vaginal opening; deep at first, while his tongue searched thoroughly and his nose nudged and played with her clit. Then onto the surface where his rambling tongue licked her puffy wet lips and clitoris simultaneously. Over and over and over, his tongue slushed into her groove and under her large swollen clit. Wider and wider her lips became as her peak neared; she joyfully felt the warm smooth movement inside of her and she wanted more. She wanted it deeper, and used the muscles of her interior walls to pull him deeper and deeper. Breathing and sighs became louder and she wanted her clit massaged by his mesmerizing tongue some more; she wanted it deep, she wanted it deeper, she wanted it massaged, she wanted it all. Henrietta twisted her bottom and twisted her overheated and widely spreaded saturated vulva in his face, getting everything she wanted.

No sounds came out of Ilique's mouth but those tongue lashes against, upon and through her tender succulent flesh. An orgasm was near as his tongue caressed her to perfection, bringing her to a point of screams and nerve ending – toe-tightening yells. Time was near and they both knew it was time; time for his long bigness, which she had observed all the time. Each time he raised his head for air, she saw his long rod helping prop up and stabilized his weakened knees, as she begged for more and more. The perfect time for entry was after a few more moments of tongue swishes under her clit, where she was most excitable, which brought Henrietta to total exhaustion and a real genuine craving for Ilique's large throbbing tool. Multiple orgasms were now occurring as Ilique devoured her tender sweet flesh with a relentless vigorness; Henrietta's vaginal folds gapped and flapped around his cheeks as his mouth ate her gourmet dish to their gratification. Her seemingly life threatening screams flowed into Ilique's ears almost as fast as her succulent juices down his throat. She knew Ilique was now in charge and let him have his way; as long as she could supply him with her magnificent substance, she promised to let him eat. Maybe, she thought, it was a mistake telling Ilique she was leaving. Her throat dried from screaming and calling his name, but her orgasms continued to be enjoyed by Ilique; he continued to eat nonstop. He was eating her gourmet dish more ways than she ever imagined, touching and caressing sensitive spots which, she never knew existed. Right now Henrietta felt if she died, she would be the most joyful angel in Heaven; and at times she felt

354

so sharp a stings streaking toward her heart, it might just happen. Henrietta was still profusely producing, but now began to wonder if the young man was too powerful for her; it was either that or her stuff was getting better by the minute. Just as her screams heightened for a finality and tremors were going through her thighs, she felt Ilique's strong hand grasp her buttocks. He lifted her legs upward over his shoulders, slowly easing his large tool inside; first the smooth round tip and then, slower and slower he glided deeper and deeper as she gasped for new breath. She felt his bigness on all sides as she gyrated her behind, pushing backward, until he had thrust the entire tool homeward. Only a few seconds expired before they had their orgasms together, falling asleep, totally gratified and exhausted.

And with that lasting performance, Henrietta was on her way home. Home for Henrietta was Correa, Maine, a small lobster, harbor town. The town's environment and its clean fresh air obviously had been good for her health, preserving that youthful beauty; she looked no older than her daughter Clara. Oh, she did not act the part of a bouncy young girl, but that is what Ilique loved about her; not to mention the goodness of her gourmet dish, and the way she made him hunger for her so bad. She did things, he thought, only a real woman could do, and he was willing to try anything she suggested to keep her. Their feelings of each other were mutual, but Henrietta wanted to make sure Ilique knew what he was doing. She knew Ilique had been pussy-whipped devouring her gourmet dish. She also knew she was taking a chance on losing someone she truly loved, but she was banking on her magic formula: Cook those good meals for your man ... tell him how you expect to be loved ... sit back and enjoy yourself while he eats.

Henrietta had to admit though, Ilique had put some magic of his own on her. He reminded her of the huge lobsters back home as they squirmed in the boiling water and later as she tasted the sweet fresh meat crossing her tongue. Yes, she saw Ilique as her complete package, especially since he was her quick learning pupil; performing miraculously, giving her multiple extra-

355

ordinary orgasms each and every time he crawled between her gorgeous thighs. Anyway, Ilique was left to fend for himself; thrown back to the beauties of the world; the Renatra's, the LaQueeta's, the Helene's, the others.

Henrietta had tried to minimize her daughter's principal problems of Helene's pregnancy, but once home, instinctively, the mother's protective mechanism slowly surfaced. And deep down, though she would never admit it, thinking of it bothered her. A thought or two, if it was Ilique's child; what effect it would have on her future possession of him. She still believed in her love theory, though unexpected elements could make it difficult. Staying busy always help, she thought, and this prompted her to go through Henri's personal items; in particular, a bag from the doctor's office. The watch she had given him for his birthday, five years earlier was there, amazingly on time, she thought, as she glanced at an identical timepiece on her wrist. Henrietta smiled of the precious memories, marveling at how Henri always treasured her gifts. Continuing, nonchalantly, rum-

357

maging through pockets of a suit produced an envelope, iron-ically sealed and addressed to her. It read:

My Dearest & Sweetest Henrietta:

At this moment I am the happiest person in the world. Girl, I know I should have told you, but I have been quite busy with my new lifestyle. Don't laugh now sis because you told me so, and I know you're going to be happy for me too when you read the next sentence. I met this girl, yes this girl; introduced by none other than your sweet daughter, my one and only sweet neice. Let me tell you, she is hot; her name is Helene Scott. She is a young twenty-three year old, but does she ever know what I need. I know you're laughing now because you told me about hot numbers like this. Just between you and me, the girl has been making me do and enjoy things I never dreamed of doing, especially to a girl. She has been making me eat her darkhollow; that's what she calls that gorgeous cavity between her beautiful thighs. I know you're cracking up by now my dear sister, but her darkhollow is so good and tasty; I never imagined a woman could be so delicious. One day I must have eaten it at least twenty times, and if that sounds like an exaggeration, it's probably a conservative count. (Smile). Helene can do things to my body, guys can do, and a hell of a lot better. I am so happy; she is knocking my eye-sockets out with the loving techniques she's laying on me.

It looks like our close guarded secret of my coming out of the closet is safe for now. Please pray for me Henrietta, because I know, down deep, you have always wanted this for me, though you have always loved me for being me. Also, pray for my recent headaches to go away; I have a doctor's appointment to-morrow. Probably caused by my new lifestyle, huh; burying my head too deep in Helene's darkhollow, perhaps. (Smile). I see what you mean now by a woman hooking a guy with that vagina of hers, if it's good and he loves it; especially if he loves it. And let me tell you this, as if you don't know already; it takes a certain kind of woman to make you love it. From day one,

Helene told me what she expected; and of course, when I found out how good it made her feel and how good and tasty it was, I was sold or as you say "hooked." Good thing for me, huh? A new secret for you girl; Helene's darkhollow taste better than honey; its mushy-gushy, and sweet syrupy-sticky. (Giggle).

Sis, I know I tell you all the time, "I love you," and I know it sounds so redundant by now, but I really and honesty want to tell you now; I love you so much for standing with me all these years.

Love Always and Forever
Your ever loving brother
Henri

P.S. Had to unseal this letter. Helene came by and told me what we both expected; her doctor says she's pregnant. More on this later girl; you know I'm sho-nough happy now. This is too much; girl I'm happy. Will call you tomorrow, as soon as I leave the doctor's office. Get use to being called aunt. (Smile).

I love you again!
Bye

Henrietta was all tears; precious happy tears. This was indeed enlightening and beneficial news; good news, she would be an aunt and that Henri was happy when his time on earth ceased. She sensed something going on, not quite right with Helene, and now she knew. Meanwhile, as if mental telepathy had roots, Helene was thinking of Henrietta real hard; deep inside she really envied her, partly or mostly because of Ilique. Helene had got to feeling bad about the lasting trouble she could cause with this untruthful pregnancy. The remarks she had made especially the threats to Ilique. The betrayal of Henrietta, who had taken to her so kindly, was becoming disturbing and the thought of losing Clara's friendship forever would devastate her. So there was only one thing to do; start apologizing immediately. Henrietta would get the first call:

"Why hello Helene, I was just thinking about you in the worst way."

"If worst is bad, I deserve those kinds of thoughts, for what I've done; the baby I'm carrying really belong to your brother Henri."

"Yes I know Helene; I just finished reading his letter. It was in his jacket pocket. A bitter-sweet letter for me to read because he expressed how you were changing his living habits and how happy he was when you told him of his child on the way."

"That is the truth Henrietta; please accept my apology for lying on Ilique, but I was afraid of bringing his baby into the world, especially if it is a boy. The thought of that became scary, and I sort of lost myself in future embarrasing situations, if you follow me."

"Not really, but go on!"

"You see Henrietta, I did not love Henri; I was just playing around, trying to prove to myself that I could change this fine hunk of a man – his lifestyle you see. I never intended to get pregnant though, and I am sorry if I ran you out of town."

"Oh, I accept your apology Helene, and you did not run me out of town. I left because of personal reasons; well, I can tell you. Ilique feel he's in love with me, and I feel he needs more experience, to really be sure. It's no secret, I'm older than him, and might have overwhelmed him with a thing or two."

"Yeah, but don't you stand a chance of losing him Henrietta, if you really care for him?"

"No, not really Helene, because like you I have confidence in my ability on men, especially the ones that I want. Matter of fact I don't have any hard feelings on you loving him that night. He needs that, and more, if he is to even think about spending the rest of his days with an older woman ... do you follow me?"

"I understand, but you could be playing with your life; there are a lot of women out here Henrietta who might give you a real battle."

"True; those are precisely my intentions. Listen Helene, I know you want to apologize to Ilique, so I'll call and tell him you're coming by tonight. Oh, he might need some extra convincing on the apology, so do what you have to do. And don't worry about me; like I said earlier, he needs the experience."

"Okay Henrietta, it's your life."

Helene hung the phone up and immediately began to feel Ilique's hands upon her as he had comforted her during the funeral. Tingling sensations drifted through her darkhollow as she recalled that stormy night. She could not believe Henrietta had just given her approval to seduce him. "As horny as I feel right now," she said to herself, "getting him to do anything, even kiss me, would be a sweet male relief." Helene's pregnancy had made her sexually extra sensitive and she had been quelling it with a bit of self-pleasuring.

Later, when Ilique met her at his door, he turned agitatedly and flopped down on his sofa. Helene followed and did the same, right beside him.

"Please accept my apology Ilique. I lied, plain and simple, and I'm so sorry." Her warm hands now rested upon his and she looked directly into his eyes.

"Why Helene; how could you accuse me ... you don't love me ... I do know that much!"

"So true Ilique, but during the funeral, I felt you inside of me, and I don't regret that part of it. Henrietta has forgiven me; she says the experience is good for you; that and more, to quote her directly."

Yeah, she thinks I need some more experience to prevent a serious mistake with her."

"What do you think Ilique?"

"I don't know ... she could be right. Anyway, Henrietta says she is not coming back until she feels I have it."

"Well, I could help ... somewhat ... you know."

"Boy, you sure don't waste any time, do you Helene? Besides, you're pregnant."

"Well, when you are as horny as I am Ilique, time is not the thing to waste; and for your information, pregnant pussy is the best kind, it's much much warmer."

"What crude language Helene, and you never paused when you said it."

"Why should I, but if you like, you can refer to my goodness as your sweet darkhollow."

"Sweet huh ... how would you know about something like that?"

"Well – I should know my own stuff – shouldn't I? You'll tell me how sweet it is yourself, later on."

"You think so huh? You sound so confident Helene."

"That's my nature. Tell me Ilique, is there any paticular experience Henrietta had in mind?"

"Who knows, that whole thing is confusing ... my youth and all, she says. Of course, she was supposed to be helping me write a book on oral sex."

"You are kidding; I love me some head Ilique!"

"Girl, you are really crude; and it wasn't exactly that way ... it was sort of for the guys ... that wondered about it – you know. Henrietta was – sort of teaching me – you know."

"Well – well – well, that's even better Ilique; like I said you'll love my sweet darkhollow. I can teach you everything you need to know about going down on a chic. You shouldn't sound so shy when you mention someone teaching you something like that; you aren't afraid to learn, are you?"

"No, not at all Helene."

"Well, this is your lucky day Ilique. I would have never figured you for wanting to know about crawling between these gorgeous thighs of mine. Like I said, you're going to love eating this pussy of mine."

"I can't get over how forward you are Helene."

"Well, that's the first step to being successful Ilique. You can't be bashful at a thing like this, but I'm sure you know that already. Because I'm sure you know a little something already. Anyway, don'y worry about it, 'cause I'm going to love giving you all the experience Henrietta wants you to have. You are really fortunate to have an experienced lady like me in this capacity."

Helene thought; this was working out far better than if she had planned it herself. She had taught one man how to eat her sweet darkhollow, and he had gone and left her pregnant, horny, and without a replacement. Now, here she was, being asked, practically begged, to teach another man to do what she really loved; volunteer his tongue to sensationalize her body.

"Why Ilique, I had no idea you were off into that type of lovemaking!"

"Well, I want to learn ... you see ... a lot of brothers want to, but they are fearful ... and I want to be able to tell them in my book what to expect. What or how to do it ... and well, how to approach the lady, when that's on his mind."

"Hmmm ... you are so smart Ilique ... getting first hand experience is the way to go. The approach part is the easiest – usually you just slide in that direction, and she'll stop you if the answer is no. That will not happen here – stopping that is. I want you to know, teaching you how to eat my darkhollow will be extremely easy, if you're the willing subject you say you are. Because that is the first step; you guys got to want to eat the pussy – oh I'm sorry Ilique – some habits are just hard to break."

"Yeah, I see."

39

Helene was more than willing to help Ilique in such an important adventure; offering additional pointers to show her keen interest.

"The curious fellow is the one you could really help in this area Ilique."

"How's that?"

"Well, basically by telling them not to be afraid of trying; they just might like it. Oh – and in your case, you should plan on much practice if you want to get it down right Ilique. Of course, I will let you know when that long awaited time comes.I feel this is going to work out much better than I ever thought it would; are you sure this is what you want This does not sound like you at all."

"I know, but Henrietta thinks I should roam around a little."

"I'm all for you to roam around in my pussy Ilique, but I would not let Henrietta do my thinking. I mean – I would never talk you out of doing what I love, but -."

"Then don't Helene; it's what Henrietta believes is best for me, so -."

"So you're going to be stupid and do it for that dumb reason."

"I love that woman Helene and believe in what she tells me."

"I'm trying to warn you Ilique; because once you bury that head of yours deep in my darkhollow, you're going to be in trouble. You might just forget Henrietta, is what I'm saying."

"Maybe – I'm glad to see you so confident; I have that same confidence, you know."

"Well – just thought I'd warn you Ilique. You certainly won't hear me say anything else to turn you against your friend. Especially since your decision is so much in my favor."

"I understand."

"And just between the two of us Ilique, I'm going to do everything I can to make you enjoy crawling between these thighs of mine. You certainly will not regret Henrietta's decision if I can say it like that."

"That's fair enough with me Helene."

"Just don't go licking on me like I'm your Henrietta; I prefer to teach you the hot zones on my body. All women are different, you know, plus there's certain little things I like that makes me feel extra special."

"Different huh!"

"Yeah – you'll see what I'm talking about when that tongue of yours start that roaming; probably what Henrietta had reference to. She wanted you to experience something different. I can see her point too, because when you ultimately settle down with her, your mind shouldn't wander or wonder about other gorgeous women, you're bound to meet. The girl is taking a chance though."

"You think so huh?"

"Sure is Ilique, because there is some good pussy out here in these streets, and mine just happen to be one of them. You'll see. Don't look so sad; I'll be one of the best treats you ever had. You will tell me as much later on, when I'm done teaching you. Yeah – you'll be wanting to eat some of my good stuff every day; that's just how good I am."

"We'll see."

"Put yourself in reserve Ilique, not me, cause I know what I'm talking about. You'll see when we're done showering; matter of fact, you'll see before then."

And Helene was right. With the soothing warm water hitting their bodies, she slid down his front to her knees, holding her palms to his buttocks until she was comfortably in place. Then her palms cupped his scrotum sac, massaging his jewels. Even the splashing sound of the water could not drown out the mellow sighs of Ilique. He felt energy going into his body as she continued her massaging with one hand and softly squeezing his penis with the other. So much strength was going into Ilique that his throbbing rod felt as hard as a frozen slab of baby back ribs. And almost simultaneously, she had him inside of her cheeks, vigorously massaging him some more.

Poor Ilique was holding onto the showerhead making strange vocal sounds well above the noise of the water. She tightened her palm around his scrotum, squeezing gently, but firmer and firmer. Ilique was gasping and hissing simultaneously. Her lubricative lips slid out and in over his knob; everytime outward, she engineered her tongue into a zapping-licking-twirling, non-stop motion upon it. Helene could feel his tension; his hardness felt good inside of her. She was loving his reaction. It was making her excited; she did not know if she would be able to wait on Ilique's tongue. His screaming and yelling was getting to her; suddenly her enjoyment was overwhelming. She heard her name between the hissing; she could feel him giving way; she could feel herself giving way. He was making so much racket with his high pitched screams and sighs, that she deep throated him for the first time, gripping both hands around his buttocks.

Ilique cried out horrendously; Helene's warmth and grip was overbearing. Never before had his body and brain been so pressurized; so into a sensation. Gushes were flowing everywhere; he was gushing, Helene was gushing. This was the first time Helene had ever had an orgasm while holding onto a penis. Yes, her first and she enjoyed it immensly. She said to herself. "The exchange was still unfair because I'm enjoying this man's stream of goodness ... damn it's warm – it's good – it's filling. I bet poor Ilique has never had it so good, and to be honest – me neither. I could really get use to eating this guy, with all his carrying on ... damn I come ... I come... can you believe that. His juices are so good." And Helene strained and drained poor Ilique as he swung on the showerhead. Unintentionally, Helene was leeching the life out of poor Ilique as she was steady coming herself. Finally, Ilique's knees gave out and the water pounded upon them as she still held on to his throbbing and still productive knob. Helene was enjoying herself; they both were still coming. Neither wanted this to end. And suddenly she thought of something sort of wild.

Helene was imaginative enough to do the darndest thing with her sexy body. She pulled Ilique from the water, sitting on top of the commode tank top, inviting him to sat on the commode seat facing her sumptous looking darkhollow. He could do no more than send his tongue caressing her outer lips, but that was exactly the teasing Helene wanted. Ilique could taste her flowing sweetness immediately; the exotic flavorful juices and tenderness of a seasonable honeydew melon, he thought. She had often wanted to come with a tender tongue touching and teasing of her vagina's surface layers. Her imagination had told her, it would be nice, and she found that right now to be correct. It feels like the real thing, she thought. It is the real thing, she thought, as Ilique now had it going on, licking her swollen lips to ecstasy. She could feel the curls and swipes of his tongue, along with her expected jubilant juices jamming his jaws. Ilique could not help but swallow and smile at Helene's unique love adventure. To himself, he said. "I love it – I love it."

And just when Ilique thought there was no more to come from Helene, she hopped to the floor, turning him around, straddling her wide vaginal opening onto his throbbing knob, garnering all of his large shaft. She knew she would come several more times, especially if he kept loving her this way. In actuality, it was she who was twirling and swirling her behind. The fullness and hardness, she thought, gives me no choice but to screw the living daylight out of this man.

"Damn – this is good Ilique – damn – this is -." Collapsing around his neck. The timing was perfect because Ilique was with her. She felt his powerful terminating ending thrust and those sudden helter-skelter jerk-jerks, just before he also cried out. Something incoherent to the both of them and unlikely to be repeated until another sensuous-scintilating-sex screwing session-surfaced. And before morning and into the next several weeks, there were numerous repeats of their torrid lovemaking, but it finally came to an abrupt halt.

It seemed almost a shame she thought, to let Ilique off the hook so easy, especially since she had promised to teach him the indulgeness of her sumptuous darkhollow. The thinking was as if she had received no benefit herself. And the truth; she enjoyed his company and he was a fast learner, but he lacked that extra tongue stroke that really set her on fire. Helene wanted the type of unpredictable lip and tongue action that made her sizzle. With more training he could have been a fair lover, she surmised ... but only fair. Men her age, she thought, was probably better off, learning from an older women, than one their own age; older women no doubt had the patience to nurture the young. She was sure however, what Ilique had learned from her would be extremely useful on an inferior being – one entirely unaware of greater expectation.

Besides, Helene knew what she was doing was wrong; infringing upon the rights of Henrietta by dating Ilique. She thought of her unborn child and the child that Uriah's wife bore to David that became ill and died. And though this was in Bibilical times, she thought of how a curse might befall her. She also knew this road was leading nowhere fast and it was time for a change – a prayerful change. And this is where we find her at this moment; asking the Lord to help her find somebody – a man – a good man – a good caring man; a good caring man who is going to help her take care of her child. Helene ended her prayer saying, "Thank you Lord, and please forgive me if I hurt anyone – Henrietta, Ilique, Clara, Henri, - anyone ... and oh – I almost forgot – Lord please help me with my crude language around the men I meet." Within minutes she had fallen asleep, but woke up during the night with things on her mind – sensual things.

Helene knew there was no future with Ilique, and this moment she was overcome with heat of another suitor. She had inquired of Ilique about his cousin, Dulique; when awakened, lying there clothesless in her soft comfortable bed, he was heavily on her mind. Even her shapely legs had kicked the covers into a roll near the foot of the bed, as she allowed Dulique to love her in her thoughts. It was physical. Everything with Helene when it comes to lovemaking is physical. She placed her hands gently, the areas, she knew his hands would be caressing her; smoothly and slowly within her inner thighs, over her labia minora and labia majora; slipping one hand upward to cup and massage her breast. The feeling coming upon her was every bit as sensual as if Dulique was really there. Tomorrow, she promised herself to take steps in making him a reality, but for now her fingers began to touch her nude body, in the places she knew Dulique's tongue would roam. She loved the feel of her sensitive labias; that swollen puffy feel, because she knew he would love the excitement generated when his tongue eased all over them. Helene knew when she screamed, he would aggressively do more; and she now felt his tongue easing inside of her, slowly and thoroughly. She could hear him grunting, as she abruptly locked her thighs around his head, loosely though, giving him the room she knew he needed to fully explore her darkhollow. Her fingers were roving as Dulique's tongue would rove; her fingers slushed gently inside, as she knew his slippery tongue would. Prolonging a climax has never been a strong suit for Helene and she hastened to get one. Her gorgeous thighs were still upward when she slid her extremely moisture filled fingers from her vagina to massage her fiery crimson clitoris. Helene felt Dulique's lips enclose her clit and felt his warm wet tongue gliding all around it. And before he even thought of caressing this sensitive object, she had one big orgasm. Resting comfortably now, with several fingers moving slowly between her saturated vaginal lips, Helene thought of how Dulique would love putting a little light in her darkhollow. And too, she thought, it was a shame he was not here tonight to munch on some of her goodies. She knew he would love what she had to offer and it was up to her to make sure he got that opportunity.

When morning came, Helene found herself in the assistant principal's office, inquiring about maternity leave. Dulique's heart softened when Helene's words and tears of her lost-love surfaced, allowing her to be comforted within his arms. Actually the grief was overbearing and she managed someway, through it all, to ask him to take her home. His warm arms, around her was everything she had hoped ... er ...prayed for. Once inside her apartment, she relaxed – loosening up, becoming jovial; telling Dulique, she never could have made it the last few moments without him. Naturally he told her, he was glad to be of assistance, offering help into the future upon leaving. And whether he meant it or not, Helene called later, that same day, asking him if he could bring her something to eat on his way home. She of course was starving and indeed would be grateful if he could do so, promising to pay for his also, if he was hungry.

When Dulique arrived with two dinners, Helene had time on her side, and made it no secret, she was going to need a replacement for her lately departed love. There was no way, she told him, that she would be able to raise a child alone. To Dulique, she seemed extraordinarily nice; even looked extraordinarily nice with her low cleavage showing blouse. He even noticed a boost in his appetite; eating part of her food. A sensual warmness emanated from his body, perhaps due to close quarters; his eyes became starry. Helene softly complained of stiffness in her shoulders, telling him to rise and massage them. She was surprised; not for the massage, but for the rising bulge in his pants. For tonight, Helene thought, she would be very pleased to have his seemingly large tool inside of her. And before morning, as Dulique did spend the night, she had her wish. This was the beginning of a beautiful relationship, which led to their marriage later on this very month. The one immediate good thing in this wedding was that it temporarily saved Clara A. Feldon from some of old man T. Metfield's pressure.

40

Prior to Helene's marriage however, Renatra and LaQueeta was obviously belabored on another conclusion:

"Girl, let me tell you what I just heard!"

"What is it Renatra?"

"You had better have your seat LaQueeta; this news might just floor you."

"Okay Renatra, lay it on me."

"Do you know LaQueeta, while Ilique was running from us, he has that Helene pregnant."

"You are lying girl ... no you're damn serious, aren't you Renatra? Why that bastard!"

"Uh huh – 'fraid so!"

"Not goody-goody Ilique ...whoever told you that story Renatra is lying on the boy!"

"I could not believe it either LaQueeta, but I heard it from Helene – well – sort of -."

"Sort of – some of that good grapevine gossip – I suppose. Girl, you know you can't believe that shit. Not even if Helene did say it ... with her lying ass. Renatra, you know that Helene will lie just to lie – she loves the excitement it causes – child has been like that ever since I've known her. And for some reason, the girl always, come out on top – people sympathize with her lying ass.

"Look LaQueeta, I'm telling you, the girl is pregnant ...hold it, here she comes now ... look at those large breast and that protruding round ass of hers."

"Hell Renatra, Helene has always had that; we both have that and we're not pregnant. We sisters are just fine like that girl."

"Look a little closer LaQueeta."

"I still cannot see anything different Renatra ...the sister just has a fine body. Even if she said it, believe me, it's not true ... Ilique is definitely not off into that flakey broad."

"Things do happen LaQueeta when men and women get together, you know; their dick get plenty hard and our pussy get plenty wet ... think about it."

"Sure Renatra, but if you remember, Ilique promised us we would have first choice after that old Henrietta dumped him and left town."

"Well, he said that in a jokingly kind of way; or if he just happened to be serious, maybe he forgot LaQueeta, or maybe he got tricked by Helene."

"Now that could be the case Renatra, because men are always getting tricked by women."

"I don't know LaQueeta ... we have not been able to trick him; are you saying Helene is smarter than the both of us?"

"Now you know better than that girl ... look, we are still in the running ... it's just a matter of time Renatra; we'll have Ilique eating on us, big time. Or have you given up?"

"No, not really, but he is such a good friend and we do -."

"We do not have anything going on Renatra, compared to what we can make that man do for us. I thought we both agreed not to get comfortable with each other."

"Well LaQueeta, you're not so bad; I feel real good when you are kissing me on my thighs."

"And I feel good when you are kissing me on mine Renatra, but that's not permanent."

"Nothing is permanent LaQueeta."

"Well, act like it Renatra; we'll get our chance with Ilique."

"Not if he has Helene pregnant!"

"Look girl, you just said, nothing is permanent; we'll trick him into the same thing Renatra."

"I don't want to be pregnant LaQueeta!"

"I know that goofy; I thought we were talking about Ilique crawling between our thighs, doing what we wanted him to do. Have you forgotten what you want him to do Renatra?"

"No LaQueeta, but it seems like it's not going to happen anytime soon."

"Don't dissappoint me Renatra by giving up so easy. You will be thanking me when it happens."

"You sound like you have some kind of a secret formula LaQueeta."

"Girl, what ever happened to your confidence … remember when you use to be the one saying, it was a sure bet on having Ilique's lips wrapped around those juicy folds of yours. Whatever happened to that spirit Renatra?"

"That seems like ages ago LaQueeta; do you still think Ilique remember what he promised us?"

"Who knows … who cares … it's up to us Renatra to not let him forget … whatever happened to that stamina you had?"

"Well LaQueeta, I like Ilique … I think he's a perfect gentleman, and I wouldn't want to trick him into anything."

"Well – well … look who has turned to MS. Good girl. Renatra, you will never get what you want like that. What ever happened to that fire you had, of making the brother eat, your way?"

"I really like Ilique; we have become real good friends."

"Okay Renatra, I suppose now you feel you can just ask him real nice to do what you want, and he'll respond."

"He probably will LaQueeta."

"Girl, you are dreaming; Henrietta is the only old bag that can do that Renatra. When were you planning on doing this monumental feat?"

"Maybe today LaQueeta; I had not decided."

"That is quite obvious Renatra. I suppose you'll invite him to your place and then tell him nicely to lick that froggy tongue of his over your poor hot vagina."

"Why not LaQueeta!"

"Well, get ready because here he comes."

"You don't think I'm going to ask him that in front of you, do you LaQueeta; matter of fact, he will not make it this far, Helene has stopped him. See, I told you ... there is something going on with those two."

"Well I hope you don't let that lying Helene stop you from nicely asking your good friend to do what you want Renatra."

"Why are you laughing LaQueeta? I'll stop by his classroom later on and ask him. Just thinking about him has made me wet for tonight."

"Well don't get too wet; you might want to save some of that good hot juice for him Renatra."

"You won't be laughing when I tell you tomorrow what happened tonight LaQueeta. Anyway, I must be going ... see ya tomorrow girl."

LaQueeta laughed harder as Renatra rolled her fine body pass Ilique and through the cafeteria's door. Ilique glanced in her direction, noticing her twirling buttocks, but she never turned around to see what she felt. On her way by his classroom, she placed a note on his desk, which read: Ilique, I would like to talk with you tonight, at my place. Eight o'clock is fine; please call before you come. Your good friend, Renatra. Renatra hoped this would work. She had nothing to lose; either he did or he didn't. Before school was out, around three in the evening to be exact, he had responded with his own note: Renatra, I will be there. Your friend, Ilique. Renatra could not wait to get home and clean up her place and her body. She prepared for a more sensuous wetness, bathing in some sweet scented oil, and putting on a short red negligee. With her long robe securing her beautiful body, she opened the door when Ilique rang.

"Hello Ilique, come in, have a seat …there's some champagne on the coffee table."

Renatra was smart enough to know, a little wine loosens the tongue; and that is exactly what she needed tonight. She needed a very loose and roving tongue; one that moved all over her gorgeous body or roved exactly where she directed it. Ilique could smell her sweetness. Pouring both of them a glass – full to the top did not seem quite proper etiquette to him, but Renatra's robe fell from around her beautiful legs as she sat across from him. He nervously downed the bubbles as her robe strayed some more. Renatra smiled and happily poured him another round. When she sat back down, her robe had completely opened. The bright red negligee left nothing to the imagination. Ilique downed his second glass.

"Ilique, I will be honest, I need you to tie your own bouquet tonight … put your head to the task if you will. I will be in the bedroom when you shower."

She tossed her robe on a chair; his eyes followed her nude behind as she strolled by, placing a bright blue ribbon across his hand. Ilique thought of the green, yellow, and red ribboned curly locks of hair he had received from her. There was little doubt what she wanted him to do. He entered the shower, hard as a brick, but departed from the warm relaxing water as soft as he could be. With his clothes in his hand he approached Renatra's bed to tell her of his intentions. She looked at him as he stood along side the huge bed. Her negligee lay at his feet on the seemingly warm floor; her nude body, in the bright light, sent out a very strong seductive invitation.

"I am physically free Renatra, but my mind is not free. Do you understand?"

Renatra was not only sensual she was also calm. "There is no way," she said to herself, I am going to let Ilique leave me high and dry … high and wet."

"Sit down Ilique." She patted the bed beside her, grabbing his hand at the same time. "No, I do not understand, but I'm willing to go along with your program, if you're willing to help me out."

For the first time Ilique noticed her beautiful body; her gorgeous breast, her nest of curly locks. He could smell her sweetness; he could now feel the softness of her fingers rubbing his hand. Vibration crept into his arms, legs, and a great arousal came upon him. Renatra felt movement in his hands as his fingers squeezed hers. She would not rush him, but she wanted his mouth to be sucking her swollen nipples; she wanted his tongue to start caressing the inside of her thighs. She wanted his lips upon her saturated folds and whatever else his mouth, lips, and tongue were capable of doing in her genital area. She wanted him to tie the blue ribbon around her curly pubic hair. She wanted anything, but to be sitting there, hot and bothered, holding hands. Ilique thought of what Henrietta told him before she left, "Experience some younger woman Ilique, then let me know if you really love me." He had told himself, he would pretend to make love to someone else and lie to her. He was still thinking when Renatra started talking softly.

"I need you to love me Ilique. I need your mouth upon me; I need your tongue inside of me."

Ilique already knew what she wanted; she had made it clear the day she got Henrietta's letter by mistake. She had thought he was experienced way back then, and little did she know, he knew nothing in comparison to now. But all that would have to wait, as Ilique threw on his pants and shirt and headed out of there. Renatra was furious and expressed herself to LaQueeta the next day.

"Laqueeta, let me tell you, that Henrietta or somebody got Ilique's mind all messed up; there I was, lying there, all nude and presentable and the fool walked out."

"Did he say anything?"

"Nope, just grabbed his clothes and left LaQueeta; and girl, you know I was looking good. Hell, I could have eaten me myself."

"I can imagine Renatra, but there will be other times."

41

The sight of the large gray envelope was enough to let Clara A. Feldon know it was from S.T. Metfield. And inside, the letter with a brief message was every bit as recognizable. The message simply said. "I know your school is new, but your test scores are much too low. In another several months, there must be a drastic improvement or changes will have to be made."

Clara knew this was another step to get her out of there. What surprised her though, was the time limit, "several months." Next month sounded more like his doing. Still, she thought, it's short – this year – early next year.

Priorties are priorties. Clara A. Feldon had planned on covering some other topics in this morning's meeting, but test scores would work.

"Listen up teachers, I have a notice here from, you know who, stating what we already know; our test scores are too low. The letter however has an ultimatum of several months for a drastic improvement. Personally, I don't like threats, but we are professionals and should treat this as a serious challenge."

"To accomplish this goal we must work together harder. For instance; Ilique, your math scores are extremely high, so I want you to get with Renatra and LaQueeta. In six weeks I want to see an improvement ... there must be an improvement ladies. Before the day is over, you will all be assigned teams to work in. This meeting is over ... let us join hands. Father, just let us work together on one accord; thank you for inspiring the children to learn. We ask these things Father for the benefit of your children, from us who neither can do nothing without you. In Jesus's name, we pray, Amen."

The meeting was quick, but quite effective. Clara had work to do; she needed to review the scores again to get the appropriate personnel in teams. It came as no surprise to her that T. Metfield was pulling another stunt to get rid of her. She thought to herself, saying, "the man must think he is dealing with some weakling or something."

After they wiped the surprised look from their faces, Ilique, Renatra, and LaQueeta started conversing. They moved down the hall, setting dates and times when their first meeting would occur. In the cafeteria later, Renatra and LaQueeta discussed it further.

"Girl, I cannot believe she assigned us to work with Ilique."

"Yeah Renatra, especially the way he has been snubbing us lately." Each had a mischievious silly grin on her face.

"LaQueeta, I have an idea if you're game."

"You know me Renatra ... and to get even with that scoundrel ... count me in. What do you have in mind?"

"Well, since Ilique is avoiding our love, let's team up on our team leader."

"What do you mean Renatra; love him at the same time?" Renatra nodded her head, smiling cunningly. "Hey, that's a great idea; he deserves it too, after leaving you, hot and wet, and not even showing up for me. We can plan it and knock his frog-ass eyes out during our very first session."

"Yeah, I bet he has never received a double dosage of fine lovemaking. I am getting excited just thinking about his punishment LaQueeta."

"Me too Renatra … this should be good … this should teach him to ignore us."

The first meeting, a dinner meeting, the ladies insisted, be at Renatra's place. They also insisted on preparing the meal. Ilique willingly went along. He however began to think, they might be up to something, when Renatra met him at the door wearing a robe and LaQueeta at the table in nothing but a negligee. Both of them were smiling. Ilique spoke to LaQueeta with a weak, "good evening," and she dipped her head slightly downward and back into place without changing expressions. Renatra pointed her hand at a seat across the table opposite them, for his head of the class lecture. Ilique knew he was in trouble, but decided to act as normal as possible and await their next move. There was no indication of food other than the sweet pleasant aroma of the two delicious looking ladies before him. He tried, but was unable to keep his eyes from dashing upon LaQueeta.

"Well ladies, Principal Clara A. Feldon sort of put me on the spot … besides the spot I put myself in; I see you both agree. And I am willing to make amends as you deem necessary … or as you two are provoked to administer."

Ilique surprised himself with those remarks; having no idea how such enticing words flowed out of his mouth. LaQueeta and Renatra turned and looked at each other; said nothing and refocused their attention back on Ilique. They had planned a surprise for him and to their surprise, Ilique was willing to accept his share of their punishment. Well, so much for normal action and reaction. Ilique proceeded since neither of his co-workers said anything.

"The first thing I do in my classroom is to make sure there is a high level of concentration. It's a dual thing, you know. I concentrate on the students and inspire them to concentrate on their lessons. So, I guess you could say there are two ingredients for success – concentration and inspiration."

Ilique to this point had been doing a masterful concentration job himself with the display of LaQueeta's beautiful breast gleaming through the negligee, but Renatra's sudden removal of her robe created a much harder circumstance, if that was physically possible. Under her robe was absolutely nothing but her fine naked body. And to make matters worse for poor Ilique, their additional plan became operative, with each standing and bending over, revealing their gorgeous nude buttocks and sumptuous portions of their heart pulverizing vulvas. Never before had Ilique seen two tasteful looking treats together, causing his mind to almost lock up. Renatra spoke:

"There Ilique, concentrate on this ... which pussy are you inspired to eat or will you eat them both at the same time!"

Ilique was silent; no doubt in a little shock. Poor Ilique could see more than a mouth full as his mind tried desperately to figure out something.

"Sounds like you need a little help man ... you can start with me with LaQueeta holding your head to make sure you make amends as you say."

And with that said, Renatra proceeded to crawl upon the large dining table, pillow and all resting under her buttock. Her delicious looking thighs were gapped open; to Ilique she reminded him of the strawberry sundaes he loved so much. The strawberry freckles on her folds beckoned his lips, but his body would not move. That is, until LaQueeta practically bodily lifted him onto the table, saying:

"Go on frogman, you know what she wants; put your head in there or I'll do it for you. We are sick and tired of the shit you have been putting us through."

This shouldn't have been a problem for Ilique since he had eaten Henrietta's gourmet dish many times, in almost the same fashion; and it wasn't, once he got his mouth onto her delicacy, forgetting LaQueeta standing over him. Renatra's reaction produced the immediate effect of his tongue, slithering about her. He was apparently eating her fruitbowl exactly the way she loved it. LaQueeta stood nearby helplessly, until jealous envy got to be too overbearing, not to mention being horny as hell. Suddenly she pulled Ilique out of the way, hopping in his exact position, pointing her nude beautiful round buttocks in his direction. His eyes peered inside her largeness, reminding him of one huge delicious banana split with triple dippings. Renatra felt the gentleness of LaQueeta and screamed Ilique's name. Ilique had never seen a woman love another and exploded with new excitement. He stood there in amazement; LaQueeta ate on and continued to show him her creamy split. His mouth watered and he placed his hands on her cheeks, licking his tongue into her creaminess and eating her banana split, satisfactorily he presumed, as LaQueeta responded with loud moans and more vigorous eating of Renatra's fruitbowl. She also responded favorably to Ilique as seemingly his favorite caramel syrup flowed his way. Her sweetness was overwhelming. He could hear LaQueeta moaning fervently and Renatra screaming frantically. It appeared as if his eardrums would burst or they would lose their breath any minute, or both.

The night became longer than they had anticipated as they took leave to Renatra's roomy bed. Ilique found himself stripped of his clothes, lying on his back, still making amends. Renatra sits atop his torso, thighs straddled, resting comfortably around his rod, facing LaQueeta who sits in his palms atop his face, where he continues to eat her oversized banana split. The ladies are massaging each other's sensitive breast with the smoothness of their hands and fingers, simultaneously joyfully sucking each other's high-spirited nipples. Such alternating was so pleasurable, especially feeling Ilique inside of them. All of their movements are slow and easy. The ladies are making sure Ilique never forget his punishment. Oddly enough though, he is taking it like a man.

Henrietta had wanted Ilique to get some experience, but this is probably not what she had in mind. His face was saturated from LaQueeta's constant barrage of liquidity; she could not help herself and felt sorry for inflicting such pain upon him. Renatra also felt bad for making Ilique screw her so long. Each received orgasm after orgasm; never simultaneously, which seemed to spur the other to another one. An endless stream of orgasms. Clara A. Feldon would love the way this team was geling together; and just think this was only their first session.

On Monday, in the cafeteria, Clara A. Feldon inquired of the ladies, as to how they were coming along. They both agreed that Ilique was head and shoulders above anyone they had ever worked with, and they looked forward to their next meeting. In Renatra's words:

"I can tell you this Clara; that Ilique is like a two headed cobra. When he finishes with you, you are totally exhausted."

"I figured as much Renatra; how about you LaQueeta?"

"I am impressed Clara; he has a better head on him than any man I know. What I like about him most though is the way he gets into things and analyze them. That was a good idea to team us up; how long will we do this?"

"For the rest of the year for sure; depends on how fast you get those test scores up, really. And if you enjoy working as teams, we could leave it like that indefinitely. What does Ilique think about it?"

"Here he comes now Clara; you can ask him yourself, but personally I think he loves teaching us his method. He really concentrate on us and has taught us how to concentrate ourselves, especially when he's mouthing that good stuff off to us."

"Hello Ilique, I was just asking the ladies how the team effort was going, and if you thought it would be successful."

"Oh, without a doubt Clara; LaQueeta and Renatra are good subjects to teach. They have willingly accepted my methods. Surprisingly, I'm using my head more than I thought though; getting a feel, more or less, as to their concentration levels. But like I said, they are both really good and I love the way we interact."

"That is what teamwork is all about Ilique; I am glad you three are geling."

"It is going far better than I ever anticipated Clara; the ladies have me in a groove. If they keep up their high energy level, I'll have their deficiencies completely licked in no time."

"Uh … Ilique … Clara said we would be a team at least the rest of the year."

"LaQueeta is right Ilique. As a matter of fact, I want you three to develop weekly sessions. It is extremely important we get the children's test scores up and keep them up."

"Whatever you say Clara, but LaQueeta and Renatra are beginning to come around precipitately already; weekly might be more than they can take or I can digest."

"The principal is right Ilique … you know that math … you eat that stuff up … and we are just beginning to learn and love your teaching techniques."

"Renatra's right Ilique, plus things will go smoother as we open up to you more."

"Those are my exact thoughts LaQueeta; I was a little tight this first go round. Weekly sessions would put me in a more comfortable mode, and like you say, enable me to concentrate more. Clara, the weekly sessions sounds simply gratifying to me."

"Thanks Renatra; okay, then its settled gang … weekly it is … remember it's for the kids."

"What happens if the scores are up prior to the end of the year Clara?"

"Relax Ilique … I'm hearing here that the ladies love working with you."

"Yeah Ilique, relax; it's for the kids, you know. If me and LaQueeta is willing to give of ourselves for our profession, and an extremely worthy cause, so should you."

"I will see you guys later; I have a whole school to run."

"See ya principal." A whole chorus rang out.

"What are you two trying to pull; I know you don't expect me to be loving on you each week!"

"Seems like we settled that a minute ago Ilique."

"Renatra's right man ... what the hell are you complaining about ... you told Clara yourself ... our stuff was good."

"Well, it was; you were like my favorite banana split and Renatra was like a strawberry sundae, but -."

"But nothing Ilique; LaQueeta, did you hear that? That was cute – a strawberry sundae – I love it!"

"Yeah but -."

"No buts Ilique; there were no buts when you were sliding that tongue of yours between our thighs this weekend. Now, if you have a problem with the day that's fine, otherwise Friday night, we expect you to be eating another sundae and my split – banana split again – I love split better. Look Ilique, if Renatra loves it and I love it, and you love it, why not. I can tell you did by the way you were eating everything in sight ... there is no reason to change anything."

"Well, I just felt uncomfortable; well at first anyway."

"To be honest Ilique, I did too, but you make love so wonderful, I forgot all about it after awhile, especially when LaQueeta hooked up on me and you hooked up on her. The girl had me going crazy, and I know it's all because your mouth, lips, and tongue were hitting her in the right places."

"You can say that again Renatra; Ilique is better than he thinks he is ... he eats my split like it's the best in the world."

"It's pretty good – well – it is real good, and so is Renatra's sundae. And I just love the sweetness you two give me. But you know this can't go on forever."

"Who said anything about forever Ilique; can't we all just enjoy something for a change."

"I guess LaQueeta ... so we're meeting at Renatra's again, when?"

"Horny as I feel right now, how about tonight!"

"Sounds good to me LaQueeta; how about you Ilique?"

"Well, since it's for the kids ... I'll be there, but I'm bringing my clothes for tomorrow. Because if I know you two, there will be no leaving early."

"Lay it on us if you want to Ilique, but you were the one eating like a hungry bull."

"Yeah, me and LaQueeta, she really had you going. I believe that girl could teach me a thing or two. I could watch you two all night ... well, part of the night anyway."

"You are too good to be on the sidelines Ilique; I could never perform that well without you. Everytime you stroked me with that tautological tongue of yours, I double-stroked Renatra. There is no way I could do that without you eating my banana split the way you do."

"Well, you girls had me fired up ... say, my lunch hour is over ... see you two tonight."

Ilique was already electrified when his finger hit Renatra's doorbell, but when the door opened and he saw the two shapely nude beauties greeting him, his mind and body gravitated to an ecstatic rage. Thoughts flowed into his brain of dinner again being served at the large dining room table; very appropriate since LaQueeta and Renatra had attached themselves to each arm and was ushering him in that direction. Once inside the room, they commence to undress Ilique until he stood there naked, and in his opinion, beautifully three-legged. As they led and seated him at the table, he wondered whether he would be ceremoniously eating a strawberry sundae or a banana split; it really made no difference, as they were both excellent choices, and his appetite was greedily growing by the seconds. It was too bad, well almost, that he would have to wait before licking his tongue upon one of these delicacies, because the ladies had other magnificent ideas.

LaQueeta slid under the table and began steamtoweling his throbbing shaft and knob, and Renatra began tenderly massaging his shoulders, neck, and head with soft hands. Ilique felt soothing grips and sensational ripples in his stomach as the heat from LaQueeta and the relaxation from Renatra met there. He had temporarily forgotten about his dinner until Renatra proceeded to spread her flavorous strawberry sundae before him upon the table. She pulled his head into her as she lay back to enjoy her sundae with him; while LaQueeta eased her salivating mouth over his palatable knob. Concentration for Ilique was easy, his naturally strong suit, as he devoured Renatra's delicacy. Impressed with his artistic tongue she moaned louder than the last time because, thanks to LaQueeta's gentle strokes, his tongue was dynamically swishing inside of her sundae. It appeared as if both of Ilique's heads were going to explode, and they did along with Renatra's enjoyment, as a multiplicity of lip synchronization occurred. Dinner was being served in a wholesome fashion, as he and LaQueeta had a head up on Renatra who lay passionately succumbed upon the table; giving freely. Ilique graciously ate Renatra's tremendous serving as he abundantly gratifyingly served LaQueeta.

Renatra had again received a thunderous loving impacted again by two people. Last time it was provided as LaQueeta ate her sundae and Ilique ate LaQueeta's banana split. This evening it was executed with Ilique happily devouring her flavorful sundae, as LaQueeta masterfully eliminated Ilique's hunger pain. When they finished lustfully toying with each other in the shower, there was only sleep ahead, as Ilique slept in the center of these two gorgeous women. The next day he wondered if Henrietta would approve of his new experience. It appeared after their two sessions, the ladies were becoming serious. Evidently they liked what Ilique brought to the table or they liked what they brought to the table for him to eat. Either way, they wanted him more and more; and poor Ilique agreed to everything, even to being available anytime during the week that they wanted him. For the first three weeks they dined together for almost every night. Ilique had never eaten so many strawberry sundaes and banana splits in his life. His diet practically consisted of these lovely meals; ironically he gained weight, though he did feel a bit weak at times.

Into the fourth week when the ecstatic newness wore thin, their dining habits dwindled also; their test scores, by the way, for their pupils were extremely high. It appeared that old T. Metfield would lose another battle. It would be interesting to see how he tried to get her fired next. The ladies, Renatra and LaQueeta had also come to the conclusion that they were entitled to some individuality from Ilique. Ilique was nervous of their decision, wondering whether he could actually satisfy a woman all by himself. To himself he said, "I have never satisfied anyone by myself; not Analicia, not Henrietta who was teaching me, not even Helene who merely tolerated me before moving on. If it were not such a shame on my part, I would call Henrietta. She told me women were different and I have found that to be tastefully true, but she obviously meant more than that."

When Ilique took everything he could remember from Henrietta's teaching, he recalled her telling him to learn a woman's body, especially the vulva; and more importantly, to listen at the woman when a love session was in progress. "They know what they want," he remembered her saying. So as they neared the Christmas holiday season he guessed at what the New Year would bring in the form of an independent Renatra and LaQueeta. Renatra thought most though of working on her father's family tree during the break. When she called him with her jubilant news, Metfield was more than flustered, saying.

"Renatra, I don't think that is a good idea, taking the dirt off dead folks and all. We didn't send you to college to learn something like that; leave that to other morons. That is even foolish of you to think of such a thing after the comfortable life style your mother and I have provided you with -."

"But daddy, mama thought it was a good idea; she has almost completed her side of the family. Anyway, what harm could come of it; I am so proud of being a Metfield." And in her exuberance hung up the phone after saying. "What a wonderful tree this will be, you'll see ... gotta go daddy ... talk to you later."

Renatra only thought she got the last word in over the phone; Sauninger cried out with her click.

"Damn, what the hell!"

42

It was thirty minutes before midnight and the fireworks had already started; though most of the noise sounded very much like the sporadic gunfire, heard every night – just much more of it. Why couldn't they wait until the dong hit twelve, thought Clara A. Feldon, is that not asking too much. The last day of this year was ending the same as last year; her man Rory Davanpourt was not there; no man in sight and only promises to cuddle up to. Rory had promised to be there between one and two a.m.; that was as definite as he could be. After all, mother Davanpourt came first in his life.

Mother Davanpourt, even now at ninety-five, was a charmer or better still, a superstitious leftover from the nineteenth century. She had Rory convinced, it was good luck to have him with her the first of each year. If she could this was the only thing Clara would change about the sweet old woman. And so it goes, another year for Clara and Rory to get started late for their own celebration.

Though a bit irritable, Clara suppressed it into another one of those old books or the real love of her life. This was nearing the beginning of the year, and if she was to equal the one hundred ten books read this year; now was a fine time to start. Curling up, with a good book, on a rainy night did not exactly describe Clara A. Feldon. One would have to expand Clara's readings to inclement times and good times. After all, books had proven to be far more challenging than men and a lot less unpredictable. Clara however had not completely closed her mind to the absolute denial of a consistent reward of the latter. So, as the pendulum struck midnight and people on television sang "Auld Lang Syne;" Clara removed the bookmark from page 205 and began to enjoy the words, as her bright brown eyes danced across sentences, plunging her thoughts into the author's triple and quadrupled meanings. Clara had learned that the simple-surfaced words had far-reaching depths into an author's sub-conscious. "The obvious never quite measure up to the reality," was Clara's, famous remarks.

As it neared two o'clock in the morning, Clara remembered a book from last year that got she and Rory off to a good year. It was the "Persian Letters," and that is what she was so engrossed in when he did finally arrive. Since that time, Rory had been calling himself the Black Eunuch for Clara. Of course in his case he would do the guarding and the moral integrity that left Clara happily helpless. So she flips to her favorite letter CXLI, and began to read. Clara thinks on Anais and cannot help but shed a tear before she burst into a cheerful smile. And it was none to soon, for Rory was arriving; and Clara was more than ready, having been in abstinence with the move in of Tashanesha. Tonight though, would mean a special celebration since she had persuaded the mother to give Tashanesha a second chance, letting her come back home. She could feel Rory already.

"Aye, the Black Eunuch is finally here."

391

"Hello Clara, I will make it all up to you one day; maybe today." Their eyes lovingly met each other's.

Their communication was good tonight, as they read each other perfect; oral make-up was definitely written across Rory's thick lips. Maybe this is how rituals get started or in the least – a jubilant celebration. Clara dressed, only in a sheer breast covering top, was hopeful of either; and from the Black Eunuch, the throwback of a year ago caused a swelling in his mouth.

"Tonight is all you will need to make up Rory!"

Rory was not a talkative person, especially if the point of view was explicit. There was an exchange of smiles as Rory slowly undressed. Clara was busily pushing her books to the floor on the side of her bed. The bearded Black Eunuch was about to bring comfort to her alluring zabaglione. Rory remembered last year and decided to do the same. After sitting with mother Davanpourt over half the night, he knew the best action for a youthful Clara was to face it head on. His head remarkably filled the gap between her curvaceous bowlegs, crossed at the ankles around the back of his neck, pulling him slowly upward. Moisture on her inner thighs heated as his hot breath passed over it, in pursuit of her delicious zabaglione. This moisture sweltering delicacy waited patiently to be devoured; succulent tastiness bubbled within its boundaries, as Rory's mouth eased closer and prepared itself to eat. An abundance of liquid flooded his mouth when he paused, staring at Clara's sumptuous chocolate pudding. His palms held her delicious hot zabaglione closer and closer to his mouth until at last they touched. His broad lips were the first to touch, followed quickly by his long smooth tongue, gliding over the outer creamy surface. Rory then gently placed his bearded face in her enchanting pudding and lay still. Clara started rubbing and pulling his smooth earlobe until she felt a sensational craving. Rory's lips were pressed firmly upon her enticing pudding as it began to dilate and seemingly breathe life. The seductive pudding slowly opened his taste buds and he felt extreme warm moisture upon his lips. Without moving his face, Rory extended, what Clara thought to be a ten-inch tongue into her luscious zabaglione. Rory still did not move his face and one would have thought him asleep, if observing the exercise.

Rory's tongue penetrated the softness within; a softness sensationalizing, his entire body. A softness that melted in his mouth, yet was still there; a softness in which the real meaning could be grasped in no other manner, than with the erectness of his tongue. There was a tenderness within this warm-soft-moist pudding that made Rory want to lie there forever, and respond as Clara wanted him to. It was still quiet – very quiet – even as Clara slowly moved backward and then slowly forward; moving ever so slightly. She could feel the swollen object against the walls of her throbbing zabaglione, but continued to move very slowly. This would be her auld lang syne, and Clara wanted to savor the beginning of the New Year. She held Rory's head still as the slow swishings and ins and outs continued. Clara was giving herself a treat that no penis could ever remotely match. Rory's harmonically tuned tongue had plenty of heat and Clara could feel it swelling even larger. Clara's robust zabaglione came alive gripping Rory's tongue firmly and pleasurable. Each centimeter forward or in, Clara released the grip on Rory's tongue, but a suction occurred that pulled him in deeper; and each centimeter backward or out, the grip was tighter, and Rory once again was pulled in still deeper. Like quicksand, the more movement, the deeper Rory's tongue eased into Clara's gripping lips. Rory was now really enjoying Clara's flavorful sweetness.

Clara was feeling good, but the right depth had not been reached. Each grip and suction hit a new spot and produced a greater feeling to Clara. Each grip and suction also widened Clara's gorgeous brown thighs and made Rory more ecstatic. He was now swallowing Clara's sweetness with unutterable fondness and joyfulness. His lips had now completely disappeared into her beautiful creamy pudding. Rory had experienced this before and knew when Clara did not release her hand from his head, it was definitely her night or their night for the max. It appeared time consuming, but within a teasing-period of time, the max, or a total of six climaxes would transpire – three each.

Rory and Clara knew the time was near. Rory's thick lips and broad nose was now completely submerged, as Clara hit an ecstatic double suction, and they both had their first tremendous orgasm; though not simultaneously – she was naturally first. However when the hot mushy juice gushed into Rory's mouth he was overpowered and couldn't restrain himself. Yes, tonight, Clara was in an extraordinary mood and held on to Rory's head. She held on and immediately commenced a circular motion of her hips and a savage assault upon his tongue. Savage, only in the sense that the circular motion, though slow, was not only upon his tongue, but Rory had not been given adequate time to savor her sweet liquid. Rory loved Clara and let her have her way when producing juices so thick and sweet.

What happened – did Clara think of Anais and decide to obtain some enjoyment on her behalf. Anyway, it did not matter, as Rory quickly adjusted and before long, another gush of hot spicy substance arrived. Rory was doubly excited; he was surprised the dosage was three-folded as before and seemingly more tastier. Rory slowly slurped Clara's pulpy juice on one end and quickly released himself on the other. This was certainly one of Clara's best outings and she still was not finished. Clara suddenly opened her fine thighs even wider, pulling Rory's head and tongue in deeper; this time locking her strong bowlegs around his body. She again assaulted his tongue with circular movements. Rory made only slurpy sounds as his throat seem to fill prior to him swallowing. The sweet warm juices traveled onto his tongue and quickly downward. That sound upon Clara's zabaglione was driving her *summa libido*.

Rory loved the taste and dranked as fast as he could, because he knew it was not long before another tide came in. Clara pulled Rory's head in even deeper, as she began feeling spots, which had gone untouched by his large-long tongue. Still, no words were exchanged as Clara's saturated thighs tightened up around Rory's stiff tongue, squeezing it like a sponge. Rory knew to get ready again, as Clara's luscious vulva felt like an oven and immediately, gushed, hot tasty syrupiness straight into his mouth. Rory guessed Clara's show to be over as she lay back; relaxed and all gapped open. The only thing left to do was to clean up. Rory lay still until the last gush of sweetness came through; then he removed his tongue and commence to lick the outside of her delightful zabaglione clean. Rory performed this task slowly as he was also enjoying his final climax. Clara twitched involuntarily, releasing even more nutrition, but he kept pace, as it was only a trickle. Clara was now snoring, displaying a stunning afterglow, as Rory gave the piping red-hot zabaglione a final cleansing, a gentle kiss, and crawled along side her for another slow, but fruitful beginning for the year. Rory had played auld lang syne with Clara's chiming zabaglione and she now lay still, savoring what was likely to be repeated many times all year long. Even Anais would be proud of her.

When morning came, Clara A. Feldon's mind quickly reverted to the usual.

"Rory, do you ever think old T. Metfield will ever lighten up on me?"

"It's hard to say, but I doubt it if he thinks there is a chance of getting you out of there."

"Well, my test scores are up Rory; better than 50% of where they were. There is still lots of improvement to be made though."

"I think you just answered your own question."

"I see; you know Rory, I really think he is peeved that a woman is doing so well. Maybe these Christmas holidays and New Year will have a softening effect upon him. I cannot see a person being so downright acerbic day in and day out, when it comes to the female gender."

"Oh, before you get worked up Clara, mother wanted me to wish you a Happy New Year; she also said not to worry about Sauninger T. Metfield. She made me give her an update on what's been happening at the school."

"I can really appreciate mother Davanpourt being so concerned. You know Rory, I thought a lot of you when you were with her last night. You bring good thoughts to mind."

"How's that?"

"Everytime I think about you, I think of something good."

"I can't imagine what you mean Clara; it's that good huh?" Rory was smiling cravingly and she knew what he meant.

"I really love the way you play on words; of course I love the way you love the most. Is it reminiscent of anything to you Rory?"

"It sure is; both now and long ago."

"But we did not know each other long ago Rory."

"You did say reminiscence, remember -." Phone rings.

"Hold on Rory, I have got to hear this ... sorry, no one's here by that name ... okay Rory, let me hear the double-good things you were about to tell me!"

"Well, years ago reminds me of eating the heart out of a melon in my granpa's watermelon patch ... so red, so sweet, so juicy."

"And lately?"

"Well Clara, you're the same as my delicious cup of coffee every morning ... when I'm pouring it I notice the rich black-ness and smell its unique aroma; then when I add my ingredients and ease my lips into it, I taste its smooth creamy sweet flavor. And for your information, every bite and sip makes me want more and more. In other words, I can never get enough of your goodness, especially when you're holding my head in place and making those funny sounds."

"Funny huh ... can't help it, the way you move that tongue of yours."

"Well honey, you know the Black Eunuch has no balls." Rory was laughing.

"Uh huh, you neither; yours belong to me. I love you so much Rory."

Before they could get all into each other once more, the phone rings again.

43

"Hello mother Davanpourt, didn't you call earlier?

"I realized it was your number Clara after I hung up; must be getting old. I was trying to call someone else, but is Rory there?"

"He sure is; hold on."

"It is not necessary Clara; tell him Sauninger called; and if you two are up and about today, please stop by."

Whenever mother Davanpourt sounded like that, it only meant one thing; she expected you as soon as possible. Rory interpreted the message to Clara, and we find them with her now.

"Rory, Sauninger called asking for my help and forgiveness. I never told you this, but he is my nephew."

"I figured something, but how can that be mother!"

"The story is too long to tell right now son. Sauninger wants me over to his house later this evening to finish clearing the air with his family. This is the day I have looked forward to for a long time. The day I have lived for; please take me by there immediately. There is no point in waiting any longer."

Mother Davanpourt explained on the way, how Metfield feared her divulging the truth, one day, especially since she was living so long. But what he feared most was Renatra finding out the truth with her genealogy trace; the pain his wife and family would be strickened with. Even now, she said he feared what a devastating effect it was bound to cause. And for the love of her brother, Rafeal Meadlarkin and the times she cried, she wanted to be there. This indeed would comfort some if not all of the pain she carried through the years. She felt blessed and asked the Lord this day, to forgive all parties involved in such a terrible tragedy. This prayer was the same one she used the day, that wagon and old man Thomas Brontlier took poor Leslie Mae, down that red-dirted country road and eventually to her grave with that broken heart. It was her same daily prayers all of those years.

When they arrived at the Metfield's luxurious residence, there appeared to be a somberness in the air; it certainly was in the living room, as no one was standing. Renatra burst into tears at their presence, and her mother reached over to console her; herself not exactly in an altogether state of mind. None of the family wore a good news – good news expression; the two boys hung their heads close to the carpeted floor. Downward. If there was a glimmer of light, it was the relief-free face of Metfield. He rushed to mother Davanpourt and held her in his arms, patting her back, whispering an, "I'm sorry," that only she could hear. He later managed a louder one to the other newcomers. Rory and Clara were smiling inwardly, as neither wanted to show their exurberance.

When Rory Davanpourt and Clara A. Feldon returned home and cleared the bathroom, rinsing the Metfield filth from their bodies, the bed awaited. They slid upon its sheets and their exurberance came forth. Clara could faintly be heard saying, eat slow and deliberate, Rory ... eat slow and deliberate. Clara's body gave Rory's nostrils an appetizing fragrance; a sensual scent and extremely mouthwatering which lubricated all that it touched. Her neck, breast and stomach were still moist as she slowly guided his head pass her gorgeous spiral-dimpled navel toward the tasty angle of her thighs where their moistures would meet. Her throbbing tingling nerve endings sensed another one of their astonishing love making sessions.

Clara could feel his wide palms around her smooth irresistible bare brown behind. Rory's firm manipulative fingers were caressingly massaging each glossy round cheek. She could also feel a warm broad fleshy object slithering slowly and thoroughly about; truly the beginning of an ultimate oral massage; and he was on the way to graciously eating her delicious zabaglione. Rory had the perfect expansive mouth and broad lips to cover a large area with his tongue as he ate. Most, of the time now, Clara had numerous instantaneous orgasms which, gradually progressed to a stormy screaming passionate frantic sensation, but today she had instructed Rory to eat slow and deliberate. For some reason she wanted to nurture and savor this one; obviously a woman's choice. Rory loved nothing better as did Clara for kisses to be planted upon her vulva. Seductive, lip and tongue kisses which gave quivering pleasure, touching her luscious outer and inner labia, prowling inside her delicious vaginal opening, and ultimately pursuing her clitoris at her request, but with an aggressive enthusiasm that always quelled his appetite. Early on, Clara massaged her breast when Rory ate her zabaglione, but later directed her palms against his cheeks to make sure both got their fill of her powerful orgasmic delicacy.

Clara's tender sweet folds were swelling and opening generously to meet the challenge of Rory's long skillfully roving, teasing, devouring tongue; a juiciness penetrated his taste buds, bringing greedy eating habits to her genital area. Alternate thrilling wet kisses between each swishing titillating wandering movement brought her now gyrating energized body to a new arousal point. She loved his gentle aggressiveness upon her, as was evident by her constant sighs and moans; his head was weaving, slow but to perfection, enjoying her soft marvelous appetizing delicacy, she thought, the last time she opened her eyes. The unhurried vigorous intensity of Rory's exquisite performance had her naked arms and fine bowlegs moving wildly. In this pleasurable excitement, Clara's lovely thighs flew attractively apart; his saliva drooling mouth lowered to a new depth of carnal enjoyment. Her colorful pink puffy rounded sensitive lips now surrounded his thick lips, and her sensation heightened; her flexible palms, those passionate embraces, gripped his non-resistant head, pulling him further within her sumptuous fleshiness. She could feel his magnificent tongue flicking, wonderful spots, leading her to breathless ecstasy; his powerful attached mouth quivering like she'd never felt; his astounding nose caressing her ravishing red clit ... numerous clitoral kisses ... and then it was over.

Anyway, life had to go on for Sauninger T. Metfield; so a few days after the holiday's food and festivities ceased, he again apologized.

"You know – sometimes the truth hurts ... however I feel free ... the truth shall set you free ..."

Sauninger T. Metfield was speaking as he stood before the group of people he had assembled at the Ordon T. Metfield Junior High School. The group consisted of his entire family; his two sons, Sauninger T. Metfield Jr. and Ordon T. Metfield II, sweet Renatra, and his darling wife Charmayne. Also present were the entire board and their wives, and the entire faculty of the school. And last, his special-special guest, Rory's mother, Mrs. Rachel Meadlarkin Davanpourt who sat beside Renatra, holding hands and exchanging congenial smiles with their eyes and lips; extending into their puffy cheeks. Yes, these two women, the old and the young were grinning from ear to ear.

"This is a different moment in my life, and I'm sure, for my family; but, yet it is sort of a pleasant one. Some of you are looking at one another wondering just what is going on; no, you're not being transferred nor is Ms. Clara A. Feldon being fired. Although I was pretty skeptical of her at first and to be honest, has given her a hard time, I feel she is definitely the principal for this school. And before I go any farther, Ms. Feldon, I apologize to you for any inconvenience I have caused you."

"Well, to cut my story short, I have been living a lie with my family name. My real legal name is Metfield, but biologically it is Meadlarkin. And for the kind gentlewoman sitting next to my daughter, that is extremely important. It is also important to her great-neice sitting next to her. Most of you know her as Rory Davanpourt's mother, but she is also Mrs. Rachel Meadlarkin Davanpourt; my aunt. I really want to thank her for keeping my secret, sacrificing her happiness and not exposing me to you kind people." The crowd looked on, definitely awestricken. "My greatest problem in all of this, as my wife so dutifully pointed out to me, was letting the Metfield name go to my head, thus controlling my actions – my life. I knew long ago of the erroneous deed by my forefathers, but elected to do nothing about it, primarily because of the status of the Metfield name. Sure, even to me now, it makes sense to be the offspring of an educator to that of a farmer, but it doesn't make it right. The worst thing I feel at the moment is having denied my children and myself the opportunity to mingle with their rightful relatives. Again, I apologize to my family as I did when I decided on this revealing. And again, Mrs. Davanpourt, my deepest apologies also go to you. I can never make up for my stupidity, but in my years left on this earth, maybe – just maybe, I can make small tokens of repayment."

"Again, Clara A. Feldon, please forgive me for being so hard on you, in doubting your ability. From now on, you have my full support as I would give any of the male animals."

The crowd laughed at his last remark, not so much as its connotation as its tension remover. Metfield or Meadlarkin as he now wanted to be called, strolled wearily to his seat. He reached for his handkerchief as water formed in his eyes. He had tried to be strong, but in the end, he could not overcome his emotions, folding his face into his large palms upon his lap. Rory G.

401

Davanpourt came forward, patting him on the back, in passing to the podium.

"Please give this great man a round of applause." The crowd stood in doing so as Rory continued. "Well brother Meadlarkin, we did not intend for the dragon to slay himself." The crowd roared with laughter. "Now if you can come forward, we would like to put some of that fire back into you."

Rory looked at the teary-eyed Meadlarkin, took his right hand in his and said. "Brother Meadlarkin, on behalf of the rest of the board, we have made a decision, with your final approval of course; to name the new elementary school in your honor – the Sauninger T. Meadlarkin Elementary School."

The crowd roared its approval, and Meadlarkin and Rory were hugged together, like men do in some of those foreign countries. Sauninger realized, a farmer's offspring could indeed become a proud person after all.

44

During her father's revelation and or publication, Renatra had tried to show her happiness. Even when she later visited mother Davanpourt to obtain the rest of the family tree, she tried to be as jovial as possible. And she was happy, but it was for her aged aunt only. For herself, she felt miserable for being, not who she thought she was. Downheartedness had set in; she talked to LaQueeta about it, to no immediate satisfaction. She even talked to herself, trying to understand if these blues of hers could last forever. Renatra kept wondering how her father could deceive their family – his wife and his three children; how could he even prepetrate such a falseness upon himself. After rationalization of her father's behavior, she still could not shake the hurt from her body; though she discovered self-pleasuring gave her some relief, especially since LaQueeta's introduction of her own vibrator.

This night however, nothing worked to console Renatra, so calling her friend naturally came to mind.

"Hello Ilique, could you come over for awhile." Sex was not on her mind; she just needed someone to listen while she talked and probably hold her in his arms while she talked. Afterall, their study sessions no longer existed, and the likelihood of a sexual encounter was nil. Two friends is how she looked at it.

"Well, I was busy, but you sound awful." In the back of Ilique's brain, sex slightly formed. He thought of how making love to her alone would be; her fruity freckles consumed him. And it was a fact, Henrietta was not going to take him back without more experience of a one on one nature.

Somehow, Ilique expected a naked or negligee clad Renatra to meet him at the door. Thoughts of the dominant LaQueeta being there even crossed his mind; though that was clearly in the past. Nervousness rose in his stomach at that thought, because he felt their episode really did nothing to help him with getting Henrietta back. When the door opened, Renatra was fully dressed and there was no LaQueeta.

"Thanks for coming over Ilique." She led him to her sofa. "I feel terrible at what happened with my father. My father is not who he suppose to be."

"But he is your true father; what if he had not been your real father -."

"So he is, but I am not who I am Ilique -."

"Hold it, you are still Renatra through and through; so your last name is not what you thought it was, so what. That does not change you being you; what's in a name anyway?"

"Everything for me."

"Oh, I see Renatra, you are just like your father."

404

"What are you talking about Ilique?"

"Remember when your father said your mother told him he had let the Metfield name go to his head, that is the same as what you've done. Let me tell you something; without that name, you are still the same sweet Renatra to me."

Apparently those words were strong or soothing enough to Renatra's ears because her head fell into Ilique's lap. He could feel her breath bouncing against his stomach and see water streaming from her closed eyes. This reminded him of when he first consoled Henrietta and he leaned and kissed her cheeks. They both knew where this was going and continued kissing as they undressed and headed for her bed. Renatra remembered her letters and curly bouquets to Ilique and told him again.

"You'll have to tie your own bouquet tonight Ilique." She rolled onto her back and positioned her beautiful thighs for him to do so. Her broad-rounded-puffed pear shaped vulva, angled traingular to the center. The inlaid freckles residing here extended an attractive invitation to Ilique's tongue; beautiful tiny freckles, all appearing to have the shape of miniature apples, oranges, and bunches of grapes, resembling a fruitbowl at its best. Just exactly he imagined, why she called it so. An appetizing looking fruitbowl, encouraging one to select his favorite fruit and eat to his delight. That is what Ilique aimed to do, but his lubricous tongue slid involuntarily down the angle and buried itself in an extraordinary sweetness. The fruitbowl's inside was indeed endeared with a thick nectareous fruit punch; retrievability at this point was virtually impossible. The sweetness and distinct flavor upon Ilique's tongue was unlike any that he had ever tasted, even better than her previous strawberry sundae. There was an unexpected goodness about Renatra. She could tell, something nice had happened as an elongation slithered within. Renatra could feel a gentle warmness touching her all about, as Ilique's tongue slowly moved, savoring her rich-creamy tasty delicacy. He was very much surprised as to how delicious and appetizing Renatra's fruitbowl was. Though she was not a Henrietta, he felt Renatra had something exceptional to offer. Ilique had hoped there would be nothing here. He was trying to oblige her, going through the motion, initailly, to get her out of his hair, or to forever remove himself from such wonderful soft curly strands. After all, Renatra had promised to no longer bug him after, a one time alone, with her. This he thought would be that time; now it looked as if a dilemma was about to take place between Renatra and Henrietta. Ilique was astonished as he continued to allow his tongue to be saturated with Renatra's goodness.

Ilique could not help but think how Renatra was surprising him. The first surprise had come with her beautiful pear golden vulva; even without the freckles, it would have been gorgeous. And though the puffiness was displayed vividly through Renatra's panties; in nakedness, Renatra's lovely vulva was truly unlike anything Ilique had ever seen. Henrietta had even warned him that women were different, but Renatra's sumptuous pear-shaped attractive vulva had gone beyond the imagination. Then there was the surprise upon entering such a fantastic object; he could now understand why LaQueeta never really let him get into it. There was an unusual freshness to Renatra's fruitbowl and a very distinct sweetness; a distinctive sweetness with a difficulty to explain the exactness of its flavorful taste. It was without question, very very good to Ilique. So good in fact that Ilique made up his mind to remain in this position as long as it was humanly possible.

Ilique instantly thought of Henrietta and how she had taught him to eat her gourmet dish. Of course, anything of that nature here, he thought, would be more than Renatra could stand and would surely blow her mind. Ironically, for some reason, he couldn't elevate his tongue from the sweetness being consumed. His lips were were stuck to the beautiful freckles. Ilique opened his eyes to see such beauty, but the closeness only allowed him a blur. One blur atop the beautiful fruitbowl was a thumb-sized short stubby clit resting against his nose. Unable to pull out and grasp this attention getter, he merely shook and twirled his head in amazement. Blurs and all, Ilique was enjoying himself, but suddenly Renatra was enjoying herself more as Ilique's tongue got the best of her; and the best of her warm wetness was released graciously inside of Ilique. Renatra had never experienced such an orgasm and such flooding from a man. She flooded more when she heard the gurgling sounds in Ilique's mouth, his throat and beyond. She could feel the tremendous excitement she generated within Ilique as his entire mouth was spinning and circling inside her fruitbowl; he was eating like he would never – could never get enough. The frustration, tension, and the terrible feeling about the family tree stored in Renatra's body was now gone, and she spoke cheerfully.

"That was not like the letter Ilique! I mean, it was far more personal; what happened?"

"I don't know; just you I suppose."

"What are you going to do with Henrietta; I mean – I can live with your decision, but I feel what I feel – I love you -."

"I don't know – I'm confused – let me think – I need time to think."

And think is what he did when Henrietta later appeared into town, months later.

45

Ilique immediately tried in his own way to steer Henrietta in another direction; for her, to make a decision and release him.

"Henrietta, have you ever been involved in a threesome?"

"What do you mean; three women – with two men – or another woman and man?"

"uh huh." Ilique still felt a bit naïve around the older woman.

"Well – which one Ilique?"

"The last one; you with a man and another woman."

"Is that what you've been up to while I was gone Ilique; you have had some experience, haven't you. What did you think?"

"Well – it was different – fantastic at first, tiresome after a while, and a bit boredom as it went on Henrietta."

"That's generally what happens to most things after the newness wears off. Unless there's something else of real value or substance to hold you there, those types of new adventures always peter out."

"So have you been in one or not Henrietta?"

"Not really Ilique; you remember, I'm from the old school."

"There's nothing old about you Henrietta, and besides, things like that have been going on since the beginning of time."

"True – true Ilique, but I would rather put all my energy into making you happy."

Ilique had not really noticed, but Henrietta had slowly been removing piece after piece from her gorgeous body, until all that was showing was her beautiful sensuous nakedness. She was ready to let Ilique know what he experienced in her absence was ... well ... child's play, compared to what he was now about to receive. Her motto on competition; "cook those good meals for your man ... tell him how you expect to be loved ... sit back and enjoy yourself while he eats," always gave her the edge. Placing her hand in his, she led him into the dining room; this was to whet his appetite and stimulate his mind, as to what he had really been missing during her short leave. Strolling away briefly and returning with a bottle of vintage wine and two long-stemmed glasses was a way to stimulate Ilique's body. Especially as she sat in his lap, holding, pouring, refilling and encouraging him to drink at will. Henrietta could feel his throbbing penis pressing against her behind as he downed glass after glass. She could see that sexual hungry look in his eyes, knowing that Ilique was reminishing about how he had previously eaten her gourmet dish, from atop this very table. Henrietta could see the urgency crawling into his body and creeping across his face. She even heard him say, under the effect of the wine, no doubt, "honey, let's make love."

At this point Henrietta rose, leading Ilique into the bathroom, allowing the warmer than warm water to run in the tub, as she slowly undressed him. When they slid into the hot soothing water, she still held his glass, pouring, refilling, still encouraging him to drink at will; even sipping from it herself, in between his constant swigs. The water obviously wet his body as his whet appetite continued to soar. Henrietta held his hands as he cupped her gorgeous breast. Later, when they crawled into bed, it seemed as if they had never been apart, but something did appear to be missing.

Ilique in the days ahead tried time after time to shake himself loose from Henrietta; he constantly called Renatra and told her how overwhelming his desires were for Henrietta. He explained how he did not love her as he once thought he did, but somehow could not tear himself away from her. Matter of fact, his last words to Renatra before the wedding day was. "Renatra, I melt in Henrietta's presence, but I am totally consumed in you when I'm alone; I wish Henrietta would release me." Yes, a wedding was about to take place – a double wedding; Clara A. Feldon and Rory G. Davanpourt was also to wed. At this moment, Clara and her mother were together.

They sat in the chapel's room, holding tank if you please, the two of them, engaged in a lowly conversation – as to sound only. The organist played according to the preprinted program; a musical selection signifying love in the surrounding midst of things. Certainly a beautiful choreographed piece which sent a melodious sonance to the ears of Clara A. Feldon and her dear mother Henrietta; two brides to be. If not for a private ceremony and a different one of sort, there would have been a capacity crowd of bridesmaids and the like; and of course a lot of chatter of another kind. Weddings, afterall, are for being happy and having people pawing over you – in admiration – we truthfully hope. But here, we have mother and daughter, two lovely-beautiful and gorgeous women, to give emphasis to their loveliness, conversing on the merits of matrimony. They sat in the small pastel blue room of immodest light; sunrays screened through the heavily lined curtains and the two small candle-bulbed lamps gave their share of dim shadowy brilliance.

The organ played on as they amused themselves in words of a warming proportion; still within the allowable time restraints. Their smiles and gesturing signified an understanding of what was before them; their conversation did likewise – words that told miniature stories of true feelings and togetherness forever. There too were exchanges of ideas as any mother and daughter would do on such a ceremonial occasion. Words and more words filled the tiny room, saturating its walls, floor, and ceiling, with startling secrets. The essence of which flowed from their lovely crimson-glossed lips:

"Tell me Clara, what is it really that make you want to marry Rory; is it love or loving to be more specific?"

"Strange as it seems mother, it's both and certainly there's other intangibles."

"I love Ilique too, and his loving is superior, thanks to me of course, to any I have experienced, but I feel guilty because of what I'm doing here today."

"Why is that mother?"

"Because I realized the other day Clara, I have been selfish in comparing the young Ilique with the young husband I lost years ago. In truth I feel I have been, loving another person; I know I haven't physically, but my mind has always been on your father. I -."

"That's it mother – that's it – that is what I have been trying to grasp! My father! I have been seeking in Rory, that father image – that longing to be held in his lap – the protectiveness I feel. Those were the yearnings inside of me I could not touch until just now. I still believe I love Rory though, in spite of that paternal affection."

"And I do believe my love for Ilique could be genuine."

In the confines of their pre-nuptial quarters, the mother and daughter talked of the wedding, happiness, their life. And within these precious moments they faced the truth. Each of them was really living in the past. Clara admitted she was loving a man; a father she never had. And Henrietta admitted she was loving a young man of yesteryear's reality.

There was much more chatter concerning the intricies of love and its seemingly overwhelming state of desirous affairs; the obvious sensuality tingles of one's fingers and toes forged inward to squeeze the heart, creating an illusion of true love. The organist played on; the tune on the program, which told of two gentlemen standing in the chapel – at the altar. The highs and lows of the fine musical instrument comforted the smiling Rory and Ilique, and gave too a signal to the smiling and overjoyed women; Clara and Henrietta, who were ever more strikingly beautiful in their captivating white and blue wedding gowns respectively. It was a lovely day for saying one's wedding vows; the sky was blue with those gorgeous puffy white clouds, a fitting of sort for the colors upon these ravishing brides to be. Their limousine to the reception stood, awaiting – white and shiny.

"Well, it is time to go Clara."

So Clara A. Feldon and Henrietta Feldon stood and embraced; still smiling as only happy brides would. The music, seemingly, was louder as they opened the door to the chapel's corridor. Nowhere in the world, at this moment, was there a happier mother and daughter, as they marched down the corridor and outside to the waiting limousine.

"Those who live as their human nature tells them to, have their minds controlled by what human nature wants. Those who live as the Spirit tells them to, have their minds controlled by what the Spirit wants. To be controlled by human nature results in death; to be controlled by the Spirit results in life and peace."

Romans 8:5,6